FOR THE TAKING

A GAMING THE SYSTEM NOVEL

Brenna Aubrey

SILVER GRIFFON ASSOCIATES
ORANGE, CA, USA

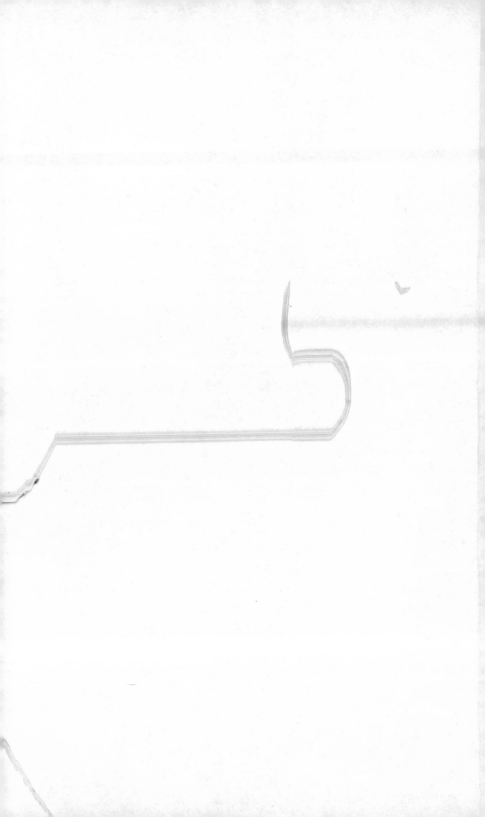

Silver Griffon Associates
P.O. Box 7383
Orange, CA 92863

Publisher's Note: This is a work of fiction. Names, characters, places, and incidents are a product of the author's imagination. Locales and public names are sometimes used for atmospheric purposes. Any resemblance to actual people, living or dead, or to businesses, companies, events, institutions, or locales is completely coincidental.

Trademarked names appear throughout this book. Rather than use a trademark symbol with every occurrence of a trademarked name, names are used in an editorial fashion, with no intention of infringement of the respective owner's trademark.

Book Layout ©2020 BookDesignTemplates.com
Cover Art ©2020 Sarah Hansen, Okay Creations

For The Taking / Brenna Aubrey. – 1st ed.
ISBN 978-1-940951-75-1

www.BrennaAubrey.com

For all my lovely family and friends who live in the Great White North. I hope Katya does you proud.

ACKNOWLEDGEMENTS

There's no way a book like this gets done with just the work of one little author. Especially one of this size. I owe many thanks to:

The professionals: K Keeton Designs and Okay Creations' Sarah Hanson for a breathtaking cover image and design. Kate Mckinley, Sabrina Darby and Eliza Dee, first eyes on the draft. Kelly Allenby for all the hats she wears cheerfully and all while looking so cute.Thanks Kate and Viv for a wonderful blurb.

Canadian help: Vivian Arend. Deborah Geary, Jo Anne Baharie, Kerri Favelle, Sara Castille.

Moral support: Soo many to name. It's been a tough couple years and I'm so glad for you, the chats, the virtual hand-holdings, the understanding. Old friends and new My humble gratitude to every one of you.

Thank you for your patience, dear readers. I know it took a while to bring Lucas & Katya's story to life but I hope you'll agree with me that the wait was well worth it.

PROLOGUE
KATYA

I GOT MARRIED IN A FAST-FOOD RESTAURANT BOOTH, ON AN extended lunch break squeezed into a sixty-hour crunch workweek.

Not gonna lie, this wedding was far from the stuff of dreams. My soon-to-be husband on the other hand? He'd probably starred in several—or even dozens—of fantasies. Not *mine*, of course.

This marriage was strictly a professional transaction. *Ahem.*

Lucas Walker, my co-worker, erstwhile nemesis and now bridegroom sat across the Formica table from me. He was tall and broad shouldered, with sultry eyes the color of melted chocolate. *And* he had that angular cut to his scruffy jaw that transformed a good-looking man into a remarkably handsome one.

My future husband. When we walked out of this burger joint, Lucas would be my legal spouse.

And I'd be his wife.

"Okay, let's do this." My friend and roommate, Heath Bowman, cracked his knuckles. Then he pushed aside the receipt for our lunch order so he could spread out the marriage license paperwork on the table. He turned to dart a glance at me beside him. "Thanks for filling all this out, by the way. That's going to

1

make this go a lot quicker." His blue eyes flicked back to the page and he tensed as if remembering something. "Oh shit, I forgot we need someone else."

Lucas leaned forward, staring through narrowed eyes at Heath with that intense gaze. "Someone else? Why are we involving anyone else in this insanity?"

Heath looked up. "At least one witness. It's California law."

We all froze and stared at each other. Should we call in a co-worker? No, definitely not. A friend of mine or of Lucas's? My gaze flicked to his and he stilled. I knew he was going to blame this on me somehow. I saw it in his glare. He did it at work often enough.

Cranberry, you are always getting into these weird-ass situations, he'd intoned at me when I'd proposed this whole thing at a coffee shop the week before. *Now you're dragging me into it?*

I blinked, my eyes focusing on the stylized red palm trees lining the tiled walls all around us.

Record scratch. Freeze Frame.

Yep, that's me. You're probably wondering how I ended up in this situation...

So yeah. It all started about three weeks ago. Just before New Year's, I'd left the U.S. to go to my friends' fancy Caribbean destination wedding. As you do. But Customs and Immigration nailed me when I came back into the country.

They made the wild accusation that *I*, a hardworking, somewhat innocent Canadian girl, who minded her own business, had been working in the US illegally. With no special visa or permit! And no legal residency!

The actual nerve.

They were correct. No alternative facts. But damn, they didn't have to be so mean about it, threatening to kick me out of the United States of America for good.

The feds didn't care that I'd rebuilt my life anew, kissing the old one goodbye—for so many reasons I was grateful they didn't dig into. In the US, I was working my dream job and putting past troubles behind me. I had a new group of friends here who loved me probably more than my own family did.

But to them, none of that mattered.

In that tiny room at the airport, they'd threatened me with deportation. And I'll admit, I panicked. In the heat of the moment, with all their fingers pointing straight at me, I'd blurted out the first lie that popped into my head: I was getting married. To Lucas, my team member from work. An American citizen.

And boy, did that lie multiply and divide and reproduce like a feverish virus. Since popping the question, my life had taken an even crazier turn. Once I'd explained my predicament in intricate detail, to my shock Lucas had agreed to help me.

Heath spoke again. "In order to be legally married in the state of California, you're required a licensed officiant." Heath placed a large hand on his own chest. "That's me. Then you need to declare out loud, when asked, that you take each other as your legal spouse. And we need a goddamn witness to sign this license."

Someone from the booth behind Lucas jerked his head in our direction. His look said it all... *WTF?*

Yeah buddy, I'm right there with you.

Lucas looked like he was ready to bolt, so I had to act fast. At that moment, I recognized our new eavesdropper's uniform. He wore the white collared shirt and matching white nametag complete with In-N-Out Burger logo, the remains of his lunch on the empty tray in front of him. An employee on his lunch break.

Slipping out of the booth, I asked Heath, "You got cash on you?"

"I have a couple twenties, why?"

"Be right back with a witness," was all I said while my future husband stared at me, wary and wide-eyed. Deer in the headlights.

In less than five minutes, I returned with our new "witness" who I instructed to squeeze into the booth beside my bewildered spouse-to-be. His nametag read *Rob*, so I introduced him to the other two.

"I gotta be back at work in fifteen," Rob said in a tight, high-pitched voice. "You said there's forty dollars in it for me?"

"Yup! Heath will pay you when you sign. This shouldn't take that long, right?" I arched my brow at Heath, silently demanding he agree with me.

Heath blinked a few times, mouth opening at least half a minute before he spoke. "Uh, yeah, sure, sure. Fifteen minutes for the long version. You can split after you sign."

Rob glanced between the three of us while tucking a longish strand of dark blond hair under his red cap. "Okay, then."

Heath's gaze flicked to me. "Do you, Katharina Rose Ellis, take Lucas Walker—" Heath squinted at the name I'd squeezed into the form. Until yesterday, I had no idea that my husband-to-be had another last name and Walker was his middle name. And that last name, it was a doozy. I'd run out of space in the blank while filling in the *surname* box, the letters spilling out into the margin.

"Lucas Walker van den Hoehnsboek van Lynden," Lucas rattled off.

"That's enough names for four people." Heath snorted.

Lucas only responded by rolling his eyes and making a gesture that clearly meant, *Let's get on with this.*

Heath's gaze flicked back to me. "Okay, so Katya, do you take Lucas to be your legal husband?"

I couldn't look Lucas in the eye, even knowing that he had his own good reasons for helping me. Things just got *weird,* so I stared at the tacky plastic tabletop and croaked out a quick "yes." If I could've gotten away with a mere nod, I would've.

Heath moved on to the next question. "And Lucas, do you take Katya as your wife?"

His hands on the table, where they were laced together, seemed to tighten, the knuckles turning white. Other than that, he made no movement. He gave a sharp nod and an even sharper, "Yes, I do." He stated with the same tone he might use for announcing that he'd contracted an STD.

Heath nodded, satisfied "Okay so… by the power invested in me by the state of California, yadda, yadda, yadda, I now pronounce you husband and wife—"

"Number ninety-three, your order is ready!" came a disembodied voice over the overhead speakers.

"Ooh, that's us." Heath offered the pen to Rob. "If you'll kindly sign right here…" He dug out his wallet to pull out some bills.

Rob had slid out of the booth, checked his watch and then with a sigh scratched his name out on the table. "Weirdest thing ever, but yeah, witnessed it."

Shit, what if immigration asked for Rob's testimony for whatever reason? I reached out and covered Lucas's large hand with my own, squeezing it. "I'm sorry. We're just so desperately in love that we need to be married *immediately.*" I sent a warning glance to Lucas, who grunted and nodded along with what I said. Yeah, he'd never be in danger of winning an Academy Award, for sure.

Rob handed the pen back to Heath and as he scooped up the cash, his phone bleated out the cheesy synthesized beat of Rick Astley's *Never Gonna Give You Up.*

Heath pushed out of the booth. "Gotta go procure the wedding feast. You two sign here while I'm gone."

The rick-roll was the *pièce de resistance* to add to the surreal list of this strange day. The semi-hostile bridegroom. The yadda-yadda-yadda-ing of our marriage vows. The interruption over the loudspeaker. To say nothing of the imminent marriage "feast" of Double-Double burgers, milkshakes and skinny fries.

Our witness, Rob, answered his phone, sauntering away without a further word of congratulations or thanks for the easy forty bucks. And I was left to stare awkwardly at my bridegroom.

Shit. He was my husband now. Didn't feel that different, though. He still glared at me with the same nonchalant annoyance as before.

With almost robotic jerks, Lucas reached over, dragged the form in front of him. He signed with quick, decisive flicks of his pen scratching across the surface of the table. He then scooted the paper to me.

But instead of signing right away, I held up my waxy paper cup of soda and tilted it toward him in a clear sign of a toast.

Our gazes met. The air between us crackled and popped.

My gaze flicked to his hands, fingers laced together tightly atop the table. My eyes lingered on them, realizing for not the first time how much they fascinated me. They were strong, masculine. Long fingers, prominent veins crisscrossing lightly hairy hands. My gaze traveled up the solid, muscular arms under his flannel shirt.

Try not to focus on that. I forced my attention elsewhere to prevent meeting his gaze again. He had the loveliest big brown eyes. They looked sleepy, even when he was fully alert. And they were fringed with dark lashes. And his mouth...

Stop it, Kat!

I cleared my throat and brandished the cup at him. "Come on, we should at least toast, right?"

He flicked his gaze back to mine, appeared to fight the temptation to roll his eyes. But he complied, tapping his cup of Coke against my sugary pink lemonade.

"And what are we toasting? Excellent deadline margins? To an early beta-release bonus from our bosses?"

I smiled. "To *us.* Mr. and Mrs. uh, van—van Hoehns—"

He sighed and put his drink down, cocking a brow at me. Letting his eyes drop slowly, they trailed down the line of my long hair, past my shoulders, down my arms where it nearly brushed the table.

His gaze warmed everywhere it touched. But I'd never in a zillion years let him know that.

"*Walker.* Let's just keep it simple. And I thought you were keeping your name?"

I shrugged and nodded. "Yeah... sure. Unless it makes a stronger case with immigration to change it. I'll have to talk to my lawyer."

"Since this isn't lasting long, I'd say the less work you have to do to change it all back when this is over, the better."

I slurped on the last of my lemonade and watched him with wide eyes. "It's a good thing that I was never all that attached to the typical dream of a big wedding. Expensive dress and bouquet of half-bloomed flowers, a glamorous first dance in front of a roomful of mostly drunk friends and family. This is about as far from that as you can get."

This time, he did roll his eyes. "Totally overrated anyway. You're not missing anything. Even if this was for real."

I twitched my brows, wondering what that cryptic remark meant. I'd have to get used to it. My now-husband was fond of making dry remarks that no one got. At least I knew mostly what I was getting into with marrying Lucas. We'd worked together for over a year and sparred regularly.

His eyes flicked away from where he'd been studying my fidgeting hands, then checked his watch. "We don't have time to wax poetic with the *could have beens*, anyway. When we get back to work today, we've gotta hit it hard. You promised."

I raised my right hand as if solemnly vowing—because there hadn't been quite enough of *that* today, I guess. "All of my lunch breaks and overtime and all-nighters are yours until we make this deadline."

He nodded grimly, satisfied. "Good. Because this—" he motioned between himself and me "—is a business transaction."

I waggled my head, tiredly nodding in agreement. I'd heard this repeatedly in the past week. "Yeah yeah yeah. I get a certified Yankee husband to put on my immigration forms for a green card. *You* get all my help to make the deadline so you can impress the big bosses for that new promotion you're coveting. I've *got* it, Lucas, like I had it the twelfth time you told me."

"Hmm. Well, a few more times can never hurt."

As game testers, our department at Draco Multimedia Entertainment had to assure the software was clean of bugs and glitches. It was especially important due to the upcoming release of the new Dragon Epoch expansion, *War of the Sunderlands*. For a game as massive and complex as Dragon Epoch, this was no simple task.

Our bosses had given us a nearly impossible deadline to accomplish this. But instead of pushing back and asking for more time, Lucas, our project manager, had accepted the challenge. Because he had something to prove.

He pressed his index finger into the tabletop between us. "*Right?*"

I gritted my teeth. "Yes. Right. *Jeez*. I'm well aware of how much you want the new job. I'll do everything in my power to help. You know what they say about immigrants getting the job done."

Damn, he was infuriating and also hot when he got this way. Bossy and insistent with a healthy dose of cranky—that was Lucas in a nutshell. Too bad he was also wrapped in a pretty package that I couldn't help noticing. Over and over. It'd be so much easier to be irritated by an ugly asshole rather than a beautiful one.

It didn't help that his bossiness always had me wondering if he was that way in bed, too. *Stop it, Kat!*

I was lucky, really. So far he hadn't asked many questions about why it was so vital I stay here in the US and not go back to Canada. My heart raced and my stomach dipped even thinking about that possibility. *No.* He was helping me stay here and putting himself on the line to do it. So for that, I'd overlook the asshole-ness and be grateful.

My home country was a wonderful place. But the specific situation I'd left... not so much. I fidgeted again, plunging the straw in and out of my empty cup to produce a wailing squeak. After a minute of this, he shoved his hand on top of mine to stop me, that fabulous jaw tensing.

"*Cranberry,*" he muttered between his teeth. "Calm down."

His hand was warm and calloused—apparently from years of rowing crew in college, he'd once said. Warm tingles raced up my arm from where our skin connected. *Holy crap.* Tingles... shocks... goosebumps. I gulped loudly and extricated my hand from under his. Then I scooped up the pen and added my signature to the license.

After reading over the form again, I sat back, glancing up in time to catch that he was staring intensely at me, his eyes somewhere on my neck or hair. But as soon as I caught him, everything changed. By the time he met my gaze again, that usual granite veil had been replaced in seconds.

He gave me a not-so-convincing nonchalant shrug and looked out the window.

"So when do I move in?" I bounced cheerfully. I already knew the answer to the question. But as usual, I found it almost impossible to avoid the temptation of pushing his buttons once in a while.

His face darkened. "You said—"

I held up my hand. "Kidding. I'm kidding. But I need to make it look like I'm living there with you. I'll have all my mail sent there, if you don't mind. But never fear, I'll keep living with Heath at his condo."

He turned back to me. "We should also get a joint bank account and I'll add your name to my bills. You won't have to pay them."

I snorted. "Good, because I'd never afford the mortgage on your fancy house."

"Whatever."

"I'll put together a photo album. Can you send me any pictures you might have? I've got some from past work parties. We should pose for a few, too. I'm afraid I'll have to ask you to do something rare and possibly painful, though, and actually *smile* in the photos."

He sighed. "Fine, if I must."

I couldn't resist picking up my phone and snapping one of him now, complete with scowl. Then I took a moment to study it. Even with that scowl, he was way too handsome—a fact I once again reminded myself to ignore. "Well, this won't help me give us a glamorous, romantic wedding for the immigration officers. We'll have to work on that."

"You're filing the paperwork right away?"

I glanced down at the marriage license between us that bore both our signatures. "I have to. By court order. I'll get it all done."

"Good. There shouldn't be any problems with that then. And of course, we have rules for everything else." I raised my brows at him, almost as if to challenge him to *dare* to go over that BS yet again. "You *do* remember the rules, right?"

Aaand here we go...

I shook my head, gaze flying out the window. Jedi Boy and his damn rules. "Yes, I remember. You're not going to make me repeat them."

His eyes narrowed. "Wanna bet?"

My gaze snapped back to his. "You're annoying."

"Don't care." He stared me down.

I blew out a long breath. "Fine. But this is the last time I speak them out loud, got it?" No reaction. I bit my lip and continued. "No acting like a married couple at work, at home or ever. No joking about being married. The secret does not go beyond you, me and Heath. No dating other people." I slurped at my drink noisily to piss him off. "And I get all the wedding presents."

"Wouldn't it be easier to convince the powers that be that your marriage is for real if you *don't* keep it secret?" Heath stood at my shoulder with the laden food tray. I had no idea how long he'd been there—long enough to hear me recite Lucas's ridiculous rules, apparently.

I scooted over to give him room to sit, and he set the food tray down.

"Sorry it took a while. Had to send my burger back. The cashier didn't put down that it was supposed to be animal-style."

Heath bit into his hamburger—priorities, after all—before flicking a glance from me to Lucas and back, still waiting for the answer to his question.

"I've got my reasons for keeping it on the down low," Lucas finally answered, his dark eyes avoiding my gaze. "Namely, I'm up for an important promotion and Kat is best friends with the CEO's wife."

Heath swallowed his massive bite of burger and snorted. "Wouldn't that be a good reason *not* to keep it secret? Hell, I'd advertise it freely to anyone who'd listen."

I already knew the answer to this, and I sensed Lucas was getting torqued, so I stepped in—magnanimously, I might add, because Lucas was equally annoying. *But* he was also doing me a huge favor. "Lucas doesn't believe in nepotism. He wants the job for his own merits."

Heath shrugged. "Okay, so keep it secret at work but—"

"The family angle is also complicated," Lucas cut in before Heath could even ask. "Believe me, it's just easier this way all around."

I quirked a brow, curious, but resisted the urge to ask the obvious question. I actually knew nothing about Lucas's family, but if not asking him meant he wouldn't ask me about mine, then so much the better. Scooping up my double-double burger, I lifted the bun to make sure they hadn't spread it with the "special sauce" that I didn't care for.

"It's easy enough to keep things on the down-low." I said. "Especially when all I'm doing is sending in documentation and then we appear for an interview." I guess we'd have to know the basics about each other's families for that... but not for months.

One step at a time. A month ago Lucas and I were at a cabin in the mountains with co-workers right before Christmas. We'd had no idea of what the crazy future would bring.

Now, here we were. Husband and wife.

"I guess that means no wedding rings, then, which was on my list of questions," Heath asked between bites.

Lucas shook his head decidedly. "No rings."

Sure. No outward signs of being married for various reasons. It's not like either of us had much free time for dating because of our hectic work schedule. Dating would make things messy and complicated, to say nothing of making this appear less real. And with his conditions on keeping things secret, we needed all the help we could get.

After we finished our "wedding feast," he wasted no time slipping out of the booth and prompting us back to work. I took a moment to thank Heath for coming all the way to Irvine from Orange, where we lived, to do this for us on our lunch break. Because it was going to be another long night at work tonight—and probably for the rest of the week.

Heath carefully wiped the grease off his hands before taking the paperwork and signing it. He tucked it away in an envelope that he assured us would be mailed to the county recorder as soon as possible.

And from where he stood, Lucas watched his every move as if he didn't trust what Heath was doing. As if he'd just signed his own life away. Because in actuality, for the next year or so—come hell or my green card—he *was*.

"Keep me posted on any developments or appointments I need to make," Lucas grunted as we left.

I fought the urge to give him a mock salute in reply.

Not even an hour later, back at the job, it was kind of weird trying to maintain the illusion that nothing had happened. It wasn't actually an illusion, though. Since nothing really had, except on paper.

I studied our Mission Accomplished leaderboard. It displayed the ranks of a running tournament among my co-workers. These were gamers who, upon feeling overworked, under paid, and undervalued, took a break from debugging Dragon Epoch to play yet another game. Mission Accomplished was incredibly outdated now, but Lucas was a longtime fan of it. Plus, it was the very first game our boss had ever worked on by himself as a teenager.

In the past twenty-four hours, Lucas had moved past me to become the high-scorer on the makeshift whiteboard-and-peg chart we'd devised to measure these things. I cocked my head, chewing a thumbnail, and squinted up at it. Lucas and I had been nudging and one-upping each other on that board for months. The third place holder wasn't even close.

"You gonna let that stand? You two are so obsessed with beating each other that no one can keep up with either of you." My coworker Joel's snarky musing pulled me out of my quiet reverie. I glanced at him as he was pointing to Lucas's winning score. It was temporary and we all knew it. I'd blow past him the next time I sat down to do another run on the game.

Except... except maybe I wouldn't. Not anytime soon, anyway. As a silent way to thank him for all he'd done for me, I might let it stand. Even if he only had to miss a few lunches for the marriage license and "ceremony," it was still a very kind thing he'd done.

Yeah, he needed me to help with the expansion, but... he probably could have done that without me.

I realized that I was smiling, a moment of tenderness tugging at my heart. In his own gruff way, he'd shown me some kindness.

With a shrug, I left Joel's question unanswered as I drifted back to my desk, taking a few moments to do some full body stretches before I sat down. It was going to be another tedious crawl until quitting time so I had to take these chances where I could.

When I came up for air, pivoting to sink into my chair, I noticed that Lucas had entered the room. His gaze traveled from the leader board, down the length of the room lined with workstations. Most likely he was surveying who was still here and who was packing up to go.

When his eyes met mine, I sent him a tentative smile and a wink.

His neutral expression morphed into a scowl, eyes narrowing. With stiff shoulders and even stiffer bearing, he moved past my desk and grunted out a brusque "Back to work, Cranberry. If you've got time to daydream, you have too much idle time on your hands."

I glared at his receding back, my own eyes narrowing as I sank into my chair. *Happy wedding day to you, too, asshole.*

Opening up my queue file with gritted teeth, I resolved to blast his lead out of the water as soon as possible.

CHAPTER 1
LUCAS

Six Months Later...

THERE WERE WHISPERS ALL AROUND ME. THAT WAS THE first thing I noticed upon removing my headset. My eyes skimmed our corner of the Draco campus, not-so-affectionately dubbed the Den by its dwellers. It was an appropriate nickname, given that those inhabitants were the game testing department for Draco Multimedia Entertainment. Mostly the employees here looked deserving of hanging out in a place called the Den. Their dress and hygiene habits fit all too well with a place far from sunlight, in an underground habitat strewn with debris from past meals.

Rubbing my eyes to refocus them after long hours staring at the screen, I scanned the room to see if everyone was where they should be. Empty workstations lined the distant wall along the large bay windows. The team-leader's desk, where I worked, was in the middle of the room. On the far side was a floor to ceiling scrum board covered with massive amounts of multi-colored sticky notes. This was marked into sections denoting where each task was in process toward completion: *planning, in progress, complete, sidelined, escalated.*

It looked like a drunk unicorn had wandered into The Den and puked a rainbow all over the wall. My eyes darted back to the cluster of people by the door—the source of the not-so-discrete whispering.

My colleagues were casting occasional glances my way as I watched them. Perhaps they were expecting me to break up their impromptu rally, but I was feeling generous. We had just come in under a nearly impossible deadline last week. It had been a long, hard push and many of them had pulled all-nighters in here to get it done.

So they were taking a little longer on their lunch break today. I didn't sweat it when we weren't under the gun.

During crunch time, there were no lunch breaks, no dinner breaks, no coffee breaks. Nor were there more than two minutes to spare for a desperate dash to the bathroom to pee out all the Red Bull, coffee or Mountain Dew. Sure enough, the next list of bugs would be waiting. And the cycle of finding everything wrong with the game before it went live would continue.

During quieter times, like this week, I eased up on watching the clock and they knew it. But their spontaneous coffee klatch was irritating me right now. *Or* I was just paranoid thinking they were talking about me.

Everything changed the minute the door opened again. Katya walked in and strode directly to her workstation without even acknowledging the cluster of her coworkers.

They, however, looked at *her*. Then, looked at me, looked at each other, and abruptly scattered like cats who'd just had a bucket of icy water dumped on them.

My eyes darted back to Kat. I caught the silky fall of long, fiery red hair to her waistline, the way those jeans hugged her ass.

Before I could even catch my breath, that familiar rush of attraction threatened to take over all thought. I swallowed. Then my automatic suppression system kicked in and I forced myself to look away before I spent too much time drinking her in. It was one of my most important rules. I called it the six-second rule. It was a little like gazing at the sun. I should never stare at her for longer than six seconds. But rather than having my retinas burned out, I risked my mind wandering into dangerous territory. Inevitably, I'd start dwelling on the fact that she had the most gorgeous ass in those new dark blue jeans she was wearing today. Or I'd obsess about the stretch of t-shirt fabric across her perfect chest. And thoughts might lead to actions.

And actions would definitely cause drama and bullshit that I'd said goodbye to years ago.

With the co-worker whispering gone, I still felt the odd inquisitive glance thrown my way from the other workstations. Whenever I caught one, I glared in return and was left in peace. Slowly, I turned back to my screen and replaced my headset. Time to scan the first bug reports sent in this morning from our beta testers.

I wasn't at it five minutes before that forbidden distraction brought herself to me. I had to spend much more than six seconds thinking about her because she was in my face. Her soft, sweet-smelling hair brushed my cheek as she bent over my workstation to murmur to me.

"I found something I think you need to look at," she said a little louder than normal, as if she wanted everyone nearby to hear. I shot a questioning glance at her. "Section 583-A. Can you pull it up?"

What the hell? I'd signed off on that days ago as clean. With a frown, I did as she asked and pulled up the notes on that section. She bent even closer to me so I could feel the warmth of her body near mine. It irritated me for some reason. Probably because her nearness—and her hotness—had been bothering me over the past year. Because I couldn't have what was so near— and I'd resolved that I *would* never have it.

Her long, glorious hair brushed my face again and—good God, that smell. The scent was this intoxicating mix of coconut, lavender and other spices I couldn't name. Maybe nutmeg. It was subtle. And heady.

And it caused a surge in my blood pressure every time. She placed a hand beside my keyboard to support herself as she pointed to the screen. I focused on her thin hands, her long, graceful fingers. Her nails were trimmed short so she could type faster but with chipped blue nail polish and little glittery charms. She was the perfect mix of tough tomboy gamer girl and dazzling feminine beauty.

And I'd resolved, months ago, for the sake of my sanity, to stop thinking about her like this, secret wife or not. Frustratingly, it hadn't been a successful resolution so far.

I chided myself for finding her scent irresistible and fought down those beginning tendrils of arousal. It had been too long a stretch since I'd had sex. The haze of desire was so strong that I hadn't realized that she was talking. I also hadn't realized that she had no intention of discussing the supposed bug on section 583-A.

"—setting up an appointment with the immigration office for our interview." She was talking in a low voice. I blinked, crashing back to earth as I pulled my face away from her silky hair. A sudden pang of lust jolted me out of my seat.

Goddamn it. Trust me to get into a situation like this, secretly married to a sexy as fuck gamer chick with whom I worked long hours every day and sometimes nights. Who had curves that threatened to drive me insane if I thought about them for more than a few minutes at a time. Who I constantly wondered if she was as good a kisser as her luscious lips promised.

And I was all too aware that she got me hard way too often from just being in my proximity. And at this moment, was threatening to do so again.

I shook my head and started breathing through my mouth so I wouldn't smell her. "*What?*" I snapped.

She sighed, apparently impatient that I was slow today and not catching on to her ruse.

"I said this isn't about a bug, but I didn't want everyone to get suspicious. I've been getting some weird looks every time I pull you out of the room to talk. Today at lunch, I had to return a call to my immigration lawyer. He got us an appointment in two weeks for an interview."

"Fine. Okay. Is that all?"

She darted me a puzzled look, flicking her hair over her shoulder—and into my face. I recoiled. Though what I really wanted was to wrap my hands in it, pull her head back. I wanted to stare into her beautiful face and put my mouth all over her gorgeous, plump lips.

But that was beside the point.

She didn't have to know that. *Nobody* had to know that.

Jeez. I needed to get laid again. This secret marriage—along with the hours-intensive, sometimes mind-numbing job—was giving me an epic case of blue balls. Perhaps after the interview, we could start seeing other people.

I leaned back in my chair to give myself a bit of a break and caught three heads pointed our way. When I jerked my gaze toward them, all three pulled back and started feigning work again, typing unnaturally fast and staring at their monitors.

I frowned. What the hell was that? Had the Den of mighty, unrelenting and detail-obsessed, hardy game-testers somehow transformed into the Lair of Gossip Girl or Gawking Rubberneckers United?

Frowning, I turned back to Katya. "Did anyone overhear you on the phone at lunch?"

She frowned back at me before an auburn eyebrow arched over her bright blue eyes. "Do you think I'm some kind of amateur, Jedi Boy? I was in that back hallway that leads to the side parking lot where no one parks. It was very private and empty. No one could have overheard."

"—That you know of."

She rolled her eyes at me. "Jeez, I'm sorry I said anything at all. But you *did* ask me to keep you informed."

My jaw tightened. "Just text me next time. No need for the full report, Cranberry. Or are you looking for every excuse in the world to come talk to me?"

In response, her face flushed a satisfying deep red. Though it wasn't exactly the source of the blush I'd like to see on her. I'd rather it be from her being intensely turned on than from being angry. But it was almost as good.

Her eyes narrowed, and she straightened. "In your wet dreams, Buttercup."

Oh, how very close to that truth she was.

I just smirked. "Be here early tomorrow. Jordan wants you and me to give that VIP tour. Not my choice."

She responded by flashing me her middle finger and turned to go back to her workstation. Thank God, though I had to forcibly remind myself to pull my eyes away from her amazing backside as she did it. Damn... that hair brushing my cheek, her nutmeg smell. All I needed was an innocent brush of those full breasts up against my arm or back to complete the trifecta of frustrated attraction.

I was finding it hard to think about much else these days and resolved that it had to be the blue balls. I'd find a tree stump attractive nowadays.

With a small smile, I returned to my work. It was safest to keep her pissed at me. She'd maintain her distance, and that's what I needed right now to keep my own head clear.

I had a meeting with the big bosses later this afternoon, and I had to get my mind back in the game.

***

When you worked in Quality Assurance for a thriving and immensely popular gaming company, you were always behind schedule. Or you were never caught up with regular duties. Or, thanks to our ever-so-thoughtful game developers, you were on a last minute crunch deadline. And when we bothered to complain about this ridiculous dev behavior to the management, it never failed. Management favored their sob story over ours.

Now that the new expansion was complete, Dragon Epoch: The War of the Sunderlands was nearly ready to be rolled out. And we were on the eve of that release. And here I was, in the boss' office, waiting to hear if he'd come to the decision I'd been waiting over six months to hear. That he'd chosen me to head up the new Virtual Reality division that Draco Multimedia Entertainment was soon integrating from a separate company.

"Lucas," my boss said from the spot where he was perched on his expansive desk in the fancy CEO's office. "I'm going to put it to you straight. I didn't pull you in here at this late hour to listen to you bitch about the devs."

I blinked, straightening in my chair as if I weren't already sitting upright. "And I'm sure that you've heard plenty of bitching from them about QA."

"Always." Adam Drake's face split with an understanding smile. This wasn't his first rodeo. Or even his fifth. He wasn't even thirty years old and yet here he was at the top of his game, CEO of multiple companies and on the Board of Directors of several others.

He was living the dream of a self-made man. My dream.

If I was being honest, I had a bit of a dude-crush on him. Adam Drake's trajectory was the perfect example of work industry goals. I'd followed his career since the days of his first game, Mission Accomplished—a game that had obsessed me as a teen. And over the years, I'd used him as a model of what I wanted to do with my own life and career.

Everybody had to have a hero, right?

I flicked a glance over at Jordan Fawkes, CFO of the company and a close friend. He twitched his eyebrows at me as if to say, *Well played*, then flicked his gaze back to Adam.

Adam's foot swung where it hung over the corner of his desk, his arms folded across his chest. His eyes went to the window as if thinking about how to say the next part. I tried hard not to grip the arms of the chair while I willed him to continue.

Just say it, dude. Just say I got the job. It won't kill you...

Adam cleared his throat and turned back to me. "The position is down to two people. And I've got to say it's been an arduous process to winnow it down to just that."

Not exactly the news I'd been hoping to hear, but good enough for now. I shifted in my seat. "Hopefully that means I'm one of the two."

Adam laughed. "Yes, of course."

I fought against the impulse to release the breath I'd been holding.

He continued, "You did an amazing job with the QA on the expansion. I know we gave you an extremely short time window. I was expecting pushback on that and you never gave it. You hit that deadline and made it your bitch. Well done."

I nodded, gratified by the recognition. It had been an exhausting six months. Seventy- and eighty-hour workweeks on my own part, and as much as I could push out of my team. And Katya... well, she'd been my secret weapon. She was beyond qualified and with a keen eye for detail that made her talented for QA. Because of her strong understanding of back-end code, at times, she'd been able to work at triple and even quadruple the speed of my other testers.

She alone had carried us through that deadline and rallied many other testers along with her. Just as I'd known she would.

Which was why nearly losing her at the beginning of the year, when she'd informed me of her possible deportation, had spelled near-disaster for my goals. They would never have given me the budget to replace her with three new QA people. And I would have been required to spend costly weeks training the newbies. All valuable time I could have spent furthering that goal to hit the early deadline.

Adam mused with a smile, "I'm not sure what you did to sweet talk your team into pulling that one off, but it was impressive. Don't think I didn't notice or am inclined to let that go without an appropriate reward."

I beamed. Yes, we'd all worked hard. But this never would have happened without Kat. She didn't know it, nor would I ever tell her so, but she was my secret weapon. And she'd worked like a charm.

"I appreciate that." I nodded. I'd worked with Adam for years. And though we knew each other well, we'd never been super close. Maybe my idolization had somehow impeded that. For his part, he wasn't the most approachable person, either—a formidable boss, yes, and a coding god. But also an outstanding leader.

And he'd started his empire by putting out games as a teenager, writing code in his bedroom late at night under the cover of darkness. At one time, I'd been so obsessed with Mission Accomplished, that I'd hunted him down at a tech conference and almost gotten myself arrested for stalking him.

Not all of those memories were something I was proud of. But I was young and hungry then. Now I was older and even hungrier.

Adam had given me a job with his fledgling gaming company after I'd bent a few of my own rules and pulled a string or two. And I'd vowed I'd never do it again. Everything from here on out would be on me—and on the team I led.

But I'd been lucky as hell to come by Kat and was willing to go to drastic lengths to keep her here. Hence the reason I chose to flout a bullshit institution I no longer believed in so I could help her get a green card.

I swallowed, lacing my fingers together to give my hands something to do. "Can I ask who's the other guy up for the job?"

Adam shot Jordan a long look, but Jordan stayed quiet. He then turned back to me. "Sure, I'll let you know as long as it's okay with you that I tell him about you."

I nodded. "That's fine." *Please don't let it be Jeremy.* I was thinking it so hard I had to will myself not to say it aloud as I tightened the grip on my own hands. Every other candidate out there was inferior to me in suitability for the position.

Except for Jeremy, who had been hired years after I had but had advanced through the ranks as a developer. He excelled at what he did. He also had ideas on how to integrate the VR technology into our existing games.

And since he was a developer, I knew that Adam favored him over me. Honor amongst coders and all that. In their world, game testers were the enemy. I'd sometimes detected a bias in Adam's decisions because of it.

Adam shifted in his seat atop the desk. "Okay, so the other candidate is Jeremy Holme."

My innards took a nosedive. Well, shit. That meant that all this was a formality. Jeremy had long since been a favorite of our illustrious CEO. I resisted the urge to fidget or show my emotions. I also fought the urge to catch Jordan's eye.

"So how will you proceed with the final decision?" I asked.

Adam cocked his head to the side as if thinking. "I could tell you, but then I'd have to kill you."

I fought to suppress a sigh of frustration. "Okay, then how about you tell me what's next?"

Jordan spoke up. "Part of it will be convincing the Board of Directors. A presentation of your clear vision for the direction of the Virtual Reality division."

I nodded, absorbing that. It shouldn't be too difficult to solidify my vision. Coming up with actionable steps toward that vision might be more challenging. I'd have to draw on the help of others for inspiration.

After asking a few clarifying questions, we quickly wrapped things up. And minutes later I was pushing out of my seat and shaking both their hands and thanking them. "You're still taking care of that VIP tour tomorrow morning?" Adam asked just before I turned to leave.

"The astronauts? We're on it."

Adam's eyebrows rose. "We?"

"I suggested he bring Kat with him," Jordan chimed in. "She's a lot of fun and it won't hurt to have a pretty girl for them to look at."

"Sexist," Adam chided him.

Jordan shrugged. "Take it up with your wife. She already thinks the worst of me."

I'd fought to keep myself from reading too much into Adam's request that I run the tour for the astronauts. They were here because they worked with Adam in one of his other endeavors. They were also avid fans of the game and would be working to promote the expansion, including several TV and internet commercials.

Jordan and Adam were continuing their usual shit-talking exchange, but I wasn't listening, already focusing on what I needed to do to push this to the final stage. I needed that job. It would be the culmination of years of strategically planned educational and career choices. It was the main reason I'd taken the grunt job in QA and worked my way through to develop a better sense of game design and playability.

Yeah, this new position would allow me to do what I'd dreamed of doing for years—making games of my own. And doing it in partnership with a man I'd admired for a long time.

What could I do to push this decision over into my favor?

I was a Quality Assurance manager. I did my job efficiently and *very* well, but my job wasn't flashy. A developer could stuff his resume with an innovative Dragon Epoch storyline, a nested chain of quests. Or he could develop a new game mechanic for the next expansion.

Me? I made sure there were no errors in the gaming program, no bugs to screw up game enjoyment. I was the janitor, so to speak, the guy who cleaned up the devs' messes.

As I left Adam's office, Jordan grabbed my arm and pulled me into his own office, just adjacent. I shut the door behind me as he started a podcast playing loudly on his phone, set it down on his desk. Then he motioned me toward the wall furthest away from the one adjacent to the CEO's office.

"Safety precaution. He has the ears of a bat," Jordan explained in a quiet voice with a grimace.

"This isn't good news," I replied.

Jordan's brows furrowed. "You shouldn't be surprised that he wants someone from development in that position. But I've been campaigning for you all this time, and he does admire your work. He *especially* couldn't believe you made that deadline. Can't stop talking about it."

I nodded, enjoying the sense of gratification that the hard work had been appreciated.

Jordan continued. "I don't think he was bullshitting you back there when he said that this will be a tough choice for him."

My lips pressed together. "If you say so."

Jordan lifted a brow at me. "Don't get all belligerent on me. He's never been the most effusive person with praise. Trust me on this. And the great news is that it's not a hundred percent up to him. I've been thinking about this strategically."

My brows rose. This came from the man who was almost single-handedly responsible for the company's triumphant bid to go public, making me, among others, a millionaire. I wasn't about to discount Jordan's strategic thinking.

"I'm listening."

His eyes flicked to mine. "Two things, actually. You need something flashy. Something new that will catch his attention. Preferably something irresistible in your plans for the virtual reality company. A new game that will sweep through the industry." I pondered this. On top of everything else, I had going on... well, who needed sleep, right?

I nodded. "Okay. That's something I can think about. What was the other thing?"

Jordan straightened, his features sobering. "Well, you're not going to like it."

I rolled my eyes. "Great. Can't wait to hear it, then."

"There's always the influence angle. You have some... ah, impressive family ties." He waved a hand up to stop me when I opened my mouth to protest. "Hear me out. A new investment. An influx of cash or sponsorship."

I drew back. "From my father? Are you out of your mind?"

I could scarcely believe my own ears. If anyone on this earth understood about fathers who had no boundaries, it was Jordan.

"I know. I know. I told you that you wouldn't like it."

"You know me well enough. I like it about as much as you would if someone suggested you get *your* dad involved in your business."

He nodded and let go a long sigh. "Yeah, I know, I know. Just think about it. I really want you in this position, too. I've gotten you this far, right?"

I huffed out an indignant breath. "Curb the ego, bro. I got *myself* this far, but I appreciate your support."

Jordan's gaze intensified. "Just think about it."

Yeah, think about getting my dad to buy off Adam. Two words: *Fuck* and *NO*.

I wasn't thrilled when Jordan had figured out who my father was. I never did ask him how he knew. But Adam clearly *didn't* know, and I never wanted him to find out. The fact that my father could buy and sell Adam *and* Jordan, both billionaires themselves, several times over, was not something to add to my resume.

But I did as Jordan asked and I thought about it... all the way back to the Den.

I had my own work to do, and now I had to magic some kind of special project to wow Adam's and the Board of Director's socks off.

Or something.

CHAPTER 2
KATYA

I NEVER THOUGHT I'D START OUT MY VERY ORDINARY Tuesday morning surrounded by four hunky astronauts. But here we were, walking together down the corridors of Draco Multimedia Entertainment Inc., and through the displays of Dragon Epoch, our most popular game.

"Whoa," one of them said. I wracked my brain to remember his name. Colonel Noah Sutton. Tall, dark-haired and with arms like tree trunks where his tight gray NASA t-shirt hugged them. Holy Moly. He had stopped in front of an as-yet-unrevealed exhibit in the back hall that was part of our promotion for the new expansion on Dragon Epoch. "I don't recognize this area in the game. Is this something new?"

The diorama showed an icy snowscape—a frozen world that would soon be discovered by players all over Yondareth, the name of the world depicted in our game. The Sunderlands were located on the polar continent of that globe, lava-heated realms existing under kilometres of thick ice in the polar caps. Only in fantasy.

I twitched my brows, impressed by the astronaut's knowledge of the game. Who knew they had enough spare time during all their hours of training to play our game?

I darted a look at my co-tour guide. Oh yeah, Lucas was also with us, oddly quiet except when lapsing into lengthy explanations to the astronauts about what they were looking at. He seemed distracted and out of sorts, though I couldn't put my finger on why. He also wasn't doing much to engage personably with our guest celebrities.

No, he left that up to me. Which was not much of a hardship after all. I was swimming in a sea of hulking muscles and alpha male testosterone. Nevertheless, it was necessary to dial up the perkiness to make up for Lucas's grumpier-even-than-usual demeanor. The only problem was, the more I flirted with the astronauts, the grumpier he seemed to get. Which, of course, egged me on even more.

It was almost like a challenge. How grumpy could Lucas get? That's just how the two of us interacted. We seemed to enjoy pushing each other's buttons.

So why not just irritate the hell out of him by flirting with a couple or four guys who were extremely easy on the eyes?

"How long have you worked at Draco, Miss Ellis?" another one of the hot hunks—er—astronauts asked. He had a sexy Russian accent and was beyond huge. At least two metres tall and what a body! I'd forgotten his name. It was something unusual and Russian-sounding.

"Call me Katya," I said.

"Short for Ekaterina?" he raised his brows. "A good Russian name."

I smiled. "Katharina. My mum just liked the name."

He laughed, his eyes taking me in with obvious appreciation. "Too bad."

I winked at him. "I haven't gotten any complaints yet."

"Back to the display," Lucas said between his teeth with another dark look at me. "To answer your question, Colonel Sutton, this is part of the new expansion and you are getting a sneak peek."

The only reason they were getting even that was that they'd left their phones in the front, as requested. They'd also been asked to sign NDAs agreeing not to discuss anything they saw here today.

Another astronaut hit Noah Sutton on the back. This one I recognized immediately, being the real celebrity of the group— Commander Ryan Tyler. But he was famous for a sad reason. He'd been involved in the awful accident last year on the International Space Station. Who'd have thought he'd be here, walking around on a tour I was giving at Draco? I was a little star-struck about it, truth be told. So my nervousness just forced me to be even more bubbly and outgoing.

I had the best job ever. Playing video games, one of my favorite things ever, check. Working in tech, like I'd studied for years to do, check. Hot guys all around me? Today that was a big yes.

Today Lucas didn't count. His grumpiness was outweighing his hotness.

A girl could get into trouble quickly with Lucas. Not me. No. We weren't right for each other, anyway.

Sure, I'd blurted his name out in the immigration office when I'd been put on the spot and threatened with deportation. It was because he'd been pestering me about work, anyway. His name had just been handy. He was the first single straight guy I'd thought of when push came to shove.

But I wasn't looking for a love connection—now or anytime in the near future. I was too focused on my job. I had goals. A new home, hopefully, here in sunny southern California and a whole new life for myself that didn't involve that hot mess I'd left behind.

It was good for me to be single for a while.

But that didn't mean I couldn't flirt a little and enjoy the side benefit of provoking Lucas, one of my most favorite pastimes.

Lucas spoke again, fielding questions about the new expansion. "I'm not going to give away the story line. That would ruin it for you all."

"Isn't the game ruined for you, a bit, I mean given that you have to play it over and over again to find all the bugs?"

Lucas smiled. "I guess it's kind of like asking you if space flight is ruined because you spend years training on the same equipment before you can launch."

The fourth astronaut, the one they all called Hammer, laughed. "Point taken."

As he spoke to the guys, I studied my colleague-slash-secret-husband under my lashes. I'd mastered this subtlety that he had never picked up on. Several of the new batch of University interns had a thing for him. One even left him anonymous love notes that I intercepted when I could—to save face for her, of course, and to save Lucas from the requisite embarrassment.

Okay, I'd admit to myself—if no one else, *ever*—that I found Lucas hot.

And never ever would I let my friends learn of that. After a year and change of making it clear that Lucas drove me crazy, I'd never hear the end of it if they knew. Or if they found out we were secretly married. *Gah*. That would be the period on the end of the sentence. Bzzzzt. Game over.

We made our way into the warehouse where there was a full display of virtual reality testing equipment from our sister company, PurVizion. The guys all immediately brightened.

"This is the same equipment we use at XVenture," Commander Tyler said, pulling a headset off its pedestal. "Adam wrote the programming on our simulator. We can interact with all kinds of surfaces and conditions using this, even simulate weightlessness when we are up on a swing and pully system. Are you putting this into the game?"

"We hope to," Lucas answered, brightening. "Still in the early phases of development."

Hammer chimed in. "Let me know if you want some expert advice. Especially if it's a first-person shooter type of game."

For the first time all morning, Lucas cracked a small smile. "I may just take you up on that."

The VR system was one of his favorite subjects lately. After all, he was up for the position to run the new VR division of Draco Multimedia. He'd told me so yesterday as we'd walked out to our cars. "We're currently researching avenues on how to integrate it with our game interfaces while still making it affordable for all our players."

I had to admit that it was fun to watch him become so animated when he got fired up by this subject. He was passionate about gaming and always pitching an idea here or there. Some ideas sucked—and I never hesitated to tell him that—but some of them were pretty darn good. He had a great imagination.

Lucas was such a cool cucumber that he rarely became animated or visibly fired up about mostly anything. Except gaming.

"Why don't you demonstrate it for us, Katya?" The handsome Russian asked. "I'd like to see how this works for games instead of how we're using it to train." He flashed me a huge smile, and I grinned right back at him.

Pretty. So pretty. Damn… how long had it been since I'd had a nice, hot fling?

I couldn't hit him up for a date—even if I truly wanted to—because I was secretly married to the grump across the room. And we couldn't date other people because *rules*.

I put on the light helmet with attached headset and goggles and slipped on my special shoes with sensors on the bottom. Lucas helped me onto the circular treadmill that simulated the ground movement beneath my feet as I ran around in the imaginary world.

Lucas was attentive as he helped me into this, double checking everything. But at one moment, when he stood between me and the other four guys, he muttered under his breath—and, freakishly, without moving his lips, "Knock it off."

When Lucas looked into my face, I pointedly rolled my eyes at him and his olive-toned skin darkened with a flush of… irritation? Anger? Oh boy, that reaction was catnip to my inner troublemaker which felt very gratified in this moment.

I poked my chest out and widened my grin. Then I waggled my eyebrows, scooping up the virtual rifle. Striking a sexy badass warrior-girl pose, I aimed it at Lucas, Lara Croft-style.

"The fake gun is for first-person shooter games, which is by far the most popular type of game being used with virtual reality equipment at the moment. We call them FPS," Lucas started.

"They know what FPS is... They're all gamers and in the military for that matter," I said. Hey maybe after this secret-marriage gig was up, I could get me some of that. Mia didn't have to be the only one of my acquaintance to score a hot nerd. I could one-up her billionaire with an astronaut.

Lucas responded by turning on the game system and turning up the volume so I would only hear him when he spoke on the voice-over mic. Petty of him, of course, but I was warmly satisfied that I'd pushed his buttons enough to crack the veneer of his control. It had become like a game to me.

I'd feel worse about that if he didn't take the same satisfaction in regularly doing the same.

So I hammed it up for the guys... demonstrated the software on the simple demo game. The software had been ported over to the Virtual Reality operating system in order to show how someone could use this equipment with a Massive Multi-Player Roleplaying game—MMO RPG. I threw my everything into it, for the business, of course. I even included extra dramatic hip swings, butt waggles and movements that would make me extra, uh, jiggly in my t-shirt.

Just imagining Lucas's face getting redder by the moment was enough to keep me going.

I ran down virtual trails in the woods, sauntered through desert sand, where the treadmill made it harder for me to walk, simulating trudging through unsteady ground. I swung a rod in my hand that appeared in the game as a simulated sword. The guys, presumably, watched my every move interacting on the screen.

"We're done, Cranberry." Lucas's voice cut through to me on the voiceover. "You can stop hamming it up now and let the guys have a chance to try."

We both helped the guys get into their equipment. There were enough demo rigs for each of them. Let's just say it was no hardship getting up close and personal with all of that hard muscle. Commander Ty had a famous actress girlfriend, Keely Dawson, as their romance had been detailed all over the news. He was still hotter than lava and rather kind to boot. A regular guy for all that he was world famous as an international hero.

Lucas and I stood back and watched the astronauts get involved with the gaming environment, exploring tentatively. With their headphones on, they couldn't hear me so I smacked my lips obnoxiously as if enjoying looking at their hard butts. Beside me, Lucas appeared more and more annoyed. Ahh, sometimes it was just too easy.

"Just remember that you are *not* available," he muttered, his arms folded and his posture tense.

I looked up at him. Lucas was so tall, it was a strain to my neck to meet his gaze when we stood this close. I could smell him—a subtle scent like suede with a tinge of bergamot. "How could I forget, *husband dearest?*" I batted my eyes at him and he jerked his gaze away quickly.

Buttons. Buttons. Between the two of us, we had more buttons to push than the cockpit of the Space Shuttle. And sometimes we risked igniting an explosion as monstrous as something that could shoot you into orbit. It was this constant back-and-forth and I couldn't put my finger on why—no pun intended.

I cocked a brow at him. "As long as you keep remembering that *you're* not available, either."

He smirked as he continued to monitor the guys' progress on the large screen near us. "How could I possibly forget that?" But he mumbled it in such a way that it was obvious that that phrase had way more meaning for him than for me.

"Well if that's supposed to mean you're sick of the blue balls, maybe you should bend your own rules and go on a date or something."

I wasn't oblivious to the hardship he was enduring by staying celibate while he married me as a favor. I mean, I'd feel relieved if he was getting sex regularly on the side, wouldn't I?

But for some reason, that thought actually just made me feel worse.

He gritted his teeth, eyes quickly scanning the room. "You shouldn't be joking about it. What if someone heard you?"

I laughed. "We're stuck at work so often and so late that people already refer to you as my work husband. No worries there. They just take me for what I love to do best—joke around."

He rolled his eyes again. "It's not the only thing you do best."

Before I could reply, I noticed that, since it was lunch hour, other employees had entered the warehouse and were watching the proceedings with interest. Some of them were pointing at the guys and I had to admit, they were quite an impressive sight for any person who was into the mountains of man muscle.

Soon we were helping the guys out of the gear and the clusters of people now crowded around us. Some of them were quite obviously star struck. I bit my lip and asked my co-tour host, "Did Adam and Jordan say anything to you about them signing autographs for the employees?"

Lucas's eyes narrowed, scanning the room as he wound a long cord around a headset in preparation for packing it away in its cozy storage container. "No. We should probably get the guys out of here and up to the atrium. Adam and Jordan should be back from their meeting soon if they aren't already."

Not a bad idea. Hiding them in the CEO or CFO's office would be a handy solution. However, before we could squirrel the astronauts away from the crowd, the men had waded in. They were now talking to our work colleagues, kindly signing autographs and posing for selfies. Too late.

It was a half hour of that goings-on before Adam and Jordan showed up and did their magic to break up the crowd. The guys thanked Lucas and me for our help and fun tour. The Russian had murmured something quietly to Lucas which had him glaring in return, visibly upset.

Hmm. *That* was interesting. Then the Russian approached me and, after thanking me, asked for my number.

I blinked at him in surprise, heart racing, opening and closing my mouth a few times before squeezing out an "I..."

He was hot in a way that the younger version of me would have jumped on in a second. But the reality of going out on a date with him was not as appealing as the fantasy of it—as handsome as he was.

"I, uh, don't even know your name... or I didn't remember it," I stuttered.

The Russian astronaut grinned. "I'll teach you how to say it over a drink. What do you say?"

I blushed, flattered, but ultimately, not super interested. These guys were fun to ogle, but they just weren't my type. It didn't help that Lucas was staring daggers at me from a few yards away while he conversed with Hammer, presumably about game ideas. "I, uh. Thank you, but I can't."

The Russian raised a brow and slid a glance at Lucas out of the corner of his eyes. "Ah I see, not available. Well, maybe you will change your mind. Then..." He pulled out a card from his jeans pocket and handed it to me.

My fingers numbly closed over the card and I smiled, thanking him. My eyes followed the guys out and when I turned, Lucas was practically in my face.

"Well?" he snarled.

I blinked. "What?"

"You gonna throw that away?"

Scowling at him I said. "You're not the boss of me. I mean, not of my personal life."

One dark brow arched over his large brown eyes. "You can't date."

I scowled back at him. Sure I had no intention of going out with the guy, but Lucas didn't need to know that. "He just asked me out for a drink!"

"You can't drink. Not with other men."

I folded my arms over my chest. His eyes flicked down, lingered a little too long on my rack then he pulled his gaze away with an evident struggle.

"Now, now. Don't be sexist. I told you that you could go find yourself a date. You have your wifey's permission." I held up the card as if to read it just to tweak him a little further. His hand flew up and wrapped tightly around my wrist.

I yanked, and he tightened his grip. We struggled like this in a sort of awkward midair arm wrestle, our fiery gazes meeting over the struggle. His eyes narrowed. Mine did the same. He scowled, I bared my teeth at him.

"Domestic violence is frowned upon," I growled.

"So is cheating on your spouse," he snapped back just as quickly.

With that, he reached up with his other hand and plucked the card right out from in between my fingers. When I lunged at him to get it back, he stuffed the damn thing down his pants. *Down his pants.* Like a bully in grade five trying to keep the stolen lunch money away from the scrawny kid on the playground.

In response I slapped his upper arm. It was surprisingly hard under my touch. I knew he had gorgeous arms but in the long sleeved raglan t-shirt he wore today, his muscles were not completely obvious. But when he wore short sleeve t-shirts, I noticed how the sleeves wrapped snugly around his biceps. Even when I nagged and pleaded with myself *not* to notice, I couldn't help myself.

Things would just go easier if I refused to acknowledge that I—very grudgingly—found Lucas attractive, and infuriating, and annoying and... fuckable.

I sneered at him as he gloated. Damn. The asswipe had stolen my bra trick and used the guy version of it. And damned if I didn't want to go digging into his jeans to find that card and fish it back. Purely so I could get the number, of course. And maybe so I could frustrate him.

He shook his head with a laugh. "Don't even think about it. You get this back when we sign the divorce papers. It's for your own good. If immigration found out you were dating someone on the side, the whole thing would be screwed up. And frankly, I didn't go through all this BS and put myself through six months—and *counting*—of celibacy to see it fail."

I blew out a breath and held my hands up, fingers spread wide open. "Fine. Fine. I have a vibrator, anyway. I don't need a dude."

And to my utter satisfaction, his face flushed red. Score one for Kat. Instead of responding, he narrowed his eyes at me.

As I turned to go, I smirked at him over my shoulder. "If you're a good boy, maybe I'll buy you a blowup sheep doll for your birthday."

He responded with a gesture that implied he'd be fondling himself later, poor sap. So I fired off my parting shot before turning to head back to the Den. "Remember to use lube to prevent chafing."

"Hold up, Cranberry. I have a piece of mail for you in my car."

I spun back to face him, brow arched. He'd just given me a handful of letters yesterday. He wasn't due for another mail drop until next week, if at all. It was all business crap and junk mail at this point. A few bills, or the occasional package from online orders.

"Well considering how you hate breaking the rules, I doubt that's an invitation to check out the back seat of your car."

He rolled his eyes. "I would have sat on it and waited until next week but it looked important. It's from Canada."

My jaw involuntarily clenched and I could feel the rest of my body following suit. Mail from Canada couldn't be good... unless one of my old friends had tracked me down and even that held its own problems.

I blinked. "What kind of mail? Like a letter?"

He shrugged. "I didn't open it. It just looked... important. Maybe an immigration thing though I don't know what official mail you need from Canada to do that. It is clearly from a lawyer's office, though."

My stomach dropped, and I fought to unclench the fists at my sides because he was now taking in my posture with a frown of his own. Drawing in a deep sigh, I tried to calm the racing of my heart. A lawyer's office in Canada could mean only one of a very few things—*none* of them good.

My stomach felt like lead but I turned away from him to prevent him from seeing anything more of my reaction. With effort, I effected a shrug and cleared my throat. "I'll stop by your car after work same as always."

After a few steps, where he awkwardly trailed me at my heels, he asked the question. "Is everything okay? You suddenly got really tense."

Huh. Just like him to act all nice after being a jerk for the past half hour. I stepped up my pace because we were about to hit the door of the Den. I'd have an excuse not to answer him once I had it opened. I'd find some peace at my workstation, cocooned in the peaceful bliss of headphones for the rest of the afternoon.

I never got there. Because the moment I entered our workspace, I stopped short, even preventing Lucas from coming up behind me. Holy crap. There was a banner and streamers and balloons. And... a cake sitting at the table for the central workstation.

It was white, trimmed with blue and silver frosting wedding bells. Atop, it said, *Congratulations Kat & Lucas!*

Our colleagues, having noticed our entrance, turned toward us. Warren grabbed a noisemaker that was sitting close to him at his workstation. He started blowing on it so excitedly that I was certain he'd pass out from hyperventilating. A few other bleating sheep followed suit.

Bloody hell.

"What the fuck is this?" I heard Lucas murmur under his breath directly behind me. Taking one step back, my shoulder blades bumped his chest, and I was not unaware of the electric spark that arced between us when that happened. I pulled away almost as quickly, my pulse leaping.

"It's a surprise wedding reception in response to the surprise secret wedding!"

Joel, one of the QA team leaders, popped up from his workstation beside my empty one. Others approached us, immediately surrounding us. My stomach dropped into my shoes and I found it impossible to look at Lucas.

How the hell did all these people find out? And when? And why? And... *how?*

My eyes flew back to the cake again. It was a giant white sheet cake decorated with big bright blue lettering. And standing in the middle of it, a LEGO bride and groom. A shimmery mylar banner had been taped to the table underneath it that read, *Congratulations Mr. and Mrs!*

I'd groan at the cheesiness of it if the gesture hadn't been so incredibly sweet.

Of course, in this joint, any excuse to binge on cake during business hours was an excuse to celebrate during high stress deadlines and late hours getting projects done. We had an oft-repeated motto in the Den. *"Mmm, Cake!"*

And for good reason. We brought in cakes for Arbor day (covered in trees, of course), Grandparents day (so we'd remember them and eat cake in their honor) and even Groundhog Day.

I could feel the tension and animosity radiating from the man standing behind me, so I reached out and put a hand on his arm. My previous stress from the news about the lawyer's letter had now evaporated. I was now in management mode—as in managing the sudden tension of the man behind me. Judging from the reactions of my co-workers, this gesture was interpreted as a tender touch between lovers—married spouses. Ugh.

Well obviously there was no way out of this but through. Not unlike that famous quote about getting out of Hell.

"How—how did you find out?" I blurted in a breathy voice.

My co-worker Joel darted a sheepish look at Warren. "Uh, well… you made a phone call yesterday in the back hallway. I was running an errand out to shipping and, um, overheard. I wasn't eavesdropping, I swear!"

Warren stepped up, scratching at his shaved head. "We thought it would be a nice way to show you that we know. This way, you won't have to keep it secret while angsting about how to tell us. I've seen a lot of rom-coms. I know how secret marriages work. Sometimes they can be a trap that breeds even *more* secrets!"

"How thoughtful of you," Lucas bit out in a dry voice. My fingers tightened where my hand rested on his forearm as a warning. We'd have to be very careful about this. *Very* careful. There was the upcoming interview at the immigration office, after all. We'd have to play along, but there was no easy way to tell this to Lucas in the middle of a cluster of our co-workers.

Joel was grinning, scruff covered dimples deepening. "I called this last year. I mean not that things would happen this fast but... you know. We all figured there was something going on with you two." Several others nodded. To our shock.

Well shit.

And, wait... *what?*

"It was a spur-of-the-moment thing," I heard myself say. "We were impulsive!"

Angie, the only other woman who worked in our department, darted an unreadable look at Lucas, biting at her lip stud. "We kind of knew it was coming. So hey, let us eat cake!" She gave that last line a sing-song tone, another one of our mottos, actually.

While everyone huddled around the cake, I met Luke's gaze. He returned it with a desperation in the back of those deep brown eyes—a deer in the headlights, sure. But even more prominent was the coal of simmering anger. *Gulp.*

Yesterday, he'd specifically asked me if I'd been overheard and I'd said no. Because as far as I knew, I hadn't been. I'd taken all my usual measures to ensure privacy. Apparently that hadn't been enough.

Faster than you could say "shotgun wedding," we were being handed slices of white cake on non-eco-friendly plastic plates. They were decorated with yellow and pink flowers and scrolled *I love you's* in gold on the edges. And people were handing us clear plastic cups of sparkling apple cider instead of champagne. "We're at work. Much as it would be fun to hit the booze, maybe we'll do that at happy hour on Friday," Joel said.

Oh yeah. More fun than getting a tooth pulled. *Egads.*

The truly awkward moment, however, came a few minutes later as we all stood around forking the cake into our pie-holes and sharing coy glances at each other. Lucas never looked up once. And to be honest, I don't think I'd ever seen someone shovel in cake that fast. He looked like he was trying to figure out a way to inhale it. Joel stood at his shoulder and had asked him a question, which only caused Lucas to shovel it in faster.

He was going to choke to death. Or give himself severe diabetes.

And either one of those possibilities would make me a widow. At the ripe age of twenty-six.

I opened my mouth to give him an excuse to leave, not even sure what I'd say. Maybe ask him to grab something out of my car for me.

Before I could, Warren was hitting the side of his plastic cup with his plastic fork. I frowned at this odd behavior as everyone else beamed at us with cakey mouths.

"You know what that means!" Joel chimed in, cheesy grin widening.

"I actually have no—" I began before being cut off by a bizarre chant that started faintly and grew.

"Kiss, kiss, kiss. KISS. KISS!"

Eww. No. "Gotta do it for good luck," said Joel.

Now I was sure that I was the one with the deer-in-the-headlights look on my face as I turned to Lucas.

Woodenly he bent and pecked me on the cheek. His rough, whiskered cheek grazed mine and my heartbeat raced. He smelled... clean and subtle. Like soap and suede. Mmm. It was a good smell.

But our colleagues weren't satisfied. "Dude," another co-worker snarked at him. "Kiss her like you mean it."

"I don't do PDA," Lucas snapped back.

"Me either," I nodded vigorously. "I'm not the romantic type."

Angie frowned. "But you're in love, right? Why aren't you wearing wedding rings or... just generally acting married? I mean, you say you're not romantic, but you ran off and did a really romantic thing. I assume you went to Vegas over the weekend?"

I blinked, my mouth dropping. "I—we—yes, of course we're in love!" I said, my eyes avoiding everyone else's gaze. "We were just being impulsive. And we ordered rings online. They haven't come in yet."

Crapola. How did I get myself into these crackpot situations? Was the red hair a curse? Was I constantly going to pull a Lucy Ricardo—or Anne of Green Gables—because of some bizarre redhead curse?

With a blank face, Lucas set aside his plate and then turned to me. "Maybe just this once." Before I could even figure out what he was doing, he hitched an arm around my waist and bent down to kiss me.

The minute our lips touched, everyone around us let out a whistle, or a cheer and applause. It was embarrassing as hell and I felt the heat in my cheeks, my neck... my lips. Okay maybe the heat in my lips was coming from contact with another set of lips. I could feel the rough around the edges where his whiskers from his perpetual scruff scratched me. That only added to the sensation flooding through me.

It felt like I was soaring down the steep part of a roller coaster at maximum speed, my breath catching, my heart sprinting, everything tingling. Everything feeling alive, straight down to the deepest parts of me. Heat formed there, boiled and roiled. His lips moved on mine and—*holy crap*. Was that his tongue?

As everyone around us egged him on, his tongue was suddenly on mine. The tips touched and pushed together, fencing against each other, vying for position. His kiss tasted like the vanilla from the cake and something hot, spicy. Like cinnamon. To my everlasting embarrassment, I let out a little squeak of surprise and pleasure that I desperately hoped no one heard. But Lucas. He heard. His breath hitched and his hand on my head shifted when he heard it. And for just a second, he slipped that hand lower, to my neck, lacing those fingers through my hair. He stroked the side of my neck before abruptly pulling away.

Our eyes met and—*wow*—*heat*. Like something inside me had melted and taken on a new shape type of heat. His eyes locked on mine, reminding me of a freshly ignited flame. Raw, hungry, licking the surrounding air, desperate for more oxygen.

What the hell just happened?

My husband of six months had just kissed me for the first time since we'd exchanged vows. And though it had been brief, it had been incredibly hot, which explained the liquified sensation deep in my belly... and lower.

Cripes. Had Lucas turned me on? With a single goddamn kiss?

Lucas and I ripped gazes away from each other and he pointedly looked at the clock on the wall at the far end of the Den. "Okay, party time is over. No more questions. The cat's out of the bag—"

"Literally!" someone chimed in.

My face flamed even hotter at the insinuation. "—and you all know, so let's get back to work. We still need to categorize all the bug reports from the beta testers."

After the requisite groans and complaints, our co-workers obeyed. Lucas and I shared another look, one where I was desperately trying to ask him WTF with my eyes without saying a word. I'm sure I looked as panicked as I felt but his face was calm, that same blank he was so good at doing. Very deliberately, he turned from me and went to his workstation.

I had too much nervous energy to sit down. Instead, I picked up all the cups and plates and stuffed them into a trash bag to take out to the dumpster.

When I returned, there were a bunch of guys from development clustered around our wedding cake like a flock of vultures. They were forking cake in and chatting with the game testers. Lucas was nowhere to be found and when they saw me, they all looked extremely guilty.

Obviously they had been talking about us when I'd entered. The cluster quieted after I ignored them and went back to my workstation. When Lucas re-entered the room—presumably after having gone to the washroom—the devs scattered like wet cats under a bucket of ice water.

Well shit. Here we go. I predicted that the news would be out and well-circulated within the next quarter of an hour. I could practically hear the entire Draco campus buzzing around me with it even now as my mind raced. I looked at my phone.

It was quickly lighting up with all kinds of text messages.

And before he hit the off button on his phone, Lucas's device had practically vibrated itself off the surface of his desk. Our gazes met again, and I opened my eyes wide. But he shook his head and went back to work.

He clearly did *not* want to talk about what this all meant. I could try to send him a message, but he was decidedly ignoring his phone right now. Which was probably the best idea.

I turned mine off as well. Mind racing, I grabbed a pen and spare pad of yellow sticky notes to make a quick list. It wasn't long and had the names of everyone I needed to reach out to soon, before the shit really hit the fan.

As I was brainstorming—and then doodling while I pondered all the ramifications of this recent development—more people entered to gawk and grab some cake. Before they could, however, Lucas shooed them out with a forceful and grumpy growl. Then he muttered, with an acrid eye cast around the room as if daring anyone to challenge him, that he wished there was a bolt lock on the Den door. Someone suggested wedging a chair up against it and, though he didn't follow through, he did mutter something about maybe he'd try that next.

Except the next person to whip through the door was someone he couldn't do anything about. Because it was Mia, my best friend.

And from the look on her face, she'd already heard. And she looked hurt.

Damn. Damn it. Dammity damn.

Lucas shot out of his seat and whirled on her before realizing she wasn't just another pesky co-worker come to interrupt our bug hunting.

Nope. She was the CEO's wife, the newly minted Mrs. Drake herself.

And Lucas wouldn't be able to scare her away as he'd done all the others.

"Mia... hi," he said and then immediately turned toward me with an alarmed look on his face.

Mia's eyes dropped to the half-eaten sheet of wedding cake, the Lego bride and groom now positioned like they were having missionary sex by some cheeky, immature idiot. Then her wide brown eyes flicked back to me. "Wow, so it's true? I thought it was a joke."

It was... kinda. But it wasn't a joke I could let my boss's wife in on. Even if she was my closest friend in the world.

But yeah, how could I tell her that when her husband had generously offered me a job, I'd faked my credentials to be able to work in the US illegally?

Guilt stabbed at me for not the first time when I contemplated the risk for the company with my sketchy escapades. There was no way to explain all the complex whys and hows of it to Mia—not now. It'd been easier to work here illegally than to apply for a work visa, given my special circumstances. The possibility of alerting the wrong people of my whereabouts was a constant source of anxiety for me.

If the lawyers on that letter in Lucas's car were who I thought they were, it was very possible that jig was up, anyway. So much for hiding out south of the border. I swallowed a lump, shoving that worry aside as I looked up at Mia and steeled myself.

Criminy. This thing was like the proverbial snowball rolling downhill out of control. It grew bigger than a skyscraper, threatening to take out an entire village upon meeting its demise at the bottom of the mountain.

I briefly contemplated telling Mia the truth because I knew I could trust her. But asking her to keep such a huge secret from her brand-new husband, my boss, wasn't fair. I couldn't ask that of her.

So it was time to lie my ass off, yet again.

I popped out of my seat, flicking my hair behind me. "Hey babe! What's up? Are your med school classes over for the day?"

As I hadn't seen her in a while, I gave her a quick hug. She didn't hug back. Instead, she stared at me like I was a crazy person.

"Wanna sit with me for a minute in the Pit?" I asked.

She made a face. "Has it been thoroughly sanitized recently?"

I led her to the far end of our workspace. The Pit was an arrangement of mismatched couches, overstuffed chairs, two semi-folded futon mattresses, a couple leaky beanbags patched with duct tape and a currently occupied dog bed. We typically used that area to crash for a few hours during long workweeks. It was a necessary refuge for occasional catnaps to help us through the long nights, often stretching well past sunrise.

Mia's aversion to it was borne from the usual décor. Crumbs, odd bits of litter, spilled snacks, empty pizza boxes and other detritus. With all these twenty-something, barely civilized and predominately male occupants, the trash accumulated at an exponential rate. Fortunately, it had all been cleaned up since we'd met our big deadline.

I sat beside Mia on the leather couch. Max, Lucas's dog, looked up from the dog bed but only beat his large fluffy tail on the ground, begging for a free pet. He frequently hung out with us in the office. Employees in our department loved having him around. As a group, we lavished him with pets, playtime and several walks a day. It was to our benefit, too, with much-needed opportunities for occasional fresh air and exercise. Or even just a chance to rest our eyes from the long hours of staring at monitors. We liked to refer to him as QA's emotional support animal and he was happy to oblige. We were the only department at Draco allowed our own regular mascot.

All the humans within earshot were working hard at their workstation—or appearing to work hard, at least—with headphones on. Mia turned to me the second my butt landed on the cushion. "What the hell is this all about? I thought you and Lucas—" she paused to look around and make sure said person was nowhere he could hear us. "—hated each other."

I bit my lip and then faked a grin. "Well you know what they say about the fine line between love and hate, right?"

She arched a brow at me, clearly unbelieving. Damn, this was going to be harder than I thought and I was unprepared for it.

In my perfect world, I wouldn't have to explain this to anyone because it would be over as quickly as it had begun. We'd never have to act like we were married for anyone but the interviewers at the immigration office.

No fakeness. No lies. Just discrete paperwork, a green card and subsequent divorce decree. And all neatly wrapped up without any of the messy personal bullshit involved. And no one had to get hurt.

A nice tidy business arrangement. Lucas wanted that job badly—and I was happy to help him get it. It was only fair, since he was helping me out too. So far we'd stuck to each other's end of the bargain. He was this-close to getting what he wanted. And, hopefully, so was I.

We'd come way too far to mess this up now. I had to see it through.

"What is *actually* going on, Kat? Is he blackmailing you or something? Did you lose a bet?" She snorted a little when she laughed.

I suppressed a grimace. "It was impulsive. Just something we did on a lark."

"On a... lark?" If her eyebrows climbed any higher, they'd vanish into her hairline. "It, uh, it didn't have something to do with catching the bouquet at my wedding, did it? I promise I didn't engineer that. I was trying to aim it at Jenna."

Suddenly the image of that bouquet caught in my long hair while I panicked and fought to free it came back to me. Despite the panic I'd felt then, I couldn't help but laugh at Mia's insinuation. "You mean you think I got nabbed by the special magic of the uber love bouquet from the super-couple wedding?"

She stared at me, baffled. "I didn't mean it like that. I just mean—"

Time to go on the offensive. "Not everyone dreads marriage like you once did, Mia. I'm thrilled. Lucas is thrilled. We're both blissfully happy. We didn't do it the way normal people do, with a big fancy party but we're both computer nerd introverts and just wanted something quiet."

Wow. Who knew that it would be so easy to tell such a big fat lie? If I were Pinocchio, the tip of my nose would be halfway to Toronto by now.

Mia shook her head, her long brown hair floating down her shoulders. "Yes. Sure. Of course people do things differently, I just—" She stopped herself and then hesitated for another long moment while she studied me. "I'm sorry. I'm just surprised. But if you're happy, then so am I. Congratulations."

I grinned. "Thank you."

She bent forward and hugged me, pulling me in tight. When she pulled back, a lot of tension that had been there when she first came in seemed to have evaporated—or at least I could hope. Mia was very smart and so I'd have to be careful or she'd easily catch me up in a lie. And since I sucked at lying, that could be scarily easy for her to do.

"Who'd have thought it... Cranberry and Jedi Boy." Then she snorted again that cute little snort she often did when she laughed.

I rolled my eyes at her in response because yeah, I had no good logical reason to explain it. Always blame it on something ooey and gooey that a newlywed like her would buy. Blame it on the "power of looooooove." Since I didn't believe in such a power overtaking my own treasured sense of logic, it became even easier to lie about.

I'd learned far too long ago that the people who were supposed to love you the most were the ones who could also hurt you the most. And I didn't want anyone to have that power over me.

I glanced at my smartwatch, hoping that this would remind her I was still on the clock—the same clock that her husband was paying me by. She took the hint.

"You need to get back to work, but we should get together soon. It's been too long. Since Adam and I got married and I started third year, I haven't been keeping up with my social life. Are you doing anything tomorrow night?"

I sat up, excited. "Coolness, the four of us could get our group together and play DE. It's been ages. I'll let Heath know when I get home—"

The words were out of my mouth the moment I realized what I'd said.

Mia's features clouded. "You're still living with Heath?"

Oh. Shit. Shiiiiiit. Ugh. Yes, boys and girls, Kat officially sucks at lying.

"I haven't had the time to move my stuff over to Lucas's house yet. You know, I've got my Twitch streaming set-up and all that equipment. And we've been working hard on the expansion. I, ah stop by his condo each night to say hi and grab my stuff for the next day." Wow... it was like once I opened up the spigot of lies, they just poured out with almost no effort.

She shook her head. "You can't keep living like that. You *do* have friends. If we band together, we could have you moved in half a day. I have this weekend off. We'll get your stuff moved over."

I wasn't sure if she could see me pale—since I'd been born pale. Being a ginger from the Great White North only compounded my whitey-whiteness. So she may not have seen me lose my color but I could definitely feel the blood draining from my face.

"Uh—oh you guys are so busy. Don't worry about me—"

She waved her hand. "Nonsense. It's not even that big a deal. We'll get it done for you. You shouldn't have to live like that. And I want you guys to come over for dinner once you're settled in and we all have more time. I don't know Lucas very well and we should get to know him better as soon as possible."

My jaw dropped. "I'll have to check with Lucas's calendar but..."

Mia's eyes-caught on a movement off behind my shoulder and nodded, her smile widening. "Ask him now. Or I can. Lucas are you free sometime next week in the evening?"

I heard footsteps behind me and fought the urge to tense. Max immediately sprung from his dog bed and went to Lucas, tail wagging furiously like a banner in the wind. Lucas reached out to pet the dog absently as he glanced from Mia to me and back again.

"Uh, yeah, nothing big. Just cleaning up on the last of the bug reports. Why?"

"Because you and your *wife* are invited to have dinner with Adam and me as soon as you can fit it in."

"Uh," he blinked and looked at me. "Well..."

I clenched my jaw before darting a hand out to grab his and squeeze it—maybe a little too tight. I could feel Mia's eyes on us, drinking in every single detail of the interaction.

"Honey, wouldn't it be fun to hang out with another couple? Don't think of it as dinner with the boss."

Mia smiled. "It's all good. I'll text you with the date and time." She pushed out of her seat. "I've got to go but I'll be in touch about this weekend, too. Gotta see who I can round up to help with your move."

"Your move?" Lucas asked as I stood, following Mia's example. Mia was momentarily distracted by patting Max on the head and I shot Lucas a meaningful look. He frowned, clearly not understanding. Typical male.

"Uh yeah, Mia thought it was weird that all my stuff is still at Heath's condo. I was explaining that we hardly had the time, what with all the deadlines and productivity marks we had to hit for the expansion."

Lucas blinked. "Uh yeah, yeah.... That's... yeah." He ran a hand through his hair, shoulders stiff again.

"Anyway, I'm off." She checked the time on her phone. The monstrous rock on her left hand nearly blinded me as the diamond caught the late afternoon sunlight. Which reminded me... we needed to get some sort of rings to wear to keep up appearances now. "Gonna go give the hubby a quick peck and take off. See you guys soon!"

The minute Mia had vanished through the Den door, Lucas's hand was clamped around my upper arm—and not terribly gently, either. "Can we have a quick chat in private, sugar buns?"

My brow shot up. Despite the ridiculous endearment, his tone was anything but light. In fact, he sounded incredibly pissed off. I supposed I didn't blame him. That was a lot to dump on him all at once.

Shit. I was certain there was going to be yelling involved with this, too. With a not-so-light tug, he pulled me in the direction of the exit. Max, with a lack of humans to entreat for pets, went back to lounging on his dog bed. As we exited the Den, I overheard a comment about the two "lovebirds" going to "make out."

Jesus Murphy. Some of these kids were sorely in need of getting their cherry popped. Way to uphold the geek stereotype, dudes.

Lucas didn't let go of my arm until we'd gone to the same deserted hallway where I'd had my phone conversation—and was, apparently, overheard—yesterday. It was our go-to place for privacy around here. But apparently not a good enough go-to place.

Or too many people knew about it.

But Lucas didn't stop here, no. He led us to the glass door that opened out to the side parking lot, equally deserted at this time of day as that's where the maintenance people parked. He pushed us both through the door, waiting until it banged shut before letting me go. It was almost as if he thought I might flee screaming into the horizon.

I kinda felt like fleeing, to be honest. Especially because of the stormy look on his face.

"What the ever-living fuck, Kat?" he ground out between clenched teeth.

I rubbed at a knot of tension between my eyebrows where pain seemed to be blossoming out of nowhere. Which was weird, because I never, ever got headaches. Studiously avoiding his gaze, I stared at the asphalt in front of my feet. "It's not my fault."

"The *fuck* it's not. You weren't careful enough and now the beans have been spilled. Everywhere. They haven't just been spilled. They've exploded all over our lives and everything is a shitty mess now."

Despite his rant, I laughed, unable to suppress the image of a disastrous Mexican restaurant kitchen mishap with his metaphor. I wondered how you said "exploding beans" in Spanish?

"As usual, you aren't taking this seriously. Why am I not surprised? When I agreed to do this for you, we made rules for it."

"*You* made the rules and I'm sorry. I didn't do this on purpose. I had to give the immigration office your info for the appointment. I had to make that call during business hours because the office is closed during the scant few hours that I'm not working or sleeping. I made that call right over there." I pointed just inside the glass door we had exited. "Since I practically live here, there was no other option."

He shook his head. "Well obviously you weren't careful enough. Now—"

I held up my hand to stop him. "Is this productive? You talk all the time in our meetings about not wasting time with who or what is to blame. That we should just focus on working the problem and getting it cleaned up. So how do we clean up the exploded beans?"

He put his hands on his hips and shifted his stance from one leg to the other. From the look on his face, he was none too pleased about having his own words repeated back to him to shut him down. But it was true. We had a massive problem on our hands and no time to shout at each other about whose fault it was.

So I folded my arms, squared my shoulders and waited for his reply.

CHAPTER 3
LUCAS

I TRIED TO IGNORE HOW HER SWEATER TIGHTENED OVER HER chest and emphasized her perfect boobs when she folded her arms like that. I *tried*.

And failed. And this only served to piss me off more and make me more exasperated with myself. Even at a time like this, I couldn't ignore how hot Katya was. My now, not-so-secret wife.

A wife I couldn't see naked or touch. Or take to bed.

A wife I was currently yelling at in the back parking lot where hopefully no one could overhear us.

It was like I was stuck inside some insane marriage nightmare. In this case, I was forced to endure all the disadvantages of being married without any of the advantages— like, say, regular sex with a gorgeous, naked woman.

I'd been on the damned marriage merry-go-round once before. At least that time, I got sex. Until the end, of course.

This time, I was like the cat who could never get to that singing canary up on the pedestal as she sang in her gilded cage. I could only watch her from afar and drool. Jesus. Even in my head, I sounded like a creeper.

"Fine," I said, my fist closing at my side as I willed myself to stop thinking about what she might look like naked. "Fine. Let's examine this gigantic mess you've just created for both of us. Because now, apparently, you're moving in with me?"

She looked up at me, wide-eyed with those big baby-blue eyes of hers and nodded like a chastened child. "You have a big house. You have a couple rooms that you're only using for storage. I could move my mattress over—or just sleep on an air mattress. You have a *big* house. You'll hardly notice me."

Oh, how very wrong she was about that. I'd notice her constantly. Even when she wasn't in eye shot. "I'll even pay you rent!" she added hastily.

And that was probably the funniest part of this entire thing. She had no idea how little I needed the money. And not just from the millions I'd earned in Draco stock, either. But all the money I'd had before that—which I now refused to touch.

Which brought me to the next facet of this entire bullshit mess—

My family. God. With this out in the open, I was now going to have to come clean and tell my family that I'd up and married again. At least this time the wedding hadn't cost them millions of dollars that they'd hardly noticed spending. And Kat. She had zero idea about the family that she'd married into.

Not that I'd even planned on ever having them meet her. This was all supposed to be long over and behind us before we had to meet any relatives.

"Our families," I finally said out loud.

She raised a dark red brow. "What? What about them?"

I gave her a look like I thought she was an idiot for even asking the question. "We're going to have to tell them, Kat. And I'm sure your parents are going to want to meet me."

She rolled her eyes. "Don't be so sure. They've got too much other crap to worry about."

Huh. That was weird. It occurred to me then that Kat almost never talked about her family and I knew little about them beyond the necessary facts. And those I only knew so we'd be good to go for the immigration interview. Her dad was a documentary production assistant and her mom was a nurse. They'd been married a little over thirty years and lived just outside of Vancouver, British Columbia in the suburb of Port Coquitlam. Sounded refreshingly honest and middle class to me.

She also had a brother, just under a year older than her. I knew hardly anything about him except that he hadn't gone to college and did not appear to be gainfully employed, still living at home at the age of twenty-seven.

I frowned. I'd have to investigate all of that later.

For now, I was too busy chastising myself for being so intent and focused on that job promotion that I hadn't considered all the ramifications. I'd taken drastic steps to keep Kat here because with her very particular talents, she was going to help me hit the deadlines and as a consequence, get this job. Kat was my secret weapon—even if she didn't know it.

With her talent, we could not have made the deadline without her. I was certain of it. So if it meant I had to mock a certain institution I had no respect for anyway to keep her here, I hadn't hesitated to do it.

Maybe I should have hesitated a little, because obviously, I hadn't thought this through as thoroughly as I should have.

I cleared my throat. "Well I'm going to have to tell my family because it will almost certainly get back to them—and soon.

Brace yourself because they'll insist on meeting you immediately."

She blinked and then shrugged. "Okay. That's fine. I can do a family meet and greet, no problem, unless... unless they're serial killers or something."

Worse. They were rich. As in loaded. As in stinking ridiculously goddamn wealthy.

And until now, and with the exception of Jordan, around here, that fact had been my best-kept secret. Now, who knew what would happen?

"Listen." She spoke after I hadn't answered her rhetorical question. She looked down, pushing a strand of glossy flame behind her pale, delicate ear. "I'm sorry this happened. I took every precaution I could. The same precautions that have worked well for the past six months. But I got unlucky. Once we do the immigration interview, and I get the green card, I promise to move out as soon as I can. In fact, I've been scrimping and saving. Once we get the closing bonus for the expansion, I'll have enough for a down payment on a place of my own. It won't be a big house like yours but it will be mine. I don't really want to invade your space but, yeah... we're kind of stuck, now."

I took a deep breath and let it go. Yeah. Stuck. With her gorgeous face and her sexy body walking around my house... *Jesus.* My thought processes were completely clouded by sexual deprivation, apparently.

My jaw tightened. "I have rules, then."

She raised a brow. "Why am I not surprised? You always have rules."

"Enough with the snarky remarks."

She blinked a few times as if unable to believe her ears. "Do you even know me? And... and is that a rule? Because, I can tell you right now—"

I held up a hand to stop her. "It's not one of the rules, no. First rule is that we'll sleep in separate bedrooms, of course. We both agree to be fully clothed while in the common areas of the home. The kitchen, the living room, and all the rest."

She nodded. "Okay, easy enough to do. Lucky for you I'm not a nudist. We had nudist neighbors growing up, and that shit was all sorts of crazy. They were not young and, well lots of things sag. And, you know, Vancouver winters are not warm." She faux-shuddered. "And gardening, that was a whole other kettle of fish. I'm not even a little tempted to do the nudist thing."

Thank god. Not that I wouldn't love to see her naked, of course, but even imagining it wasn't good for the level of sexual frustration I'd been suffering from lately. And having sex with my hand was only succeeding in taking the edge off. But I anticipated things were only going to get worse with her under my roof.

"Okay so no getting naked except in the shower or in our own rooms." She nodded decisively, as if I'd been giving her instructions for work. "Fine... what else?"

I gulped, then stiffened. "Pick up your messes."

She scowled. "I'm not *that* bad."

"You're the queen of clutter. If your room at home looks anything like your work desk, then you better keep that shit contained in your bedroom at my house. With the door closed at all times."

She frowned. "It's just organized chaos. I know where everything is."

"And as I've told you before—"

"'Chaos on the outside reflects the state of mind.' Yes, I've heard that about eleventy dozen times. Fine, I will endeavor not to trigger your anal retentive OCD neat freak tendencies with my clutter."

Instead of rolling my eyes, I cocked my head at her and stared her down. Our gazes clashed, and she jutted her chin out at me defiantly. Then she raised her auburn brows at me, as if to ask me, *Is that all you've got?*

Oh dear Ms. Ellis, you just have no idea, do you?

My mind was drawing a blank now. The main condition had been the naked one. That one was really the most important regulation I could think of, anyway. I grasped for anything. "Take the trash out when it's full."

She just rolled her eyes. "I'm not uncivilized."

I sighed. "You do come from the land of Tundra, hosers and ice-hut dwellers."

She rewarded me with a scowl. So I decided to poke at her some more. It was a pastime of mine. "It's okay, Cranberry. One day Canada will rule the world and then everyone else will be *sorry*." I made sure to give that "sorry" a marked Canadian pronunciation.

In truth, I actually liked her Canadian accent. It was subtle. Almost unrecognizable from the typical west coast American accent—except for slight differences on some words that you only heard if you spent time around her.

On those words, the vowels were softer, more clipped. And there was a slightly different cadence to some of them. But just those tiny giveaways on words like *sorry* that, for her, rhymed with *story*. And other words like *about, house, out*, which sounded way less harsh than their American counterparts. Those tiny clues were enough to reveal that she wasn't yet another pretty California girl.

Nope, she was an absolutely stunning Canadian girl.

An absolutely stunning and *exasperating*, Canadian girl.

Her eyes narrowed. "At least I come from a country that knows that beer isn't supposed to taste like cow piss."

"Beer and poutine. The staples of all fine haute cuisine."

She shrugged, putting her hand on the doorknob. "You forgot moose steaks. And elk hoof soup."

Elk hoof soup? I scoffed. "Is that really a thing?"

She blew out a breath, shaking her head as she yanked the door open. "Of course you would ask me that."

I followed her down that back and somewhat private hallway, trying hard not to focus on her ass as she strode in front of me. *Eyes at eye level, Lucas.*

Just as we were about to turn the corner, however, she stopped and spun on me. It happened so quickly that I almost collided with her. As it was, by the time I stopped we were mere inches apart. She locked gazes with me and then reached out and flicked one of the buttons on my shirt with her finger. "One last rule. There will absolutely and under no circumstances be sex, right?"

I blinked. "Are you asking me or are you telling me?"

"Well, I mean, we already aren't having sex with other people but—" she gestured between the two of us. "—as a married couple. One might expect..."

I shook my head and swallowed. "There are no expectations."

Her face was unreadable as she nodded. "Okay, I guess we won't need a rule."

I licked my lips and shrugged. "I guess not." But I could always fantasize. That didn't break the rules. Of course fantasizing always made it more difficult to *keep* the rules so fantasizing was out.

Note to self—no more fantasizing.

Did I read a little disappointment on her face as she turned to round the corner ahead of me? Perhaps she'd misunderstood me, though I'd spoken the truth. There were, indeed, no expectations of sex. She'd asked me for a favor and she was at my mercy to go through with it so she could get permanent residency and stay in the country. For me to ask for—or worse, expect—sex would make her feel obligated. And that would be gross.

But that fact didn't preclude my interest in her. She didn't need to know that. And I was good at keeping secrets. I'd had a lot of practice.

As I rounded the corner, I caught Jordan just leaving the Den with a plate full of cake. He was speaking to Kat and when I came into view, caught my gaze with a pointed raise of the brows. *Oh God, here we go.*

"Hey Lucas, I was just congratulating your blushing bride here on your surprise nuptials." He shifted his cake plate to his left hand and held out the right one to shake mine. I gripped it, giving a quick pump before dropping it. Kat thanked him and slipped inside, shooting me another unreadable look. I wasn't sure if that was in reaction to what I'd said in the hallway or to this fresh development.

I knew I wasn't going to get off with a mere thank you like Kat had, but I tried it, anyway. "Thanks, bro. I gotta get—"

As I went to move around him, he held out a hand and pressed it on my chest, blocking me. "Nice move. Didn't think you'd anticipated me. Or did this all go down last night after I talked to you?"

I frowned, trying to read him. He had a teasing grin on his face, brownish-green eyes dancing. Jordan loved to tease and mock and sometimes he was a pain in the ass. But he was also a good friend.

"What, you think I got married to increase my chances for the promotion?" And that's exactly what I'd been afraid of, of course.

He gave a noncommittal shrug, a curl of his lip as if to ask, *Why wouldn't I think that?*

"That seems like a drastic thing to do," I continued.

Jordan laughed. "Marriage, by definition, is a drastic thing to do."

I blinked. "Have you shared that opinion with your girlfriend?"

"April knows all about my opinions."

I blew out a breath, ready to blow *him* off before he dug any deeper into uncomfortable territory. "Well you know what they say about opinions being like assholes. Everyone's got one but I don't necessarily want to know about yours because it most likely stinks."

He nodded, taking my crap in stride like he often did. For as much as Jordan liked to dish it out, he could also take the shit directed his way equally well. In fact, he was the type of guy who respected you for giving it back to him, as long as it was properly meted out and well-deserved.

Jordan leaned in and lowered his voice. "Listen. You know and I know that you are way over-qualified for your current job.

Even Adam knows that. Any extra push you can give to let him know of your commitment, has my full support. Even if it means marrying the boss's wife's best friend."

I clenched my jaw, irritation boiling at the base of my spine. Jordan drew back, studying my reaction. "I know you hate the whole nepotism thing. But sometimes... when you need a slight edge. Sometimes things like this can help."

"I don't need or want that kind of help. And you of all people should know that damn well."

A smooth smile, a knowing nod. "Understood." And when I went to grab the doorknob to enter the Den, he stopped me again. "Don't hurt her or I will be forced to break both your legs."

"Right on. I'm shaking in terror already. Enjoy your cake." I made another note to myself. Once this was all over, Kat would have to go around trumpeting about how our "conscious uncoupling" had hurt no feelings whatsoever.

No hearts would be bruised in the making and breaking of this marriage. Guaranteed.

That night, I hit my front door with a plan on how to carefully spread the news to everyone else in my life. I'd have to do it fast but first, I had priorities. It was nearly dinner time, and I had to feed a hungry, slobbering dog almost immediately.

Max waited patiently as I dished out his food and I nuked myself some frozen dinner while he noisily gobbled his in three seconds flat. I was composing a mental list of everyone I'd need to reach out to about this whole mess. My family would be hearing soon about the sudden marriage so I needed a hastily crafted story to head off the shitstorm at the pass.

I scrolled through the various stunned text messages on my phone, resolving to answer them later when a new one popped up.

Michaela: We still on for piano lesson Sat. and WTF holy crap did you and Kat actually get married or is that some crazy ass rumor someone is pranking me with?

Michaela, my former roommate until recently. Well, might as well start here. I keyed in my reply.

Lucas: No prank. 100% serious. We eloped last weekend.

I took a breath after typing that. What was one more lie, really? Kat and I had spent a few minutes after I'd handed over her mail inventing a new timeline for the secret marriage. Might as well try the story out on Michaela.

Lucas: Gonna need to give you a rain check Sat. cuz we're moving her stuff in. Would you mind watching the dog that day? He's prob gonna get over excited with all the activity.

The microwave beeped, and I waited a minute to pull the steaming tray out. Salisbury steak again. Oh well, someday I'd have time to actually have a real meal. Michaela's reply zoomed back to me faster than I thought she could thumb-type.

Michaela: We're, uh, talking about the same Katya, right? Red hair, works with you in QA? You 2 usually hate each other?

I heaved a sigh. This didn't bode well for the rest of the people to whom I'd have to spread the news.

Lucas: Yep, one and the same. Will you take the dog? Promise you extra practice time on the piano, happy to give you all the lessons you want.

Since she'd moved out, we'd been trading dog sitting favors in exchange for my giving her lessons. It had been nice to keep some small semblance of a social life outside of work. Michaela didn't work at Draco, though her boyfriend, Jeremy—my competition for the big job—did. Nevertheless, I still counted her as a non-work friend.

Michaela: I knew I was right… when I said that you two need to boink and get it over with. Talk about keeping the secret of the year! O_o I'm still in shock! Huge congratulations on the marriage though. And yes, happy to watch Max during the move-in.

Well I guess shocked amusement was the best I could hope for from among my friends.

My family, on the other hand…

With a resolved sigh, I opened the phone app and clicked on my mother's name in my contacts. The weight fell in my stomach as I put the phone to my ear, listened to the rings and hoped it would go to voice mail.

Max lifted his soggy muzzle from the watering bowl and plopped beside my chair. As usual, his uncanny ability to sense my mood was accurate. He readily offered comfort when he judged I needed it.

Instead, my mother's voice sang out after the second ring. "Lucas. Finally. I've been waiting for days for you to get back to me."

I cleared my throat and straightened my spine even though she couldn't see me. Then I braced myself. "Mother. I hope you're sitting down. I, uh, I have big news..."

Then I swallowed the sudden bile rising in my throat and spilled it all... or our own manufactured truth about the romance, the wedding, everything.

CHAPTER 4
KATYA

I FINALLY MADE IT HOME FROM WORK AROUND EIGHT P.M. with my phone still turned off. I pulled into the darkening parking lot of the condo I shared with Heath in Orange. Gathering my things, my mind raced through the crazy events of the day, still in disbelief of all that had transpired.

Almost absently I studied the single piece of mail Lucas had delivered to me from his car an hour before. As I'd suspected, the return address on the envelope was imprinted with the logo of a familiar law office in Vancouver. With no desire to know its contents, I stuffed it in my bag, vowing to feed it into the shredder as soon as possible, unread.

But I needed a moment to catch my breath as I fell back against the raggedy seat of the old 90s Honda Civic I'd inherited from Mia. Straightening my shoulders, I decided the best way to distract myself was to brave the messages on my phone before facing my real-life—and likely very irate—roommate.

Holding my breath, I turned on my phone and began to scroll through the scary amount of text messages queued up in my text app.

So many messages, in fact. Some from people I barely knew. Some from a few numbers that weren't even in my contacts that said "Congrats!" and "How wonderful!"

But the ones from my closest friends, I saved those for last.

Mia had only sent me some info about the move to Lucas's house on Saturday and when she and Adam would be showing up to grab my boxes. But the rest... they were a mess. Most of them included the letters *WTF?* A whole lot of question marks and even more exclamation points.

Rather than repeat myself and copypasta a generic message for each of them, I opened up a group text instead, to April, Jenna, Alex and yeah, even Mia and Heath.

Katya: Hey all, thanks for the wonderful well wishes. Yep, Lucas & I did tie the knot. I know that's hard to believe but... whirlwind romance and all that. And maybe the curse of Mia's bouquet getting caught in my hair at her wedding.

Mia: Heyyyy no fair. I didn't do that on purpose.

Alex: I can't believe you did it. You married Jedi Boy! Does that mean you get your own lightsaber? Did he use a Jedi mind trick on you?

Jenna: Sounds like it was probably more like a Jedi sex trick.

April: Damn it, Mia. I should have slipped you a few hundred to aim that sucker at me so I could at least savor the terrified look on Jordan's face when I caught it.

Mia: You enjoy tormenting that man so much. I love every minute of it.

Jenna: Kat, least you coulda done was warn us so we could have given you a bachelorette and hired a hot male stripper.

Heath: Did someone say hot male stripper?

Alex: I can't wait to see your ring!!! Send us a pic ASAP!

Mia: Heath did you know about this secret romance all along and kept it from me?

Heath: This vault holds many secrets, dollface. Do you really want that door opened?

Mia: Hmm. Maybe not.

Alex: No really, I need a pic of your ring. Like... NOW.

Kat: Not available yet. They're on order. Will do as soon as we get them. I'm exhausted, ladies and gent. Gonna go hit the sack.

April: What? It's still super early

Jenna: Must be from all that hot newlywed sex she's having.

With a sigh I tucked my phone in my bag, hopefully having mitigated that disaster for the evening. There would be more, though, certainly.

Like facing the roommate. He'd probably be as little amused as Lucas was that the secret was out.

I opened the front door of our condo softly and shut it, while walking on tip toes, as if that might help at all. If only I could make it to my room unnoticed, I'd bar the door and have some physical protection. As bad luck would have it, Heath sat on the couch watching some survival reality show on the History Channel, his back to me as I snuck through the room. I was halfway into my bedroom doorway when he spoke loudly in his deep baritone between clenched teeth.

"You owe me big time for this, Kat."

Well he was right, I did. And then some.

***

"Did I buy these or did you?" A few days later, Heath stood in our kitchen holding a set of drinking glasses edged with blue and orange wavy lines, one in each hand. I stood facing him, packing tape gun in hand, in preparation to seal up one of the boxes I'd just filled.

"I bought them but you can keep them. I'm going to get a new set when I buy my condo." Without a word, my brawny, six-foot-five roommate replaced the glasses in the cupboard by the sink.

"Oooh, while you're here, I could use your height to grab me some of that crap on the top shelf."

He opened the next cupboard and cocked his head. "Way up there? How the hell did you get it up there in the first place?"

I shrugged. "You, probably. That mini food processor and the juicer are mine."

"There go my plans to start the new cleanse diet." He pulled the seldomly-used appliances down, dutifully wrapping the cords around them to prepare for packing.

"Like you needed an excuse," I replied without mentioning that I'd purchased and then used them exactly three times for that exact purpose. Then I thanked him and tucked the appliances into the next empty box.

Heath squinted as he watched me. "Just...uh... how much of your stuff are you moving over there?"

I darted a quick glance at him before grabbing the marker to label in great detail the contents of the box I'd just sealed up. "All of it."

He frowned. "But you've got the interview soon and if all goes well, it should only be a few months at most for your green card to go through. Do you really need to go through all this? Why not just pack up a few of your clothes and toiletries?"

I bit my lip, capping the pen, squeezing it tight, so it made a satisfying click. "Aside from it looking really suspicious to my movers that I'm only taking a couple boxes, you mean? It can't just look like I'm over there as a guest or as a temporary hook-up."

"Yeah but... who's looking?"

"Well Mia insisted on helping me move all my stuff over. And Adam got involved and... well you understand I have to make it look real." I hesitated, then crossed to check the rest of the cupboards. Meanwhile, Heath had plopped himself down at the kitchen table and was running his long fingers through his dark blond hair.

"Are you that depressed that I'm going?" I asked. "I would have thought you'd be jumping for joy that you can turn this place back into your wanton love pad."

Heath cast an acidic eye in my direction, so very opposite of amused by my joke. In fact, he'd been quite the hermit, lately, not dating much at all. The previous week, I'd convinced him to set up a profile on a new dating app just for shits and giggles. Nothing had come of it yet. But it was still early days, as I reminded him daily.

At least nowadays he was hanging out with friends again and he wasn't as morose as he'd been the previous year while recovering from a bad breakup.

Heath cast an assessing look over the small cluster of boxes. "You know, for having lived here for, what, a year and a half, you really don't have that much stuff."

I smiled. "I showed up from Canada with just a suitcase of clothes and haven't been back. I have much more crap back home but I haven't missed it."

Heath tilted his head at me. "I never hear you talk about home, ever. Don't you miss it at all?"

I hesitated, setting down a white mug imprinted with the logo of a popular bug-logging software. It had been free swag at the last training conference I'd attended. I pondered Heath's question. *Home.* It had been a long time since I'd thought about the place I left behind as home. Sure, I'd grown up there and my parents' house was there but....

I missed Canada, to be sure. BC and California were so close culturally that the differences were minimal—one place used metric while the other used the old school system. One placed loved baseball and basketball while the other worshipped at the altar of the Stanley Cup and all things hockey. One place rained a lot more than the other, but had gorgeous green vistas and mountains to show for it. Both had equally sucktastic traffic.

But there were so many things I didn't miss about home. And all it took were random legal letters showing up out of the blue at my brand new address to remind me of that.

"One thing's for sure," I sighed, hedging at his question. "I'll be relieved when I finally have that green card in my hand and therefore won't run the risk of getting Draco or you and your friends in trouble. That was a huge favor I still owe you for, by the way, getting me the paperwork fixed up for me so I could get the job."

Heath smirked. "I got friends in low places."

I smiled. "You sure do. But things will be so much easier once I'm legal."

"You should be thanking Lucas for that, not me." Heath shrugged, studying me with curious eyes that revealed he wasn't one bit fooled by my sidestep of his question.

"Yeah well, I'll figure that one out later."

His blond brows raised as he looked over my already-packed boxes. "Are you sure about all this?"

I raised my brows. "What, moving in with him? We already did the hard part and got married—"

He laughed. "Getting married is *not* the hard part. The hard part is all about living together—without committing a felony. It's a whole different ball game. And you two will have an especially hard time of it, seeing each other 24/7. Both at home and at work. I just don't want to end up watching this on *20/20* as a cold case with you dead and him on the lam."

I raised a brow at him. "What makes you think it wouldn't be vice versa?"

Heath returned a wicked smile. "Yeah, actually as soon as it came out of my mouth I realized that the more likely scenario would be the reverse."

I winked. "You know me so well."

"How are you going to manage not to kill him? You two don't get along very well."

"We get along well enough at work to get a lot of shit done. Our department has never been more efficient, actually." Then I pushed out of my chair, on my way to start packing up the living room. "Besides, if he gets too mouthy, I could always just break his jaw, so it has to be wired shut and he can't talk. Then we'd be just fine."

Heath followed me through the swinging door into the living room. I just had a few baubles and tchotchkes in here, not even enough stuff to fill one box. Heath, as the typical bachelor with some money, had filled his pad with every state-of-the-art electronic device and gaming console known to man. My few souvenirs and glass items were all but lost in here, anyway. I grabbed some bubble wrap to keep them from breaking and started enveloping each one in way too much of the stuff.

"As long as neither of you give in to the UST, you'll be just fine."

I hesitated, frowning. "UST? What's that stand for?"

"Unrealized sexual tension," he stated matter-of-factly, handing me the tape gun I'd forgotten—but he had remembered—from the kitchen.

I hesitated, brandishing the thing at him like a weapon. "And what the hell is that supposed to mean?"

Heath rolled his eyes. "It means exactly what you think it means and if you don't acknowledge it, I'll call you on your denial."

I jerked the thing at him like I was firing from a pistol, then bent to seal up the box. "I summarily reject your ongoing and very annoying hypothesis about all that. Lucas is a work friend— and sometimes rival—who is doing this to help me and himself out."

"Uh huh," he said, clear skepticism written all over his face.

I inspected the packing tape closely. "Hmm. I wonder if this can be used to seal up humans. Want to be the first to try it out? Or maybe I could break a bone or two to get my message across."

He smirked. "Save that for your hubby. You're gonna need plenty of it. Or maybe save it for yourself. If your lips are sealed up, you won't fall prey to the temptation of kissing him."

I stiffened, remembering the scorching kiss between us that afternoon that had so overwhelmed me. It had come on so suddenly, when he'd pulled me into his arms to offer our doubting colleagues "proof" that we were now a couple. By the looks of his calm and collected exterior when we had come apart, that kiss hadn't affected him the same way it had me.

Or had it?

Lucas was always so good at hiding his emotions. Hiding what he was thinking. It was nearly impossible to tell what was going on beneath that placid surface.

Heath was still flapping his jaws, pulling me out of the recollection. "C'mon Kat, haven't you wondered why his was the name you blurted out when the immigration people were giving you the third degree? I mean, it was amazing quick thinking on your part, sure. But there had to be a subconscious reason Lucas was the first name you blurted as your supposed soon-to-be fiancé."

I eyed him and then gave an over-exaggerated shrug. It probably revealed that I was anything *but* nonchalant about that question. I'd asked it of myself more than a dozen times since it had happened.

Put on the spot, cornered and facing deportation, I'd formed the lie so quickly, so perfectly and apparently, so convincingly that it had saved my bacon. But why Lucas?

There was an answer in there somewhere but I wasn't willing to dig deeply enough to find it. Not yet.

Instead of indulging in Heath's speculation, I returned to my mock threats to get him to shut up already. "If not broken bones, then I can always super glue your ass to the toilet seat for sure."

This time he seemed to take the hint. "You'd do it, too. You're evil."

"*Chaotic* evil, yes. So watch out."

Heath took a long breath and let it out, looking away.

"What?" I cast him a quick glance under my lashes. "Figuring out how you're going to take a shit standing up from now on?"

"No. Just dreading how quiet this place is going to be without you."

My mouth curled up into a sad smile. Poor Heath. He'd been lonely lately. "C'mon, dude. Think about all the hot guys you'll get to bring home without having to worry about working around the annoying roommate."

His lips thinned. "Yeah. Well maybe I've got some UST saved up myself."

I waggled my eyebrows at him. "I recommend a sex toy or two. It helps a lot."

We were both silent as I labeled that last box. I misspelled *tchotchkes* three times, crossing out each attempt before giving up and just writing it out phonetically.

Straightening, I finally cleared my throat. "What is your honest opinion about that, anyway?"

He was watching me with one dark blond brow raised, his head propped up by the arm resting against the back of the sofa. "About sex toys?"

"About sex."

He laughed. "I have a very positive opinion about sex, yes."

I shifted from one leg to the other, trying to find a more careful way around the question but failing, much to my frustration.

"Ohhh. You mean... sex between you and your husband? As in 'consummating your marriage?'"

I avoided his gaze, wiping some dust off the end table with a rag and shrugging to make the question appear extra casual. "I mean, would it be that bad?"

"I don't know. Lucas is a really good-looking guy and you're attracted to him. It wouldn't necessarily be bad... for het sex, anyway."

I turned my back on him, still "dusting," and hesitated before continuing. "That's not what I meant. I mean...would it necessarily be a bad thing to happen?"

Heath was reflective, and I darted a look at him over my shoulder. He seemed to be contemplating the question before discarding it with a shrug. "How the heck am I supposed to know? I mean... as long as neither of you got emotionally attached. And you both agree that there is an expiration date on the relationship. But you do work together so if it ends badly that could make things miserable for you both, after the fact."

I pondered that for a moment, resisting the temptation to heave a sigh. It wasn't like I'd been planning on hooking up with Lucas. Yeah, I'd thought about it more than once. Maybe even wondered what it would be like to feel my skin on his skin, the weight of him on top of me. Maybe even got a hot, tingly feeling when imagining it. But that meant nothing. That was just biology.

I hadn't gotten laid in almost a year and the dry spell was getting rather old. But this girl had willpower, and she'd power through.

And once I was single again, it would be *game on.*

The packing had taken half a day. The move took maybe an hour. On Saturday afternoon, Adam's assistant, Nate, showed up with a truck that was more than twice the size for what I needed. About a half hour later, Adam and Mia were on my doorstep. In fifteen minutes, Heath, Adam and Nate had loaded my mattress and bedroom furniture. I'd purchased those with my first check from Draco after sleeping on Heath's den couch for a month. Then came my few measly boxes of books, keepsakes and appliances. A few suitcases with my clothes in them. And that was it.

As it drove off, the truck rattled from being mostly half-empty. We could have easily done this with a pickup truck. I followed that truck in my Honda the full twenty-minute drive to Lucas's house in Irvine. And it took even less time to unload and stack my worldly belongings in one of the empty bedrooms—which I'd hastily explained would be used for "storage." No one had to know that I'd be sleeping in the guest room. I'd ask Lucas's permission to set this room up for my Twitch TV livestreaming channel.

"Yeah, just load it all in here and then I can unpack from here later."

Lucas got home from work about five minutes into the procedure and he didn't seem surprised to see us. Though he was a little nonplussed to see Adam there actually pitching in to help. They almost ran straight into each other before Lucas silently set his bag aside and pitched in himself.

"Honey!" I said, trying with every ounce of my measly acting ability to make it sound genuine. I leaned in for a quick peck but we even screwed that up. He aimed for my mouth while I aimed for one of his whiskery cheeks and our noses ended up colliding.

Adam and Mia both started laughing. "Going to need to perfect the *Honey, I'm home* greeting," Mia said.

Afterward, we hit a nearby restaurant—there were no neighborhood pubs in this part of Irvine—and had some drinks at the bar.

"Thanks for all your help moving her in. Drinks are on me," Lucas offered generously.

I reached out and squeezed his hand where the other two could easily see the affectionate gesture. It felt—weird. Not just because we were playacting but because it felt like I was lying to two of my closest friends. Which, in fact, I had been doing for some time now. But this lie felt more real.

But there *was* something... the way it felt when I put my hand over his where it rested on his hard thigh. My hand curled around his—for authenticity of course—and for a split second, I felt him respond. The thigh muscle under his jeans hardened, his thumb hooked around my hand, and very quickly, almost automatically, the pad of it stroked my finger.

Yeah, there were tingles all the way up my arm from just that simple touch. It was just the dry spell talking. The long slog through the desert before I got my divorce papers. Then I'd be able to go out and have a proper hookup and sow those wild oats. My wild oats were raring to go and didn't like being held back. And they very much liked that simple touch from the man who was, in name only, my husband.

"So why haven't you been wearing a ring?" Mia joked. "Were you planning on staying secretly married or something?"

Lucas stiffened beside me as he swirled his whiskey on the rocks. "I've got the rings at our house. This all happened so quickly that we haven't decided what we're doing."

Mia frowned and looked at my drink, looked at my waist, then back at my eyes. Holy shit... did she think I was pregnant or something? To counteract any question of *that* I held my mug of beer up and took a deep draught from it. Then I licked the foam off my top lip with a satisfied sigh.

"Yum." I said, barely holding back the burp that wanted to rise up and be set free. Thank God this bar had Canadian beer on draught and I didn't have to drink the donkey pee that passed for beer in this country. I'd sooner have wine.

Mia sipped her cosmo, then set it aside and bent over the table toward me, her long brown hair hanging around her face. "So are you keeping your name or are you going to be Ms. Walker?"

"Actually it's not Walker it's—"

Lucas's hand leapt up and squeezed mine hard. "No, actually she's keeping her name, aren't you, sweets?"

I blinked. He sure was sensitive about his name—that other name. Like it was some kind of secret. Shit that Dutch name was a mile long and practically unpronounceable, so I could understand why he'd prefer to use Walker. It was much simpler. But if it was just for simplicity's sake, then why avoid even mentioning that he had another last name?

I shrugged. Adam was his boss, too. In all probability, he probably already knew Lucas's legal last name. Adam held up his chilled mug of beer. "All right then, how bout we just toast to the newlyweds?"

Mia snickered. "Which ones? We're newlyweds, too."

"We've actually been married almost eight months, four days and..." he paused. "Sixteen hours."

She raised her brow and turned to me. "See what happens when you marry a child prodigy genius? He never forgets dates. I'll never have to remind him about my birthday or our anniversary—"

I laughed. "But will *he* have to remind *you?*"

Mia sat back, eyes wide with a faux look of offense on her face while Adam laughed into his beer mug. "She's acting innocent, but you totally nailed it. She'll be the one running out at midnight the night before to buy me something."

Mia put her hand up, palm out at eye level as if blocking Adam from speaking to her.

He threw her a sidelong glance. "Am I in the doghouse now?"

"Would be more of a threat if you actually had a dog." I snorted.

Lucas looked from one of our friends to the other and laughed. "That's not just a figure of speech at our house."

Our house. I watched Lucas as he continued to chat with my friends, warming up. And I marveled at how easily that phrase had rolled off his tongue as if he already thought of the place as ours.

I blinked. This was certainly going to be the weirdest few months of my short life so far, that was for sure.

"That's going to take some getting used to," Lucas muttered as they dropped us off. We stood on the front steps to wave goodbye, Lucas's arm wrapped around my shoulders, mine around his solid, hard waist. The perfect picture of spontaneous newly-weds.

Lucas's home was gorgeous, over eighty-years old and had once served as a farmhouse for the surrounding area that had once belonged to the Irvine Ranch Company. As such, the rest of the homes on the block surrounding us were much more modern clone-a-homes. But this house had a broad, wide porch supported on thick columns and a whole lot of charm.

Inside there were multiple built-ins, beautiful finishes and trims, real plaster moldings, chair rails and picture rails on the walls. There were even craftsman style fixtures—beautiful tiffany lamps and exquisite hardwood floors. Such a house was a rare find in Southern California. I longed to have the kind of money to own a place like this of my own someday.

But I'd settle for the starter condo I had my heart set on as my first purchase. Some place all my own that I could take pride in as a new legal resident of the country.

I shot a sidelong glance at Lucas, beside me, who had just pushed open the front door. For an awkward moment we both seemed frozen there, at a loss for what to do or say. This was our first time alone as husband and wife in his home. For some bizarre reason, my heart was pounding like a virgin on her wedding night. Which was hilarious to me in the back of my mind because I was so not a virgin.

Lucas took a breath and entered the house without waiting for me. There'd be no carrying me over the threshold. Not that I really cared about that shit. Now that we were alone, we didn't need to fake it for anyone but the mites and dust motes. Oh, and for a few minutes, we'd play along for Michaela when she delivered Max from his day at her house.

In spite of the playacting, I had to remind myself how ridiculous it was to think of Lucas as my *husband*. Okay, so we'd said vows aloud to take each other as a spouse. Aside from the fact that we'd signed a piece of paper for the government. Aside from the fact that everyone we knew besides Heath thought or soon would think—once they found out—that we were married for real. Aside from the fact that we'd live together in this house and go to work together in the same car.

Aside from all of that, we weren't *actually* married. Were we?

I rubbed my forehead as I followed Lucas into the house. All of this thinking and pondering was making my head hurt.

Lucas moved with direct purpose toward his room—the master. When I hesitated in the living room, he called to me from down the hall. "Come here for a moment."

Huh... I trailed after him slowly. By the time I entered his room—which was immaculate, by the way—he was digging a box out of the closet. A beautiful wooden box that was polished and inlaid with different colored wood and mother-of-pearl in patterns. And though it had been in his closet, it wasn't even dusty.

This dude took clean freak to new levels. Or else his housekeeper was extremely detail oriented. Or both.

Lucas gently set the box on his nightstand with great care. I glanced around his room. I'd been to the house several times before briefly, either fetching something from him, or dropping something off. One time, he'd held a backyard get together for the entire QA department. But I'd never been in this room. The dark wood furniture that appeared to be from the early part of the 20th century seemed to fit perfectly in this house. Either the furniture was antique or well-made copies. Whoever had helped him decorate had done a wonderful job. Immaculate hardwood floors were covered with gorgeous middle eastern rugs. The house was so cozy.... homey.

Two of the bedrooms were completely empty. But this room had dark wood carved furniture and a four-poster cherry wood queen-sized bed with a royal blue and white bedspread. The wide-screen TV attached to the wall opposite the bed and beside the stone fireplace seemed completely out of place.

Through the doorway, I caught sight of a gorgeous marble washroom counter with basins that looked like earthenware bowls. They sat atop the counter and large goose-necked brass faucets arced over them. I also caught a glimpse of the very end of an elegant claw-footed tub. Wow. I'd always thought the house was beautiful but hadn't had much chance previously to appreciate these details.

Either Lucas or the people who'd lived here before him had put a great deal of work and thought into the restoration of this lovely place.

Lucas paid no attention to my inspection as he sifted with purpose through the wooden box.

"Here," he finally mumbled as he pulled out a red velvet-covered jewelry box that looked worn and old. He popped it open and looked over the contents, then turned and looked at me, brows raised. He twitched his head, beckoning me over to where he stood.

"I'm hoping it won't need to be resized," he added as he reached in and pulled out a ring and held it out to me. Without touching it, I looked it over. It was gorgeous. Just flat out beautiful...not like any jewelry that had been fabricated in this century. It was clearly as antique as the house and furnishings around us. The piece, clearly an old-time engagement ring, had a diamond in the center. It didn't sit high like modern rings but was recessed. There were tiny triangular emeralds on either side and wrought platinum or white gold worked in a tiny grill and filigree design. The style looked very much like art deco.

"This was my great-grandmother's wedding ring. It's from the '20s. My grandma gave it to me a while back. I know it's old-fashioned and all but..." he shrugged.

My mouth dropped. The round diamond at the center caught the overhead light and sparked gorgeous colors from within—red, blue, pink, purple. "Are you kidding? It's breathtaking." It was actually the most beautiful ring I'd ever seen.

But I shook my head when he extended it to me. "I can't—I can't wear that. It's too special. It's a family heirloom."

His eyes locked on mine and I swallowed. He clearly wasn't going to take my no for an answer. "You're my wife, Kat. Take it. It makes sense for you to wear it."

"We could just go get something at a pawn shop."

He blew out a breath and laughed. "That won't work, especially if we're going to have to convince my family. You'll just have to wear this."

I took it from him slowly as if it might vanish, then inspected it closer, studying the intricate filigree work on the side. "Is this... are these shafts of wheat on the sides?"

"Symbols of fertility, I think. These old rings were full of all kinds of symbolism."

I grimaced. "Well that's not exactly applicable symbolism here. We need a ring with three-dollar bills or unicorns on it to properly symbolize our marriage."

"Does it fit?"

I looked up at him. "I have no idea."

With a deep, frustrated sigh, he snatched the thing from my fingers and wrapped his hand around my left wrist. "Hold out your hand, we'll see."

I relaxed, and he pulled my hand toward him, then slipped it onto my ring finger as the diamond winked at me in the low light. Slowly he slid the ring up toward my knuckle as if anticipating at any moment that it might catch. It was slightly looser than a ring I would normally wear—which was rare since I wasn't a big fan of jewelry, especially on my fingers.

As a gamer girl, I used a keyboard a lot and kept my fingernails trimmed down to nothing. It didn't give me the most picturesque hands for fine jewelry display, to say nothing of the scar across my knuckles. That was a trophy from my childhood when I'd tried to punch out my brother. I'd cut my hand on the railing behind him when he'd ducked, avoiding my blow. Twenty stitches later, I had a long, fat scar for life. It leant well to my image of a tough girl, so that was awesome.

But with this delicate, one-of-a-kind piece of jewelry on my finger, it looked out of place. Like a tiara on an orangutan.

I admired it, turning it this way and that under the overhead light while Lucas, apparently did the same. "Wow, it fits nicely."

"Just a tiny bit loose but I can put something on the back so it won't slip off."

He shook his head. "I can get the jeweler to resize it for you."

I frowned, pulling my hand away. "Uh, no that's not necessary. I'm not going to be wearing it that long. You definitely want to save this for when you get married for real." My voice died in my throat as the look on his face darkened. I'd said something wrong.

"You do—you plan on getting married for real someday, right?"

His cheeks bulged where his jaw tightened. "Marriage is a fucked up and outdated institution that I don't ever hesitate to mock. For your benefit, I might add."

My brows twitched. Wow. Those were some, uh, strong feelings. I'd have to ferret out sometime why he felt that way. But clearly now was not the time.

"But mocking marriage and giving me your great-gran's wedding ring—"

He shook his head. "It's no big imposition. It would only be sitting in this box gathering more dust." He waved to the big box that, in fact, had no dust on it at all.

"What will you wear?" I asked in order to diffuse the sudden tension that had erupted from nowhere.

He turned back to the velvet box and pulled out a man's wedding ring. "My grandfather's ring." Without waiting for me to look at it, he slipped it onto his left finger.

I raised my brows. "Wow. It's a perfect fit."

Lucas clenched his jaw, glancing down at the white gold band that was simple but engraved with etched patterns on it. Masculine, elegant and otherwise unadorned.

Huh... well... "Oh, put your hand down on the bed for a minute and I'll snap a picture. I've been putting together a photo album of stuff for documentation of our relationship. In case we need to show anything for the interview. This will be a good addition."

Lucas made a weird face but did as I asked, placing his hand down on the beautiful bedspread. I pulled out my phone, then I put my left hand down on top of his, angling it so that both wedding rings could be seen in the photo. It was an easy matter of snapping a few from different angles. My head bent close, focusing. I shifted and—the back of my head bumped his nose slightly. He sucked in a breath.

"Oh! Sorry." His hand tensed under mine and I pulled my hand away.

He seemed... angry. Or at the very least, tense. I knew that this whole situation had blossomed into more than he'd bargained for and he was probably still pissed about it. I ventured a look up into his face. Then I drew back, slightly startled at the intense look in his eyes. He was looking at me like... like... he wanted to either punch me or devour me whole.

I pulled back with a soft gasp. We held each other's gaze for long tense minutes, my eyes drifting down toward his full lips. In that moment and for no logical reason whatsoever, I really, *really* wanted him to kiss me.

I wanted him to kiss me so much that I leaned in and opened my mouth slightly—

Just as he jerked back, the doorbell rang.

He stiffened and blinked, as if snapping out of a trance. Then tore his eyes away from my face and said, "That's gotta be Michaela bringing the dog back."

I blinked, pulling myself out of my own weird trance. As he turned and left the room, I shook myself as a reminder of how bad things might have gotten if he'd kissed me. If I'd kissed him back. If our tongues had touched and danced and our bodies had pressed too close.

We might have lost our clothes and... and fallen onto the bed and... ended up in a sweaty and breathless tangle as a result. We might have strained muscles or even sustained more serious physical damage. There might have even been some biting and scratching. Definitely some moaning and panting...

So I guess it was a good thing we didn't go that route.

Too damn bad.

The front door opened, and I heard the telltale patter of pawed feet and the click of toenails on hardwood floor and heavy canine breathing. I met up with the new arrivals in the living room where Michaela was talking to Lucas. Max, a large and exuberant golden retriever, bolted at me the minute he caught sight of me.

"Hey, Katya!" Michaela greeted me with a tentative smile.

I bent to scratch my old buddy behind his ears. He was soft and smelled good, having just gotten a bath. Unfortunately he also breathed his hot moist dog breath right into my face. I quickly straightened and turned back to Michaela. We'd met before on a few occasions. Her boyfriend, Jeremy, worked at Draco as a developer so she'd attended work functions as his plus one.

Also, we'd spent a few days together at a cabin last winter during a holiday retreat with several other co-workers.

"Hey Kat! Congratulations to you, too. What a shock that's been."

I had no idea how to answer her, but as far as I could tell, her congratulations were genuine. Our eyes met and as I hesitated, hers widened. "I'm sorry—I just meant I didn't see it coming. You guys were that good at keeping it on the down low, but I'm really happy for you."

"Oh," I laughed, darting a nervous glance at Lucas who, as usual, had a neutral expression on his face. "Yeah, well thanks. And, you know him." I jerked a thumb at him. "My husband is the secretive type. And *surprisingly* romantic. It was all his idea."

He arced a brow—all stoic and Spock-like—but didn't contradict me. Nevertheless, I could detect trace evidence that he was irritated by my embellishment.

I fought a smirk. *So much the better.* "In fact... he thought we should honeymoon in Japan so we could start our training to become actual ninjas."

Michaela looked from Lucas to me and then back at Lucas, then laughed. "I could actually see that..."

"*And*—" I leaned forward conspiratorially.

Lucas cut in, leaning forward. "Well look at the time. I owe you dinner for watching Max all day."

She shook her head. "Thanks, but not necessary. I like the arrangement we've got going. Maybe you can give me a little more time on the bench. And of course, more lessons are always welcome."

I frowned looking from one of them to the other. On the bench? Lessons? What on earth did that mean? Was Lucas some kind of secret Dom or something? A bench, as in a spanking bench? Lessons? What the *what?*

Was he about to show me his "playroom?"

Michaela noted my confusion immediately. "The piano. I don't have one at my place. Just a tiny keyboard. When Lucas and I were roommates, I used to listen to him play, and it made me want to learn. So I'm a late bloomer but determined to learn."

I darted a quick glance at Lucas who had a strange look on his face. It was almost like he was holding his breath, as if he was afraid I'd blow our cover or something. He played the piano?

Of course, I'd noticed the instrument in the alcove of the living room. I'd never connected its presence to the fact that he might have some hidden talents besides being good at video games.

"Oh that's cool. I can see how he inspired you." I cleared my throat and my heart sped up. I knew a lot about Lucas. But clearly not *everything*.

Soon after, Michaela excused herself to get back home to dinner with Jeremy. She gave Max a big hug around the neck and then left. The dog, after sniffing me thoroughly, then jumped up on the couch. Lucas quickly chased him off to his doggy bed, though. So apparently the dog lived under the same neatness rules that I did. Poor guy. We'd have to commiserate later.

"So, ah, apparently you're some kind of piano virtuoso?" I raised my brows at him.

He rolled his eyes. "My parents forced lessons on me from when I was four until I was seventeen. I get by. But no, not a virtuoso."

I stared at him, frowning as I gnawed on my lower lip.

After a minute of silence, he shook his head at me. "What?"

I fluttered my eyes in irritation. "Well, I mean. That's probably something I should know, right? For the interview?"

He scowled and turned, heading for the kitchen. I followed at his heels.

"Do I know everything else?"

He darted a look at me and then ducked into the fridge. "It's impossible to know everything about a person," he replied.

"Well, are you at least going to play something for me? So I can at least talk about it if they ask?"

His brows scrunched together. "It's a screening interview consisting of only the most basic questions. What are they going to ask you that would be even relevant?"

I shrugged. "I dunno. Does he play a musical instrument? Is he any good? Simple enough questions. I mean, like you said, did you put yourself through all this only to have us screw it up on the interview?"

He scowled, slammed the fridge door shut and spun on the ball of his foot. "Fine."

A second later, I was the only one standing in the kitchen, my jaw open. I trailed him into the living room where he was now sitting down at the grand piano. It was a lovely, dark wood instrument that rested inside the raised alcove behind the living room. Lifting up the wooden key cover, he put his right runner-bedecked foot on one of the pedals. Then he stretched out his arms and rolled his shoulders. I bit my lip watching those hands, slightly curved fingers barely touching the keys.

Without a flourish or any type of show-off gesture, he then proceeded to blow me away by playing a famous classical piece I instantly recognized but didn't know by name. His fingers rushed up and down the keyboard as his toe bounced up and down on the pedal.

He read no music nor did his facial expression change at all. Well, no, wait that wasn't completely accurate. His features, though still blank, seemed to relax a little, as did the rest of his body posture, especially as the piece continued on.

And as I watched his strong, long-fingered hands glide over the keys, it... did something to me. Watching a man's hands glide over the piano keyboard was infinitely sexier than watching hands on a computer keyboard or game controller. *Wow.* How did I not know that my husband was a man of hidden talents?

A rush of heat scorched through my insides wondering what other special skills he might have. Maybe even in the bedroom?

He played beautifully, and those hands had to be good for more than just the piano and computer keyboards. Like... what if *I* was his keyboard? I all but resisted fanning myself with my open hand just picturing it. Who'd have thought a man's sexiness could be increased by an exponential factor by playing the piano so masterfully?

Well.... I'll. Be. Damned.

Suddenly he was standing, closing the piano up. "No commentary from the peanut gallery needed. Now you know. And I'm hungry."

With that, he stood and left the room to go back to foraging for dinner.

"Wait..." I trailed after him as I followed him to the fridge. "How... what...? Can you explain that please?"

He put a hand on the fridge door and turned back to me, a dark eyebrow raised. "I thought I just showed you everything you need to know."

"Well no. You said you took lessons for most of your childhood. You played some Beethoven and then—"

"Mozart," he corrected. "*Eine kleine Nachtmusik.*"

"If you're some kind of musical prodigy, then why—"

"I'm not. I have a near-flawless technical style but with no emotion or color." He sounded like he was repeating someone else's critique of his work.

"It sounded amazing to me."

"No offense, but you don't exactly have the refined ear to hear what I'm describing. You didn't even know it was Mozart."

I shrugged. "I know what sounds good. I'd kill to be able to play like that."

His gaze intensified on me before he tore his eyes away and turned back to the fridge, opening it. "If you really want to, then do what Michaela is doing and take lessons."

I stared at his back between narrowed eyes, burning with irritation. He could also teach lessons in earning a kick in the ass. I imagined myself doing it right then.

He sighed heavily and muttered about how he needed to hit the grocery store before shutting the fridge again, empty-handed.

I shook my head. "But why—"

"Why am I not on the tour circuit wearing a tux, carrying a candelabra and playing for thousands?" he laughed acerbically. "It's a skill. I took lessons because it was expected of me. I quit the minute I could. Yes, I can play. That's thirteen years of lessons and daily practice you hear. Nothing more."

I shrugged. "Okay. But…it was really good."

He sighed and rolled his eyes. "Well, thank you. I suspect you have hidden talents I don't know about."

I laughed. "Well a former boyfriend or two has informed me that I give next-level blowjobs."

His features froze for a moment, as if he didn't trust his ears. I laughed, hoping that would have at least got him to crack a smile. Instead, he narrowed his eyes and blushed.

Then he visibly swallowed. "Well, I'd ask for a demonstration but… rules and all."

I took a deep breath, meeting that gaze and dizzy with the tension building between us. Was he angry? Was he annoyed? Who knew?

"So your parents forced you to take piano, huh?"

He shrugged. "It looked good on the college résumé, as did the private school and the rowing crew. They got their wish. I got into Cambridge. Hated every second of that two years before I transferred to Berkeley. But hell, at least I can play the piano."

My brow twitched and suddenly any sympathy I had for him dried up. "Well at least yours supported you going to university. Be grateful for that. Mine blew my tuition savings, and I had nothing. When the time came, they told me to get a job at the local supermarket and go to vocational college. They also said it'd be a huge waste for a girl to go into computer science, since it's such a male-dominated field."

He looked at me like I'd grown another head. "What the hell is wrong with your parents?"

I suppressed a biting retort. *How much time do you have, buddy?* But I was even more annoyed by the clear sympathy on his face. No, I didn't need sympathy from the Grump-master General. Not now.

"Eh, like any typical child I ignored them, rebelled and went into computers, anyway."

He blinked. "Good thing you did. But jeez—"

"Anyway," I cut him off before we started drifting into territory I did not want to discuss—namely my screwed-up family. "I'm not like a musical prodigy or anything but... I can fix us some dinner. I can cook a mean meal. And you're clearly hungry."

He waved at the refrigerator. "There's nothing in there to eat."

I moved around the center kitchen island. It was a gorgeously equipped room, despite the age of the house, with all the modern conveniences. I nudged him out of the way and he jerked away from me like I'd given him an electrostatic shock. Yanking open the large fridge, I took a moment to assess the situation. He was right. There wasn't much. A few bits of high-end fancy cheese. Half a dozen eggs. A few assorted vegetables that were still good—a green bell pepper, half an onion, some fresh mushrooms. Two small tomatoes. Half a carton of milk. At least he bought groceries, though I wondered when he even had the time to cook for himself since he lived at Draco even more than I did.

I started gathering ingredients and formulating a plan. "You like omelets? I can whip us up something."

"Uh yeah..."

"Eggs, peppers, a little bit of onion. Some of this yummy cheese. I can even finish it off in the oven as a frittata. You have any potatoes? And a big ol' pan?"

He pointed to the pantry. "I think there are one or two in there."

I instructed him to grab them and start washing and peeling while I chopped. He came back with a few potatoes that had roots sprouting out from them. Still good to use.

About forty-five minutes later, I was dishing pieces of steaming thick and fluffy frittata onto our plates. We set them down at the kitchen table with casual place settings.

Only then did Lucas notice the bit of rearranging I'd done during the move-in. At the centerpiece of the table stood a small potted cactus sticking straight up. I'd found it set out on the back steps with a few other sad-looking potted plants. But this fellow had special meaning, so I'd brought him inside. I'd never pass up a chance to torment Lucas, to be honest.

The cactus' pot still had a Christmas ribbon tied around it. The fact that Lucas had received this little guy in a white elephant gift exchange last Christmas was entirely my doing. Now he had his very own "pet cactus." I'd teased him mercilessly about his phallic-looking new succulent sidekick. In fact, I'd even given him a name, much to Lucas's chagrin.

We'd had no idea, during that short cabin stay with a few work friends, that we'd end up legally married a month later. Who could have ever predicted such a crazy future?

Lucas eyed the plant but didn't seem too surprised to see it there. "Ah, I see you located it."

"You've been neglecting poor Cocky the Cocktus." I threw him a cheesy grin. "Can't have that! Cocky is your best bud."

He eyed me. "If you hadn't just made me dinner, I might be tempted to plant Cocky in your bed sheets for a nice prickly surprise."

"Don't even think about it, Jedi Boy. Now eat up."

He sniffed at his plate. "It smells amazing. You didn't poison it, did you?"

I only arched my brows mysteriously at him. He dug in and then sat back, clearly stunned. "I guess I'm not the only one with surprising talents."

I started laughing so hard I almost choked on my eggs. "It's only a frittata. They're super easy, as you saw."

He started forking in bites as fast as he could sustain the pace, talking in between swallows. "Your special talent is way more practical than mine is." He waited a beat while I looked up, then waggled his brows. "Oh and the cooking's really good, too."

I flashed him a cheeky smile. "Too bad you'll never get to witness the other talent firsthand." Or would he?

Damn... I had to stop thinking about how hot it was that he played the piano. How together his home life seemed to be compared to mine. How he was just a little older than me and yet so much better at adulting than I was.

I had to stop thinking about *him* as sexy. And a good kisser. With elegant, long-fingered hands that could move their way across any keyboard the way I wanted him to move them across my body, over my bare skin.

On top of all that, he was also an accomplished gamer, as well, as evidenced by his ever-present name near the top of our department's leaderboard. So he was sexy, accomplished, an actual man who could adult semi-decently and on top of that, he was just as nerdy as I was.

Damn. Time to get my mind out of the gutter and back to reality. This was a sexless marriage, as we'd both agreed it would be—*and* would remain. The circumstances of us both being forced to live under the same roof together notwithstanding.

"How'd you learn to cook so well?"

I grinned. "The Food Network. I had to cook often. My parents were gone a lot in the evenings and I got sick of freezer food and leftovers."

He nodded. "I suppose it will be useful to have these odd bits of knowledge of each other for the interview. Just in case."

"Are you nervous? About the interview?"

He shook his head. "I've done some research. I don't think the questions are that hard. This first interview is very broad and general. Those questions like what kind of face cream you use are the stuff they talk about in the movies. I think we'll do fine. We know each other well enough and our relationship is documented."

I, however, was starting to feel dings in my confidence about this same interview. I was learning all kinds of new stuff about him after mere hours in his house. What if there'd been something we'd missed? I'd thought I knew him well before this. Hell, we'd been married for six months now. But I was only just now finding out new things.

"Besides," he continued. "Now that we have to go meet my parents tomorrow night, that interview is going to be nothing in comparison."

My fork clattered loudly against my plate as I dropped it. "When were you planning on telling me *this*?"

He shrugged. "Tonight. I didn't want you to get the jitters. There's really no need to be nervous."

I blinked. Logically, he was right. But that didn't preclude the sudden butterflies. "I mean, should I bring something? Are we ready for this?"

He shrugged his characteristic low-key shrug. "Just dress nice. They're old school and family dinner is a formal affair."

"Uh... oh. Okay."

I guess time would tell if we would be convincing or not. If we failed this initial interview, they'd call us in for follow-ups that would probably be harder to answer.

I blinked. Until then, I had a lot of studying up to do in the next two weeks. And tomorrow night's Meet the Parents event would be my initiation.

My baptism by fire.

CHAPTER 5
LUCAS

"SO WHICH IS IT GOING TO BE, A FLIGHT SIMULATOR OR A first-person shooter?" Hammer raised the paper coffee cup to his lips, took a sip, then set it down.

I stared across the table from him, and up from my currently blank paper, which was supposed to hold the notes from our brainstorming ideas. Except that in here, so far, it had hardly started sprinkling with no storm whatsoever imminent on the horizon. And no ideas for the game that would make me the first director of Draco's shiny new virtual reality division.

I flicked the pen in my hand and sat back in my chair. The surrounding workstations in the Den were all empty. It was just him and me at the scrum table (so we called it) and a pen and blank sheet of notebook paper between us. "It's true that both formats are ideal for the virtual reality interface format." I answered neutrally. Neither of those ideas excited me, even if they did make sense.

Hammer nodded. "Well, I can give you advice on both. I have combat training as well as being a pilot."

"Exactly the reasons I asked for your help on this. I really appreciate it, man." I threw a glance at him and shifted in my chair. "But I'm looking for an idea that will blow them away. Something different and unique."

"—And doable." He nodded. "You definitely have to pitch something that will be possible to produce. Adam Drake is a genius when it comes to programming and games. If you go to him pitching something pie in the sky, he's going to recognize that immediately."

I rubbed the sudden tension knotting the back of my neck and glared at the ceiling. "I know... that's what's got me drawing a blank."

"Well there's Battle Royale, which is the most famous of the VR first-person shooters. We could try some twist on it. Maybe more players at a time, or a scenario mode or—"

I scribbled down those suggestions and then dropped the pen so it rolled across the notebook.

Hammer frowned. "Do you wanna do this another time? You seem distracted."

I returned my gaze to him, straightening from my previous dejection. "Nah, man. That's okay. Thanks so much for coming in to help."

He smiled crookedly. "I'm a big fan of video games, especially Draco products. I had the time. And I had to admit to hoping to see some more of the place."

I stood. "I can do that. In fact a walk around might help get the blood circulating and the ideas flowing."

So once again, I was escorting an astronaut through the corridors of the Draco campus. Only today, I had him to myself so I could pick his brains, for whatever good that would do.

"I hear you just got married. Congratulations," he said.

I raised my brows in surprise. It seemed weird, hearing it from someone I barely knew. Even weirder than hearing it from my closest friends. I wasn't sure why. It hardly seemed real to me at all—mostly because it wasn't. And I'd never mentally prepared myself for having to go through all this painfully awkward playacting about it.

"Uh yeah, thanks. So here's the ideas room." I led him past a room that had no windows open to the outside world besides the small one in the door. I couldn't let him inside. During business hours the room was used for groups to work in. But when unoccupied, the doors were open for any employee to post notes or write on the walls with productive ideas for games or for running a better company. Once a month the ideas were printed up, collated and presented to the officers in summary form. From there I had no idea what they did with them. Probably round-filed.

At least none of my ideas had seen the light of day. *Yet*, I reminded myself. There was a first time for everything.

This new job would be my chance to finally make a difference.

Hammer peeked through the window into the ideas room. "Do I have to bribe you to get entrance so I can read the stuff? Maybe add a few notes of my own?"

I laughed. "Non-employees are welcome to submit their ideas through our company website. There's a whole tab and form for it."

We made our way quickly through most of the boring areas—workstations, cubicles, areas like Human Resources, Risk Management, etc. But the warehouse... that's where the fun began with the experimental and prototype equipment.

"So your new wife is the cute redhead who helped you show us around?" he asked later, then added with a laugh. "Kirill's going to be bummed."

The Russian cosmonaut who had been hitting on her? Well, so much the better, then. The guy was built like an oak tree. Against my better judgement, I might have been tempted to take a swing at him for his blatant flirting with Kat during the tour. The dude had a steel pair, that was for sure.

"I doubt he has trouble finding willing single women," was all I said. As usual, nothing to give away the violent tendencies of my thoughts regarding that matter. Yeah, I could envision smashing his head like a melon every time he leered at her but that was unproductive.

"How about covert operations or special forces?" I changed the subject back to what we'd been discussing before—my new project. "A twist on the first person shooter format. Instead of running around just shooting whoever you want, like with Battle Royale, it could be covert agents amongst the friendlies. You'd have to figure out who the undercover agents were."

He nodded. "Not a bad idea. I don't know much about covert operations, though. But Noah is a big fan of DE, too. And he was an Army Ranger. He might be able to help."

I scratched my chin and mulled that over, then we pulled out the VR equipment and played a quick FPS game. He, naturally, won.

"I don't know what guns these virtual weapons are supposed to be imitating but I'm an even shittier shot with them than with the real thing," he laughed. "There's a reason I went straight to test pilot school right out of the Air Force Academy."

I laughed as we removed our helmets, goggles, game paddles and gloves.

He threw me a sidelong glance. "Tough gig, marriage. Especially when you work together." He sighed.

Dude. Tell me something I didn't already know.

"How long have you been married?" I asked, mostly to deflect. He seemed willing to talk though and building relationships was important in business. Might as well run with it as long as it didn't get too personal. Hammer was a nice guy, and I genuinely wanted to get to know him better. He might be my ace in the hole when it came to dreaming up a new and exciting game for this new platform.

"I *was* married. Past tense. The beginning is the fun part. The stuff that comes after..." he gave a rueful shrug.

"Have any advice for a newbie?" I didn't feel like getting into the fact that I wasn't actually a newbie. But that first time had been short and rough and I chose to ignore that part of my past most often. It had taught me one thing, though. Marriage—real marriage, not this fake farce—was definitely *not* for me.

Good thing Kat and I understood perfectly going into it that this would definitely not last. There wouldn't even be time to mess it up.

Hammer tilted his head thoughtfully, his expression deadly serious. It almost made me feel guilty. "Give each other breathing room—especially when you get home from work after a long day of seeing each other under stressful circumstances. Just let her breathe."

"So your ex is an astronaut, too?

He shook his head. "A scientist, but we were in the Air Force together before I joined NASA. Before—" he cut himself off, frowned at something that only he could see, then just shrugged "Before we split up."

I frowned. He had a weird way of talking about his ex. I expected bitterness or negativity there but there was none. "Seems like you're on good terms with each other. Are you two still friends?"

He shook his head. "Haven't seen her in years. Just hear things.... The military world isn't really all that big."

We spent another half hour or so in the warehouse bantering ideas back and forth. I had enough to fill a half page of notes, anyway.

We made plans to get together again as his schedule permitted. Then it was time to go home to the li'l wifey and see what she'd done with the place...

Knowing that exasperating redhead, it couldn't be good.

CHAPTER 6
KATYA

M Y GUEST ROOM BED WAS NOT HALF BAD—QUEEN-
sized with a fluffy mattress topper that made it feel
like sleeping on a cloud. In fact, it was rather comfy
and so I didn't mind that my twin mattress had been left leaning
up against the wall in one of the empty rooms. It took me a
minute to remember where I was as I reached my arms above my
head, knocking my hands against the carved hardwood
headboard. I studied it for a moment as my blurry vision came
into focus and I cleared my throat.

Lucas certainly had a good eye for fine things. Pretty things.
There was a definite aesthetic to his house that I had not
anticipated. It wasn't flashy or ridiculous. It wasn't white walls
stripped to the bones of anything but electronics and leather
lounge furniture, like the average bachelor pad.

It looked like he had taken time and consideration in putting
things together. He had good taste. The house itself was
gorgeous and the history behind it rare in this area. And he had
filled the lovely house with equally befitting things.

Maybe he'd had a previous girlfriend help him with the
decorating? Hmm. I'd have to ask him about that. But who knew
with Lucas? I probably wouldn't get a straight answer without a
heavy dash of salt and disdain.

119

I reached over to grab my phone, as was my habit when I first woke up, to check for updates, texts and the news. The first thing I noticed was the text from Lucas telling me he'd gone in to work for a few hours and would be back some time after noon. Then he wished me luck unpacking.

I might have stayed in bed, luxuriating in the comfort for another hour or so. But I was interrupted by a dog. Max somehow knew how to headbutt his way in through the bedroom door and approach the bed. He pushed his cold nose at me, insisting I give him loves.

I patted him for a while, scratching his ear, where he grunted his approval. But every time I tried to pull my hand away, he'd shove his big black doggy nose at me, looping it under my hand insistently. Apparently I was open game to dish out the doggy love while I was prone and within reach of the dog nose. So apparently I'd have a furry alarm clock to back up anything else I might sleep through. Good to know. With a groan, I pushed out of bed and padded across the hall to the washroom. Thankfully Max didn't know how to headbutt his way through that door. There was no way I could handle that level of canine interference.

It was time to get going and get my things unpacked. His kitchen needed the most help. He had gorgeous appliances but was clearly someone who didn't cook for himself. Not many pots, pans or even things like spatulas and baking spoons. Since I had my fair share, I unpacked my kitchen boxes to fill out his bare marble countertops.

After that, I opted to pull out my electronics equipment, a few personal items for my room, some keepsakes and my clothes. I wouldn't be here long, anyway. Would I?

For breakfast, I searched in vain for tea bags, then gave in and fixed myself a cup of coffee in Lucas's fancy one-cup latte machine. To eat, I grabbed a banana. Then, still in my pajamas and housecoat, I started sorting through the boxes, deciding what I'd shove in the spare room closet for storage and what I could pull out.

I'd been studiously ignoring my updates and my inbox, complete with steady flow of messages asking why I hadn't livestreamed on Twitch in days. I'd posted notices all over my channel before I'd unplugged my equipment to pack up for transport. Still, followers were clamoring for Persephone's Corner starring yours truly, the amazing gamer girl.

Sometimes it was tedious to be so awesome. But only sometimes.

I had a smallish but fiercely loyal group of followers who watched regularly. They liked my snarky remarks and my chatty gamer gossip. Most preferred my witty advice and commentary on the games I played—and played well. I couldn't complain. On Twitch, I received donations and subscription money—along with a small supplement for ads that showed on my feed. I made some nice supplemental income from streaming my gaming, much to the dismay of several jealous colleagues.

Of course, I never streamed playing Dragon Epoch. That would have put my job in jeopardy. None of my random followers even knew I was a Draco employee as that was top secret info.

Given that the channel had been down several days, I was feeling the pressure to provide some sort of content for them. An idea occurred to me—why not stream while I was setting up my rig here in the new place? If I got my cameras and mic up first, then I could talk to my followers, broadcasting while I plugged in equipment and set up the room. That way, my followers had live proof of my work in progress and I'd have something to stream even though my rig wasn't ready for game play.

Before that, I vowed to start the day off right with a little yoga to work out the kinks in my muscles from all that moving. To say nothing of the need for stress relief from the events of the past week! I slipped into my bright green and blue leggings with my black tank top and did an entire hour video from my favorite Yoga instructor on YouTube.

Feeling energized and full of excitement to get this new section of my life started, I went into the empty spare room Lucas had told me I could use. The other spare room was a den with his exercise equipment in it—weights, barbells and a massive and expensive-looking rowing machine. I tried not to spend too long picturing those arm muscles bulging as he used it. *Hmmm.*

For today's stream, since I'd be moving boxes and equipment around, I opted to use my headset mic. Since I was a seasoned pro, I got my desk and computer hooked up in less than thirty minutes. Then I set up my two cameras—one atop my monitor and a GoPro mounted high up on the other side of the room.

I inputted the information for Lucas's WiFi—which he'd already helpfully supplied me with—and then I was off to the races. The little green light flickered on, indicating that I was now live streaming once again.

Standing back away from the monitor so I could fit my entire body in front of the webcam, I smiled and waved. "Hey guys! *Surprise!* Your evil overlord, Persephone, has returned much sooner than anticipated. I'm starting to settle into my new digs. Do you like?" I opened my arms and turned around, indicating the spacious room. "Nice and big and full of so many possibilities." After catching a glimpse of myself on the monitor, I smoothed a strand of hair out of my face.

Then I set to work opening boxes and pulling them out. I plugged in wire and connected auxiliary equipment—controllers, lighting, speakers—chatting away as I went.

I talked about everything—the components of my rig, which were exactly the same as the setup in the corner nook of my bedroom where I'd streamed from Heath's place.

"So what was I saying?" I prattled on after being distracted by the surprising response I was getting on my chat stream. My followers were overwhelmingly enthusiastic about me being online again! There were donations coming in and the new subscribers count climbed quickly.

"Oh, I was talking about my latest gaming obsession, Covert Ops. I got to sample it at the last E3 convention and I can't wait for its release. Just ten more days 'til that puppy is live to download on Steam!"

I turned and opened the small box labeled game controllers. I had all kinds, actually—thrust master, paddles, steering wheel, old school joystick, PlayStation emulator, Xbox and Virtual Reality wands. I kept them all organized on their own little stand, ready to grab whenever I needed them. I also had to set up my PlayStation and flat screen TV, too. All of which I got done while babbling away to my unseen internet audience and not playing a single damn game.

I didn't have time to read the chat stream but I could see from across the room that it was a banner day for new subscriptions.

I was up several hundred new followers from this morning alone. Who knew that watching someone set up their new rig would be so interesting?

"Some of my suggestions for setting up your monitor revolve around ergonomics, of course. Gotta make sure you're not craning your neck or getting gamer's elbow or any—"

Suddenly the door to the room whipped open and Lucas bust through so quickly he was a blur. He was holding something gathered in his arms. I turned to face him, putting my hands on my hips.

"What—"

But he shoved himself between me and the camera and threw a blanket over my head, wrapping it quickly around me. *What the...?*

I stumbled back with a shriek and fell on my butt, the blanket obscuring everything. Dumbass! This was not an amusing joke.

"Lucas, you dickhead!" I yelled before I realized he was talking.

And he wasn't talking to me.

"You uncivilized little shits need to go wank off to PornStop and leave *my wife* alone."

I fought through layers of blanket to free myself from my sudden oppression. He was *so* getting his ass kicked.

I poked my head out in time to see that he had thrown a sweatshirt over the camera. Now, he was searching for the button to switch off my video feed.

"Lucas!" I shouted again, pulling myself up to stand, spitefully kicking away his stupid blanket. "What the hell are you doing?"

"First, I'm shutting this shit down. Then, at my earliest convenience, I'm going to hunt down some IP addresses and deliver payback to certain little horny douchebags."

I moved up to stand beside him where he bent over my keyboard furiously typing into it. Whoa. The chat feed was going a mile a minute and Lucas's lines were in shouty all-caps.

Still the subscriptions kept pouring in...along with the donations. One popped up on the screen as I stood there, trying to gather my bearings.

LuvDosBewbz(.)(.) has donated $10.00. [Please come back, pretty lady!]

I blinked, completely confused. Lucas was still pounding away furiously, his teeth gritted, his facial features tight with anger. He still hadn't said a word to me since shutting off my feed.

But the tone of that chat was... ugh. Full of comments about how great my ass and boobs looked in my yoga gear. How my followers were steadily messaging their friends to come check out the latest gamer hot girl. Tons of people stated they couldn't wait to watch my regular stream. Many were assuming I was a newbie who'd never done this before and had resorted to showing off my assets to gain viewership.

Yeah, *yuck.* There were channels like that but mine was *not* one of them.

"Wait, what is that?" I said, pointing at a thumbnail pic someone had posted in the comments section. Lucas clicked on it to expand the screen capture someone had caught. I leaned in close.

"What the...?" I squinted and turned my head sideways.

"They're your breasts, apparently," he drawled.

And he was right. In their full glory, up close and personal. A perfect shot of my cleavage as I bent down in front of the camera to fix the mic. I'd been way too focused on having something to talk about and getting my stuff set up. I definitely hadn't thought about the fact that I was still wearing my yoga getup nor about how that would look on camera.

He grimaced and clicked on another image, expanding it. "And here are several shots of your ass. This one looks like you were fishing something out of a big box on the ground." The camera got my most popular angle, apparently, as my butt was front and center in the photo.

I leaned in to read the caption, *Dat ass!*

Heat crawled up my neck and my throat felt tight when I swallowed. My eyes flicked to Lucas's. "I, uh, I guess I didn't think through my wardrobe."

He blinked, his face flushed with barely contained anger. "There are a lot of dirty pubescent children out there, both physically and emotionally. Do yourself a favor and don't read the chat."

So of course my eyes flew immediately to the chat box. Before he could put his hand over it to block me, I caught a glimpse of someone dubbing Persephone the newest addition to the "Camgirls of Twitch TV."

I drew back, frowning in disgust. "What a bunch of bullshit."

I didn't have to rely on wearing tight clothes and showing my cleavage to get attention. It worked for others, and that was fine, but it was so not my style.

Lucas was flushed and grim-faced with obvious anger when I moved over to the mouse and clicked the window closed.

He stiffened and then turned to me. "Those disgusting idiots were just fantasizing about all the parts of your body they want to bathe with their spunk."

I wrinkled my nose. "Ewww. Disgusting little shits."

Some of those gamer kids on the internet could get particularly raunchy when shielded by their anonymity. And sexism in the gaming community was real. There was a chance I'd spoiled some of my cred as a legit gamer girl with this stunt.

Well shit, at least the live streaming was a side gig and not my full-time job.

Lucas straightened from the keyboard and stood stiffly facing me. His obvious displeasure was making me feel a bit sheepish. "I'd done yoga right before and I got the idea to stream my set up. That's why I was dressed like that."

He shook his head. "You should know better, Kat. You should also know about the dangers posed to any internet streamer. Calling SWAT teams on people just so they can watch streamer get 'swatted' on live internet. That's dangerous shit. To say nothing of stalkers."

I frowned. "A wee tiny mistake I won't make again. But I'm not going to curb my streaming out of fear. I definitely won't wear my yoga stuff again even if it was a banner day for new subscribers." I stuck my tongue out at him and he rolled his eyes as he left the room.

In spite of my surface irritation, though, I was grateful that he'd raced in and put a stop to it when he did. I had no idea he even followed me on Twitch. Likely he'd gotten the notification that I was livestreaming on his way home and realized what was going on. It could have gone on for another hour had he not shut it down.

Thank goodness he had.

Out in the living room, I turned to him. "I don't need to use my rack and my ass to get subscribers and donations. I'm just myself on my channel—a funny, quirky gamer girl. I don't get all glammed up or wear a push-up bra."

He blew out a breath. "Please tell me you aren't so naïve you think every single one of your subscribers are there for your gameplay instead of because of how you look."

I spun on him, hands on my hips. "How do I look, Lucas?"

Might as well call him on his shit, right? His eyes narrowed and slid down my form slowly. It wasn't lewd or leering, the way he looked at me. But it warmed me up like the lightest touch, nevertheless. I found I wanted him to look at me, notice me.

I waved a hand in front of my chest. "Is that all my worth? My face, my tits, my ass?"

He blinked. "Exactly the opposite. But the fact that those horny little shits see only that and not your actual—and considerable—talent pisses me off."

I sighed. "Welcome to being a woman in the gamer community. We are constantly objectified as well as having our abilities questioned. People assume the only reason we get ahead is because we purposely use our bodies and our looks to replace real ability."

"Well you know *I* don't think that way. But not acknowledging how your looks play into it is disingenuous. You're way too—" he cut himself off, flushing as if whatever he was going to say would embarrass him to admit.

I stared at him expectantly. He blinked, then returned my stare for long, tense moments.

Then he cleared his throat. "I still plan on hunting down those little shits and infecting their machines with undetectable malware."

A smile tugged at the corners of my mouth in spite of everything. His protectiveness toward me was more than a little endearing. It almost—*almost*—made me forget about his implication that my looks played a part in my online popularity.

I would be naïve to think otherwise, I suppose. And his implication wasn't one of finding fault or finger pointing. It was just stating a fact. If his beliefs had aligned with the stupid little woman-hating incel gamer-gate shits out there, then I would have long known that by now.

"You're just making peace so I don't embarrass you in front of your parents tonight."

He cracked a smile at that. "Just wear a nice dress and use your best manners and you'll make it through unscathed."

I raised a brow, contemplating that. "They sound really old-fashioned."

"You have no idea."

I eyed him suspiciously, deeply aware that there was more that he wasn't telling me about himself, his family and this evening in general. "So how nice should I dress?"

He checked his watch. "Think formal."

Hmm. "Well I have the dress I wore to Adam and Mia's wedding. It's island-dressy."

He raised his eyebrows. "Which means?"

I straightened. "Well it's very pretty and for warm weather. The weather is nice out today so I won't be cold. And it's classy as far as I'm concerned."

He shrugged. "If it's pretty and you like it, then wear it."

I made a mock sniff of irritation and snarked. "So glad I have your approval." But suddenly a wave of nervousness boiled up. His skepticism and mysterious behavior was only making me more aware that I probably shouldn't screw this up.

His smirk widened. "Don't jump the gun. I haven't seen you in it yet."

I had a little over three hours until we had to leave. Under normal circumstances that would mean I'd have at least two hours to spare in order to get ready. But his talk got me so nervous that I took a lot longer to prep than usual. I spent extra time with my makeup, doing my eyeliner with a slightly shaky hand. Was there any way they'd know that I didn't buy my non-designer makeup in some high-end fancy store?

I also spent time on my hair, brushing it until it gleamed, way past my shoulders and halfway down my back. I was overdue for a trim and suddenly nervous that they would look closely and find split ends. I opted to fish out my curling iron—that I hadn't used since the aforementioned wedding—from a cardboard box helpfully labeled *washroom*.

Finally, every curl meticulously planned was then strategically implemented. After a slight tweeze of my brows and the best makeup job I could manage, I was ready to slip on the dress.

Fortunately, I'd immediately hung it up in plastic after having it dry cleaned, so it was ready for me to wear. The dress was a strappy number made of milled silky fabric in a delicate ice blue. I'd planned it that way—to attend a winter wedding, even if smack dab in the middle of thirty-degree Celsius Caribbean weather. It hadn't felt too much like winter but I'd wanted to acknowledge that beautiful New Year's Eve joining in some way.

Plus, this color looked really good next to my skin. Gave it a glowy, porcelain appearance. I was pale, both due to DNA and the country of my birth. And living a few years in California had only served to remind me of that. The southern California sun could rip the hide right off anyone not used to it. And even then, the use of sunblock and sunscreen was a religion here. With my skin, I had to be extra diligent.

I took over two hours to prep and primp, unheard of in my normal regimen. But I was ready, slipping my feet into glittery high-heeled sandals.

Feeling like a princess, I actually giggled at myself in the mirror. Getting dressed up like this was so rare that it was almost a treat. I wasn't so much of a tom boy that I didn't like being a pretty girly-girl once in a while. But no more than once in a while. Doing this every day would be too damn exhausting. And boring, too, to be honest. I rarely spent more than a half hour on my daily beauty routine mostly because I didn't find it interesting to spend any more on it.

My heels echoed on the hardwood floors as I walked down the hallway to the front room. I was a few minutes early, hoping to one-up Lucas, who, I knew from work, very much prized punctuality. He'd factored in the length of the drive, the time he wanted to arrive and given me a time by which I needed to be ready.

And here I was, five minutes ahead of schedule and hoping to be here first. But no, he was already there, standing near the door and looking at his phone.

I could hardly be stealthy when my shoes made the same amount of noise on his floor as a galloping baby goat. But I stopped when I entered anyway because...

Because he looked so incredibly hot that it took my breath away.

Lucas was wearing a dark charcoal gray suit, a lighter colored grey shirt. The only splash of color in his entire ensemble was from the deep blue silk tie. But wow. I'd never seen him in a suit before. All of us employees in the Den were casual at work and in most functions surrounding work.

That suit was tailored to fit him perfectly. It accentuated his fit build. Having rowed crew in college, he had a well-developed upper body while also having to maintain a certain weight for the team. He obviously kept himself in shape on that rowing machine, even with the demanding job. Impressive. My eyes glided down his form from head to toe. I'd wondered more than once what he must look like under his clothes. And then I'd chastised myself for not keeping it one hundred percent professional even in my thoughts.

I cleared my throat. "You look handsome," I said with a small smile.

But the way he was looking at me right then said that I wasn't the only one who wasn't keeping it one hundred percent professional...

CHAPTER 7
LUCAS

I WAS PREPARED FOR HER TO LOOK HOT. KAT WAS ALWAYS hot without even trying. But I wasn't quite ready for this. She looked...

My mind ran through a litany of possibilities from basic to flowery—gorgeous, radiant, stunning, ravishing. Beautiful. Her dress was short, resting mid-thigh and hugged her curves. A glittery light blue with silver accents. It complemented her coloring beautifully. The top of the bodice was held up by thin straps over her pale shoulders. It dipped into a plunging neckline, showing about as much cleavage as she'd inadvertently given to her audience of horny gamers this morning.

But I pushed that thought aside quickly before the irritation flared up again. Her beautiful dark red hair gleamed against the color of her dress, spilling over her shoulders in thick, loose curls. I'd never seen hair that color on a person and at first had been convinced that it wasn't her natural color. It wasn't until I'd noticed that her brows and eyelashes, when not wearing mascara, were the exact same color that I figured she was a natural redhead.

It gave her an otherworldly appearance, like one of the ethereal and mysterious elves out of our Dragon Epoch game. Like a fey creature from deep in a dark forest who wielded nature magic and was as wild and as powerful as the land and trees that surrounded her.

My eyes settled on her cleavage. The dress showed off all her stunning assets.

And they were amazing, perfect assets. The round curves of her breasts, the glow of her skin there advertised all on its own a creamy softness that screamed to be touched. Along with a sweet, sweet flavor I longed to taste. I was obsessed with the thought of running my tongue there, along that silken valley, those pillowy crests. The state of things below my belt was suddenly uncomfortable, pulled like a knot wound tight. I was rock hard at the thought of touching and tasting her. I gripped my phone so tight that I almost dropped it.

She was looking like *this...* and I had to share her with my family tonight.

Which was probably a good thing because I was so damn tempted to do something that would feel very good, but that I'd regret later. I'd already endured the shitty conclusion of a terrible marriage once. No need to tack a similar messed up ending onto this fake one.

Tonight, I had a new wife I needed to present to the whole damn family. Of course, they'd insisted on it the minute I'd been forced into revealing the surprise marriage. So bogus or not, we'd have to go through with the charade of pretending to be new husband and wife.

Yeah, sure, I never turned down a chance to mock the institution of marriage when I could. But there was no way I'd consider getting tied into another disaster like the first one had been, even if just legally and temporarily.

Regardless, looking at Kat right now, I couldn't help but wish there was more between us than a sham marriage. Because... *wow*. It took me a moment to catch my breath and calm the beating of my heart. I was grateful for the front flap of my jacket covering other, more visceral reactions.

"You look good," I heard myself utter. Understatement of the year. She looked good enough to eat and boy was my mouth already watering. Hunger pangs screaming for her, demanding, insistent. So loud they almost combined into a chorus all their own. One that threatened to own every thought until I finally got to touch her, undress her, taste her. Bury myself between those warm, curvy thighs.

Fuck. I really needed to touch her. And any excuse would do.

"Shall we go?" I said after another pause where I fought to collect myself. Jesus. I'd seen a pretty woman before. I'd seen lots of pretty women. I'd been married to a pretty woman.

But... it was hard to remember all the rest. All those in the past. The past I'd wanted to forget. Right now, Kat was making that *really* easy.

Usually, she was just needling me and making it her mission to irritate the crap out of me. And aptly succeeding in doing so. Tonight apparently, her mission would be to unknowingly drive me crazy.

I held the door open for her, like a gentleman—like I'd been trained to do automatically in my past life. Old world manners died hard. She walked through the doorway in those clicky heels with glittery straps that snaked up around her thin, sexy ankles. I couldn't help pressing my hand to the small of her back to guide her though.

She didn't need it. Probably would never thought of asking for it.

No that small, simple touch was for me. As if to reaffirm to myself that she was real and she was, indeed, this beautiful on top of all her other admirable—and not as visibly obvious—assets.

And that for a short while longer, she was *mine*.

My fellow co-worker. My sometime partner-in-crime. My erstwhile nemesis. My wife—whom I couldn't touch. And no, not by some arbitrary law or regulation. Not even by her own insistence. No, that stupid-ass stipulation had come from me and I had no one to blame for suffering with these blue balls but myself.

Unfortunately, I had no time to wallow in my misery. I moved to the passenger side of my midnight blue '80s era Mercedes Benz to open the door for her.

"Wow, such a genna'man," she drawled, surprisingly, with little of her characteristic snark. She looked at me and gave an exaggerated wink.

I had little occasion to drive her places. We only rarely interacted in a social context. Sure, we'd spent nights and nights on top of each other—unfortunately not literally—in the Den during crunch time. We'd done occasional happy hours with the department or a house party. I rarely got the opportunity to show off my own unique skill set to her. But it had been so ingrained in me growing up that I really didn't have a choice whether or not I wanted to show it off.

As I helped her into the car, I was privy to the wonderful fringe benefit of a full view down the front of her dress. She slid into the seasoned leather seats and smiled up at me, which did nothing for the condition of things below my belt.

No wonder all those little shit bottom-feeders watching her on Twitch had lost their minds today. Shit. She was so goddamn sexy it hurt. Even when just wearing her yoga clothes.

Damned if I wasn't also secretly gloating at the thought of showing up to the family dinner with this hot as fuck woman on my arm, calling her my wife.

My cousin would openly flirt with her in his usual over-the-top fashion. Father would probably spill his cognac and make quite the mess. Most likely both of them would be thinking dirty old man thoughts the entire time she was present.

But she was *mine*. Even if it was just on paper. And even if just temporarily.

"So I can't believe I've never asked this but... where do your parents live?"

"South county. Coto de Caza."

From behind the wheel, I threw a furtive glance at her to see if the name rang a bell, but she didn't make any sound of recognition. Good. So much the better. Her ignorance of the local geography would serve to make her less nervous. That community easily housed some of the wealthiest people in southern California. She'd figure it out the moment we hit all the massive homes and gated security. Fortunately, by then she'd only have minutes to get worked up about it.

Turning the ignition, I eased out onto the driveway and hit the button to close the garage door. Her sad little '90s era Honda Civic sat in the driveway, looking forlorn in this neighborhood amongst all the hybrids, Mercedes and BMWs. Nevertheless, the car still seemed to be holding up.

Soon we were on the freeway. I glanced at her as she watched the dried summer hills of southern California chaparral slide by her window. Her hands were folded quietly in her lap, no sign of fidgeting or nervousness.

"This shouldn't be too big a deal tonight. My parents have only known for a few days, after all. But they insisted on meeting you this weekend as soon as I told them. Couldn't really avoid it."

She nodded, gazing down at her tightly folded hands. "No worries. I get it."

"How did your parents react?"

She hesitated in answering and I threw her a follow-up glance. Surely she'd told them... But it was still unclear exactly what her family situation was. She didn't seem close to them at all and I was once again curious. Maybe she hadn't even bothered to tell them?

She cleared her throat. "I haven't heard back from them yet."

My brows shot up in surprise. "You, ah... you emailed them the news?"

"Something like that."

Wow. I threw her a sidelong glance, determined to get her to fess up about this. But now wasn't the time. She glanced at me, then turned to look out the window.

When I opened my mouth to reply to her, she beat me to it. "I miss the trees sometimes," she said out of nowhere.

"I beg your pardon?"

She turned to look at me. "The only big trees here are palms. They are everywhere, of course. And they fit in here, but I miss the trees in the Pacific Northwest. There's just something about them—firs, maples, birch. It's so brown here in the summer. But that's the greenest season in the PNW."

I kept my eyes on the road. "I grew up here. I'm used to it."

"So do your parents still live in the house you grew up in?"

One of them, I thought, but I only nodded in response. Again, the less info I spilled about all this, probably the better.

I exited the freeway and wound down the familiar thoroughfares and byways, ending on a two-lane highway. That road led to one of the gated communities that made up Coto de Caza, nestled up against the dry hills and the canyons of Southern California back country.

We wound our way up the hill from the freeway through not one but two guard stations. If she didn't freak out now, then we'd probably be good for the rest of the night.

CHAPTER 8
KATYA

H E WAS SUBTLE, BUT I NOTICED THAT HE THREW THE occasional glance my way as we exited the freeway. The car followed a twisty two-lane road that wound high into the hills. Was he testing my reactions? I made sure to drink in my surroundings but keep any inner responses low-key.

But that was getting a little more challenging to do as we made our way to the first gate. It was automated. Lucas pulled out a metallic card from behind the car's sun visor and waved it past the machine. An automated gate slid aside to allow the car entrance.

The homes we passed were large and beautiful with carefully maintained front yards and expensive cars in the driveway. It was a quiet and rather snooty-looking neighborhood—fountains, statues and fancy topiaries in practically every front yard. There were homes like this in the richer parts of Vancouver, but I'd never found myself in or even near any of them.

But the real nerves—the sweaty palms and the racing heartbeat—kicked in when we hit the second gate within the first gated community. And this one was manned by several uniformed guards. Like the freakin' Tower of London or something.

Lucas braked and lowered his driver-side window. "Van den Hoehnsboek van Lynden."

After angling a camera at the car and scanning in the license plate, one of the guards nodded. His white military-style hat bobbed up and down in the late afternoon sunlight. "Of course." And he let us through the gate.

Well just... holy crap. Where the hell were we going *now*? We were running out of hill to climb.

If possible, *these* homes easily topped the other beautiful homes we'd just passed.

And they definitely should be labeled mansions by any and all who had ever been introduced to the concept of what a mansion was. Adam and Mia's place would fit in easily here. Of course I was sure they preferred their little private beach on a semi-private island in the back bay but... *this view!*

I looked out over the lowlands of the cities of south county below us as we ascended further up the hill. For every foot we scaled, the homes increased in size and volume and in value by hundreds of thousands of dollars—or so I guessed.

Wow. They really didn't want the riff raff getting into their nice little haven, did they? Two different gates... armed guards. How'd these residents get their hands on their yearly fix of Girl Guide cookies in this neighborhood? To say nothing of trick-or-treaters.

Lucas had grown up... *here?*

"You okay?" he finally asked after long silent minutes of driving. "You're very quiet over there. " *For once.* I knew he was thinking that last bit though he hadn't actually said it. But yeah... he'd finally found a way to shut me up.

I'd practically bitten a hole through my lip and, with my arms folded across my chest, my fingers were now squeezing bruises into the flesh on my upper arms.

When I figured there was hardly any hill left to climb, Lucas pulled down a private road. It led to what could only be described as an estate, not a mere mansion.

Fuuuck. What the ever-living hell?

I'd think this was some kind of joke if he hadn't been waving cards in front of machines. To say nothing of calling out his last name like he was a goddamn Rockefeller or a Carnegie.

The driveway was long, lined with a seemingly endless row of palm trees, culminating in a decorative circular plaza set before the sprawling home. A valet raced up to open my door as Lucas parked at the curb. I looked toward the driver side where Lucas was letting himself out and, curiously now, avoiding my gaze. He handed his keys to the valet who greeted him by name and pulled the car away to park somewhere else.

Then I turned to gape at the house before us. "You didn't tell me that your family lives in a hilltop resort. Is—is this a hotel?"

Lucas did not respond, glancing up casually at the massive structure that towered above us, all stone, glass and sleek, modern lines and curves. The home itself was a work of art.

My head tilted as I continued looking up and up and up. There were at least a dozen slender, circular chimneys scraping the late afternoon sky. Uh. Gulp.

I wiped sweaty hands across the material covering my thighs. Lucas's great-grandmother's diamond ring winked, catching in the sunlight. When I stopped to study it, I fixated on the horrid state of my cuticles and chipped nails. My breath seized. I'd never been more self-conscious in my life. Most likely the family would be asking to see the ring on my finger tonight. I hadn't thought about how crappy this lovely piece of jewelry would look on my unadorned hand.

"I shoulda got a manicure. Or at least painted my nails."

Lucas seemed unconcerned about the state of my hands as he held out his to me. Slowly I took it and his fingers engulfed mine, holding firm as if reassuring me. "There's no time to be nervous. Just take a deep breath and go with the flow."

Go with the flow. Riiiiight. I sent him major side-eye for that. He caught the expression, eyebrow raising. Oh, I promised him payback for this bullshit. It would be swift and painful, too. I hoped he read that in my eyes. We'd just see how easily he got through the flow when recovering from a non-metaphorical swift kick in the nuts.

We climbed the shallow steps down the walkway of geometrically fitted slabs divided by shallow trenches of trickling water. It was designed to look like we were walking on the stepping stones of a stylized stream, driven by a fountain near the front door. Instead of knocking, Lucas turned the doorknob and entered. I half expected a uniformed doorman.

We stepped inside and I had to remember to breathe because the place was even more exquisite inside than out. My head tilted back to take in the massive chrome-trimmed winding staircase, the huge crystal chandelier that towered over the colored glass-lined reflecting pool in the entry way.

An older couple—probably in their fifties or so—approached the front foyer to greet us. How they knew we were here, I had no idea and figured it must have been that valet dude radioing back to the house. Or maybe even the guards at the gate.

Or maybe the invisible butler did it.

I had no idea if the Van Den Blah Blahs had a butler or not. At this point, it would be the least shocking revelation of the evening if they did.

It was quite involuntary, of course, and purely due to the overwhelm that I let slip a "Holy fuck." Some moments just required that universal—if profane—exclamation. And this was definitely one of them. I'd muttered it under my breath but apparently the woman heard, her perfectly penciled brows climbing in her botoxed forehead.

Her dress was a glittery non-color, likely by some famous designer. She also wore a necklace that was probably worth more than my entire house back home. Her ash blond hair was short, just around her ears and curled up. Matching god-awfully expensive-looking earrings nestled in each of her ears.

After giving me the once over, she turned to my husband. "Lucas, you're finally here."

She kissed both his cheeks instead of wrapping him in a hug. It was a very European style of greeting. She struck me as highly sophisticated in her manners even though she sounded quite ordinarily American when she spoke.

"Mother," he said evenly. "Thank you for the invite."

Then the man stepped forward to shake his hand. "It's been too long, son." He was tall and finely built and Lucas resembled him a bit—coloring and build-wise, anyway. Their features were markedly different.

And the coolness in their greeting wasn't lost on me. After the awkward handshake, both parents looked expectantly at me without saying a word. Was Lucas supposed to introduce me? Why was everything so uptight and formal? Even the way they'd called each other, "Mother, Father, Son," was weird.

Well, screw that shit. That was *so* not me.

I pasted on a giant fake smile and stuck my hand out to shake. "Hi, I'm Katya."

To their credit, they didn't clutch their proverbial pearls over my casual greeting. The woman took my hand and smiled. "I'm Elaine and this is my husband, Arent." She then leaned forward and putting her hands on my upper arms, touched her cheek to mine and kissed the air. She repeated this action on the other side before taking a step back. I stood still, bathed in her expensive perfume before pulling back stiffly.

Lucas's father followed up by taking my hand and shaking it. His eyes slid down my form almost lewdly before he sent a quick wink to his son. Was that a wink of approval? *Yuck.*

"It's short for Katharina, no?" Elaine asked.

I nodded, that ridiculous smile still fixed on my face. "Yes. Katharina Ellis."

Without changing her neutral expression, she turned to Lucas. "She's keeping her name?"

"It's the twenty-first century. That's what women do now," Lucas's father replied before either of us could. "Especially when our son prefers your name over mine."

Lucas grimaced. "Not something we really need to talk about now."

I frowned. Hmm. There was a story there. Van Den Dad seemed bitter about Lucas not using the extra lengthy Dutch name. But it was more than just for mere convenience. Obviously, my new husband was not good at coming clean. This mansion and estate were quickly revealing what I suspected was merely the tip of a very big iceberg.

Let's hope all our carefully planned schemes and agreements were not going to suffer the same fate as the *Titanic*.

Lucas's mother turned to me amidst the ensuing tension between her husband and her son. "We are so thrilled to meet you. What a wonderful surprise. We're all looking forward to knowing you better but for now, welcome to the family. We're serving champagne at the outdoor bar beside the pool. Lucas will show you."

With no small relief, we turned from the chillingly formal parental greeting. I felt Lucas's hand on the small of my back again, like when he'd escorted me out of his house earlier today. I could feel it resting there, maddeningly and inexplicably possessive. The touch burned through the cool silk of my dress.

We passed through the archway into the back part of the home and toward a huge set of open glass doors to a stone terrace. I muttered under my breath, "I'm going to fucking gut you later, dude."

A quick expulsion of air, as if covering for a surprise bout of laughter was his only response. His hand on my back moved, the pressure deepening. I longed to bat his arm away but for some reason, didn't. Regardless of how annoyed I was with him right now, we still had to keep up the appearance of a deliriously happy newlywed couple.

We moved through the high stone archway and through the glass walls to a sprawling terrace that overlooked the valley laid out below. If this was a mere family dinner, then Lucas had the biggest ass family I'd seen in a long time. There were at least fifty people here, with drinks in hand listening to live music. They ringed the gorgeous glass tile-lined pool full of floating flower arrangements. In fact there were white floral arrangements everywhere, perfuming the air with the scent of roses and hydrangeas. And even an intricate ice sculpture and silver champagne fountain.

What the...?

"*This* is your small family gathering?" I asked in a harsh whisper as he directed us to the outdoor bar manned by two uniformed bartenders. They passed us each a flute of champagne, informing us not to drink until the "special toast."

Special toast? What the hell was this? When had I crossed the magical threshold and stepped into a real-life version of *Lifestyles of the Rich and Famous*? And would those champagne wishes also be accompanied by caviar dreams?

Gag. I'd never had caviar before but the mere idea of eating fish eggs made my stomach roil. Sure, we British Columbians loved our fish but give me a nice freshly baked Sockeye over hoity-toity fish eggs any day of the week.

I spared a glance at my husband. He did not appear thrilled. Of course, with Lucas, one never knew. He could have that stoic face even while in the throes of ecstasy. Maybe his O-face looked just like that.

I yanked my gaze away from him—and my thoughts away from what he might look like during the height of pleasure. Just not a good place to go, mentally, when you were sexually frustrated and stuck under the same roof with a handsome and maddeningly annoying man.

Lucas's parents swiftly followed us to the bar and were presented their own glasses of champagne by the bartenders. I glanced at the pile of napkins on the bar—decorated with silver congratulations and stylized wedding bells. Movement out of the corner of my eye had me turning my head, only to be blinded by multiple flashes from the largest camera I'd ever seen. Two professional photographers did a small dance around each other to capture every moment.

Holy shit... Lucas's parents were going to toast us in front of this huge crowd. All this meticulous décor, the drinks, the food and this party had been thrown together at the last minute.

Suddenly self-conscious, my gaze dropped to the ground. Lucas's dad took up his glass and tapped on it with a spoon to get everyone's attention. In no time, everyone was staring at us. The head of the Van Den Household spoke in a clear, well-trained, almost Shakespearean voice. "Let's start this off right. We may have been taken by surprise about this lovely new addition to our family but we'll welcome her right. Everyone, this is our new daughter-in-law, Katharina Ellis. Please join me in a toast of congratulations and well wishes to the newlyweds. To Lucas and Katharina."

Everyone around us echoed the toast, clinked glasses and we drank. Murmurs echoed the new father-in-law's well wishes. Then some rando in the crowd called out, "To Baron and Baroness van den Hoehnsboek van Lynden."

More mutters and another sip from everyone. My arm froze before taking a second sip. That had been a joke, right? But if so... why was no one laughing? I glanced at Lucas to confirm that was, indeed, a joke. But he wasn't laughing. Instead he was gazing daggers in the direction of whoever had said it. And Lucas's dad looked like someone had just stomped on his foot. He, pointedly, set down his champagne glass, not drinking to that toast, whatever the hell it meant.

His son then downed the remaining contents of his own glass and pointedly refused to look at me after that. Maybe he could use a good stomp on his foot, too. Dude had a lot of 'splainin to do.

Someone banged their own glass with a spoon—and unlike the plastic cake fork against the plastic juice glass in the Den, this one rung out. A woman called out from the crowd, "Kissing time!"

Lucas turned to me and lifted his brows in a question. Despite being extremely annoyed with him, I sidled up to him, merely for appearance's sake. But I sent a heated glare at him as his face came closer to mine for the kiss.

Whether or not he noticed, he did not react. At least he was consistent. Lucas's hands came around me and pressed on my back to pull me against him. My fingers curled around the lapels of his jacket. Then he leaned in and pressed his mouth to mine.

People clapped and cheered and... well I didn't pay much attention at that point.

The minute his tongue entered my mouth, I stiffened. The hands on my back pressed a little harder and his mouth did the same, deepening the kiss. For a guy who didn't show much emotion on the surface, he really did know how to kiss like Cassanova. This wasn't a cold peck to satisfy the masses. It wasn't an act. He wasn't good enough at that.

No *this* was something more.

Our tongues tangled and heat flared between us from my simmering anger to something hotter. His smell, his taste, the warm pressure of his mouth on mine. Desire crackled between us, alive and palpable, threatening to seize the moment. With the last shred of my anger and self-consciousness at the crowd looking on, I nudged him away.

He gave me the slightest bit of resistance, so I had to push a little harder. And I could see in his eyes the second our mouths parted that he wasn't ready for it to be over. Our gazes held and locked and even if it had been an amazing kiss, I still hadn't forgotten that I was pissed at him.

And I was frankly getting tired of having to kiss him for others' amusement and satisfaction. Newlyweds did it all the time, yadda yadda yadda. But we weren't your average newlyweds and unlike average newlyweds, we never got to kiss unless it was for show or to make a point to onlookers. It was frustrating, in more ways than one.

My cheeks were still heated, but whether from anger, embarrassment or that kiss, I couldn't say. Probably a clever and confusing stew of all of the above. My eyes narrowed at him again, putting extra venom into this glare. He fully pulled back then, and I immediately felt relief due to the distance between us—both physically and emotionally. I could always count on Lucas to keep his emotional distance, after all.

Thank goodness for that failsafe.

It wasn't that I didn't trust myself enough. Hardly. But it was always good to have a backup. Lucas's reserve, his gift for keeping people at a distance, was our ace-in-the-hole. I couldn't have picked a better person to pull off this scheme with. Even if I had done it on the spur of the moment and completely subconsciously.

But still, his reserve had aided him in keeping almost everything about his personal life from me. And *that* was annoying.

It would have been useful to know that the Van Den Parents were richer than God. And apparently foreign royalty? What. The. Hell.

Lucas's parents—or, as I should start thinking of them, my mother- and father-in-law—started to mingle in the crowd and the large group broke up into clumps. Soon every stranger known to mankind who shared even the tiniest micron of DNA with Lucas was welcoming me into the Van Den Richfucks fold. I pretended I was like Princess Diana, with a pasted-on smile and gracious handshake. At least I hoped to hide the internal screaming and the fact that I wanted out of this damn place *toute de suite.*

A familiar-looking tall, willowy blonde woman in her mid-thirties approached, a big smile on her face. Beside her was a fairly good-looking younger man who held both their drinks while she shook my hand.

I'd seen her before but I couldn't place where I knew her from. My mind immediately started racing to remember where and in what context.

"Hi there! I'm Lindsay Walker, Lucas's cousin on his mom's side. You look really familiar to me. You work at Draco, don't you?"

That's where I'd seen her! I wanted to say she was Adam's friend or... maybe Jordan's? Or both?

I nodded, tucking a loose strand behind my ear and suddenly wishing I'd worn it up in a messy bun. But that probably would have garnered disapproval from all the foreign royalty present.

Suddenly I recalled where I knew Lindsay from. "Yeah. We've definitely met. Wasn't it at the VR demo last year? Not too long before the company went public. You're a friend of Adam's, if I remember correctly."

She smiled and darted an enigmatic look at Lucas, who, unsurprisingly, stone-faced it. Wait, hadn't Mia said something about her and Adam dating a long time ago? I couldn't even picture that if I tried.

"Lucas, here, owes me for that little favor." She shot him a teasing smile.

He blew out a breath but didn't seem offended. "I earned that job on my own."

She winked. "Of course you did. But *I* made the introductions. Just remember me when you're a world-famous game designer."

He rolled his eyes.

"It's not what you know, it's who you know. I guess that's so true," I said with my own snarky smile at Lucas. He seemed far more irritated with me than with Lindsay.

Although I shouldn't talk. I got my job because Adam had offered it to me after I'd left Canada to come down to Southern California. I had given up a good job when I'd come to be with Mia during her cancer treatment and recovery.

But it hadn't been the only reason I'd left. It had been an all too convenient time to leave the land of my birth. I'd needed to make a fresh, new start where the past and all that stress wouldn't follow me. For a long time, it hadn't, thank the Flying Spaghetti Monster, the Great Cat Goddess, Pan and all the other pantheons. I tried not to think about that legal letter I'd never looked at. Hopefully it was just a one-off.

Lindsay smiled, blue eyes darting from one of us to the other. "So I guess I get indirect credit for this adorable little love match of yours, since you met each other at work?"

Love match, yeah right. As in love-to-hate-him match. As in I'd love to stomp on his foot right this very moment but couldn't. Jesus Murphy. I downed the remainder of my champagne in one gulp while she chit-chatted with her cousin.

Another guy, shorter and fairer than Lucas, appeared on Lindsay's other side while her bored date had wandered off to grab some more drinks. The newcomer sent me an obnoxious wink and a flirtatious smile. I suspected that he'd dipped heavily into the libations long before we'd arrived.

The new guy bumped his shoulder against Lindsay who gave him an exasperated look and batted his hand away. "Don't be annoying," she said.

"It's a brother's number one job to be annoying," he shot back.

Lucas jutted his chin out at the new guy but didn't smile. "Hey, Henry." Then turned to me and, without meeting my gaze, gave the quick explanation. "Lindsay's younger brother, also my cousin."

Henry bent exaggeratedly over my hand when I offered it to him. He then one-upped his cheese-factor by kissing the back of it and sending me another wink. Eww this one was a creeper all right. "Since you are Dutch nobility now, my lady baroness."

Lucas stiffened. When he straightened, Henry sent a smug grin to his cousin, brows bobbing up and down quickly. That must be bro code for me meeting the requisite minimum hotness level, according to him. Jeez. Dude-bros were so gross.

"Oh hey Lucas, head's up. I'm pretty sure I saw your ex-wife here earlier in case no one else warned you."

Lucas's shoulders went rigid, and he looked much like someone had shoved a stick so far up his ass it was poking out his nostrils. Then his eyes scanned the pool area as he pointedly avoided my gaze.

What the...? Suddenly there was an ex-wife now? What the hell was this shit?

Lucas had never been married before... had he? Was Henry just being cheeky by referring to an ex-girlfriend like that? My eyes flew back to Lucas. It was time he offered me some explanations. And I wasn't going to wait until we got home. This was bullshit and it wasn't fair of him to keep me guessing all evening.

I forced myself not to grind it out through my teeth, *barely*. But I did interrupt Lindsay telling a funny story about a past client who sued his neighbor's dog for chewing a garden hose in half.

I loudly cleared my throat. "It was great to see you again, Lindsay, and nice to meet you, Henry. Now I have to excuse myself to visit the washroom if that's okay. Lucas? Can you show me?"

Lucas took my empty champagne flute from my hand setting it on a nearby tray. He then excused himself to his cousins and forged a path through the clumps of people back into the house. I followed on his heels and luckily, he walked fast enough that we weren't stopped by anymore well-wishers.

Once inside the house, I clamped my hand tightly onto his solid arm. He turned to me, mildly startled. "I need to speak with you in private, *sweetheart*," I muttered between clenched teeth, my eyes driving darts into his. He shot a glance at me and had the gall to hesitate. As if he was afraid of what I'd do to him in private.

Be afraid, dude. Be very afraid.

Too bad I wasn't wearing my pointiest of pointy heels. I could have really done some serious groin damage with those. Unlike most newlyweds, I had no use for that part of his anatomy. He just needed to be verbal and breathing at that upcoming interview. I could turn him into a eunuch and no one but him and me would know.

He was already escorting us to a quieter part of the house. Down a plain hallway in what I could only described as a "service" wing. Likely an area into which the blue bloods of the household would never deign to venture.

There were no staff here. Just the evidence that they worked out of this area—a washroom with schedules posted. A calendar on the wall with notes or messages attached. And a ginormous laundry room, which we entered.

I'd seen public laundromats smaller than this one, for Van Den BlingBling's sake. Lucas swung the door almost shut and turned to me with a sober expression.

In response, I stiffened and folded my arms across my chest. "What the fucking fuck, Lucas?"

He shrugged. "I'm sorry. My family always goes over the top. They said 'family dinner' and I stupidly assumed it would be *just* a family dinner—not the social event of the year."

I blinked. Wow. Talk about clueless.

"I couldn't care less about the party, Jedi Boy. But I would have appreciated, ya know, a decent warning about all the Downton Abbey bullshit."

He frowned, but did not answer.

"I mean... *this* is your family? Crazy Rich Caucasians? Who the hell *are* you and why am I only finding out about all this now?"

Infuriatingly he shrugged again and looked away from me as if I bored him with my feminine hysterics. "I didn't think it would make that much of an impact for the one or two times you're likely to see them before this is all over. I mean, had things gone according to plan, you would never have met them in the first place."

I gaped at him and gestured wildly. "Way to turn the blame back on me. *Again.*"

His gaze was straight and sharp, like an unforgiving arrow shot across front lines. "I'm only stating a fact."

"An *alternative* fact."

He ran a hand through his hair, rolling his eyes.

"What on earth were you trying to accomplish by keeping me in the dark and failing to prepare me for all of this? To teach me a lesson for letting the cat out of the bag?"

He sighed. "I'm just trying to minimize the impact of this night on any future repercussions for you *or* me."

What the hell did that even mean?

"I'm just saying that you had almost an entire week to clue me in that I'd married into the Royal Family of the Netherlands."

"Okay so... my family has money. Does that make any difference? They'll all be strangers to you next year."

"What about this baroness thing? What the hell even is that? Why did they call us Baron and Baroness Van Den LucasSucks?" His jaw tightened, displaying his clear irritation with my newest iteration of his family name.

He reached up to pinch the flesh at the bridge of his nose, the dim light gleaming off his wedding ring and expensive-looking cufflinks. "You should probably learn the name since you are, essentially, part of the family now."

"You don't even use it. Why is that? So you can be royalty walking amongst us commoners and unwashed masses?"

He clenched his jaw. "We aren't royalty." Then he reached up as if to loosen his tie slightly while clearing his throat. I blinked, nonplussed. Then he spoke again. "My father is a baron."

"*What?*"

He heaved a sigh, again as if I were boring him. "Immediate family members and their spouses have the title as a courtesy. That's how it works when you're part of a noble family. My grandfather emigrated to the US from the Netherlands and yes, he had a noble title but it doesn't mean anything anymore. There, nobility is just like everybody else—here even more so. They don't even use their titles in conversation which makes my cousin even more of an ass for announcing us that way."

My eyes fluttered, trying to take in that flood of new information. "But he wasn't wrong, was he? That is actually our title?"

He hesitated, hands working at his sides. It was interesting to see normally calm, collected, take-charge Lucas in this situation. But yeah, I was still annoyed as hell at him. "Yes."

My face flushed hot with anger and... shock, I guess it was. "Motherfucker."

"Yeah, you're probably gonna wanna start watching your mouth. Nobility frown on excessive swearing."

Oh he was trying to be funny, was he? I balled a fist and held it up, taking a step toward him about to ask him their take on domestic violence. His eyes widened comically.

Damn it if I didn't need him bruise-free in a few weeks for our interview. And if it weren't technically spousal abuse—I'd kick his ass right this very minute. "This is not a time to joke about this. And what the hell was that little tidbit about an ex-wife?"

He shook his head. "Nothing I even have the time to go into right now."

I held my hands out, palms up, gesturing around us. "What so you're just going to brush me off after withholding that little detail? Jesus, Lucas—"

"I'll tell you everything later. But if Claire approaches you tonight, avoid her like the plague."

My face burned even hotter. How the hell was I supposed to do *that*? I had zero information and he wasn't being fair. We had an interview in two short weeks. Not only did I know hardly a thing about his family background, but he had an ex-wife. One that I could be put on the spot about! "Fucking-a. I'm going to seriously—"

This time I did take a swing. In spite of my words, it wasn't a serious one. It was actually my shot across the bow because he clearly was not absorbing the depths of my anger.

He easily stepped out of the way just in time to avoid my fist, staring at me like I was a crazy woman.

He never got the chance to respond because we were interrupted by a manufactured, yet polite cough in the doorway. Both our heads craned toward the interruption.

A young woman, about the same height as me, stood there. Her dark hair was pulled into a sleek updo with one artful tendril hugging her jawline. She was dressed highly fashionably from her sparkling crystal-covered three-inch Louboutins to the orange-red off-the-shoulder mini dress. Like she'd stepped off the page of a *People Magazine* fashion feature page. Or like she'd been plucked right out of a Kardashian-Jenner family outing. If by family outing, they meant clubbing until four in the morning.

Was this the ex-wife herself? My stomach dropped.

Her big brown eyes carefully studied Lucas and then me and then back. "Uh, hey. They sent me to fetch you two for dinner. Everyone was worried and thought you two had escaped out the back way. Which wouldn't really be surprising."

Nope instead she'd witnessed our "lovers quarrel" complete with my swing at Lucas. *Great.*

Lucas rubbed at his jaw awkwardly, as if I really had punched him.

"Well, I won't lie and say it didn't cross our minds."His face split into an uncharacteristically a wide grin. "Hey sis. Great to see you."

Her dark brow arched. "You've been a stranger."

I was at once relieved she wasn't the ex-wife but mortified that this newcomer was my sister-in-law. Inner sigh. The young woman's eyes flicked to me and then she threw a pointed look at Lucas, as if prompting him.

He jerked toward me. "Oh, this is my sister Julia. Julia, this is Katya, my wife."

Julia seemed to fight rolling her eyes at her brother as she stepped forward to take my hand. "My brother always had wretched manners. So wonderful to meet you." She smiled tightly and gave my outfit a once over before turning back to her brother. "Secret wedding? How romantic. I'd be more pissed I didn't get to help out with the wedding. To be honest, I got my fill on your first one. I hope you two had a lovely wedding."

Lucas and I met gazes, and I had visions of red palm trees on white tile in my head. And that stupid jingle from the In-N-Out commercials. *That's what a hamburger's all about.*

"Uh yeah, it was a great wedding. Simple. We had the most important ingredient there. *Love.* That's what a wedding is all about." I was so incredibly tempted to sing that last line to the tune of the jingle. It might have been worth it to see the look on Lucas's face.

"Good," Julia said, with another carefully controlled smile. "I look forward to getting to know you better. And hopefully this means we'll see more of you, Lucas. But right now everyone's waiting for you two before we go in to sit for dinner. We're kind of formal around here with these types of events," she explained.

Julia turned her back, probably to roll her eyes and disguise her disdain for me—that certain was I that she hated me already. The minute she did so, I sent Lucas the most withering stare I could muster.

He grabbed my hand anyway, laced his fingers between mine and tugged me after him.

A procession into dinner. How very Van Den Downton Abbey. I half wondered if Her Majesty The Queen would be in attendance.

CHAPTER 9
LUCAS

"CLAIRE IS HERE," JULIA WHISPERED AT MY SHOULDER and from the way Kat's head turned, I could tell she could hear. "I'm sorry. I invited her before Mother informed me this was about your surprise wedding."

Because of course she did. *Damn.* My relatives seemed to have a strangely difficult time acknowledging that Claire was no longer a part of the family. For as short a time that she had even been a member of it, it was especially shocking.

Dinner was as formal as Julia had warned us it would be, sit down with courses, place cards and the like. I sat between my mother and Kat, while my father peppered my bride with questions on her other side. He kept a steady stream throughout the dinner—most of which I heard because my mother hardly spoke to me. Maybe she was sulking about being cut out of the wedding and the advance notice and the chance to try to talk me out of it.

Or maybe she was just putting on a brave face, ever the gracious hostess. Her top priority had always been maintaining a perfectly constructed image.

Kat's table manners were on point, much to my relief, though she didn't use the continental style of eating that my family preferred. But that didn't single her out amongst many of our guests.

"You actually work directly with Lucas at that gaming company?" Father asked her.

Kat, who'd just forked in a bite of meat, nodded enthusiastically while she chewed. "We're in the game testing department."

"So you sit around and play video games all day? I can see why Lucas loves that job so much," he said with a soft laugh and that same insulting tone he'd used my entire life. *Nice, asshole.*

"Actually it's much more than that," she responded once she'd swallowed. "It's not about playing a game. It's very meticulous work. We have to test every aspect of the game. In reality, it's our job to *break* the game any way we can in order to determine durability and clean playability after market. It takes a very good eye, a lot of patience and careful attention to detail. And it has to be done fast, usually on a tight deadline. That's why Lucas is so good at it. His ability to focus on details is amazing."

My brow twitched in surprise. I'd never heard her directly compliment my skills before. She'd expressed admiration here and there—mostly in the role of cheerleader. And I didn't think that was because she was only one of two women who worked in our department, no. Kat's enthusiasm and higher than average work ethic kept our team fueled and ready for whatever hit us. She was the perfect team player and got us through the rough spots with her ready humor and energy.

All this on top of being my secret weapon.

"He's always been like that," Father said, eyes narrowing at Kat. "And he's put it to good use, I see. Along with his impeccable taste in beautiful ladies."

Gross. I leaned in to create a distraction so Kat wouldn't have to listen to any more of that bullshit, but my mother interrupted me.

"You're bringing Katharina to the family reunion next month, I hope," she said with a nudge in my side.

I flicked a glance at her. Ah, and here it was, the reason she was likely holding any anger toward me inside. She wanted something. Our attendance at the family reunion? *Really?*

I'd rather have oral surgery without anesthesia, to be honest.

I barely felt like I belonged in this family anymore and I had severe doubts that they would make Katya feel anything close to welcome. I knew them too well. Fit in to the image of what they wanted to present to the world or dare to face their wrath.

Or do what I did and vanish for over half a year.

"Probably not. We've got a lot going on this summer with work. Kat has some summer plans as well. And there's this new position I'm—"

"It really would be a nice way to welcome her into the family, Lucas. And we'd love to see more of you, of course. Please talk to her about it?" She would not be deterred, apparently.

I gritted my teeth, still managing the irritation at having been cut off. As usual, she wasn't the smallest bit interested in hearing about my work or my plans. Or, beyond this new development, my life in general. I was foolish to have assumed that things might have changed.

"We'll see." But I had no intention of putting Kat—or myself—through days of awkward family festivities. To say nothing of the stilted relationship that, beyond the DNA we shared, gave us practically nothing in common.

"I see you're not drinking your wine, Katharina…" my father was saying toward the end of the main course.

"Oh, uh, I'm not much of a wine drinker, actually. But I do love beer."

You would have thought she had admitted to skinning small animals alive or something. Heads turned, silverware clattered against dishes, gasps all around. People stared. Father's eyebrows climbed his skull. *Christ almighty.*

"We're going to have to educate you in the joys of the grape. That glass has some of our finest Cabernet Sauvignon from the family vineyard. 2008, I believe. A dry year. The harsher the weather, the better the wine."

Kat blinked, visibly shocked. "The family vineyard… as in *your* family's vineyard?"

"And winery, yes. In Napa. *Turning Windmill Winery,* established 1986."

Kat's face blushed deep pink. "Oh well, yes, I should definitely have some wine then." She snapped up her glass and downed half of it in one gulp. I had to raise my fist to my mouth to cover the chuckle behind the back of my hand. Fortunately, Mother hadn't seen. She was more focused on her conversation with my cousin Lindsay and her new boyfriend than she was on Kat's uncouth attempt at sampling the family label.

Kat finally came up for air complete with purple moustache and nodded vigorously. "Oh yes, that's amazing wine. So good." She then dabbed at her lip with a color-coordinated napkin.

The rest of dinner followed a similarly amusing path. I was especially entertained when Father found out she was Canadian. His eyes widened and he all but asked her if she went moose hunting regularly, used antlers in all of her decorating and lived in a yurt.

Yeah. Some things just never changed.

After dinner, people filed out of the dining room and back out to the terrace to watch the sunset. Instead of moving with them, Father hooked a hand around my arm and asked me to meet him in his study. Ah, so apparently it was time for the Big Talk ™. I'd hoped that he'd decide to forgo it, but no such luck.

And as bad luck would have it, the first wife, not the second, was waiting for me in the entry hall. Though I was flattering myself to think it was by chance, because Claire stood lingering, as if waiting, while others filtered around her out toward the terrace.

"Lucas—"

My eyes snapped to her, but I quickly turned away as if I was very pressed to get to my next meeting. Unlike Kat, Claire was a reed-thin size zero with shiny dark hair. As if for effect, she was wringing her perfectly manicured hands. I'd once thought her beautiful. She couldn't even hold a candle to Kat.

Claire was also a woman that, for a long time, I could hardly look at without feeling nauseous, frustrated and angry. But that had been behind me for several years now.

Now I just felt nothing at all. *Thank God.*

We may have once been married, but since then she'd been a perfect stranger to me for twelve times longer than the marriage had lasted. Had she not somehow latched on to my family, I'd never have had to lay eyes on her again. But unfortunately, as it was, she turned up at practically every family event, which gave me all that much more incentive to stay away.

Tonight, I wasn't in the mood to spare her a hello or how are you doing. I just stopped and waited when she planted herself in my path for whatever melodramatic performance she would no doubt give.

"Um." She furiously bit her bottom lip and looked around her. "I just wanted to... wanted to extend my congratulations and wishes for your happiness. The two of you look very happy." She batted her eyes a few times, as if giving the illusion of fighting back performative tears. Non-existent tears.

I nodded. "Thank you. We are very happy." Then I turned to go.

She gaped at me. "Don't you have anything to say to *me?* Like maybe I should have gotten some warning first or something?" she practically screeched.

I turned back, completely perplexed. "Warning? About what?"

She shrugged and looked down, still blinking furiously, this time adding a tremble to her voice. "About you getting remarried. So I wouldn't have had to hear it from your family after I got here tonight."

I frowned. "I had no idea you were even invited. So no, I don't have anything to say to you."

Likely, she'd already told everyone in our circles about how unfair I'd been. Or she'd complained about how I hadn't taken her back when she wanted—no, *demanded*—it. Or she'd wished aloud that the new wife and I would split up before our first wedding anniversary. I only regretted that Claire was going to see that prediction come true. Confirmation for her that I was indeed a shitty husband.

But that still didn't make me care.

Her eyes narrowed to slits. "Well I certainly hope you don't freeze her out like—"

"We're done here." I cut her off before she launched into the blame game again. We'd been divorced over six years. It wasn't just water under the bridge, that water had flowed out to sea and evaporated into a tropical storm over the Pacific a long time ago. "Bye, Claire."

When I turned my back on her to head down the hall to the study, I could sense her standing there, staring after me.

Nevertheless, I paused at the door to the study, unconsciously straightening my jacket before entering. Father was seated at his huge oak desk that had once belonged to my grandfather and had, before that, graced the grand study of the ancestral home in Utrecht. The soft red leather creaked as he settled into his chair and gestured with a flourish at the facing seat, a comfortable wingback chair. The sight of it immediately brought back memories of his stern disciplinary lectures as a child. Or the hours of unwanted and unneeded advice spewed at me as a teen. I chose not to take a seat, but I did unbutton my jacket and stuff my hands into my pockets.

He arched a brow and without a word, pulled out a cut crystal decanter and two matching glasses. Specially aged scotch, his favorite. After pouring, he pushed a glass toward me and immediately started sipping at his. I almost laughed at what this image might look like to some outsider walking in—like Kat— and her allusion to the whole Downton Abbey thing. All we were lacking were a couple of Cubans, some fancy silk smoking jackets and posh British accents.

I left my glass on the table untouched while he sipped deeply from his before setting it down and throwing me a speculative glance. Father was in his mid-fifties and heavily favored the European mannerisms and bearing of his aristocratic old world family. Here in Southern California, he was like a living, breathing anachronism. The discrepancy wouldn't have been nearly as glaring had he taken up residence on the other coast of this country. As it was, formal, uptight and California did not mesh well.

I waited for him to speak. It was how I'd been raised and old habits died hard, even when you really, truly wished to kill them.

He cleared his throat noisily and finally belted out a blunt, "So what's the real story with this woman. Did you get her pregnant?"

I pinched the flesh at the bridge of my nose to cover rolling my eyes, unsurprised that he'd chosen to lead with that.

"'This woman.' You mean my *wife?*"

He handwaved—yeah, literally handwaved, fingers splaying through the air in a dismissive gesture. "You know what I mean. I'm just asking because everyone's thinking it."

I cocked my brows. "Oh, they are?"

He half shrugged. "Lots of pointed glances at her midsection. Maybe you hadn't noticed."

"I just noticed people admiring a beautiful woman." It was true that I could have just given him a straight answer and put his—and apparently all the rest of the world's—fears to rest. But there was no small pleasure to be had from making this man sweat a little.

The paternal figure cocked his head and shot me what I'm sure he thought was a sly glance. "It's true that your wives are getting progressively prettier, I'll give you that. Let's just hope you can make this one stick."

I ignored the obvious bait. "I'm sure you answered your own question by serving champagne the minute we walked in the door. And of course there was asking her about not touching her wine at dinner."

Another one of those infuriating shrugs. "Just want to make sure I'm not going to end up a surprise grandfather."

"Well give it time, maybe my sister can help with that." I folded my arms and leaned up against the bookcase-lined wall. The smell of leather-bound, exquisitely ornate books that he never read hit my nostrils. At least the staff successfully kept up appearances by never allowing them to get dusty.

His cold stare held mine for long minutes until I broke the tense silence that settled between us. "To what do I owe the honor of this grand audience?"

He sat back, blowing out a breath, his eyes narrowing. "You aren't sparing the sarcasm tonight, are you?"

I smirked. "Might as well cut to the chase, right?"

As he shifted to cross his legs, striking a haughty pose, the leather creaked its protest. "You're really not in a position to have this kind of attitude. You've brought this new person into our family without any warning whatsoever. Not even an introduction beforehand. I thought you'd sworn off marriage after the last one. Even when she begged for another chance. Did you see a gorgeous face and let your hormones get the better of you? Or... was it something else?"

I scratched my forehead with one nail, just above my eyebrow. "It sounds a lot like you're questioning my sanity." *Again.* "What's next? Should I expect threats of being committed against my will?"

Father's gaze narrowed. "That was a long time—"

"And yet you still bring up Claire and the theatrics she pulled when we split up. That was a long time ago too. Nice move, by the way, inviting her here tonight. That hasn't been awkward at all."

He shrugged. "Your mother's doing, not mine. She's Julia's closest friend." Father's gaze drifted away from mine and he appeared deep in thought. "I'm going to be honest. Your behavior has us concerned."

Ah. There it was. *Concern.* Lucas was having "another breakdown." Time to round up the troops and start tearing our own hair out again! What will the neighbors think?

"Last I checked, I didn't need to run my important life decisions by you for pre-approval. I'm twenty-six years old."

He didn't like that little reminder. All my choices since the day I'd left my old life behind me had reinforced that belief and it still irked him on a regular basis.

"Last *I* checked, I'm still your father and you're still a part of this family. Your introducing her to us ahead of time would have been the decent thing to do."

I stayed silent, and it was a concerted effort to keep my words from escaping my mouth. *I gave you the warning you deserved.* Damn. This was a fake marriage, sure. This shit he was throwing at me—the past, the self-interested "concern"—should have been rolling right off my back.

Instead it was making me simmer with subdued rage, doing exactly what I'd hoped it wouldn't, bringing the past up front and center and throwing it all in my face.

This prick was implying that the only reason I'd deign to marry someone like Katya was because I'd gotten her pregnant. Or that I'd allowed her to manipulate me and my hormones. Or that I was mentally ill. That pissed me off even more. He knew nothing about her nor did he appear to want to know anything about her. His own new daughter-in-law.

He brought the glass to his lips for another sip, then leaned back into the chair with a long drawn-out sigh. "I trust you have a prenuptial agreement in place."

More fuel for the rage embers that threatened to flare into full-blown flames. I rubbed my jaw and fought to keep the smile from my face before I dropped this particular bomb. "There's no prenup."

He visibly paled, mouth pursing up like he'd sucked a lemon. *That's an A plus for being dramatic, dear Father.*

"It won't be needed." I couldn't help but twist the knife a little. "I haven't touched the trust fund and I have no plan to."

He rubbed his forehead. "No one can touch that money but you. I can't do anything about that. It was your grandfather's doing."

Much to your chagrin, I know.

"It can stay in the trust fund and accrue interest. Maybe my heir, if I have one, will enjoy it."

The look of disgust on his face almost made me laugh. Who in their right mind would turn down a nine-figure trust fund? But since they'd long ago decided that I wasn't in my right mind, why not just keep them guessing?

"Your behavior these past six years has beyond baffled me. I don't understand you."

I nodded coolly. "Clearly."

He shook his head with more of that faux concern. "You treat this like a game. Even now. You need to man up. I hope this girl—"

"Her name is Katya. Your daughter-in-law, Katya."

"—is the one for you and that it works out. Maybe you've learned to be a better husband this time around. If not, that's going to be one hell of an expensive divorce."

Oh, he had no idea. *None.* A new idea bloomed in my mind. Maybe I'd sign it all over to her when we divorced. *Problem solved.*

And that bullshit about being a better husband, though it did sting, was rich coming from a man whose own fidelity over the years was at best questionable.

"Is there anything else or am I free to go back to the party and my wife?" Unfortunately I did not manage to keep my irritation out of my voice.

He stood, refilled his glass and picked it up, took another sip and watched me coolly over the rim of the glass. "You're free to do whatever you want, son. It's how you've been acting for years. Too bad divorces are only for spouses and not other family members, huh?"

He shook his head and left me standing there in his own study. Probably the only way he'd ever get the last word in was to leave the moment he'd delivered it.

Fuck you, Arent van den Hoehnsboek van Lynden.

I strode to his desk, scooped up the untouched glass of whiskey he'd poured for me and knocked it back. It burned so hard that my eyes watered as the smoky-flavored liquid seared its way down my esophagus.

Were they all thinking that? That I'd lost my mind? I unstopped the priceless decanter and poured myself another glass. Lather, rinse, repeat.

Memories of that time—the huge ball of anxiety constantly in my stomach and in my throat. The way that everything I'd bitten into turned to ashes in my mouth. The constant phone calls.

The lack of sleep. The tight band around my chest that made it hard to catch my breath and struggle even harder for the next one. I squeezed my eyes shut as if that would shut out the kaleidoscope of images, feelings and words sliding through my memory. Another drink.

I didn't stop until I'd finished the third.

The room was starting to fade into a slight blur. A warmth spread through me but it didn't manage to smother that inner rage. In a way, I still mourned the loss of that naïve young man I'd once been. He'd been killed the night the people I'd most trusted in the world had wedged a knife in my back.

Fuck you too, Claire. Mother. Julia.

I left the study, vaguely aware that I wasn't exactly walking in a straight line. Inexplicably, I wanted to be near Kat. I could trust her. Of all the people here—including the ones I'd known my entire life—she was the one person I *could* trust.

We had our moments but her dealings with me had always been on the up and up. Always honest. No bullshit.

This family needed a lot less of that. And I wanted to leave this goddamn mausoleum with Katya. *Now.*

I needed her now and for a short while, she was still mine.

Mine.

I found her on the back terrace talking to my sister Julia and Julia's two closest friends—Claire and the new flavor-of-the-month whose name I could never remember. A bubbly blonde girl with a voice that sounded like she'd just sucked in a ton of helium.

The three of them had my poor wife cornered, though Katya didn't appear to be in any way distressed. My hand tightened into a fist at my side. With that collection of harpies, I'd fear for anyone in her place.

Julia and Whatshername were nodding along, prompting her to continue. Kat took small sips of her glass of water in between talking while discreetly scanning the area around their little group. She looked like she wanted to make an exit herself.

Well here I was, Kat's white knight to the rescue. I'd even brave the harpy flock, and the dreaded ex to save her. Maybe she'd even appreciate it.

Of course, the fact that I wanted to get the hell out of here meant that my motives weren't exactly altruistic. I'd get her away from the group and then we'd plot to make our escape. I re-buttoned my jacket and approached the circle, putting a hand on the curve of Kat's back and avoiding the overtly curious gazes of the other three women.

"Lucas!" my sister said, her eyes widening. "I was just admiring Katharina's gorgeous dress." She held up her phone, which showed a flattering picture of Kat that she must have snapped just minutes before. She turned to Kat. "With your permission, I'd love to post it. My lifestyle brand followers will love it."

Julia began typing away on her phone as if starting the post without getting Kat's permission. Kat blinked, startled. "You have a lifestyle brand?"

Without looking up, Julia nodded. "Mmm hmm. Maybe you've heard of it? Fløe. F-L-O with a slash through it-E—as in 'Go with the Fløe.' I just hit over two million followers last month, so a lot of people will see your pic. Can I tag you? You have an Instagram, right?"

Kat blinked as if still absorbing all of this news. Julia had been touting herself as an influencer and brand ambassador for several years. Finally, after coming of age for her trust fund, she'd quit college and started her own lifestyle brand. At least she was interested in doing *something*—even if it just meant traveling, clubbing, shopping, partying, and documenting it all for her followers.

"Uh, yeah. Sure. It's @PersephoneGamer. It's linked to my Twitch account."

One brow rose, Whatshername whispered something I couldn't hear to Julia. Claire continued to stare at Kat and me with that weird mixture of hurt and curiosity. Awkward. God, I was so done with this bullshit tonight.

"That's right." Julia said, glancing up from her phone. "I knew you were a gamer. Will have to check out your channel sometime." Biting her lip, she continued to thumb-type her post. "Sorry just adding hashtags now. That's off the rack, right? Not a designer?"

"Yeah," Kat answered. "If I can't pronounce the name, I won't wear it." Kat laughed, I laughed. The other three stared at us with looks akin to mortification.

"Well. Sorry to interrupt but I need to steal my wife away." She turned to meet my gaze, giving a decisive nod. Kat was subtle about it, but I could tell she was still pissed at me. Didn't matter. After three and a half glasses of my father's Scotch, not much could faze me, not even an angry wife. And a butthurt ex-wife, for that matter.

I hadn't made eye contact but I could feel Claire watching every move we made. My arm hooked around Kat's waist, pulling her up against me. I could feel the entire length of her body along my own in a way I never had before. After the initial stiffness of surprise, she relaxed against me before covering the hand I rested on her hip with her own. Our fingers laced together and suddenly....

My alcohol-laced blood ignited and quickly burned for more. For *her*. Without another thought, I swept down and planted a firm kiss on that soft, sweet-smelling neck.

And then she did it.... She shivered against me. That tremor sent a bolt of desire right through me and I was hard instantly.

She sent me a questioning glance—her cheeks slightly pink, her mouth open, her chest rising quicker than before. I hadn't realized that my hold on her had tightened involuntarily so I reluctantly loosened my grip. But not without that reminder inside my head that cried out with all the sophistication of a Neanderthal. *Mine!* Mine, mine, mine.

All mine.

"Are you okay?" she whispered when the others started talking amongst themselves.

I leaned in to return the whisper, aware that the world around us was still a little wobbly. "Let's go home."

She stared, her pink lips parting again. I *really* wanted to kiss them. In my pleasantly buzzed haze, it was all I could think about. Then I wanted to feel those lips all over my body.

She tugged on my arm and jerked her head toward the house, wordlessly asking me to speak in private. Maybe she wanted to yell at me again, like she had before dinner. I suppose I didn't blame her.

And I certainly wouldn't disagree to being alone with her privately. But not because I wanted to talk.

Kat slowly slid away from me and I reluctantly released her. But she caught my hand and, with a gentle tug and a wave to the rest of the group, pulled me away.

Once inside and in privacy, she turned to me and quietly stated the obvious. "You're drunk and you reek of whiskey." I responded by reaching up to her face and running a thumb along her bottom lip. That lush, plump lip needed to be tasted. Her face clouded, and she batted my hand away. "I'm still super annoyed with you right now."

I smiled and shrugged. Her anger had to cut through several layers of mellow drunken euphoria to have any kind of sharp effect on me. I was at that perfect state of just having had enough to feel good without going over the top into melancholy.

"Welcome to being married, Cranberry."

And then I swooped in for a kiss despite her purported annoyance with me. In this condition, I found I couldn't resist her, so I chose not to. The moment there was a flicker of response from her, my hands were on her neck, holding her head to mine.

My body against her body. My mouth against her mouth. My hands sifting through her glossy, thick hair. Her hands came up first to cling to the lapels of my jacket for a few seconds before giving me a hard shove away.

I probably deserved that.

"I said I was annoyed, What I *really* meant was pissed off," she hissed in a low voice so that no one would overhear.

I swallowed. "Kat—"

Heels clopped across the imported stone floor toward us. Before I could turn to see who it was, the generous whiff of designer scent, always Chanel no. 5, gave it away.

All I could do was fumble to straighten my coat so that my current state of arousal wasn't obvious before turning to face my mother.

"I've been looking all over for you two. Aren't you just the most adorable lovebirds?" She was using her fake-nice sing-songy tone of voice that meant she was irritated or just plain angry about this situation but she was never going to let it show. Especially not to her new daughter-in-law's face, anyway. I recognized it instantly after enduring a lifetime of it.

Kat ducked her head demurely as if embarrassed and rolled her swollen lips into her mouth.

"It's my fault," I said after clearing my throat. "My wife is so gorgeous that I couldn't go another second without kissing her."

Mother laid a hand on my arm and smiled, gave a fake laugh and turned to Kat. "Of course. I was a newlywed once myself, you know. It wasn't so long ago that I can't remember how that felt. Lucas *was* a honeymoon baby, after all."

Ugh. No thanks for *that* mental image.

My mother, still focusing on Kat, gave one of her sickly sweet high society smiles while settling her free hand over her heart. *Laying it on a bit thick, aren't you?*

"I just want to let you know again how thrilled we are to have you in our family."

Kat's eyes widened, and she gave a small smile. "Oh, thank you. That's very kind. I'm happy to be here."

Mother darted an unreadable look at me and then proceeded to talk quickly. A sudden sinking in my stomach warned me only seconds before the words were out of her mouth.

"We're having a family reunion up at the vineyard next month. I have to ask, since we weren't able to attend the wedding, we'd love for you to be there—"

"Mother, I've already said we need to work—"

She pivoted on me. "It's only for a long weekend. No one—not even you—needs to work that much. And there'll be relatives you haven't seen in ages, from the east coast and from the Netherlands."

My back went rigid with anger, frustrated at her typical refusal to listen to anything I had to say. Kat's head jerked quickly to look at me. Our gazes met and there was something there. That anger from before and also a little of her signature feistiness.

I turned back to my mother to head Kat off. "For the last time—"

"We'd love to. That sounds wonderful," Kat overrode me.

Mother ignored me completely and honed in on her new daughter-in-law, whom she was, even now, most likely categorizing as an ally. *Fuuuuck.*

I shot a glare at Kat and Mother caught it. "Oh Lucas, don't be like that. It will be fun. Romantic. We'll put you up in the Lover's Villa guest house all by yourselves. The reunion is going to be fantastic with amazing food, games and there's the new spa we just had built. It will be the honeymoon you should have given her when you got married."

Great. More recrimination. Still more expectations I had not lived up to. Because why not? I hadn't already disappointed them enough, which seemed to be their unspoken message to me in practically every single phrase they uttered. And now my only ally, Kat, had become a turncoat.

"We have to go *now*," I ground out between clenched teeth. Apparently I used such harsh tones that Kat's face registered shock and Mother... Mother just drew back and gave me that look. That *Lucas is crazy* look. I'd seen that a lot in the past six years, too.

Without another word, I turned and stormed out of the room, directly headed to the front door. I didn't give a damn if Kat was behind me. I heard the word "drinking" behind me, as if Kat was making my drunken excuses.

Which pissed me off even more.

Fuck it. I might even chance a DUI if it was the only way to get my ass out of here. I was already yelling at one of the poor valets—a new guy I didn't know—to bring my car around.

Kat was at my shoulder a moment later. "Let me drive."

"Sure," I muttered. "What will you do for an encore, wreck my car?"

The valet glanced from one of us to the other when his boss, Armando, the family's regular driver, walked up. "Madam would like me to drive you both home safely. Jerry can follow behind us with your car, Mister Lucas."

Kat's eyes widened and then she shot a glance at me. I avoided her eyes and rubbed my forehead. It was, after all, the most sensible suggestion. "Yeah, all right. That's fine."

Shortly thereafter, we were seen off by my parents at the front curb. Father was still scowling from earlier and Mother had on the brave face, her mouth only trembling a little. And me, in all my buzzed euphoria didn't give a rats ass that I was the endless source of frustration, hand-wringing and sorrow for my parents. Just by choosing to pursue the life I wanted instead of the one they'd planned out for me.

We exchanged short goodbyes in which Kat, apparently had earned a quick hug from my mother and a curt 'welcome to the family' from Father for her troubles.

My jaw tightened, witnessing this. Well she wouldn't be enjoying her revenge quite so much once we were stuck in Napa, unable to escape the cursed 'Family Reunion.'

We settled into the back seat of the town car and she gave a long sigh. "Holy shit. I need a drink."

So did I. And as far as I knew, Father never stocked the car with booze. This wasn't a party limo, after all. And the last word I'd use to describe this ride home would be a *party,* pleasantly buzzed or not.

CHAPTER 10
KATYA

OMETHING WAS OBVIOUSLY BOTHERING HIM. LIKE *REALLY* bothering him. He sat in the back of that town car, elbows on his knees, forehead in palms, fingers threading through his dark hair, never looking up. Either he was about to puke or was going through some serious family-induced turmoil. Possibly both.

But things were bothering me too—*him*, for example, and his behavior this entire evening. I wanted to yell at him and fought hard to hold back, curbing my own burning irritation.

It took a minute to figure out which was the right button, before I pressed it to raise the divider between us and the driver. No need for him to know all the juicy details of our non-marriage. I'd never been in a car like this before but I'd seen enough movies to know it could be done. Then I cleared my throat and turned to him.

Lucas's hands, where they supported his head, were strong and laced with bulging veins and a light dusting of dark hair. For some reason, I found them fascinating, my eyes wandering to them even as I spoke in stern tones to their owner.

"So not like you've cared to ask my opinion, but my entire summation of this evening can be put into three little letters. WTF."

He massaged his temples with his thumbs, pressing the heels of his hands to his eyes. Still, he said nothing.

"And on a scale of one to ten, your husband rating tonight is damn low."

"Great. You and Claire can form the 'Lucas is a shitty husband' club when this is all through. You can arm wrestle for the positions of president and vice-president. Tell me something I don't know."

I folded my arms tightly against my chest. "Yeah, so when were you planning on telling me about that little tidbit? After I'd failed the immigration interview for not knowing a thing about your previous marriage?"

His head jerked up, and he peered at me through narrowed eyes. There was something there at the back of them. Some deep hurt I couldn't name and knew instinctively that it had been there long before I'd set foot into this whole hot mess of a family. Somehow, our coming back here tonight had dredged things up for him.

I could identify—all too easily, as a matter of fact. But even though I felt bad for him, it didn't give him an excuse to be a complete and total dick to me.

He spoke through a clenched jaw. "It's not like you're exactly forthcoming about your own family, are you? My in-laws—your parents, your brother—I hardly know anything about them either. I also have no idea why you're avoiding them to the extent that you dropped everything and left your country. And that for some reason, getting mail from some lawyer in British Columbia terrifies you."

I blinked, swallowing a bit of guilt at that reminder. Yes, he spoke the truth, on all counts. But tonight wasn't about me and my family.

"Nice way to turn that back to me but you didn't come face to face with an ex-spouse you didn't even know existed. Nor will you because *I've* never been married before. You might have mentioned *that*, at least."

For some reason, that revelation most of all, was the one that was sticking with me—beyond the Van Den Richie Rich parents and the glamorous socialite sister. Beyond the fancy European noble title and the sprawling mansion and family vineyard. Beyond that... was someone whom Lucas had married years ago. Presumably for love. Presumably before he became closed off, bitter and jaded on the entire idea of marriage.

His gaze intensified. "And what difference does it make to you that I was married before? *This* isn't even real. And maybe you should be thankful that I think marriage is a joke. My marriage to Claire lasted all of five months, FYI. I probably never would have agreed to do this if I took marriage seriously."

Whoa... I blinked a few times. "So this is a joke to you?"

He gave a stiff shrug. "Not you needing your green card, no. Or you keeping your job, which helped me out a great deal. But I'm all for mocking an outdated and ridiculous institution that I personally loathe. *That's* the joke."

I shook my head, frowning. "How are you so bitter about everything? You're not even thirty yet."

He clenched his jaw, cheeks bulging, staring straight ahead. "I have damn good reasons."

I folded my arms tightly and shifted, staring at him sharply. "Maybe it's about time you shared some of them, then. Since now this involves me too."

He muttered a string of bad words under his breath, threading his fingers through his hair a few more times. It was standing straight up like a fright wig. I might have teased him for it had he not been so fully agitated already.

"Fine." He let out a long sigh and straightened, falling back against the seat, posture stiff. "Why not give you something else to mock me about? When I was way too young, I screwed up and made some shitty decisions to make other people happy. Finding out it's almost impossible to reverse some of those mistakes helps you get bitter fast."

I rubbed my forehead, attempting to curb my irritation with him out of concern. His tone of voice sounded weird... flat, emotionless. And not in his typical emotionally unavailable way.

"I don't plan on mocking you about it, FYI." Then waited a moment to ask him the follow-up. "So you, uh, got married to make other people happy instead of yourself?" My eyebrows knotted into a frown. This sounded weird. Maybe people who had titles and lots of money still acted this way.

He rolled his eyes and fixed his gaze out the window to avoid turning toward me, most likely. "I was nineteen. She was my high school girlfriend. The wedding was a full blown over-the-top ridiculously expensive party that everyone wanted. Every reason why I married her was the wrong one."

Hmm. I sank back against the luxurious leather of the town car and it squeaked as I shifted toward him. "What were the reasons, then?" I asked a little quieter than before.

The more he seemed to get agitated talking about this the more I felt myself calming down. All of this in spite of the fact that I was still reeling from this weird ass night and still annoyed with him for the secret-keeping. I was willing to hear him out, anyway.

"Idiocy of youth. It seemed like the thing to do. We met during our sophomore year and had been going out for a few years. But I was on my way to Cambridge, a big unknown, foreign country. She really wanted to come along. My family liked her family. She wanted it. They wanted it."

"Everyone but *you* wanted it?"

He shrugged. "I had no idea what I wanted. I was a kid. I just wanted to make everyone around me happy. Live up to my family's expectations, toe the line. Be the good firstborn and do what I was supposed to do. Until I couldn't anymore. I figured out that making myself utterly miserable to please the world around me was not a good idea. On top of that, I wasn't ready to be a husband—hers or anyone else's."

I paused as he stared blandly out the window and my heart hurt. I found a familiar echo of his story in my own. We'd both been motivated to toe the family line and be the perfect child, even if perhaps for different reasons.

I glanced at him again. It was hard to rid myself of that image of Claire looking at him. She'd never taken her eyes off of us and it had been... uncomfortable. They'd been split up for six years, for heaven's sake.

"Could Claire still be in love with you?"

One hand went to cover his face as he laughed. "Oh don't read anything more into her behavior tonight than self-pity, and a constant craving for attention. She never loved me any more than I loved her."

I shook my head. How messed up was all this? "Well if that's the case, then your parents really didn't seem to consider your feelings when they invited her tonight."

He shrugged. "Or yours, for that matter. What if you were actually my brand new bride who cared about me? They gave us zero warning. I shouldn't be surprised. Claire's hung around a lot in the last six years. They like to keep the relationship with her parents and make themselves look progressive and welcoming. It's all about how it all looks to everyone else."

I shook my head. "Damn, that's insensitive of them not to consider how you'd feel, though."

He gave another dry laugh. "Not shocking since they'd never claim in a million years to be sensitive. She managed to get her claws into our family. She's Julia's BFF and party pal after all."

"You all went to high school together?"

He turned, watching me out of the corner of his eye acerbically. "You just saw my family house, do you think I went to a normal public high school even if I wanted to?"

I bit my lip. "Let me guess, high end prep school in New England somewhere?"

"Bingo. New Hampshire to be exact. Claire was from Upper East Side New York City. Financial district money. My parents consider themselves inclusive and open-minded enough to accept the nouveaux riches into their inner circle."

I laughed, and the car swerved suddenly, probably to avoid a pothole. The driver called something I couldn't hear through the partition, possibly an apology. I lost my balance, falling against Lucas who caught me in his arms as quickly as I fell against him.

I turned to apologize for falling all over him and our faces were dangerously close. Electricity sparked. There was no denying the sizzle and crackle between us. And then there was his smell, that clean bergamot and suede scent. So delectable, so masculine.

And drunk with whisky breath or not, he still looked magnificent in that suit.

Our gazes held, and I had to force myself to swallow even as I slowly sat back. He seemed to be holding his breath, too. And right then I knew that if I hadn't pulled away, we would have kissed in the next moment and... well I didn't want *that* did I?

Did I?

After an awkward minute where we both stared out of our respective windows, Lucas spoke again, his voice losing that previous tightness. Now it seemed like he'd gained some distance, like he was telling someone else's story.

"One good thing came out of all this, though. I learned that I'm not a good fit for marriage. I was young and stupid and didn't think through any of it. I was living someone else's life."

"Whose life?" I asked.

He gave a tight shrug. The hand that rested on the seat alongside his thigh tightened. "Lucas van den Hoehnsboek van Lynden."

I blinked. "But... isn't that you?" Jesus, was he about to confess to me that he had multiple personality disorder or something? Just how many Lucases lived inside that head?

He shook his head, lips thinned. "Not anymore."

I opened my mouth to question him further but thought the better of it, since he seemed like he wanted to tell his story in his own way.

"I don't expect you to understand based on just the tiny fraction you now know. What you saw tonight was the glittering outside, the glamorous wealth and ease in which they live. But that life comes with certain... expectations." He shook his head, still looking out the window. "I tried. My whole damn life I tried to fit myself into that framework, to do what they expected—go to the right school, study the right subjects, marry the right girl. Everything." His voice was strangled now, as if it hurt him to let that all out. He was silent for a long moment and we watched the lights of the city streak by in the window.

Suddenly the car slowed as we exited the freeway and headed along surface streets toward home. It seemed to jostle him awake from wherever he'd drifted off to.

He ran a hand through his hair and gave a self-conscious laugh. "Sorry to ramble on like that. It was a lot to dump on you in a night where you've already had a lot dumped on you."

I echoed his shrug. "Well, I *did* ask."

He threw me a quick glance, then rested his head against the seat to stare up at the darkened roof of the car. "I've really never talked about all this out loud before. Haven't had anyone to discuss it in a long time or, *ever*, really. Or maybe I've just had too much to drink."

Suddenly we were slowing and pulling up to the curb of Lucas's house. Before Armando could pop out to get the door for Lucas, he was gone and halfway across the lawn. He called out his thanks to the driver who graciously opened my door for me.

The other driver parked Lucas's car beside mine in the driveway and I was dealing with getting the car keys back and giving him a tip. At which he blanched and flat out refused to even touch the money, waving it away as if it were a lump of dog poo—or Canadian dollars. Chalk up yet another of my middle class faux pas for the evening.

Jeez.

By the time I was able to catch up with Lucas inside, he was already standing at the little wine cart in his living room. He'd thrown off his jacket and tie and tossed them on the sofa. Max had jumped up from his bed to greet his human, nuzzling Lucas's free hand and wagging his tail furiously. Lucas patted the dog on the head absently, fixated on the selection in front of him.

The cart had various bottles of liquor on it but no wine, ironically. He apparently used it as a small wet bar. It was a lovely cart, fancy and mirrored. Like maybe it had been a wedding gift. I suddenly imagined Lucas and Claire going through all their things and deciding how to split them. How much of this place had she helped furnish, if at all?

He had poured himself another drink and was halfway through it, knocking it back quickly. Shit. He was obviously still in pain and I had no idea how to handle it. Should I let him sit out here to drink and retreat to my room? Or should I be the good little wife and make sure he was okay?

He had just finished his first glass and uncapped the bottle to pour another. Max sniffed at the air but sidled out of the way while I moved up beside Lucas. As much as I would have loved to get out of the dress and wash the makeup off, I just couldn't leave him like this.

But once I stood beside him, he slipped away from me, beating a very determined path to the piano, drink in hand. Max and I both gazed after him, then the dog turned around and slipped through the kitchen and out the dog door into the yard.

After another deep gulp of the drink, Lucas settled on the piano bench. I had to admit I'd been wanting to listen—and more so *watch*—him play again ever since the first night he'd revealed his hidden talent to me.

And I had to admire, too, how he held his liquor. I mean, he was obviously drunk but there was no wobble in his walk. He still had that same upright—almost snobbish—posture that had always made me wonder if he were a secret dancer or trapeze artist. Now I knew that the so-called and fabled "aristocratic bearing" had a source, with a noble title and everything!

He began to play some morose tune I'd never heard—slow and with lots of flat notes—in what sounded like a minor key. I didn't know a ton about music but I knew enough to know that this was the equivalent of some forlorn drunken melody. I moved to stand behind him and he flicked an unreadable glance up at me as he continued.

I couldn't help it. I felt bad for him. Family could be so shitty. Complete with all the expectations heaped upon you just because of whom you were born to and whose DNA you shared. I knew enough of that, even if my family didn't have millions on top of their billions on top of their aristocratic titles. Family could pretty much suck at all echelons of society. No one knew that more than I.

I crooked a half smile of encouragement and put a hand on Lucas's shoulder. "You okay? Holy crap, you're tense." Especially for being drunk... His body felt like a thick rope twisted around rocks and tied into unyielding knots.

He did not react aversely to my touch, nor did he reply. He just continued to play his slow, sad, obscure tune.

"You—I could give you a back rub. My roommate—well my *former*—well, you know. Heath likes back rubs and apparently rates mine with two thumbs-up. It's a perk of having me in the house... if you want."

His fingers glided across the keys. He still didn't speak—just sent me another enigmatic look from those fathomless dark eyes and shrugged one of his shoulders. I frowned but took the gesture as tacit permission.

I moved behind him. Then I laced my fingers together, cracked my knuckles, rolling my shoulders and my neck like a pro wrestler about to enter the ring. Gently, I placed my hands at the base of his neck.

The sad melody continued uninterrupted, but he finally spoke in a quiet, hoarse voice. "Try not to strangle me."

"Tempting, but no." My hands worked down his extremely tight neck to where it joined his shoulders. I massaged small circles through the soft, slippery material of his shirt.

He hit his first missed note when my thumbs smoothed their way up the back of his neck, working parallel to his spinal column. His skin was flushed, presumably from intoxication. He missed his second note the moment the tips of my fingers touched the base of his hairline. That missed note came with a sharp intake of breath.

And as I worked my way back down his neck, it was clear that he was only growing more tense instead of less. Suddenly he missed a bunch of notes in a quick jumble, then stopped playing altogether. Perhaps it was when my fingers slipped around under his jaw while massaging light circles under his earlobes with my thumbs. His skin felt hot and rough with whisker growth though he'd shaved before we'd left for the "family dinner"—or whatever proper label could be attributed to that spectacle.

Lucas now sat completely motionless, fingers splayed across the keys without playing. I took a breath and let it go, allowing my hands to fall away. "I'm sorry. Did you not like it?" My hands rested lightly on his shoulders, but before I could make any other move, he reached up with his right hand and snagged my wrist within his grasp. The grip was firm, tight... possessive.

"I liked it. I liked it too much," he muttered in a thick, low voice.

Then he stood and turned to face me. Our gazes caught and my breath froze in my chest. He was visibly aroused. Though I vowed to keep my eyes fixed on his face, it was noticeable. I didn't even have to glance down *there* to reaffirm my assessment. His dark eyes were scorching me to cinders where I stood, boring deep inside of me. I held that dark gaze with my own and swallowed thickly, hoping he'd reach for me. Hoping he'd initiate something.

"Do you... do you want to talk some more about what's bothering you?" My voice was a husky whisper.

I knew goddamn well that he didn't want to talk, but what else was I going to say? *Please pull off my clothes and fuck me at last?* Yeah, I might have wanted to say that. I might have been broiling where I stood, desperate to feel those strong, capable hands all over my body. But I didn't say it. I wouldn't tell him that.

His gaze was intense, a thing alive, a palpable touch. And his voice, when he spoke, was hoarse with desire. "I don't want to talk... at all." With the free hand that was not currently clasped around my wrist, he reached up and ran his thumb along my jaw.

Then hooked that hand around the back of my neck and gently tugged, pulling my head to his.

Firm lips on mine—fire and smoke, whiskey-flavored, insistent. He had my lips parted in moments, his tongue pushing into my mouth, tasting me, taking me.

And with a startled whimper, I went along for the ride. That kiss crackled down my neck, spine and straight to my center where smoldering embers erupted into flame. My breasts ached for his touch and gooseflesh rippled over my skin.

From just a kiss, he could do this to me. I had to admit, no other guy had ever achieved that so quickly. Either he'd earned a secret PhD in kissing somewhere, or there was something about him and me and our coming together. A crackle and spark. A smoldering energy that had always been there between us and now was finally striking sparks.

Maybe it was like a chemical reaction that bubbled and smoked the moment two inert substances came in contact. We were like ammonia and hydrochloric acid—two reactants flaming to smoking heat the moment they came together.

He only pulled his lips away to speak. His breath and mine were coming fast, the warm and humid puffs of air mingling, thickening the air between us. It was a wonder he could form the words. "I want to taste you *everywhere.*"

His voice was urgent, full of need, full of heat and longing. With a loud clack, he slapped the cover closed over the piano keys. A shove of his leg scooted the piano bench out of the way. Then, without a barrier between us, he pulled me flush against him.

"You've been drinking..." I mumbled against his lips where they were fixed to my own.

"But you haven't. And I know what I've been wanting for a whole lot longer than just tonight. This is no sudden impulse out of the blue. What do you taste like?"

I gulped and everything inside me plummeted, sucked toward the ground, the world turning slightly. As if I were also suddenly drunk—intoxicated by his persistent mouth and lips. They were now enveloping my very willing and tingling earlobe.

Holy shnikes. Like... before I even realized what I was doing, my arms were locked around his neck, holding him to me. Like he was a life raft, and I was clinging on for dear life instead of for his near-perfect foreplay. This man could kiss the sizzle from a pan of frying bacon.

And he was serving me up just the way he wanted me.

And I was completely okay with that as I let the current of this river snatch me up and carry me away wherever it may take me. He wanted to taste me? I wanted to be tasted by him. *Perfect.*

His lips slipped down the side of my neck, nipping at the sensitive skin there, and his hands slid down my back to rest on my ass. He had to bend slightly to do this. Lucas was tall, and I was on the shorter side of average. Maybe I should have kept the piano bench in place after all and used it for a booster seat.

He seemed to have a similar idea when he decidedly adjusted his grip and hitched me up against him. Without thinking, I locked my legs around his slender hips, the handkerchief hem of my dress bunching up. And our mouths were locked together in a fierce battle of the tongues once more. He let out a soft growl, and I released a tiny sigh in answer.

I was on fire and hoping we'd soon be repairing to his bedroom to quench it.

But apparently he didn't even want to go that far. Instead, he hitched me higher and slid me onto the top of his grand piano. The silky material of my dress eased effortlessly along the glossy black top of the instrument and my feet dangled over the front. I flicked my toes to kick off my heels.

Sex on a piano. "How *Pretty Woman* of you," I whispered, almost shivering from the crazy arousing thought of what was to come. My panties were already soaked.

His dark eyes pinned mine down as he eased a warm hand up my thigh. "If it's good enough for that dude in the movie, it's good enough for me," he replied.

Without a moment's hesitation, Lucas hitched the hem of my dress up to my hips and pulled down my panties, tossing them to the floor. I was suddenly thankful for having been extra fastidious about shaving this afternoon. His hands glided up my smooth skin to rest on my hips, positioning me just at the edge of his piano.

Then he bent and kissed the inside of my thigh. More gooseflesh bloomed where his mouth and tongue connected and pressed along the tender skin. I let out a tight breath, not even aware that I'd been holding it until I sucked in another one. Lucas's hand cupped my knee and pushed it aside, opening my legs further apart.

Oh Lordy... Lordy. He was going to. He was... I couldn't even form the thought, my mind was swirling and my heart was pounding with heated excitement, cold thrill and maybe even a little fear. What would happen next?

I'd been craving a good roll in the hay. It had been far too long. And all work and no play made Katya a dull girl but...

Would this change things? Would we cross some line that couldn't be uncrossed? Was this a mistake? And why the hell was I angsting over it as his mouth—and that exquisite whiskered jaw and chin—crept closer and closer to my center. Oh Christ. My eyelids closed, and I slumped back on the piano, resting against my elbows.

His hands were firm, sure, but gentle, stroking me in ways that revealed his experience. He'd done this before—a lot—and if he kissed me there the way he'd kissed my mouth, I was in for an amazing orgasmic finish to my evening.

"Lucas," I rasped, my legs suddenly tensing.

He stopped but didn't raise his head. Instead he waited. When I didn't say anything, he asked. "Do you want to stop?"

I swallowed, my head now spinning, my throat tight and my body ratcheted up and raring to go. I was hypersensitive to everything around me, including the light touch of the air. "No... Do you?"

"Fuck, no. I want to taste you until you come on my tongue. I want to know if it'll be as amazing as I'd imagined it would be."

My jaw dropped. "You've—you've imagined it?"

His mouth connected at the juncture of my inner thigh, his tongue slipping out to lick me there. I sucked in a breath.

"Yes, I have. And every time, you were hotter than the last time."

He'd been fantasizing about me? More than once? With his whiskey-loosened tongue, he was now freely admitting all kinds of things to me. *Dutch courage*, so to speak. I almost laughed at the irony of that thought.

As for me, I wouldn't be putting that out there—the myriad of dirty dreams and other, ahem, private moments when his handsome face had entered my mind unbidden. But I forgot all that when his mouth hovered over my sex, hot breath bathing me with promises to come.

I sighed. "Well... that's a tall order. Not sure I can live up to a fantasy. I hope you aren't expecting—"

"You already are, Kat. You already are." A finger entered me and I gasped. Then another. He flicked his dark eyes up to look into my face, as if gauging my reaction. Then, as if satisfied by what he saw, he continued. His thumb parted me and suddenly his mouth enveloped my center, sucking relentlessly at my clit. *Holy. Shit.*

The hand on my knee pushed again to further open me and I complied with both knees, allowing him full access. My head dropped back, dangling on my neck. Behind my closed eyelids, brilliant light strobed in concert with his mouth on my sensitive center. My equilibrium spun and whirled, lost to sensation alone. Each flick of his tongue I felt everywhere, pooling into molten lead at the base of my spine.

I swear to God I almost forgot how to breathe. Pretty sure I did forget my own name. All that existed was his hand on my leg, his fingers gliding rhythmically in and out of me, his hot mouth sucking. His tongue lapped relentlessly over that sparking bundle of nerves.

Full speed ahead—from aroused to almost coming in less than a minute. Jesus Murphy. It was like the Daytona of orgasms.

"Say my name," he said roughly as I gasped for air. Jesus, I couldn't say anything at all. Nor did I even think I knew how to speak the English language anymore.

He stopped, stilling his fingers, pulling his mouth away. Everything in me was so tense, dangling on a precipice and he was toying with me, making me wait. I lifted my arm to reach so I could finish myself off with my hand. He batted it away easily. "Say it, Kat."

My tongue dragged over cracked lips, and the blood blistered in my veins. Unable to focus on anything beyond the sweet pervasive ache. I was so close to that quivering elusive edge. *So close.* "Lucas," I breathed.

He licked me again, and I cried out. So hot and yet not quite there. Not enough pressure, not enough contact. "Not enough," I breathed.

He laughed. It was a dry laugh. He seemed to be enjoying the level of control he had over me and were I not so overcome, I would have been annoyed. I moved my hand again to touch myself and he caught my wrist.

"Say you're mine," he ground out.

My eyes flew open in shock and my legs tensed.

"Lucas…"

He lowered his head to suck on me once more and my eyes rolled back into my head, eyelids fluttering. Here it came. On a monster wave that was about to crash down and swallow me whole. Oh God. Fuck. Yes. *Yes.* I'm yours, Lucas. I'm yours. Make me come. *Make me come.*

My body convulsed, driven to the heights of pleasure. Gasping, I sucked in air as if I'd been holding my breath for hours. A rush of pleasure and bliss and exhausted euphoria rained down on me like droplets of mist on a perfect autumn morning in the Pacific Northwest. Every ounce of tension drained from me.

I stared up at the plastered trim on the old-fashioned canted ceiling. What. The. Fuck. Had. Just. Happened?

Lucas straightened and stared down at me inquisitively with an almost arrogant curl at the end of his lip. As if he were quite pleased with himself for having made me lose my mind. And for having done it so fast.

Right now, lying here and feeling like I had bones and muscles made out of jelly, I quite agreed that he had the right to be a bit arrogant. Dude had skills. What else could he do with even more interesting parts of his body than just his mouth?

Slowly I propped myself up on my elbows while he quietly tugged the hem of my skirt to cover me once again. He avoided my gaze and with a heavy sigh turned to flop tiredly on the nearby couch.

I blinked. He had nothing to say after that? Where had this even come from? Last I knew, he'd been annoyed with me and practically two-fisting whiskey down his pie-hole as fast as he could swallow it.

But I'd gotten a killer orgasm out of it so who was I to protest? And the least I could do was offer to reciprocate because... if I was being honest with myself, I really wanted to. Not to mention that fact that after six months of marriage, I was beyond curious to see what kind of weapon my husband was packing.

The thought made my heart speed as a fresh wave of hot arousal seeped through my languid, satiated body. Swallowing, I sat up and carefully slid off the piano.

He was slumped awkwardly across the couch, so I came up behind him and kissed his neck, running my tongue along his ear. "My turn for a taste of that cock you were just pressing against me."

He let out a low groan, head falling to the side, and I moved around to kneel before him on the couch. Hungrily, I tugged down his fly, struggling at first to pull it taut so the zipper would move. He was silent and, despite my struggles, didn't help me. I made sure to slip an extra grope in the process. He was still rock hard and a surge of excitement rose up in my throat.

He was not going to one-up me in the oral sex satisfier department. Here was my chance to show him why my fellatio skills were considered well above average. Soon he'd be grinding and gasping under the power of my mighty wonder-tongue.

I tried slipping my hand in through his fly but that was awkward, so I unbuttoned his pants. And just as I was about to set eyes on the prize, a snore reverberated from his chest. My head shot up. *What the...?*

Lucas's eyes were closed, mouth open, head slumped to the side against the back of the couch. More snores followed up that first one. I blinked, poking him sharply in the chest a few times to jostle him awake but there was no response.

Well... *shit.*

My shoulders slumped in defeat and I conceded, carefully zipping up his pants. Then I pulled off his shoes and gently eased him onto his side. There was no way in hell that I was getting him into his bed. He had to weigh almost twice as much as me.

After having fetched a pillow and throw off his bed, I set a glass of water on the coffee table. Then, I made him about as comfy as I possibly could. Then I retrieved my heels from underneath his piano and headed back to my solitary room to collapse.

Frustrating? Yes. But I'd definitely ended up on the better end of that bargain so... I wouldn't fret too much. Tomorrow was always another day to get square with him, or maybe even... horizontal.

A hot image of Lucas and I tangling up the sheets of his fancy wooden bed. What a nice image to entertain as I slipped off into lala land hoping for another fun sex dream.

CHAPTER 11
LUCAS

SOME OBSCURE SCOTSMAN ONCE SAID THAT IF LOVE MAKES the world go round, Scotch makes it go round twice as fast. I had to say this morning that I agreed. While it had been fun in the moment, that Scotch was causing a lot of regret on a Monday, of all days.

My eyes cracked open and my lips were caked with dried drool from where I'd been mouth breathing all night. My face was probably going to bear the waffle imprint from the couch material for the rest of the day.

And we wouldn't even talk about the marimba concert currently taking place between my throbbing temples. Under normal circumstances, I'd curse the fact that I'd ever done this to myself as I coughed and rubbed the grit from my eyes. But the memory of the incredible finish to a shitty night was making that all too difficult.

I sucked in a sharp breath at the memory of Kat's smooth, soft skin. Her pale legs as they dangled down the front of my piano. The feel of her silky thighs against my cheeks, the taste of her. The way she'd responded to me. *Fuck.* She'd come so hard, so fast it had bowled me over—pretty much literally. I must have passed out minutes after that. But what a way to go...

Shit. Now my head wasn't the only body part that was throbbing.

I rubbed at my forehead, trying to ease the dull ache while pondering what the hell had led to that amazing punctuation mark at the end of the day. I should be chastising myself for crossing a boundary I'd worked so hard for months to set and keep in place. But I just couldn't find it in me to do it.

I'd been wanting to taste her since pretty much the moment I'd first seen her almost two years ago. That gorgeous burnished hair, those amazing, intelligent blue eyes. That wit, the gregarious tough-girl charm. Yeah she drove me insane on a daily basis with her teasing and button-pushing. But I enjoyed giving it back to her just as hard—or harder.

All that had proved to be a months-long, protracted and frustrating exercise in daily unfulfilled foreplay.

And finally, last night, drunk off my ass, I'd gotten the chance to hear her moan. To say my name and to watch her while she came and know that I was the one doing it to her. Damn it. I was hard and already plotting ways in which we could pick up where we'd left that *To Be Continued* caption.

My all too pleasant thoughts were suddenly cut by an unfamiliar yet persistent chime and even more annoying buzz against the wood of my coffee table.

What the—?

It was the alarm app on a phone. Diving for my device, I saw nothing. Then I turned with a groan—and the world turned with me. As the alarm persisted, I felt around on the coffee table for the other phone sitting there. For some accursed reason, Kat must have set an alarm for this morning. I frantically pressed every button available to me to turn off the goddamn thing. Jesus, Kat. Wasn't this what alarm clocks were for?

Max padded in from the direction of my bedroom, having opted, I suppose, to sleep on his dog bed despite my sacking out on the couch. He began pressing his nose toward my face, panting his hot humid breath.

Nausea roiled in conjunction with the headache. *Thanks a lot, dog.*

I blinked at the screen once the buzzing and alarm stopped. Kat's phone was locked, of course, but the bright screen stung my eyes. I pondered the time, six thirty-one a.m. on Monday morning. My eyes dropped automatically to the unread text just below. Nosy, sure. But it was an unconscious action born from the habit of looking at my own screen.

Once I read the message there, however, I immediately wished I hadn't.

Hot Russian Astro: Hey, Red. We still on for coffee after work? Need a lift?

The contact entry was *Hot Russian Astro,* followed by five shiny gold stars. My jaw clenched immediately only sending more pain to my throbbing temples. Heat flushed up my neck and if I wasn't careful, I was in danger of blowing a gasket. He'd addressed her by a nickname *Red.* And that was exactly the color I was immediately seeing as anger quickly wrapped a stranglehold around my throat.

Fuck.

Of course, this meant that Kat had gone ahead and called the Russian cosmonaut who had been flirting hard with her during our tour of the Draco campus. Despite the fact that I'd trashed his business card days ago.

Goddamn it.

I nudged Max's face away from mine, then covered my face with my hands, pressing palms to my closed eyelids, as if willing the pain away would help. Yeah sure. The physical pain, maybe. But I was seething and shaken from what could very well be, but likely wasn't, an innocent text.

We had agreed to not see other people and thus she was breaking the rules. I had a right to be irritated with her for that. But this sick roiling in my gut and the burning fire at the base of my throat was not mere annoyance. It was a volcano of fiery jealousy threatening to erupt at any moment.

It was picturing this damn Russian schmoozing her, charming her, buying her coffee and then putting his hands on her.

Fuck no. *Fuck no.*

With an aggravated growl, I bolted off the couch and stalked through my bedroom, dumping the pillow and blanket on my bed before heading into the bathroom. As I went through my morning routine, laced with much-needed tablets of pain reliever and a full glass of water, my joints were still stiff with anger.

In my brain, jealousy scorched a huge swath through my thoughts, turning everything else to ashes and dust. To the extent that in the shower I cranked the hot water to nearly scalding. Even when it was at the point of being uncomfortable, I let it run all over my body until the stream turned ice cold. I'd emptied my water heater for one goddamn wasteful shower. And I had nothing to show for it besides a fast-growing obsession picturing Kat with that Russian cosmonaut.

What the hell was she thinking, going out with him?

If it had been just an innocent or friendly thing, she'd have told me about it. No. She was hiding it from me.

And she wasn't the first woman in my life to have done that.

I dragged a razor across my jaw and chin, only to barely avoid opening my carotid by accident. In frustration, I couldn't avoid thinking about that *other* time. The morning I'd found updates on Claire's phone from one of my closest friends at Cambridge. Only to hack the damn thing open—her passcode had taken me exactly three tries to guess—and find over two months' worth of texts between the two of them. Beginning at the innocent, to the venting of frustrations, to the inappropriate for a newly married person to the unquestionably unfaithful.

The day that I'd read those, I'd felt hollow, numb and oddly, inexplicably relieved. *Relieved* that my new wife was professing love for someone else, even if it was a friend. I took a deep, painful breath, studying my half-shaved face in the mirror. Those memories arrived on a problematic wave of even darker, more unpleasant memories—the beginning of the end of my old life. I hadn't hated everything about it. And parts of my younger life I missed still.

But not enough to want them back. *Never that.*

I threw my razor down after rinsing the blood out of it for the second time—and subsequently patching up my face. I tried not to think about the difference in how finding this text made me feel from the previous time. There was no relief in finding this message on Kat's phone. No numbness or indifference. The complete and total opposite, as a matter of fact.

This *one* text had turned me into some unthinking rage-furnace and I was already plotting ways to prevent this coffee date from happening.

I actually cared more about this incident with a fake wife than I had with Claire. Because I'd fucked up.

Because I'd known better than to get involved with Katya sexually. And up until she'd moved into my house, spending time with me twenty-four-seven, I'd been successful at keeping her at a safe distance.

But less than forty-eight hours after she'd moved in, I'd had my mouth between her exquisite thighs. Had I not passed out, I was certain it would have progressed much further than that. Just thinking about what could have been, even in my fury, was making my cock ache.

I wanted her too much.

And I'd wanted her for too long.

And that right there was the biggest reason why I should never *ever* have her.

I dressed quickly in jeans and a t-shirt and grabbed a pair of sneakers, my movements still stiff and jerky. As it was after seven now, I should probably wake her up to get ready for work. But the pettier part of me didn't even want to look at her right now.

Damn, wasn't it funny? You could change your name, your goals. You could change everything about where you thought you were headed as an adult. You could change your previous vision of the future. But you still had to rely on and trust other people. And you had no control over what they'd do. And no matter how much you endeavored to change, history could still repeat itself.

Maybe I was just a shitty husband who drove his wives—real *and* fake—to cheat. What was the psycho-babble term? Emotionally unavailable. I'd heard that a few hundred times while going through my first divorce and subsequent therapy sessions.

I was stuffing the last few things into my backpack, determined to get breakfast at the Draco cafeteria and eat at my desk, when Kat came out of the kitchen. She was fully dressed for work, her long shiny hair brushed out and gleaming over her shoulders.

"Damn it. There it is." She scooped up her phone from the coffee table. Then she set those gorgeous big blue eyes on me, her sultry lips parted in a wide smile. "Hey you! Good morning. You feeling okay? I could make you a Caesar if we weren't heading to work."

"A Caesar?" I snapped, a little too quickly than I'd intended. I picked up my own phone and tucked into the front of my bag. "What the hell is that?"

"Oh, I'm sorry. I think you guys call it a Bloody Mary. Good for hangovers."

I grimaced. "No thanks." Not in the mood for any more chatter, I turned and grabbed the front doorknob to head out.

I glanced back to see that Kat's eyes were on her phone. I hesitated as she unlocked it, morbidly curious to see her reaction to the text message. Would she confirm my suspicions? I was a glutton for punishment apparently.

Her eyes skimmed the text, and she frowned slightly. Then she typed out a text quickly in return. "Shit I forgot I had a coffee appointment with the Russian cosmonaut dude."

"Hot date?" I couldn't even help it. It just jumped out of my mouth.

She gave me side eye. "Hardly. He got my number from Jordan. Apparently his friend wants to start a Twitch channel, and he wants advice from me. I don't even want to go. I just gave him a raincheck and told him I was hungover."

"You didn't drink last night," I said, fighting hard to ignore the immense wave of relief that washed over me. She didn't want to go. There was nothing between her and the cosmonaut guy.

But still, the indisputable fact that I had just about lost my shit when I'd thought otherwise was rattling me good.

"Wanna go in to work together?" She pocketed her phone and looked up at me expectantly. No discussion or even allusion to the goings on of last night. She was playing this very cool.

I swallowed, mind racing. "I'm riding my bike. See you in a few."

She extended her arm toward me. "I can at least take your backpack in my car."

"I'm good. Bye now."

She stood frozen, watching me with wide eyes as I turned and opened the door, pulling it firmly shut after me. On the front step, I halted and took a deep breath. *Damn.* This woman was already causing me to lose it. *Get it together, Lucas. Eyes on the prize.*

With stiff determination, I pulled my bike out of the garage and got on, speeding down the street like a bat out of Mordor. The ride would take longer and I hadn't planned on using the bicycle this morning. But it had been a handy excuse to avoid sitting in the car with Kat.

I didn't see Kat again until lunchtime because I was in team meetings most of the morning. Thankfully my headache had let up. But my thoughts—my quick obsession—over this morning's reaction to that innocuous text was really shaking me to my core.

And I knew, as the day wore on, that I couldn't put myself in that position again no matter what. And no matter how much I wanted to fuck her.

And I really *really* wanted to fuck her.

But I had to stop thinking about that and about the night before, when I'd had her spread out across my piano, silky smooth legs open for me...

Goddamnitfuckinghellstopitnow.

I barely looked at her when she sidled up to me at my workstation, sinking into an empty chair beside me. "How are you feeling? Headache gone?"

I stared fixedly at my monitor, logging bug reports as they came in. "Never had one in the first place," I lied.

A pause. "Is everything all right? You aren't... you aren't upset about what happened last night are you?"

My eyes dropped to my keyboard, then back up to the monitor. I wish I could close my nostrils as easily as closing my eyelids because she smelled amazing, as usual. That coconut and nutmeg scent was pure intoxication—possibly quadrupling the world-turning effect of Scotch. She bent forward and her silky hair tickled my arm. I yanked it back as if she'd burned me. Then she pulled away.

"Oh okay, so the answer is yes." As it was lunch hour, hardly anyone was in the Den and those that were all headphones on.

Her voice was still low enough that anyone around us, even without headphones, would have trouble hearing us.

Still, she paused and when I said nothing, her tone turned icy. "Wow, Lucas. Never thought I'd say this to you, of all people, but you are such a cliché."

I bit my lower lip but like an asshole, I still said nothing. Didn't even spare her a glance.

With an indignant huff, her chair scraped back against the floor and she stood, stalking out of the Den. Once the door flipped closed, I put my face in my hands. God, I was such a massive dick. I owed her the barest minimum of an explanation, at least. But all in all, this was for the best.

This *would be* for the best. By keeping her at a distance I was protecting her. Yes, and also myself.

When you played with lava, you were extremely likely to get immolated. And Kat? She was pure molten magma right down to the color of her hair.

The day became a long slog after lunch. I hadn't brought the dog with me to work because of the last-minute switch to my bicycle as a mode of transportation. I texted Michaela to have her check in on Max. She'd replied that she was already on her way to the house for some piano practice, so that was fine. When I left, it was almost dinner time. There were no plans for dinner and I couldn't find Kat before I left. I assumed she'd already gone home.

So when I walked in my front door, a fistful of the daily mail in my hand, I wasn't surprised to see people in the front room. But I expected those people to be Michaela with Kat. Instead, Michaela sat across from two guys I'd never seen before.

Shutting the door, I set down my backpack. Max trotted over from where he'd been hitting up the newcomers for attention. As I bent to scratch him in greeting, I studied these dudes.

Not friends of Michaela's, from the nervous way she was sitting on the edge of the couch. And one of them looked a little rough, like the cliché'd poster child for the kid who'd dropped out of school because he did too much pot every morning. He wore a black '80s metal band t-shirt, ripped jeans, chains hanging from his pockets and biker boots.

The other guy looked boyish and fresh-faced enough. Still not the greatest dresser in low riding jeans and a well-worn t-shirt but he popped out of his chair to approach me with a smile.

"Hey bro. You have a cool dog! I'm a big dog lover." Max turned back to the guy, and he obliged the dog with more head scratches. So far the stranger had one new best friend here, at least.

I set down the pile of mail, my eye catching on the top piece. The envelope was another one of those law office letters addressed to Katya.

Then I turned back to the visitor. "Do I—know you? Or are you here passing out religious tracts? Because... no thanks."

The boyish-faced man threw his head back and laughed like I'd just said the funniest thing he'd ever heard. Perhaps he'd thought I was joking.

"I'm Derek." He lifted his hand from scratching Max's head to hold it out to shake mine. "You must be Luke, eh? Pleased to meet you." He grinned, showing off a dimple as if he knew it was there and was his best feature.

I frowned but took his hand regardless, because manners and all. There was something familiar about his bright blue eyes...

"Lucas," I corrected, tersely. Derek? Derek who? I didn't know a Derek.

He hesitated, then his eyes widened. "Oh, sorry." And there it was. The Canadian accent on that one word was unmistakable. "I guess Kat never talks about me? I'm your brother-in-law, Derek Ellis."

"Ah, yeah." I frowned, confused as to why Katya hadn't warned me about her brother showing up. Maybe that's what she'd been trying to talk to me about at lunch today when I'd brushed her off. "Sorry, it's been a long day, and I didn't put it together. Katya's actually told me a lot about you." It could be the truth, if by a lot I meant "nothing at all."

My eyes went to Michaela who definitely looked like she wanted to take off. "Thanks for letting the dog out."

"Anytime," She sprung from her seat and grabbed her bag, heading to the front door. "Thanks, as always, for the practice time."

Michaela opened the front door but was blocked from leaving by Kat, who had her keys out as if to unlock it. Before she could say anything to Michaela or me, her eyes landed on her brother.

A dark scowl clouded her face, and she stepped past Michaela without a word. My friend promptly fled, obviously reading the room and getting the hell out. I half wished I was leaving with her. Derek's dirtbag buddy on the couch had said nothing but perked up when Kat entered. Her eyes bulged almost comically at them both.

"What are you doing here?" she snarled at her brother.

His dark brows knit in confusion. "Here I was all proud of myself for making this a surprise. But I guess that wasn't such a good idea? It's good to see you, anyhow."

"Hey, kitten," the other guy said with a wide grin. The nickname—and the way he looked at her—instantly made my blood boil.

"Don't fucking call me that, Mike." She stormed past all of us and out into the kitchen.

The guys looked at each other and Mike started laughing. "She *mad*."

Derek threw him a warning look then glanced at me. "So this is awkward."

Before I could reply, Kat was back in the room with us, having left her things in the kitchen. She stood facing her brother, her arms folded over her chest. "What are you doing here?" she repeated at her brother, promptly ignoring the gloating asshole on the couch.

Derek appeared taken aback, eyes widening. "I can't believe you're still mad at me. It's been nearly two years. We heard you got married—"

"From your lawyer? Did your lawyer tell you that?"

Mike shifted uncomfortably on the couch and Derek avoided his friend's gaze. The tension in the air was thick enough to be sliced with a plus-two magic broadsword. I instantly wanted to bail and let them hash it out, but that would be hypocritical of me, considering all my family bullshit I'd just subjected her to.

"C'mon don't be like that. The parents were worried. You took off to another country and got married. Then didn't tell us anything. It's like we don't exist anymore."

She arched her brow. "Then why didn't *they* come?"

"Mum wanted to, but she couldn't get the time off. She's been pulling some double shifts at the hospital. And dad's in the middle of a big project for a docuseries. I volunteered to come and Mum even packed you a big care package." His gaze flicked to me. "Besides, I'd like to get to know my new brother-in-law and see a bit of sunny California."

With every bit of news he delivered to Kat, she seemed to grow even tenser.

I stepped forward, glancing at their bags. "It's late to get a room somewhere. You're welcome to stay here. Fair warning, I don't have a spare room set up but we have some air mattresses."

Perhaps I did it to be nice and cut the tension. Perhaps I did it to get her back for tying me down to that crappy family reunion my mother was so obsessed with. Or perhaps I did it because having other people in the house would be safer. This one fact decreased the likelihood of us repeating last night's shenanigans. In that moment, I wasn't exactly sure which was the real reason.

Kat's eyes went ginormous and before she could speak, Derek moved up beside her and slipped an arm around her shoulders. "C'mon sis, truce? Please? I come in peace bearing Aero bars and Mackintosh's toffee. Also all-dressed chips, Smarties and Swedish berries. I heard you can't get any of those in the States."

Kat's jaw bulged where she clenched it. "You're the one who likes the toffee, not me."

"Then I'll help you eat those... or maybe Lucas will like them. Share a bit of your culture with him, eh? But you can pig out on all the Aeros and the chips and other stuff. Lots of fun junk food. Sorry I couldn't bring you fresh Timmy's donuts but they wouldn't keep."

Kat's skin appeared even paler, and she looked at the floor in front of her. I'd never seen her like this, like she had no idea what to even say. Derek must have noticed, too, a concerned frown on his auburn brow.

He glanced up at me. "Thanks for the invite, Lucas. Very kind of you and we're happy to accept your hospitality."

Kat gently extricated herself from her brother's grasp and he dropped his arm. Wow, this was so bizarre. Not only the obvious tension between them but the complete change in her demeanor.

"No offense, but I'm not quite understanding how you were even allowed to leave the country," she ground out.

Huh, this reference and the one about the lawyer had me thinking about those legal envelopes. Another one had shown up today. Did they have something to do with her brother? Or some trouble they were both in? Or maybe it was a lawsuit of some kind? Were Canadians as litigious as Americans? I had no idea.

"We got in a car and drove. It wasn't hard." He bent his head as if to catch her gaze while smiling up at her. "C'mon sis, are we cool? Because if so I was told to snap a selfie with you the minute I saw you and send it to Mum."

She blew out a breath and rolled her eyes while Derek sidled up to her again and held a camera up to their faces. Kat tucked a lock of hair behind her ear and smiled tightly for the selfie.

While Derek fiddled with his phone, presumably to send the photo to their mother, Kat turned to me, motioning toward my bedroom. "Babe, can I speak to you in private for a minute?"

I nodded and followed her down the hall to my room, shooting a look back at our strange new guests. They were each fiddling with their phones and not paying us any attention.

After shutting the door, I waited.

Kat's shoulders slumped immediately, and she ran a hand through her thick, long hair pushing it back. Like a dog tracking his favorite treat waved in front of his nose, I followed the movements. As usual, the powerful urge to touch that hair came with it. I shoved the longing aside and concentrated on the situation at hand.

"What on earth were you thinking, inviting them to stay here?" she finally asked.

I blinked. "I was trying to be nice to a member of your family. Besides, your brother seems like an all right guy. His buddy is a bit of a dick but..." I shrugged. Her gaze on me hardened, and I frowned. "What? You actually wanted me to turn your brother away?"

She shook her head absently and looked up at the ceiling. "I don't know. I just... I think it's a bad idea."

"What's wrong with letting him have a short visit? He stays a few days and gets bored. Then we get him out of here so we can get on with our work and lives. And that includes a certain very important interview coming up. It'll be *fine*."

Her gaze on me, if possible, had hardened even more. "You do realize that they think our marriage is for real, right?"

I shrugged. "Well, so does my family."

She blinked again as if I were some kind of idiot. "Which *means* that if they're sleeping over, we'll need to be sleeping in the same room. In the same bed." She pointed to my bed as if to emphasize her point.

My eyes followed where she pointed, to my perfectly made-up bed. Which, to be honest, hadn't had a woman in it in a very long time. The last woman I'd dated, over a year before, had only wanted sleepovers at her house, which I'd rarely done as I didn't like them. Since the divorce I never had anyone overnight at my house.

But now Kat would have to do just that. Through my own stupidity, I'd graduated us from playacting only for work and special occasions to now playacting twenty-four-seven.

Since there was absolutely nothing that could be labeled "playacting" between us the night before, on the piano, that was leading me to a big danger zone. I blinked, staring at the bed, then I turned back to her and took a deep breath.

"I, uh, think we can manage that for a night or two."

She snorted. "Until a night or two turns into a week or a month. You don't know my brother. He's like kudzu—hard to get rid of and turns up everywhere."

I glanced at the bed again, trying hard to put out of my mind how she'd felt and tasted under my hands and tongue the night before. The sound of her coming, deep throaty moans and a high-pitched squeak when she arched her back. *Shit.*

The bed was big but not big enough to avoid what I didn't really want to avoid. I craved her gorgeous, lush body pressed up against me in sleep. I wanted to inhale the coconut scent of her hair splayed across my pillow. Suddenly I wondered if she slept in skimpy negligees or sexy lingerie. It would be out of character for her but... once I pictured it, I could not unpicture it.

Damn it to hell. What had I gotten myself into?

Her pointer finger tapped at her mouth as she was obviously thinking and had no idea the dirty turn my own thoughts had taken. "Maybe we can have fumigators show up in a few days or something."

I laughed. "Fumigators to get rid of unwanted family members. If that's not already a business, it should be. They'd make a killing."

"Or we could always just move."

"Hmm." My mind was racing, trying to find a way to get out of us sharing the bed in here. I had no real ideas. There wasn't enough room on the floor to throw down an air mattress and I only had two, which presumably would go to our guests.

Maybe a sleeping bag? On the hardwood floor that would suck big-time. I'd be walking around like an eighty-year-old man after only a night or two of that.

I ran a hand through my hair. "Okay, you can sleep in here but... I have rules."

She blew out a breath and folded her arms across her chest, which, of course, tightened her shirt right around those perfect boobs of hers. That delectable chest that I still hadn't gotten a chance to touch, fitting those breasts into the palms of my hands, the soft—*fuck*.

"Of course you have rules. Why wouldn't you? We had rules for when we got married—"

"—And you broke the most important one about keeping it secret—"

She scowled but continued to talk over me. "Rules for me living here, which, I might add, I've kept every one of them. *You* are the one who invited them to stay and put us in this latest predicament."

I shook my head. "We need rules, especially now." I didn't need to add that we could hardly afford another slip-up like last night. That had been completely *my* slip-up, but still. The rules were more for me than for her, obviously.

"We both need to be fully clothed in bed. Top and bottom. No sexy negligees."

Her cinnamon brow shot up. "Shit, I was hoping you'd be wearing something in black lace with fishnets."

I gave her one of my not-taking-bullshit looks that I normally saved for work. And she reacted with her usual give-zero-fucks-about-your-stern-looks response.

She waved a finger in my face. "Look, I don't sleep in anything like that but I don't wear stuff on my legs when I sleep. It drives me nuts. An old cotton nightie is fine."

"Okay. Well then, you can take the right side of the bed. I usually sleep over on the left, anyway."

"The right side? Is that the side Claire slept on?"

I ignored the snarky question and continued to count down on my fingers. "I shower at night. You can either have the shower after me or you're welcome to use it in the morning."

She shook her head, rolling her eyes skyward. "Morning's fine. Anything else? Am I allowed to snore?"

"Do you snore?"

Her ice-blue gaze was as cold as the northern wastes. "No." Her eyelids fluttered. "What's next? Should I wear a Handmaid's Tale-style hood? Blessed be the fruit?"

I blew out a breath. "Chill out, I'm just... I don't want..."

"You don't want me to shamelessly seduce you like I did last night. I get it."

I rubbed my forehead. "In no way do I think that's what happened."

She threw her hands up. "Well since you made it clear you don't want to talk about it, how am I supposed to know what you think?"

"I know I screwed up and I feel bad about it. That's what I think. I'm sorry."

She blinked, shocked by my sudden admission and apology. It was not something that usually happened when we were knee-deep in our typical banter. But there was nothing typical about what happened between us last night.

"Okay," she said slowly as if she were waiting for some kind of salty punchline from me. That never came.

"I was drunk and I know that's no excuse for breaking our rules. It won't happen again."

Her gaze dropped, and she stared at the far wall, as if in deep concentration or lost in thought. But for once, she didn't bite back. Thank goodness because I honestly was putting my best foot forward.

"So is there anything I need to know about your brother and his friend?"

She pulled back from wherever she'd gone, mentally, and looked at me with a frown. "Um, like what?"

I waved my hand in the air vaguely. "Like what's his story? I mean, you made some reference to his lawyer and seemed surprised he could leave the country. Is he in some sort of trouble? And Mike looks like some failed biker gangster. Should I lock down the valuables?"

Kat's face sobered, and she darted a glance into my eyes and then away. "Honestly I don't know what Derek's legal status is right now. It's been over a year but things weren't all that great when I left. I guess I'll try to find out the details since he'll be staying here with us. And yes, definitely lock down the valuables. Speaking of which, is there a way to lock the guest room? I rather them not open it up and wonder why all my stuff's in there.

I scratched my jaw, thinking. Her evasion had been slick but it had been just that—a way to sidestep the subject without substantially answering my question. I'd have time to dig into that later, hopefully.

"That door has a key lock on the knob. I'll dig out the key for you so you can lock it from the outside."

She hesitated, then took a step toward me. "I know I was irritated with you for inviting them to stay, but it was kind of you. And, just, thanks for doing this."

Against my better judgement, I reached out and touched her upper arm. "We'll make it work, Kat. Don't worry about it. If he does happen to see your stuff in the guest room, just say I got drunk last night and snored a lot and you moved in there."

She bit her lip. "I'm not going out of my way to make them comfortable, either. Just the air mattresses and a few blankets on the floor in the dining room. Maybe that will hurry them along, too."

I nodded. "Good thinking. We'll get them out of here as soon as we can and everything will be back to normal." Whatever *normal* was.

Sharing this bed with her for a few nights while not being able to touch her was going to be an exercise in insomnia for me. But I'd helped get us into this mess. Might as well do what I could to help her out of it.

I wanted to help her. I couldn't help wanting to help her, to be honest. And I was pretty sure that if she asked me to, I'd inconvenience myself in more ways than merely having her share this bedroom with me for a few nights.

If this were an actual marriage, I'd be in trouble.

Thank God, it wasn't.

CHAPTER 12
KATYA

HOLY SHITBALLS. WHAT THE HELL JUST HAPPENED? THE Universe thought the combo of threatened deportation, a quickie wedding to fix it and a surprise marriage reveal to everyone we knew wasn't quite enough? Oh and my husband's secret European noble family. Now we had to add my screwed up dysfunctional family to the mix. All for a perfect crap stew.

Yum, yum. *Ugh.*

Mike seemed bummed there was no beer in the fridge. I interrupted Lucas before he could offer to go pick up a six-pack at the nearest liquor store. And much to my relief, neither of them pushed the issue. Derek had no reaction at all, which gave me a spark of hope despite my overarching skepticism.

"Hey, cool cactus." My brother observed, nodding at Cocky in the middle of the table. Watching the irritation slide across Lucas's face was the one highlight of the evening.

To say I had no appetite was an understatement—for crap stew *or* for the pizza we ordered to feed our new unexpected guests. It all sat like a rock in my stomach and I said very little during dinner.

I studied my brother while he was engaged in talking to the other two men. He seemed like the same old Derek. Fun and sweet and talkative. He could be a great guy when his mountain of baggage wasn't weighing him—and everyone who loved him—down.

Nobody looking at him right now, with his relaxed attitude and his smiles would know that he could also be the most selfish human being on the planet. And everyone around him who loved him waited for the much-promised but never-delivered change.

I blinked, still stung that it was him and not Mum or Dad who had come or reached out in any other way. If they'd found out my address, then they could just as easily get my phone number or email. They could have contacted me directly. Instead, they'd sent Derek and a junk food care package.

And that hurt, too. They were consumed with their work, obviously. And those fancy embossed letters I kept getting from the expensive lawyers in Vancouver were no doubt the reason why. That old wave of bitterness deep down reminded me that this was Derek's fault, too.

And there was no doubt that his visit was related to those legal troubles and all the reasons I'd ditched that bullshit in the first place. Yeah that was me, Katya the Brave who fled her homeland rather than stand up for herself.

But as Lucas had said, this visit was only for a little while. I could survive anything for a little while, couldn't I? Hell, I'd been secretly married to the grumpiest man on earth for almost seven months now. That had to be some proof that I could go the distance!

I set our guests up in the empty room just off the kitchen, the would-be formal dining room that Lucas had never decorated. It had hardwood floors and echoing, empty white walls. I gave them Lucas's air mattresses but played dumb about any type of hand pump, though I'd seen one in the storage closet right beside them. Oh well. They'd just have to blow them up with their own lung air.

My brother had the good sense to keep his mouth shut about it, though his friend Mike groused loudly. I gave zero fucks about what *he* thought. He'd always been public enemy number one and best-friend's-little-sister-tormentor extraordinaire.

Dumping the pile of folded sheets and blankets that Lucas had also offered up into a pile, I heaved a sigh. The guys looked up from their phones as I mumbled, "If you need anything else, there are towels in the linen closet."

"You have a nice house here, sis. Did you two just buy it?"

I shook my head. "Lucas has lived here for a few years. I just moved in when we got married."

"That was fast." Mike set aside his phone. I darted a sharp gaze at him, then turned away. Who really cared what this dickweed had to say? Not me. Nor did I ask him to clarify. He continued in spite of the dirty look I'd thrown him, peering up at me. "You two getting married, I mean. Like... why not just live together for a while first? What was the reason to rush getting married?"

Needling shit. He was always doing stuff like this. As if to add insult to the injury of Derek showing up unexpectedly at my door, he'd brought Mike with him. He and Derek had been tight since the early days of middle school. I blamed a lot of Derek's issues on Mike's bad influence but would my parents ever listen and intervene? Never.

"Oh, I'm sorry, Mike, are you upset that I'm no longer available? How was I to know you've been carrying a torch for me all these years?" That vague reference to the time he'd had the nerve to ask me out. He'd been gross enough to act entitled to dating me, given all the time he'd spent hanging out with my family. I was just sixteen and of course I'd never even come close to thinking of Mike that way. And predictably, his treatment had gotten even worse after I'd shot him down.

Mike laughed. "Wow, kitty's got some sharp claws. Hopefully you only use those to scratch down your hubby's back."

I ignored him, went to the closet, pulled out a few pillows and instead of dumping them on the pile of bedding, I pelted them at Mike instead. Aimed right for his stupid meat head. He snarled a *cunt* at me under his breath when one hit him square in the face and I smiled widely, pleased with myself.

"Leave her alone, man, jeez." Derek finally looked up from his phone to snap at his friend. *Thanks for stepping up for me, big bro.* I gritted my teeth.

"Yeah, so tomorrow morning Lucas and I are out of here by half past seven to go to work. I'm going to need you to vacate the house. You can go do all your touristy things. Not gonna lie, though, it's spendy to be a tourist here. A one-day ticket to Disneyland alone costs half your soul. And with the exchange rate, it's even more in Canadian dollars. Just sayin'."

I gave Derek side eye, strongly suspecting that Mum and Dad had bankrolled this trip on top of everything else. *Great.* Aiding and abetting someone to leave the country with their money. Jumping parole to do so. So typical of them. *All* of them.

Derek smiled. "Well you know I hate early mornings but we'll deal. Too bad you can't come with us to Disneyland. Mum gave me money to buy you two tickets. You can't get time off anytime soon?" I just shook my head. I probably could but I didn't want to. In response, he shrugged. "Well I'll leave the money so maybe you two can go on your own sometime."

I shook my head. "Thanks but it's okay. I doubt we'll be able to make it there anytime soon."

His gaze dropped, and he nodded. "That's too bad. You should definitely take some time to enjoy life once in a while. Good night, sis. Sleep well."

I turned to the door. Mike spoke up then, talking to Derek but clearly meaning for me to overhear. "Maybe we can hit a weed dispensary tomorrow. We'll need it after a night sleeping on the floor. That is if the lovebirds don't keep us up all night with their loud screwing."

I didn't turn around or make any other indication that I'd heard him. Nothing that might give him even the teeniest iota of satisfaction. It was tough because I wanted to kick the tool in the face. His ugly mug was right at runner-height, after all. He'd always been such a pain in my ass, perpetually egging Derek on in some new plot to terrorize me.

I quickly stopped into my guest room and grabbed my nightie and my clothes for the next day. Using the key Lucas had given me, I locked the room so they wouldn't end up snooping in there and asking questions. Then I removed all the toiletries from the nearby washroom to put in Lucas's.

When I got to the master bedroom, Lucas's door was ajar, but the room was empty except for Max who lazily gazed up at me from his night bed. I slipped in quietly and obliged him with a few belly scratches. Noticing the washroom door was shut, I laid my stuff on the bed. Then I patiently waited for my turn, but he seemed to be taking half an eon in there. He did warn me he liked to shower at night.

But what else was taking up all this time if it wasn't the longest shower ever in the history of showers? Was he dressing? Shaving? Plucking each of his whiskers out one at a time with tweezers? Counting the tiles on the floor? What?

Suddenly I pictured him with nothing but a towel draped around his waist, hard muscular chest coated with steam and maybe a few droplets of water. Even if he was taking forever in there, I mentally took advantage. Lying on the bed, I stared at the ceiling and indulged myself in a nice little visualization. His delicious arms, biceps rippling as he reached up to shave. I wondered if he had dimples in his back at the base of his spine. Did he still work out regularly or was that fit form just from having been athletic when he was younger?

In spite of this pleasant turn of my thoughts, I still seethed about Mike's shitty remark about the loud sex. He wanted loud sex to keep him up all night? I was more than happy to oblige, even if just for his benefit. Getting up, I went to the bedroom door, cracked it open a bit and began fake moaning loudly à la Meg Ryan from *When Harry Met Sally.* "Oh baby, give it to me!" I practically wailed. I tried rattling the headboard but it wouldn't budge—solid wood antique and probably made from ancient redwood trees.

I tried pounding on the wall. No luck... it being an old house meant that the walls were solid plaster. No sound carried between the walls. At all.

So I went back to the door to holler some more. "Oh, oh, oh! Yeah, baby. Harder!" And I added in an unearthly howl for good measure before shutting the door.

Silence except for the complaint of old hinges. I spun and there was Lucas in the washroom doorway. He clutched the doorknob as if it was the handle to a knight's shield brandished to protect himself from some unseen onslaught. His eyes were wider than normal.

My face flamed hot, and I blinked, scrambling to explain. "I, uh. Well, they... Mike, uh...."

His eyebrows went up, and he nodded expectantly, waiting for me to spit it out.

I blew out a huff and gestured stiffly toward the washroom. "Are you done in there?"

He stepped into the room wearing dark blue cotton pajamas. They were creased and looked stiff, as if they'd just been ripped out of the package. Like his grandma had gifted them to him for Christmas and he'd promptly dropped them in an empty drawer because.... Because he usually slept naked, or something.

He looked hotter than I'd ever expected any guy to look in cotton pajamas. There was something so... clean and honorable and upright about him normally. The pajamas just added to that image. But there'd been nothing clean and wholesome about what his mouth had done to me the night before as I was sprawled across his piano, his eyes like super-heated coals. I swallowed.

He motioned to the empty washroom. "All yours."

I didn't have much to do besides wash my face and change my clothes. I'd shower in the morning, like usual. But upon returning to the bedroom, I suddenly fathomed how small a queen-sized bed could be. Especially when sharing it with a handsome non sex-partner. In addition to a whole heaping of unrealized sexual tension.

I hovered at the edge of the bed, and he glanced up from the e-book on his tablet.

"Uh, so how should we do this?" I cleared my throat. "Like, um head to toe? Or me above the covers and you underneath? Or—"

He blinked and rolled his eyes. "Just get in. I'll try to control my urges."

I clenched my jaw, wondering if I could control mine.

As I'd come to expect from Lucas, the quality of his bed linens were freshly cleaned and top notch. Probably billion thread count premium organic Tunisian cotton hand-picked and woven by virgins. They did feel heavenly against my skin. I slid in, then rolled over on my side to face him. Propping my head up on my hand, I studied his profile for a moment as he fiddled with his tablet.

As if he felt my stare, his head pivoted, and he fixed his dark, unwavering gaze on me.

Our eyes locked and the air seemed to thicken between us. I studied the dark fringe of lashes around his eyes as his gaze roamed my face, settling on my mouth.

I swallowed. He swallowed. The silence stretched on.

The lighting on his face changed as his tablet clicked off and still we stared at each other, haunted by the ghosts of unfinished business from last night. Although *business* would be the last word in the world that I'd choose to describe the goings on the previous night.

No... no...

I'd felt him everywhere. Suddenly an ache tightened between my thighs, in my stomach, down to my core. Everything inside me heated from the memory of how good he'd made me feel. And how much I wanted him to do it again.

And how much I'd like to do the same to him.

Clearly it had freaked him the hell out, given his brusque freeze-out at work today.

Nevertheless, I wavered where I lay, leaning forward, just slightly, as if pushed by a stiff wind. And that bit of movement, right there, broke the spell. Immediately he sat up and turned to set his tablet on the nightstand.

And with a gruff "Good night," he clicked off the bedside lamp and turned his back to me. I lay there, not knowing exactly what to think, blinking into the darkness. In minutes, he was inhaling and exhaling slowly with the peaceful rhythm of slumber.

With a sigh, I flopped onto my back and stared up at the ceiling for hours. It would be a miracle if I could sleep tonight with all that had gone on. The thoughts, they were racing and jumping from subject to subject. All the past anxieties had now combined with the existing energy and tension that I'd hoped Lucas would help me release.

I couldn't get Derek's sudden appearance at my doorstep out of my head. After almost two years of hearing nothing from any of my immediate family members. Suddenly him, of all people, showed up at my door as if no time had passed at all. As if I hadn't packed up my bags in the middle of the night and taken off without saying goodbye.

This trip of his wasn't just some pleasure trip to see the sites of Hollywood, visit famous beaches and stroll around amusement parks. Something was afoot. Almost certainly it would include some kind of pressure for me to return to Canada and all the unfinished business they felt I'd left behind. That was a given.

No way in hell.

Nothing worked... not rolling from side to side, not adjusting a pillow, not getting up to use the washroom—and almost stepping on a sleeping dog in the dark. I lay there for hours, sleepless, thoughts racing like stock cars winding their ways up hairpin turns and high cliff roads. Suddenly I wished I could just give up and go blow off some steam while gaming. But I'd have to walk by the dining room and who knew what those two idiots were getting up to in there. Had to maintain the illusion that we were happily snoozing away, spooning tightly after some mind-blowing marital sex.

God, I could use some sex right now, marital, semi-acrobatic, or even boring missionary-style. I wasn't picky at this point.

Instead, I calmed myself while listening to the regular pace of his breathing and staring at the shadows that the neighbor's pool reflected on the window. I almost felt comforted. Like I wasn't in this alone.

But maybe that was all just illusion.

Nevertheless, my eyes finally closed just after four in the morning.

CHAPTER 13
LUCAS

IT WAS CLEAR THAT SHE'D GOTTEN HARDLY ANY SLEEP. I'D never tell her but, she woke me up a few times throughout the night with her restlessness. It had been a while since I'd shared a bed—as in literally sleeping beside each other in bed. Last night's experience had been a weird throwback to my married days.

Or, I guess, those other married days.

We were quiet in the morning, hardly speaking. She'd had the forethought to grab her clothes, and I let her have the bathroom first, dressing while she showered, then starting a pot of coffee.

Our surprise guests were still sleeping. I left it to Kat to deal with them—which she did, rousing them before breakfast and essentially sending them on their way after feeding them. They groused at her but eventually, with some goading, left the house when we did.

Derek stood on the front steps as we locked up. "See you back here tonight sometime, eh? When are you off work?"

"Five, in theory," Kat said drily. "Not that we ever make it back at that time."

"Traffic?"

"Long hours, extra overtime. Lots to do."

Mike snorted. "But why? You play games all day for a living. It's not like you're saving lives or something."

Dissing the job of the people whose house you're shacking up in was not a good look. Hmm. This guy, Mike, never failed to make me like him less every time he opened his mouth.

Derek patted the dog's head, waved good-naturedly and threw his friend a puzzling look. Kat's brother seemed all right but man did he have his sister tenser than my shoulder muscles after an hour of sculling on my rowing machine.

The two made their way to the curb and the beat-up sedan in which they'd just driven over a thousand miles to get here. I took Kat by the arm and directed her to my car. She glanced up with a question in her eyes but didn't ask. We had to keep up appearances after all, and not just for the two numbnuts staying in our house, but our co-workers as well.

I opened the car door for her and she wordlessly slid in. Then I moved to the back door to let Max into his usual spot, which he happily did. Going to work with me was a big adventure for him but I think my co-workers were far more bummed than he was when I didn't bring him.

"You're quiet this morning," I said finally after we'd driven for a few minutes. It wasn't a long commute to work—about fifteen minutes when we left at this time of day.

"I'm sorry about this whole surprise guest thing. Thank you for being so nice about it."

I shrugged. "Dealing with in-laws is another one of those things you can't avoid when you're married." Jeez, I felt like some great marriage-tutor, like a user's handbook with all my stupid observations. As if my first go-around in this particular circustent hadn't completely soured me on the institution, when it definitely had.

I'd vowed to never do it again. And yet, here I was.

I shot a glance at her. She had her fingers laced together tightly in her lap, clearly tense. "Are you okay? You didn't sleep much last night."

She turned to me, fresh-faced with her gorgeous hair pulled back into a single tight braid that clung to her scalp and trailed between her shoulder blades. She was also pale, wearing only the barest hint of makeup. But as always, she was still utterly beautiful. She'd have to put a bag over her head—and the rest of her body—to disguise that fact.

I gripped the steering wheel a little tighter and reminded myself for the billionth time not to dwell on how much I was attracted to her. Following that train of thought was dangerous—and headed almost certainly to dangerous derailment.

"I've got a lot on my mind. Kyle is going to ask me to sign off on his Class A quest chain. *Again.*"

I frowned, searching my memory for those bug reports. They'd been incredibly problematic when she'd initially reported the bugs. Sloppily put together and full of glitches and typos, she'd told me, when the devs couldn't hear us, of course.

Because to the devs, we were public enemy number one. We were the ones who told them where they'd messed up and they didn't like that at all.

"And you don't think they're ready to go out with the new game update?"

She clenched her jaw, then looked down at her hands, spreading her fingers wide. "Not even close."

"Then tell him that." It's not like she'd ever had a problem with that before. "Those changes can't go live until he gets your say so, and he knows that."

"Yeah, he's been really pissy about it and I just don't feel like dealing with him today."

I frowned. This was so unlike her. Our line of work required a strong backbone. We had to stand up to developers, project managers, and even, sometimes, the company officers. When we couldn't assure the quality of the product, we could not allow it to ship. It was a big reason why she was good at it. Her backbone was shiny stainless steel.

"Remind him that none of that shit goes live until you sign off."

She huffed a sharp laugh. "Oh he knows that. But instead of taking the kissing-my-ass approach to get me to, he's been acting a little..."

"Like a prick?"

"Intimidating," she concluded at the same time. Then her brows scrunched together from some unspoken concern and she stared out her window again.

"Is he being a dick to you?" My question sounded a little more forceful in my ears than I'd intended. She shot me an unreadable look but if my reaction surprised her, she gave no indication.

Suddenly she was fiddling with her wedding ring, twisting it on her finger, then smoothing a hand over the jeans that covered her long, shapely legs. Then one hand ended up on the door handle, the other one resting on the parking brake, idly pressing and releasing the button at the end of the handle. Over and over again.

Without even thinking of doing it, my hand went to cover hers, enfolding it with my own. "Don't sweat it, Kat. You've got this. And if he pulls any type of attitude, I'll back you up. You've got this," I repeated.

She turned to me, her face still pale but something new in her eyes—gratitude? Appreciation? "Thanks," she whispered.

But I knew that this wasn't what was truly bugging her. No the source of that issue would be hitting us in the face once again the minute we returned home to our unwanted houseguests. There was definitely something up between her and her brother—and the rest of her family, for that matter.

Maybe she'd come clean about it soon. Or maybe I'd be forced to ask her directly.

As usual, we went our separate ways at work. Me to meetings, her to one-on-ones with the devs who relied on her for white-box testing. Kat was a valuable asset to our department because of her extensive knowledge of coding. She was able to look at code alongside the finish product and predict potential problems. It was rumored that she'd be heading her own team of white box testers soon, if not running the entire department if, God willing, I got that much-coveted promotion.

Speaking of which, my self-appointed "mentor" for the new job showed up just after the last meeting that morning as I caught a quick bite in the cafeteria. Jordan plunked himself into a chair at my table, an apple in hand, while I finished up with some notes on my tablet. I didn't even bother to look up.

"Hey there, young padawan. How goes the married life?"

"Just dandy," I answered drily.

I signed off on what I was doing and closed the app. Pushing the tablet away, I turned to him. Jordan had an elbow on the table, his fist under his chin, staring at me as he thoughtfully chewed his apple.

"Have you done any more work on your concept for the new company? The clock is ticking and I want you to get this job."

I mimicked him, eyes narrowing, resting my own chin in my hand. "And just why is it so important to you that I get this job?"

Jordan casually shrugged a shoulder, leaning back in his chair and looking away. "Because we're friends? Isn't that enough?" He bit into the apple and chewed again, avoiding my gaze.

"I'm working with one of the astronauts. We've come up with some ideas."

At the periphery of my vision, I caught a glimpse of someone approaching us. We both looked up at Jeremy. The competition. He nodded at Jordan, smiling nervously. Jordan motioned for him to sit down but Jeremy shook his head and tapped his wrist. He must be on a deadline.

"Just ducked in to grab a bite to have at the desk while I get my stuff finished up." Jeremy turned to me. "I just wanted to thank you for those links you sent. The Unreal Engine is a great idea."

I nodded. "Sure man, no sweat. Good luck. Tell Michaela I said hi."

Jeremy's mouth twitched and his face clouded. Hmm. Was something going on there? I darted a glance at Jordan. If there was, I wouldn't ask him now. Jordan and Jeremy weren't all that close, anyway.

"Well with all these good ideas you have, I see the competition is stiff," he snorted. "I thought I'd had you beat until you made that impossible deadline. And now with this creative side showing..."

I raised a brow at him. "Don't act so surprised."

Jeremy laughed. "I'm just used to you yelling at me about my bugs all the time. Didn't know you could do all this other stuff."

Jordan watched our exchange, quietly crunching on his apple and progressively frowning.

"Anyway, I didn't mean to interrupt. Enjoy your lunch." Jeremy's eyes shifted from me to Jordan and then back again, as if his suspicions about Jordan's preference toward me were now stirred. Jeremy raised a hand and turned away and I watched his receding back for a moment.

How weird it was to be competing for this high-level job—something that I'd been working at for years—with a friend. The results of this competition would change one of our lives dramatically and possibly affect our friendship forever.

When I looked back at Jordan, he was scrutinizing me between narrowed eyes. I blinked. "What?"

"'Thanks for the tip?' What the hell is that supposed to mean?" His features twisted with suspicion. "You aren't giving him tips and ideas, are you?"

I shrugged. "He's helped me, too. This isn't cutthroat."

Jordan set down his apple core on a napkin and dusted off his hands. He turned to me with what appeared to be forced patience, as if explaining something to a ten-year-old for the fourth time. "It's business, Lucas. In the words of one of my role models, the chairman and co-founder of Nike, *Business is war without bullets*. It is, by nature, cutthroat."

I shook my head. "Jeremy's my friend. I'm not going to wage war with him."

Jordan's brow rose. "Am I betting on the wrong horse?"

I laughed at him. "I'm neither a soldier nor a horse. Get over yourself."

Jordan shook his head, suppressing a smile. "Marriage has obviously made you soft. We'll need to work on toughening you up, padawan."

"Fuck the Star Wars references, Obi-Wan." He knew, along with anyone else who knew me, that I couldn't stand the allusions. One could not go through most of his adult life being known as Lucas Walker and not hear something along those lines almost every day of the week.

Jordan pushed up from the table with a wide shit-eating grin. "Use the Force, Luke. I mean Lucas."

"Fuck off," I snorted at him good-naturedly and he waved on his way out.

When I returned to the Den, Kat wasn't at her station. I assumed she'd gotten tied up in her own schedule. Suddenly Kyle, one of the developers, appeared at my side with his tablet. "I need to get these resolved bugs signed off today."

I glanced at him and then back at the checklist on his tablet. "You're going to have to wait for Katya to do that. I can't override her."

He stared at me, as if unbelieving, for a moment, then made a sour face. "*Can't* or *won't*? What, are you afraid she's going to hit you over the head with a frying pan?"

I continued typing, not even willing to dignify the comment with a response.

He let out a frustrated sigh. "She's impossible. Can't I just work this out with you?"

I turned my chair toward him, stone-faced. "No, you can't. And if she's not signing off on your QA, then there's a damn good reason for it. It's not just some whim."

Kyle's face turned smug. "Oh, right. Gotta keep the home fires burning, right? Stick up for the little wifey?"

"Are you through with the preteen temper tantrum?"

His eyes narrowed. "Can't you just do me a favor this once? I just can't with her."

I drummed my fingers on the desk, impatient for this exchange to be over with and suddenly sympathetic that Kat had to deal with this attitude on a daily basis. I remembered her exhausted resignation in the car this morning, the way she'd nervously fidgeted, dreading Kyle's pushy behavior. Usually she was a tigress, standing up for herself and others when she felt the need. But this morning, not so much...

"Then maybe you need to put some real work into your code so it's not full of bugs. Katya does her job, and she does it well and my judgement of her work has nothing to do with the fact that we're married. Got it?" Kyle's mouth opened to interrupt me but I overrode him. "If this game ships with low quality, it's all of our nuts on the line, man."

His face suddenly split into a grin and he snorted. "Well not hers, 'cause she doesn't have any."

"Thanks for the anatomy lesson." Sexist bastard.

"I have a to-do list a mile long," he whined.

"Then you do what we do and you pull all-nighters 'til it's done. Or you tell your boss you've got too much on your plate. But when you deal with the QA on your work, you do it respectfully or you'll answer to me. Because she's a highly competent colleague not because I'm married to her. Got it?"

"Screw it. Whatever, man." He threw up his hands in surrender, then snatched up his tablet.

"That's how we roll around here," I said to his back and I swore I heard him say "pussy-whipped" in the string of words he muttered under his breath.

Because of course... Dick. Jeez. I knew that there was rampant and toxic sexism in this industry. I knew that fact intellectually but it really irked me to see it in action. To have it thrown in my face, especially about someone I cared about.

I blinked. That thought had slipped out before I could mentally reel it back in. I corrected myself forcefully—I didn't care any more about Kat than I did about the rest of my team. *There.*

Talk about coming face to face with the fact that others had it tougher than I did. Women and minorities in this industry really had to work twice as hard, or harder, to win respect. I rubbed at my jaw, then my tired eyes, resolving to talk about this with my superiors when I had a spare moment.

And if I was lucky enough to get the promotion, I vowed to do things differently with the company division, too.

I whipped out my phone and texted Kat. I wanted to be present when she spoke to Kyle about his bugs. Then, I got back to work.

A half hour later, she hadn't replied. I flagged down Warren and asked him if he'd seen her. "Yeah, man, she's been snoozing in the Pit since lunch, sacked out on the couch." Then he threw me a sly grin. "Must have been all that newlywed sex that wore her out. Did you try the Canadian sex positions?"

"The *what?*"

He nodded, completely serious. "There's a whole website about it. Canadian sex acts. Like you probably went the Full Mountie on her, huh? Or maybe tried the Polar Bear Grip? The Igloo Melter?"

I rolled my eyes and pushed out of my chair. "Grow up, Warren."

"Bruh! What about the Winnipeg in her Regina?" he called after me.

I answered over my shoulder with my middle finger.

"Exactly!" he guffawed.

What the hell even was that? Jeezus, had everyone in this place lost their minds merely because Kat and I had gotten married? Did all couples who worked together have to put up with this shit or was it just because this place was nerd-central?

Usually I was proud bearer of my Geek Card, but not today.

I found Kat splayed across the couch in the Pit, fast asleep on her stomach, her long hair, having been pulled out of its tight braid, was covering her face. Knowing she'd had a wretched night, I was hesitant to wake her up. Not that I'd slept much better than she had. The mere thought of her body lying that close to mine—in my bed—had kept me too distracted to sleep.

In the too-recent past, I'd perhaps entertained a fantasy or two of her lying there in that very spot. But not wearing that thin green cotton night gown that had only hinted at the curves underneath. No, in my headspace, she was in my bed, her creamy skin very naked against my dark blue sheets. That glorious, shiny red hair splayed out across my white pillow cases. And in every one of them, that very tempting, naked body was underneath mine. And that skin was every bit as soft as it looked.

God how much I'd wanted to touch her and see if reality had lived up to my fantasy.

Last night, when she'd sat facing me as I read on my tablet, she'd opened those lips and leaned forward—almost as if she would give me a goodnight kiss. It had been too much. Too close to where those fantasies always began. And my very physical reaction to that moment had caused me to turn over and flip off the light as fast as I could manage.

Because I knew that if I'd leaned in too, I'd be lost. With no way to pull back again.

To give in to the pull that was Kat would be allowing myself to be dragged into a vicious tidal whirlpool, risking doom. And I'd made that escape once, only because I'd passed out exhausted from the previous Scotch-aided escapade.

I wouldn't be so lucky again.

And for the next however-many nights that we would have to share a bed, it would be torture. Exquisite torture, yes, but torture nonetheless.

I predicted a lot of showers in my near future. At least I would come out of the ordeal very clean.

I sank down beside her on the couch, hoping that would jostle her, but she was soundly asleep. So I brushed the hair away from her face, slowly, delicately, as if revealing a long-hidden, delicate work of art under layers of debris. And her face was just that. Her glowing skin, the fine, slightly upturned nose, the thick brows matching her gleaming hair... those lips. Those kissable, delicious lips. *So tempting.*

Tucking those strands of hair behind her ear, I ran my thumb over her prominent, high cheekbone. She was so very pretty. *So dangerous.* I swallowed.

"Kat," I said in a small voice. "Katya, wake up."

Her eyelashes fluttered and then opened. Those blue eyes focused immediately as she squinted up at me, then proceeded to contort her body into a long, catlike stretch that pulled her t-shirt tight against her chest. Her curvy legs splaying out. And now I was doing more than just admiring her beauty... I was reacting to it in a very sexually frustrated way. Turning to hide the hard-on in my pants, I clenched my jaw, frustrated. Damn it. Even opening up this little bit was dangerous.

I stood. "You fell asleep," I snapped without looking at her again. "We're not paying you to snooze on the job."

She let out a sigh. "Sir, yessir." Then she pushed herself upright on the couch, blinking and stretching her neck from side to side. She'd really been out of it.

"Kyle came by and shouldn't be a jerk to you again. But I don't want you to meet with him without me present, just to make sure."

She blew out another long breath, then looked up at me with an unreadable expression. "Thank you."

"You're welcome. We'll go home at five." And I left.

Yeah, I was gruffer than I'd meant to be and it wasn't her fault I found her so difficult to resist. But I had a will of iron and I *would* resist her. I'd succeed where I'd failed before.

When we arrived home, the houseguest contingent were sitting on the doorstep sipping beers with a 24-pack sitting on the ground between them. Their jeans were rolled up on their calves and Mike wore a red Angels baseball cap that he must have picked up at a local souvenir shop.

"This American beer tastes like moose piss. I have no idea why we bought an entire two-four of it," Mike drawled as we approached.

"Like you know what moose piss tastes like," Kat's brother said.

"Couldn't even drink it at the beach, anyway. Such a crock."

Kat stiffened as we came to a stop, staring at her brother with hostile eyes.

"How was your day?" I asked neutrally when her silence started to make it a little awkward.

"We went to the beach. Nice beach. Something Spanish name like the beer. Corona de la..."

"Corona del Mar," Katya supplied. "And no, you can't drink alcohol on any beach here. Just like at home."

"Well, there are ways, at home." Mike said with a smug grin. "But we didn't dare over here. American cops are bonkers. Took all the fun out of the beach."

Another long awkward pause before Kat turned to her brother. "You shouldn't be drinking that at *all*."

"We're on vacation," Derek answered with a slight whine. "It's my first time in Cali. Cut us a break, sis?"

Ugh. Yeah, no one who lived here called it *Cali*. Ever. His smile looked a little defiant when he met his sister's gaze and took another pull from his bottle.

She folded her arms across her chest. "And Mum and Dad spent thousands on rehab for what, exactly?"

Derek blew out a long breath, crossing his eyes before rolling them but did not answer her. He and Mike shared a look and both bust up laughing, as if they'd predicted she'd say something like that and were mocking her.

I could feel my arms tense and I had to resist saying something I'd regret.

When Kat continued to lock him down with her condemning stare, he set down his empty bottle on the step and held up his hands in resignation. "All right, all right. That's the only one I've had. I promise to be good and not have anymore."

Mike tipped his bottle up with a laugh. "I will make no such promise."

They stood when I climbed past them to unlock the front door. I entered and held it open for them. Neither of them said another word to Kat as she stood there, stiff posture unchanged. Mike did make sure to grab the rest of the carton to carry inside with them, though.

"I'm starved. What's for dinner?"

With a long sigh of resignation, Kat bent to pick up the bottles they'd left behind. Then her shoulders sagged, as if she was wilting before my eyes. As if the tough girl had finally had enough and had to show her exhaustion. I quietly seethed with resentment.

Damn. This was going to be a long few days. I'd probably have to start guzzling something stronger than beer to get through it myself. Unfortunately, Scotch apparently made me do very inappropriate things with my wife, so that was out, too.

CHAPTER 14
KATYA

I MADE THEM EASY BOX SPAGHETTI THOUGH I WAS TEMPTED to just throw the cold pizza from last night at them again. All through it, I gritted my teeth and sifted through ways I could get them out of here. The past nearly two years hadn't changed Derek a bit. And Mike would always be his stupid asshole self even after the apocalypse.

Even as I bent over the boiling pot of pasta, tears prickled the backs of my eyes, the same old resentments rising up. Mum and Dad telling me they couldn't afford to get me the new console game I'd waited patiently for and had asked for only that one thing for Christmas. But I'd gotten some clothes, bought on sale, instead. The game cost too much money because Derek was at a new private outpatient rehab that cost a fortune. Or they had lawyer bills to cover or whatever it was that month.

Suddenly I was remembering the Sunday afternoon I'd come back from a weekend camping trip over on the Island near Victoria with my friends. I hadn't noticed that my car wasn't in its usual parking spot. But when I walked into the house, Mum had headed me off, wringing her hands. She'd tearfully told me that Derek had been in a car accident and had just been released from the hospital. But he was fine, wasn't that great?

Oh and by the way, the car I'd saved up months for and strictly forbid him from ever even going near? Yeah, they'd handed him the keys the second I was out of town and given him permission to take it out after he'd whined about it for hours. My poor little Ford Focus hadn't been as lucky as Derek. It hadn't survived being rammed into a telephone pole by my drunk and/or high brother.

Oh and surprise, surprise. The parents didn't have the money to fill in the gaps for the insurance check for the hosed car. So, I'd had to work even longer to buy a replacement. All while shlepping for months to my third shift job on Vancouver's less-than-optimum public transport system. Or bumming rides off friends when I could.

The little wads of mad money from babysitting and doing other odd jobs in high school.... I'd stashed them where I thought no one would find them. Derek always managed, though. And he took it—*all of it.*

And now here he was, having the audacity to guzzle beer on my porch and act entitled to everything I had and *earned.* Again.

I took a deep breath and let it go, vowing to find a local Al-Anon group. Those meetings had helped me get through some of the worst of it back when I was living it every day. I'd learned long ago that even if I loved him or hated him, Derek would never change.

Not when everyone around him allowed him to be the colossal selfish prick that he was.

And even now as I seethed at him, guilt also clutched at my throat for thinking the awful thoughts I was thinking about my own brother.

The kid with whom I'd shared so many adventures in our younger years. We'd been close. Learning how to skateboard together. Our first bike rides. I constantly waxed him at any video game we played. We were only eleven months apart in age. Practically twins, Mum liked to joke.

And though he was the older one, I'd always been the more responsible one. Throughout our lives, everyone had cut Derek all the slack.

And I couldn't help but feel bitter about that, especially now. Especially since his screw-ups had cost me my home, my long-time school friends, my hometown. My own goddamn country.

By the time that spaghetti was done I was boiling over with resentment like that pot of pasta.

"Are you okay?" Lucas said at my shoulder and I nearly jumped into orbit in surprise. "Sorry, didn't mean to startle you. I'm really not that stealthy."

I took a long breath and let it go. "No," I said shakily, aware that my heart was beating a thousand kilometres per minute. "Just deep in thought, I guess." Deep in seething, angry thought.

"I don't mean to offend you but... is your brother always like that toward you?"

I checked the pasta to see if it was *al dente* yet, but it was still too chewy. I turned back to Lucas. "If by 'like that' you mean entitled and a jerk, then yes. Pretty much."

He raised his brows and rubbed at his jaw thoughtfully. "Okay. Is there anything I can do to help ease the awkwardness?"

"Thanks for asking but it will be like this until they leave." He watched me work as I moved from the stove to the oven where the garlic bread was toasting.

"We should find out when that will be. I'd prefer sooner rather than later."

I raised my brows at him. "I warned you. Hopefully the sleeping arrangement isn't too heinous to live with."

When my eyes flicked up to catch his gaze, they locked and for long, thick moments there were no words. There was no sound aside from the boiling water and the sizzle of the sauce on the stove.

But so much was being said. I saw it, just for a brief minute, a flicker of that same spark that had ignited his eyes the night of his family's party. The night we'd kissed so intensely. The night he'd made me feel so amazing atop his piano.

That moment ranked right up there among the all-time highlights of my sex life so far. And to think it was one brief encounter—and a first, between us. I couldn't help but ache to know what we would be like together if we did more.

And goddamn it all, I wanted more. Apparently so did he.

But he was going to resist with every fiber of his being.

I could see that, too, in his eyes, in the distant and cold way he acted sometimes. When he held himself back from being kind and open. As if anything else would put him too close to danger.

I wasn't ashamed to admit that I craved that same danger he was avoiding. With a deep breath, I broke off the stare and quietly asked him to take the basket of garlic bread to the table.

Our guests ate my dinner with gusto, then predictably left the plates on the table. They were too distracted, apparently, having discovered Lucas's console system hooked up to a brand new 4K TV in the den and his considerable game library. Lucas, in his long-suffering, went in to get them set up on his system. Perhaps he figured that would keep them occupied and out of trouble.

He didn't know them like I did, though.

And me, I ended up clearing the table alone after having cooked everything. It gave me a chance to plot how I was going to get them out of here.

Call the fumigators?

Or an indoor painter?

Or a dog catcher to haul them off to the accommodations they truly deserved?

To his credit, Lucas came in on the tail end of me cleaning up. He finished for me, loading the dish washer and kindly thanking me for a delicious dinner. We joined the buttheads in the den for a time while they continued to game. They even had the nerve to ask Lucas for cheat codes, for which he refused to oblige them.

They both sucked hard at pretty much every game. When I told them I wanted to join in, Derek purposely started the game without adding me. But he handed the controller over to Lucas and stood up.

"I need to use the washroom and I'd like to chat with Kat for a minute if you don't mind."

I glanced over at Lucas, who gave me a look, as if asking if it was okay to *pwn* Mike into next week.

"Just wanted to catch up is all," Derek coaxed. I darted a look at him and then sighed. "Okay fine."

After he used the washroom, we met in the empty dining room where they had been sleeping. Lucas had hauled some big beanbag chairs in for their comfort. Derek sank into one of them while I grabbed a chair from the kitchen table.

If I had to storm out of here in a huff, I didn't want to have to fight my way up from a beanbag to do it. When I came back, he had his big duffle bag in his lap and was rifling through it. After a moment, he pulled out a taped-up box and held it out to me. I could see my name had been written across the top of it in black Sharpie in Mum's distinctive handwriting.

"Your Canadian junk food care package, as promised. Mum even sealed it up good so Mike and I wouldn't dig into it. Though if you don't mind sharing a toffee with me..."

I tore through the tape on the box and dug it out. My senses were assaulted with the smell of sweets—the light fluffy milk chocolate of the Aero bars most prevalent. It brought back memories of stopping at the corner store down the street to pick up milk or other groceries for dinner. I'd splurge and use the change to buy myself a little comfort chocolate. A girl had to treat herself to some quality chocolate bars every now and then.

I pulled out one of the toffee bars and gently tossed it to Derek, who promptly did the traditional thing and slammed the bar on the floor. The usual practice was to slam it on the wall but that was too far out of his reach. He then opened the inner wrapping, pulling out the bite-sized broken pieces.

He held the wrapper out to me and I shook my head. "I don't like how it sticks to my teeth." My hand sifted through the box again, past bags of chips and candies. No letter or card. I frowned. Just a box of junk food?

"Did you see? I stuck a Canucks bumper sticker in there for you, too. What's wrong?" Derek asked once he'd swallowed his bit of toffee. "Did we forget something?"

I darted a look up at him and shook my head. "Just thought Mum might leave a note or something."

Derek hesitated, his eyes on the box and then he darted a speculative look up at me. "She, uh, I think she wanted to. But...

she feels bad. She honestly doesn't know where she and Dad stand with you. You know, since you haven't reached out to us and they wanted to give you your space and independence. And..." he hesitated as if pondering something, then sifted through the wrapping to pull out another triangle of toffee and chew it slowly.

"And... what?" I prompted, lifting my brows.

"I think Mum feels a bit guilty about how everything was left. Because of the argument you two had. And you got so angry. Then she never really had a chance to work it out because... you were gone."

I blinked at Derek, watching him as he recounted this version of the events that had transpired my last weekend in my family home. He seemed so sad, both for himself and at conveying our mother's sadness, too. Did he blame himself? And why the hell was I feeling guilty? I was perfectly justified when all three of them were pointing fingers and staring me down and asking me to do something wrong, damn it.

I took a deep breath and let it go but didn't respond, sadness suddenly gnawing at the edges of my being. Did they all think I'd *wanted* to leave things that way? That I of all people would be the one who wrecked our family? Because... because... my hands on the box tightened.

"Mum did say she misses you a lot. Dad too, of course. You've always been his favorite."

How could I have been his favorite—or Mum's favorite— when they barely even knew I existed? I was that other kid, the one they didn't have to bother with because she didn't have all the problems. The one whose sixteenth birthday they'd completely forgotten about because Derek'd had to get his stomach pumped at the hospital.

My brother set aside the rest of the toffee, carefully laying it atop his air mattress and turned back to me, hands on his knees. "Haven't you ever thought about maybe coming back for a visit? We could clear things up. Stay in contact. It doesn't have to stay like this."

I folded my arms and as he spoke, I could feel my shoulders hunching protectively. My only response, though, was to vigorously shake my head.

"You haven't thought about how easy it could be? I mean, how much you could help me out—"

I tensed. Here it came, what he'd wanted all along. Why he'd driven all this way. It had to be. He was no great savior of our family. The only thing he was saving was his own skin.

"C'mon Kat, just this one thing and it all goes away for all of us. And you could do that. *You.* Don't you want Lucas to meet the rest of your family?"

I stood and set the box down on the chair. I didn't have to listen to this, and I wasn't going to. "Enough Derek," I ground out between gritted teeth. My blood pressure was starting to rocket and I could feel my heartbeat in the vein at my temple.

Derek popped off his beanbag faster than I could have thought possible and he caught my arm just above the elbow to stop me. "Come *on*, Kat. I'm begging you. I just need your help. Just this once."

Just this once. Shit. How many times had I heard *that* before? My hands balled into fists and I yanked my arm out of his grip. "Do that again and I'll knee your balls up through the roof of your mouth."

Derek's face flushed, and he opened his mouth to heatedly reply when the floor boards down the hall squeaked. Lucas emerged from the darkened part, toward the den.

Lucas looked from Derek to me and back again. "Is everything all right?"

I swallowed and Derek froze, darting me a look. "Uh, yeah," I said, my voice breathless. "He's trying to bum the Smarties off me and I told him to buy his own. He just gave me the junk food care package and now he wants to raid it."

Lucas was watching Derek the entire time I spoke, and I knew he didn't buy it. Lucas was too damn smart for that. And I wasn't nearly a good enough liar to pull it off anyway, which made this whole damn situation even more ironic.

Laughter bubbled up in my throat, borne of irony and angst and all the consequences that had sprung up in my life as a result of one decision. To run and leave my troubles behind me. Those troubles always found you, sooner or later. It didn't matter how fast or how far you ran.

I swallowed, then faked a ridiculous yawn, raising my still-tightened fists over my head. "Man, I'm spent. I think I'm going to turn in. You guys all have fun playing more games. Derek is the least lame at Mario Kart."

"Hey! I'm not *that* bad at gaming," he protested. Derek's voice sounded natural, as if nothing negative had just transpired between us.

Lucas said nothing, standing aside when Derek made his way into the den. I waved Lucas to follow him. "Go on. I'm fine."

Then I turned the other way and went to get a few items out of my room for the morning, moving them to Lucas's room again. Had to keep up appearances, after all.

I ignored the heavy weight in my belly from my conversation with Derek. I focused on what I needed for the morning instead, shoving my racing thoughts as far into the background as I could. I was not going to let Derek play me like he always did.

Damn. I needed to attend a meeting so I could get all this out. I vowed to Google for one nearby on my phone when I got back to the bedroom. Meanwhile, I had to decide on what to wear tonight and tomorrow. I definitely should not think about how much I really wanted Lucas to distract me with his hands and that heavenly mouth of his.

The little devil on my shoulder was telling me to grab a slinkier nightie to sleep in. Something silky with spaghetti straps and lace in the bodice. Would that qualify as a negligee that he'd specifically forbidden? Rules were meant to be broken, right? Maybe I'd get an orgasm out of it. Or two. I had a lot of tension that needed releasing.

I listened to the angel on my shoulder instead and grabbed the same frayed cotton nightie I'd worn the night before. It was loose and covered me from neckline to my knees. Certainly no one would find me tempting wearing that.

Despite my best efforts to beat Lucas back to his room, he was already in the washroom when I got there. Perhaps I'd taken longer than I thought to listen to the angel and devil argue with each other while I'd stood in front of my dresser, frozen with indecision.

I sat and waited for several minutes but generally, I was just so put out about Derek and his constant asks. It was exhausting to even think about. I just wanted to crawl into bed as soon as possible. But Lucas wouldn't be out for another ten or fifteen at least.

In frustration, I stripped right there in the middle of the bedroom, determined to curl onto the bed and collapse in exhaustion. But then I realized I really needed to moisturize. The dry weather here in California was often killer on my skin and it had been especially dry lately. So I grabbed the bottle of lotion and began to apply the cool creamy mixture to my elbows, arms and knees. Working it into my skin, I enjoyed the faint scent of coconut and jasmine that tickled my nose.

Apparently I didn't pay close enough attention to how long I was taking. Nor did I hear the shower turn off, because I was stark naked when the door to the washroom opened. The little devil had won out after all. I could hear her cheering from somewhere in the far corner of my mind.

Lucas halted in the doorway. I froze where I stood, full frontal pointed right at him.

His eyes swept me from head to toe and I didn't even have the decency to blush. I mean... I hadn't planned this but I sure as hell wasn't going to frantically try to cover up, scream and demand he close his eyes. Instead, I let them get their fill.

They were like flames, licking and burning me. Everywhere his gaze swept over my body, it singed me like a raging wildfire. His gaze was thirsty. Parched like the Mojave. And it turned me on like nothing else.

My nipples tightened, and he slowly averted his gaze—almost as if it physically hurt him to do so—but still said nothing.

I reached for my nightie and slipped it over my head, mumbling an apology.

He kept his eyes on the ground and stepped out of the doorway. "All yours," he said in a slightly strangled voice.

Was he angry? Did he think I'd planned it on purpose because I wasn't shrieking with faux modesty? I quickly washed my face, brushed my teeth and my hair and called it done.

The lights were out and Lucas was already in bed with his back turned to me. I gingerly slipped between those smooth sheets, taking care not to accidently brush against him. Though that devil, she sure was pushing for it, the mischievous minx.

Then I cleared my throat. "I'm sorry. I didn't plan for you to see me like that."

He said nothing for a moment, then rolled over and faced me. "Why would you think I'd suspect that?"

"I dunno. Maybe because I didn't act all scandalized and upset that you saw me?"

He paused. "And why didn't you?"

I shrugged. "It didn't feel weird for you to see me naked. It just felt natural. We are married, after all."

"But it isn't real."

"Mmm." My heart sped up. It was feeling more and more real every day, but I didn't dare tell him that. He'd freeze me out like he had the morning after the party. Lucas was a textbook case of emotionally unavailable male. Except when he wasn't. And when he wasn't, he was remarkably intriguing to me. Like a mystery I'd sacrifice sleep to solve.

"I could do with a little of the real stuff right now," I finally said in a low voice. In the dim light, our eyes met and held. Did I imagine his gaze intensifying, his tongue darting out to wet his lips?

I sure as hell didn't imagine it when he reached out to run his thumb lightly along my lower lip. It may have been an innocent gesture, but it strummed through my body like the most erotic touch I'd ever known. My lip trembled, and the thumb stopped moving. Then it pushed forward, into my mouth. My lips closed around his thumb and he let out a gruff growl, a low groan.

"We can't," he whispered.

My tongue caressed the pad of his thumb, snaking around it. Perhaps showing off a bit of the hidden skills I'd bragged about so easily days ago. I knew how to blow a guy's dick and his mind at the same time. And I was damn good at it.

And I owed him one, anyway. Perhaps tonight I'd get to call it square for that oral bliss he'd delivered on his piano.

His breathing sounded a bit more ragged now, more obviously turned on.

"We should," I said when he slowly retracted his thumb. Then, feeling bold and fully thirsty, I took his hand and brought it to my breast, pressing it hard against my tight, aching nipple.

The ragged breathing increased—some of it mine, to be fair— as his thumb rubbed against my nipple through the thin worn cotton of my nightie. I let out a light moan of my own and slowly, his head drew near mine.

Two milliseconds before our mouths would have connected, a loud crash and shattering noise sounded from the den. We froze, staring at each other in shock, our dubious house guests suddenly remembered through a haze of lust.

I popped out of bed in seconds and ran for the door, down the hall, following the sound of hilarious laughter and the familiar nauseatingly sweet smell of marijuana smoke.

Jesus Murphy. These assholes were lighting up in the middle of our house. Pushing through the door, I scowled. The guys were laughing and playing their game on the console, ignoring the mess they'd made with the smashed glass on the hardwood floor between them.

They looked up at me, then at each other, their laughter intensifying. Mike held game controls and Derek held a smoldering cigar in his hand. "Oh hey, sis, can you clean this up? It fell."

I looked at the mess of shattered glass and then back at him. "No, you can do it yourself after you put that out. Don't you fucking smoke pot in the middle of my house."

"It's legal here, right? We're in Cali. It's all legal."

"It's not legal in my house. I can't stand the reek. Put it out."

"Jeez, Kat, no need to get mean about it." But he made no move to snuff the rank thing out and Mike kept on playing his game as if I hadn't said a thing. I scooped up the half-filled glass of beer before he kicked that one over, too, then snatched the blunt out of Derek's hand and doused it in the beer.

"What the fuck!" He said, sitting up. "I wasn't finished with that."

"You are, now. Just because Mum and Dad let you do all the weed you want doesn't mean you have the right to do it here. This is *my* house. You don't get to stink it up with your fatties."

Lucas entered the room with a broom and dust tray but before he could bend to sweep it up, I held up a hand toward him. "Make them do it."

The two houseguests looked at each other and started laughing again. Then Mike turned and tried to peer around me to look at the screen. "You mind? You're blocking me."

Instead I went to the outlet and pulled out the plug to the console. "Game's over."

"Bitch!" Derek muttered.

Mike's expletive was worse, a fun word for a woman that started with c. That made two of those in two days. Lovely.

Lucas threw down the broom and tray with a loud clatter and both of the guys nearly shit their pants with shock, staring at him with widened eyes. "*No.* You don't ever, *ever* talk to her like that. Apologize."

"She's my sister." As if that gave him the right to abuse me. Derek sat up stiffly like he was entertaining the thought of confronting Lucas.

Lucas did not back down, eyes flashing with anger. "And I'm her husband. You're in my house. You don't ever call her that or you'll answer to me and you won't like what I do." He pointed to the broom and dust pan on the floor. "Get off your asses. Clean this shit up and fucking apologize to your sister. " He peered at Mike. "And it goes without saying, you too, unless you want to sleep in the street tonight. And don't ever call my wife that again."

I watched Lucas in wordless shock as he stood there, looming over my asshole brother with a tense posture. Lucas looked ready to back up his demands with something physical, if necessary.

And it did something to me. Emotion so strong and thick clogged in my throat so I couldn't even speak. Blinking, I hardly registered when Derek muttered an apology and began half-heartedly sweeping up his mess.

He did a crappy job of it, of course, but they soon cleared out of the den and slunk back to their air mattresses in the dining room. I bent to finish up but Lucas wordlessly took the broom out of my hand and did it himself.

I was so choked up I couldn't even thank him.

I got myself a glass of water from the kitchen and went back to the bedroom. Sipping at it, I sorted through this swirl of emotions overtaking me. Was I happy? Was I sad? Was I anxious?

I had no idea.

It was a unique and perfect storm of feelings swirling around like a massive tornado sweeping across the prairies.

I was standing like that, unmoving in the middle of the bedroom, when he re-entered and shut the door behind him. He stood beside me, looking into my face. "Hey, are you okay?"

And ridiculously—and as much a surprise to myself as anyone—I burst into tears. This would be more shocking to people who had known me my entire life, who knew that I never cried. Not when my pet turtle died at thirteen—though I had felt so sad and full of regret that I'd wanted to cry. Not when Derek had broken my Nintendo DS that I'd saved up birthday and holiday money forever to be able to buy.

No, my signature emotion was usually anger and my drive came from determination.

I didn't succumb, I overcame. And to me, crying was succumbing. It was weakness.

But right now, I was bawling my eyes out, much to my humiliation.

"Kat, hey." He pulled the cup from my hands and set it on his dresser. Then he put an arm around me and I immediately buried my face into his chest and proceeded to stain his pajamas with my tears and snot. There was nothing pretty about these tears. No it was damn hideous, this ugly cry—complete with hiccups, sobs and a guttural wail here and there. He stood stock still and weathered it all.

After a few minutes, I calmed down enough to notice things. The way he held me, a hand lightly rubbing my back. Back and forth, from one shoulder blade to the other without a word. *So patient.*

I started to sniffle, and that's when I knew I needed to go diving for the tissues. He anticipated me, pulling away to grab a box from the dresser. I buried my face in a wad of them, blowing out enough snot to float the goddamn *Titanic* in the process. Without a word, I went into the washroom and washed my face, checking myself out in the mirror above the sink.

My eyes were puffy and nose was swollen. I blew into the tissue a few more times so I could breathe more easily. Though I suspected that if I fell asleep soon, I'd be snoring like a hibernating grizzly. Not a good look to share a bed with my hot pretend husband.

When I returned to the room, I got my own glimpse of some unexpected skin as Lucas had pulled off his wet pajama top. Shirtless, he went to the dresser to pull out a replacement top. I stopped and watched him. He had a nice body—not rugged, but definitely athletic, defined and firm from years of rowing crew for high school and college. His arms were amazing, which made me think those weights sitting on the floor in his den weren't just there for decoration. And his chest... wide shoulders, firm pecs.

Oh. My. Yum.

Hair lightly dusted his chest and gave him a clearly defined happy trail across a flat stomach and straight down to his pajama bottoms. *Drool.* He noticed me as he pulled the shirt over his head, hesitating before putting his arms through. He'd caught me ogling him, and instead of being embarrassed and trying to hide it, I smiled at him.

Tit for tat. He'd gotten his eyeful earlier. Except he'd seen my tits, and I still hadn't seen his tat. As the brilliant white t-shirt slid across his stomach, he returned my smile with a small one of his own.

"Feel better now?" he asked.

I nodded.

We stood there in an awkward pause, apparently neither one sure what to say next. So I attempted to explain myself. "I'm sorry about that."

He shrugged. "You can't control your brother."

I shook my head. "No, I mean... that was more than an ugly-cry. It was a repulsive-cry. And you let me slime you."

He shrugged. "I guess you had a lot to get out."

I sighed and approached, coming to a halt when the bedframe pressed against my shins. We stood facing each other with only the bed between us. "Thank you."

He patted a shoulder. "It's a half decent shoulder to cry on."

I shook my head, still watching him with this wide-eyed sense of wonder I hadn't stopped feeling toward him since he'd chewed out my idiot brother on my behalf. "No, not that—I mean—thanks for that, too. But I meant the other... No one has ever stuck up for me like that before."

His eyebrows rose. "No one?"

I shook my head. "Nope."

"Not even your parents?"

I huffed a dry laugh. If he only knew. "Especially not them."

He frowned. "What, they just let him walk all over you like that?"

I rubbed my forehead with the heel of my hand. "They let him walk over all of us like that. Everyone was too afraid to set him straight because—I don't know—he can't take it or something. He got all the help and since I was the stable one, I got ignored."

His dark eyes searched my face, as if looking for something. He was so handsome it hurt. And since my eyeballs were already achy from the recent weep-fest, my gaze fell to the bed between us. I wanted his comforting arms around me again. It had felt so good for those short few minutes, to have a reminder that I wasn't so alone in the world. For those brief moments, anyway.

His face clouded, and he swallowed. "Your family sounds clueless."

I sank to the bed and sat on the very edge with a long sigh. "I guess you're no stranger to that."

"I, ah," he sank to his edge of the bed and ran fingers through his dark hair. "I overheard a bit of your conversation with your brother. I didn't mean to eavesdrop."

I sighed. "It's okay. I figured you had." My eyes fixed on the far wall because I was too embarrassed to look at him.

"Are you—are you in some kind of trouble?"

I blinked, frowning, then turned to him. He must have heard more than I though. "I'm not sure, actually."

"Is that what the lawyer letters are about?"

My mouth thinned. "I honestly don't know. I've been shredding them without reading them."

He frowned, his face darkening. "How can I help you?"

My eyes closed for a beat and then opened and I suddenly felt that wave of defeat wash over me again. "You've already helped me. Probably more than I deserved."

And with that, I flopped back on the bed and stared up at the ceiling, emotion rising in my throat again. Shockingly, tears threatened, poking little spears into the back of my eyeballs and I blinked furiously.

Lucas watched me, then lay on his side and reached a hand out to cup my shoulder. "Hey, hey. I'll be the judge of what you deserve, got it? We'll figure this out."

Without even thinking about what I was doing, I reached up and curled my hand around his. Fingers intertwined immediately. Then Lucas reached up with his free hand to flip out the light.

Once the light was out, I didn't hesitate another second. I couldn't. I rolled to him throwing my arm over him in an awkward sideways-lying-down hug. Slowly he freed his arm and lay it across my back, patting me reassuringly again.

Then he kissed my hair. I closed my eyes. *This.* This felt so good.

And that was it. I was lost with that one simple gesture as the cherry on top of his awesome caring-man sundae. My head tilted up and seconds later, my mouth was on his and we were lip-locked in one of the furiously hottest kisses I had ever participated in. Our mouths fused in a searing union, picking up right where we'd left off before we'd been so rudely interrupted.

Thank goodness. I thought I was going to be denied a hot make-out and hopefully more. His mouth moved over mine, possessing my lips with each press of his lips, each touch of his tongue to mine. And as it continued, he took more and more control, wresting it from me like the gentle repossession of an inappropriate object from a child's grip.

His mouth was sure, firm but gentle. Passionate, hot, and yet there was something else behind it—a near-loss of control. Even now as massive heat sparked between us, I could tell that he was holding back.

And the first thing I wanted to know was, if *this* was holding back, then what happened when this man let loose? And how in the hell could I get him to do that—and *soon*?

Because... wow.

He was burning me up now, just from kissing me. How much hotter could it get? Every touch of his lips zinged down crackling nerve-endings to pool in my core in a molten swirl of arousal.

My equilibrium turned on itself, the world going askew, when his hand slid down my upper arm and covered my breast, palming it expertly. Then his fingers zeroed in on my nipple, kneading it mercilessly. I arched my back and swallowed a shocked squeak.

In minutes he'd be in command of everything—my body, my pleasure, all of it. And I was ready to tender my most willing surrender. As a matter of fact, I'd be willing to wave my panties as a white flag—if I were wearing any, that was.

He seemed to remember that fact as his hand moved on, slipping past my waist to my thigh, then over my ass in a very thorough caress. With a growl from deep in his throat, he plunged his tongue in deep and moved that hand to catch the hem of my nightshirt.

Oh god, *yes*. Take command, my general. I whimpered against his lips and the pressure of his kiss intensified, his tongue tasting me deeply. It reminded me of the things he'd done to me the night on his piano with that very talented tongue. The memory of that brought a warm gush of arousal at the juncture of my thighs. If he pushed me on my back this moment and climbed on top, I'd be ready for him without a second's further preparation.

I was *so* ready for sex. For *him*, especially.

It was high time we made this marriage a real one. At least this one part of it, anyway. His hand traveled up my thigh with certain determination. Meanwhile, I decided he deserved a studied counterattack. My hand dropped from his hair to travel determinedly across his chest, his flat, hard stomach to rest on the object of my never-ending curiosity.

I'd rarely felt as much satisfaction as I did when Lucas quickly sucked in a sharp gulp of air in response to my touch. I gripped him through the thin cotton bottoms of his pjs finally becoming acquainted, after over six months of marriage, with my husband's large cock.

And holy shit, I was not disappointed.

He was long and girthy and fully rigid. More gratification bloomed, warming in the fact that my body, my kisses and my touch had evoked this response in him. Yeah, he'd gotten me wet in seconds, but I'd made him granite-hard in just as short a time.

Aside from a slight pause when I'd initially touched him, he hadn't stopped on his mission. He slid his hand up my leg, under my night shirt until it rested on my hip. Skin on skin, blistering heat mingled with sticky sweat. I arched my back again, pressing my breasts against his hard chest. If I didn't get release soon, I might explode from the pressure building inside me. Everywhere—behind my nipples, deep in my belly, knotting tightly in my core. The entirety of it screamed for release.

Fuck it. I wanted skin under my palms, too. My hand slipped into the waist of his pajamas, eased into his boxers and claimed my prize immediately. His hips jutted forward, one leg pushing between mine. His hip overlapped mine as he pressed me onto my back. I didn't let go of him. Instead, my hand slid up and down that soft skin, fingers exploring the rigid, smooth geography of his member.

The size of him excited me, I wasn't going to lie. I'd suspected he might be packing a substantial weapon but had no way of knowing until now. And yeah, they said that size didn't matter and yadda yadda yadda. But *damn*, this was... impressive. It was always the quiet, curmudgeonly ones who seemed full of the biggest surprises. And Lucas's *surprise* was indeed huge and the better for exploring.

His breathing was quick and hot, his heartbeat under my lips, where they rested on his throat, felt like it might burst through his veins. It seemed as if, for a moment, the general was going to cede his command to me.

But that was only for a moment.

Then his hand slid to rest between my thighs, his mouth dropped to suck my nipple through the nightie and he was in control again. My back arched again under these newer, more intense stimuli, then I tore at the elastic on my neckline, pulling down the material to bare my chest to him. With a gruff groan, he held the front of my shirt down and devoured my nipple, sucking it ferociously into his mouth.

In his excitement, however, he had rolled onto me, inhibiting my ability to keep my grip on him, which was frustrating. With my free hand, I shoved against his shoulder, forcing him back onto his side so I could continue my exploration.

I wasn't going to let this be another one-sided experience.

Our mouths were finding each other again, over and over in hot, wet, tongue-assisted kisses between cheeks and neck and eyelids and collarbone kisses. We were leaving no ground between us uncovered.

It was a veritable war zone, complete with tiny explosions of pleasure. His fingers were slipping inside me, now, nudging my legs apart to make room. Meanwhile, I began to stroke him in earnest. His breath was ragged, urgent and mine rose to match it.

"I'm going to make you come again," he declared.

"I'm going to make you come, too," came my riposte.

"You're coming first, Kat." To back up his words, his fingers did something inside me, twisted or curled or something. There, he reached a spot that few men—at least in my experience—knew about. *Holy shit.*

My entire body went stiff with new, more intense waves of pleasure. Damn he was right. I was going to come first—and very *very* soon. Then his thumb got involved, flicking against my clit to work in concert with his other fingers—nimble fingers kept strong and skillful from playing the piano.

They played me equally as well.

I saw burning meteors streaking across the black skies behind my closed eyelids. My breathing stopped just before wave after wave of satisfied release crashed, a climax every bit as intense as the one he'd evoked with his mouth the other night.

Um. What the fuck...

He hadn't even fucked me yet and yet had given me two of the best O's I'd ever experienced. I may have rolled onto my back and forgotten about everything, drowning in an afterglow almost as powerful as the orgasm itself. I would have done it, had my hand not been so tightly clamped around his cock. It was almost as if I were holding on for dear life—a fact that reminded me of my promise to him.

I wanted to make him come. So instead of rolling back, I leaned forward and caught his mouth with mine, then moved my lips across his whisker-rough cheek to whisper in his ear. "Now you're going to come, Lucas. Come inside me."

His breathing stuttered as if the suggestion hadn't even occurred to him. As if he'd already figured there would be no penetrative sex between us. I was about to disillusion him of that assumption right now.

"Please, Lucas, I want you inside me."

"No," he said gruffly as if it pained him to say it. He blew out a rough breath. "We can't."

I sucked his earlobe into my mouth, gathering ammunition for my own assault. "We can. We *should*. I can't wait to feel this inside me." I squeezed him to leave no doubt about what I meant.

"Fuck," he said gruffly, then put his hand over mine, showing me how to move it, how he liked it. "Like this, Kat."

"But—"

"No. We are not fucking tonight." His voice was tight and urgent. His tone—unmistakably final.

I blew out a breath in frustration and he drew back, searching for my gaze in the dim light. "Make me come like this," he said in that same voice that brooked no argument. Like a commanding general's order.

So my hand moved, stroking his cock softly, slowly, deliberately attempting to drive him to madness. His breath was ragged against my neck, his hand getting its fill of exploring my chest.

But when I wouldn't vary my stroke, he grew desperate, grinding against my hip. "Faster," he muttered.

After another half second of protest, I complied, quickening my stroke, enjoying the feel of his cock swelling even larger in my hand as he neared his own release.

But that wasn't enough for him. In the last few seconds before climax, he pushed me onto my back, set himself between my legs and ground himself against me, frenzied and raw. As he stiffened and held his breath, he found his own release, spilling his hot semen onto my nightshirt.

Welp, I guess I was sleeping naked tonight. And if that didn't lead to more sex, I'd be utterly shocked.

Almost immediately, Lucas rose from the bed and grabbed washcloths from the washroom for us to clean up with. Without caring what he'd see, I pulled off the nightshirt. "Not a bright move if you didn't want to see me naked again," I said lightly with a wicked smile. The little devil on my shoulder would have heartily approved had she not already gone to bed for the night.

Without looking at me, Lucas moved to his dresser, pulled out another pair of pajama pants and a big t-shirt, which he tossed toward me. Then he disappeared into the washroom.

I sighed, anticipating more of the post-sexual emotionally unavailable freeze-out he'd shown me before.

When he returned, it wasn't exactly like that. More like gentle awkwardness. I looked up at him before he flipped off the light, weariness clear in his eyes.

"Why couldn't we—?" I asked.

"Can we discuss it tomorrow? When I'm not so exhausted."

"Of—of course. Yeah," I murmured, still perplexed.

The light flicked off, and he was asleep in minutes. Ugh. Not exactly the roll-over and fall asleep maneuver of males from ages past but close enough. I stared up at the ceiling, still basking in my own pleasant rush of dopamine but already craving more.

We weren't even after all. I still owed him head. Maybe tomorrow.... And with a thrill of fresh arousal, I began to fantasize about how it might come about—and how it would be.

It wasn't conducive to sleep, and I ended up not being able to get to the land of nod for hours. But it was a pleasant way to suffer from insomnia nevertheless.

CHAPTER 15
LUCAS

M Y EYES CRACKED OPEN TWENTY MINUTES BEFORE the alarm went off and instead of springing out of bed and heading to the bathroom, I stared at her lovely face instead. I never got bored looking at her and, like this, I could stare my fill, no questions asked. But after a few minutes, I had to fight the urge to smooth that rust-colored hair back from her face. I wanted to touch that soft cheek, run my thumb over those full, rosy lips.

Wow, she was stunning... even with bed hair and no makeup, her long cinnamon lashes lying peacefully against her pale cheeks. Her soft breathing. And the way she'd touched me last night, something stirred, replacing those tender feelings.

Slick, hot arousal. I wanted her again. Well, actually—I amended the thought—I wanted her *still*. Last night's release had been a pale shadow of what I'd known it could have been if I'd given in to her request, if I'd come inside her. The mere thought of it crackled over me with an electric energy. The usual urges that came with morning wood knotted into something tighter, more demanding, even painful. I wanted to roll her gently on her back, part her legs and taste her again. Then I wanted to quench my thirst deep inside of her heat, riding those silky soft thighs to release.

Damn... an extra-long shower again this morning might do the trick. Rubbing one out might take the edge off, but I needed this woman out of my bed ASAP or I'd most definitely give in to temptation tonight.

And I couldn't. We couldn't. Right now she was beholden to me for this favor I'd granted. I couldn't let this happen between us because the power balance was uneven. She was not paying for my cooperation with her body.

But I was not a goddamn saint for chrissakes. I could only say no for so long.

When I got out of the shower, I remembered belatedly that in my distraction, I'd neglected to grab my clothes for the day. I usually showered at night and really had had no need of a shower again. It had been an impulse decision once I was already in the bathroom. I'd jumped into the shower in the vain hope that it would help me overcome this. It was either that or stay in bed and initiate what would certainly be some smoking hot morning sex.

With a towel wrapped around my waist, I crept back into the bedroom and glanced at the clock. She usually woke up around this time of the morning but I'd turned off my alarm early. I'd wake her up after I got dressed, so I dropped my towel and began pulling clothes out of my dresser.

"Mmm. Nice view," she murmured from the bed from which she had a full view of my bare ass. I hurriedly pulled on my boxers before turning around.

"Didn't realize there was a full moon out this morning, did you?" I snorted.

She smiled, doing a full body stretch that gave her movement an almost feline-like quality. One thousand percent sexy.

"Come here," she said.

I swallowed. I was not going anywhere near her when I was only partially dressed and she was laid out like that.

"Can we talk for a minute? Or should I get up and go over to the washroom naked in order to get your attention?"

I took a deep breath, stepped into my jeans and pulled them on, then walked over to the bed. She patted my side, as if she wanted me to sit down. Meanwhile, she struggled to sit up, resting on her elbows. Her shirt—*my shirt*—was huge on her and the neckline dipped down to reveal a large slice of her creamy breast, just above the nipple. She seemed unaware, and I fought to keep my eyes above her neckline.

"What's up?" I asked, as if I didn't know.

"Can we talk about last night?"

I glanced at the clock. "We don't have a lot of time."

"It won't take long. I just wanted to know—"

"Why we didn't go all the way last night?"

She laughed. "Jeez, you make it sound like we're still sixteen. But yeah. I mean, I'm not going to be coy and say it was because you didn't want me. Because I know you did."

I bit the inside of my lip to keep from smiling. So like Kat. As honest as ever. No pretensions, no games. No manipulations. No fishing for a compliment though she was goddamn-well worthy of nearly all of them.

"I just didn't think it was wise to jump into something like that without..."

"... discussing it first?" She nodded, her eyes widening with obvious hope. "Hence my desire to have a discussion about it *now*."

I swallowed. "I've jumped into things in the past and they were the biggest mistakes of my life. I don't jump anymore."

She frowned slightly and then nodded. "Okay. So what should we discuss? I'm on birth control and I'm clean. I've been checked since my last—since last time."

Last time. Huh. A streak of jealousy sliced through me to think of some other guy having what I'd denied myself last night. What I wanted more and more with each passing day and yet wouldn't allow myself to have.

"Uh, huh. It's not really that I wanted to discuss, though that is important. I'm also clean and it's been a while."

She blinked as if surprised.

I cleared my throat. "But there's more. I don't like—I don't think we should start anything physical."

Her face clouded. "Well, newsflash. We already did do physical stuff. And you started it."

I ran a hand through my hair, gritting my teeth so that my jaw muscles bulged. "I mean, we shouldn't take it any further."

"Because...?"

"Because we work together..."

"But we're married."

I shook my head. "But soon-to-be divorced, remember? And trust me, working together will be more than just awkward if we've had a physical relationship and then ended it."

Her eyebrows twitched together. "Why worry about awkward? I've never worried about that. Who gives a shit?"

"I don't really care what other people think." I shrugged. "I'm talking about our feelings, our..." I cleared my throat, trying to find the words.

Her eyes narrowed. "Our own emotions? You think I'm going to get emotionally involved?"

I flicked a glance at her. It wasn't just her I was worried about, but I had no problem allowing her to believe just that.

"Also I don't want you to think I expect sex as a payment for doing this whole marriage thing for you."

Her face clouded, and she pushed herself up to a full sitting position. "Uh, why on earth would I think that?"

I shrugged. "Because it's a power imbalance. Like if I was your boss..."

"If you were my boss, I'd have to kick your ass on a daily basis. But this whole *payment* thing... it assumes that I don't like or want sex and would only be doing it for you."

I froze. I guess she was right about that...

She leaned toward me and I enjoyed a full view of her mouth-watering cleavage. Reluctantly, I tore my eyes away, frustrated at my own body and my constant reaction to her. I had zero control where she was concerned. *And,* I'd just had two orgasms in the past ten hours that hadn't been enough to get my mind off how much I wanted her. I was still as hungry as an apex predator during migration season.

"Newsflash. Girls like sex, too. Some of us love it, as a matter of fact."

Oh gawd. That was about the last thing I needed to hear. Blinking, I ran a hand through my hair. It felt a lot shakier than before just remembering what she'd sounded like when she'd climaxed. "Yeah, that was kind of a stupid thing for me to say."

She shook her head. "Aren't you at least a little curious about how we'd be together?"

Curious? No. More like obsessed. I pressed my lips together. "I just think there's too much potential for problems."

"We have an agreed-upon expiration date, right? No harm, no foul." Her eyes dropped to my lips and she slowly licked hers with that pink devil tongue of hers. That tongue that had wreaked havoc on my senses the previous night. The one that had made me want to throw caution to the wind.

But every time, *every damn time,* I'd ever done that in the past, it had ended up in disaster. And trying to extricate myself from said disasters always constricted the trap. It hadn't been that long ago that I'd had to completely jettison my old life to gain freedom.

I wasn't prepared to do it again. Because this time, I had too much to lose. Too much that I cared about.

And with Kat, I knew—I just knew—that it would be worse. She'd cover me and blow through my life like a flash fire, here and gone, bringing complete destruction wherever she touched. Without even intentionally setting out to do so or even being aware of having done it in the aftermath.

I took a deep breath. "I think it's best if we go slow, no matter what we decide."

Her mouth curved—almost seductively, I thought. "Six months of marriage isn't slow enough for you?"

It's not real, I almost said. I didn't want to keep repeating it to her. She knew it damn well herself. *It's not real,* was going to have to become my goddamn mantra over the next little while, while we lived together, while we were a married couple.

It's not real. *Not real.*

"I need to think about it. About a lot of things." I shifted where I sat to avoid the view down her shirt. "In the meantime,

I wanted to ask if you would let me handle this situation with your brother and his pothead buddy."

Her brows knit. "Handle it, how? Challenge them to a duel or something?"

"No, I just mean... getting them out of here and avoiding any more crap like last night. It's seriously pissing me off how they treat you."

Her features smoothed and those big blue eyes got even bigger as she studied me. She said nothing for a while, as if pondering how to respond. Then she silently nodded. "Yeah, yeah I'd like that. Please."

I got up, grabbed my shirt and pulled it on. "Time to get going. Think we'll have to grab breakfast in the cafeteria at work."

"Barf," she said, but slipped out of bed. I left the room shortly thereafter to get my things together—and avoid another glimpse of that gorgeous naked body. I must be stark raving mad to try to avoid the sight of all that smooth, creamy skin. The curves of her hips, the swell of her gorgeous, perky tits. The pale pink color of her nipples. The thin strip of proof that she was a natural redhead where those luscious thighs met.

Remembering it made me hard yet again. I'd just rubbed one out less than an hour before. It was like I was eighteen with all systems set on perma-horny all over again.

I also went to wake up the deadbeat guests and get them roused and ready. To say they were reluctant was an understatement. I ended up blaring Queen on my speakers in the front room. They finally stirred about halfway through *Bohemian Rhapsody*.

"What the hell is a Scaramouche, anyway?" I heard Mike ask Derek as they stumbled toward the guest bathroom.

Soon Kat joined me, her gorgeous copper-colored hair brushed out and gleaming over her army-green hoodie. She twitched her head, and I saw them—the hickeys I'd left on her neck the night before.

Damn it. It turned me on like little else had—besides her hands on me, of course. Those small mementoes of my mouth tasting her neck, my hands all over her round, soft breasts. The way she'd moved against me, the way she sounded when she came to climax.

Ugh. This hard-on was never going away, apparently. She should come with that warning label on the Viagra bottles about causing erections lasting more than four hours. Looked like I was suffering from perpetual wood for the foreseeable future.

Desperate for a way to get her out from under my roof and fast, my mind raced. The first step was getting her back into the guest room. And I couldn't do that until her unwanted guests were on their way.

"Guys," I said when they were gathering up their things for the day. I reached for my wallet and pulled out a couple bills. "We talked it over and we think it might be best if you two stay at a nearby hotel." I handed them a paper I'd just printed out. "Here are five places that have good ratings and are close." I held out the bills to them. "And something to help you with the cost of the room."

The two guys looked at each other and when Derek opened his mouth to protest, I held up a hand. "No, you're going. I'm not having a repeat of what happened last night. And I don't care for how you speak to my wife. Let's keep things, cool, yeah? We'll spend time with you after work and on the weekend. We can take you out to Hollywood or to Disneyland."

Kat entered the room with her bag slung over her shoulder on the tail end of my pitch. The look Derek gave her was one of pure hurt. "It's okay with you that your husband's tossing us out?"

She paused as she locked gazed with him and I saw something in her eyes, as if she were instinctually responding to Derek's hurt feelings. Then she shook her head, as if snapping herself out of something. "Last night was too much. When you pulled out the weed, you made the decision that you weren't appropriate guests to stay here."

He took the paper but refused the money, saying he had plenty. Kat didn't push it so I tucked it back into my wallet. "I'll make us some dinner tonight. Give me your number and I'll let you know when we'll be home."

Mike rolled his eyes and Derek gave a one-shouldered shrug. "Let us treat you, to make up for it. If this town has half-decent Chinese, I'll bring your favorite. Cashew chicken." He threw a tremulous smile at his sister as she held out her hand for his phone to program her number into it. I could sense it from here, her wavering.

But there was no way in hell I was allowing them back to stay so they could mistreat her as they had the night before. Otherwise I'd be putting him in a hospital for whatever shitty thing he'd inevitably do or say to his sister. This was all so weird. Kat, who took zero crap from any of the dickheads we worked with seemed to really have a soft spot for this deadbeat of a brother of hers.

The guys proceeded to gather up their things with a bit of muttering—mostly coming from Mike. Derek seemed more resigned to his fate. But he gave Kat a hug on the way out. "See you soon, sis."

Then he left, head drooping as he watched the ground dejectedly on the way out to the car. Kat watched him with unreadable blue eyes and a complex expression on her face. As if she had fifteen things racing through her thoughts at once.

I loaded the dog and an unusually quiet Kat into the car and, aside from Max's constant panting and some road noise, the inside of the car was silent. We made our way down the broad boulevards of Irvine, all marked by artful dividers and carefully placed trees. Irvine was the quintessential planned community. Many lamented its lack of character but I liked the order that it presented. A clean, quiet city.

Kat hadn't moved, one hand clenched into a fist, the other holding a phone that she scrolled through with her thumb.

"What's up?" I finally broke the silence.

She took a deep breath in and out. "I'm searching for a local chapter meeting."

I raised my brow. "Of...? Exasperating Red-haired Expat Canadians?"

She threw me side-eye, then hesitated, lowering her phone. "Al-Anon."

I blinked. "Isn't that for addicts?" Was there something she wasn't telling me? Maybe she'd had similar struggles as her brother?

"That's Alcoholics Anonymous—or Narcotics Anonymous, or various other organizations depending on the addiction. Al-Anon, Nar-Anon, etc. is for family members and friends of addicts."

I blinked but didn't look at her. "Oh."

"I really think a meeting would do me some good right now."
I raised my brow. "You used to go a lot? When you lived in Canada?"

She shrugged. "Yeah for a while. When I started college. I'd never heard of it and there was a chapter at my college campus. I started going and talking to others. It helped me feel less alone."

I nodded. "I take it your parents never went."

"My dad went to one meeting, declared it a bunch of bullshit and never went back. Mum refused altogether. They hate anything that might even remotely resemble tough love. They prefer the mollycoddling approach because *that* has worked so goddamn well with him." Her voice was sharp and bitter—something I'd rarely ever heard.

I thought about their conversation that I'd overheard the night before, the way he'd moved up to her, grabbed onto her and was begging her to do something for him. *Just this one thing*, he'd said. *You could really help me out.*

I swallowed and decided to take the delicate approach to digging deeper into the subject she'd lightly brushed aside the night before. "Derek seems to really want you to go back to Canada. Is everything okay with your parents?"

She darted me a look before beginning to fiddle with her phone again. "I guess they're fine. He didn't tell me much."

We drove another block before the next question formed in my mind and I'd figured out how to reword it in an unthreatening manner. "Is there anything I should know? For example, why you left Canada?"

She turned her head and looked at me, then spoke in a flat voice. "I left because Mia was sick. My best friend needed me."

I'd heard about that before so it wasn't a surprise that she'd repeat it. "Is that the entire reason?"

She blinked and gripped her phone tight. "Why are you asking me all this?"

"Because I need to know. It's occurred to you that immigration does a background check on you with your home country, right? If there's anything..."

She frowned. "I got the background check and submitted it. I'm clear. I'm not some secret felon if that's what you're asking."

I rolled my eyes as I hit the blinker to turn into the parking lot of Draco. Max barked excitedly. He adored coming to work with me because that meant he got spoiled.

"I know you're not a felon. I just—I just want to say I'm here for you if you want to talk. About your brother or anything else."

She smiled faintly. "Thanks."

I frowned, mulling over the past two days as I got out of the car, grabbed my bag and the dog leash and locked up. I watched Kat's bright hair swing across her back as I followed her into the main entry of the building.

There was something up and weird going on with her family—and not just the shitty behavior I'd seen Derek show his sister. There was something about the parents. It seemed like Derek ruled the roost there, including the parents. That must have been shit to grow up with.

Of course, who was I to talk? My parents had been so busy wrapped up in their own lives and image. And they were obsessed with how their two children fit like accessories into that overall image. I doubted they'd ever seen us as real people at all.

Yeah, the trap I'd wiggled myself out of while practically having to chew my own arm off to get free had not started with the doomed marriage to Claire. My feet had been clamped inside those steel jaws long before that.

That same old oppressive gloom weighed down on me just to think about it and I had to remind myself that those things were in the past. Hopefully, soon, the distant past.

At lunch, Warren approached me with a slap on the back. "You musta tried another one on her last night. I saw her neck, bruh. Way to go." He held out his fist for me to bump. I just looked at it, gave him a grouchy sneer and he retracted it. "Tap the Maple, eh? Man, to be able to have sex with a hot girl whenever you want. It must be great to be married."

Yeah, whenever I want. *Sure.* 'Cause *that's* what marriage was all about.

"Go back to your bugs, Warren," I growled, "before I move up your deadlines."

I ran into Kat only a few times. She was weird today, distant and a little distracted. And she'd been keeping her distance.

I couldn't tell whether it was because of our talk this morning, because of what her brother had said to her or because of my questions about it. Part of me was determined to get the story behind what was going on there. But if I dug deep into her life, and she into mine, it might make it all the more difficult to pull things apart again.

As I reminded myself practically daily, this marriage had an expiration date on it. Better to keep my distance and emerge unscathed. After all, I knew I could do that well—be emotionally distant. It might make for a shitty husband—and I knew I had been one the first time around—but hopefully it would make us great exes.

I found an empty conference room to spread out my concept notes and rudimentary sketches on the VR game and worked there for an hour or so. Kat slid in to find me at around five. She glanced at the table, then at me, tucking a long strand of that gorgeous hair behind her ear. "Uh, hey. So you're still working?"

"Did you hear from your brother? Did he still want to get together for dinner?"

She shook her head. "I haven't heard and to be honest, even though he talked about getting Chinese, he's usually a lot of talk. If he doesn't text me first, I'll touch base with him later tonight about the weekend."

She moved deeper into the room as something on the table caught her eye. She picked up one of the sheets covered with my scrawl, squinting as she tried to read it.

"Is this the thing you're working on to present to the officers? For the new position?"

I cleared my throat, suddenly wishing I could yank the notes away from her. Weirdly self-conscious without realizing why. Probably because, when it came to all matters gaming, I highly valued her opinion, and this concept was far from developed enough for me to ask for feedback from her.

Kat leaned her curvy hip against the table as she pondered the notes, then without a word, laid a sheet down while she picked up another. I watched her as those blue eyes slid down the page and she chewed her thumbnail absently. She was dazzling, even when she made no effort to be...

"Hmm," she mumbled, snatching up another sheet. "I see what you're aiming for here. A cross between a Battle Royale first-person shooter and a sandbox game so you can design your own hideout fort. Interesting."

I sat back and flicked the pencil in my hand with irritation. "You hate it."

She straightened, startled. "Nooo. I wouldn't say that. I just think it could be more... original. More on brand with Draco?"

I frowned at her. "But that's just the point. I'm showing how Draco can expand beyond its original concept of Dragon Epoch."

She shrugged. "Sure but..."

"But?"

She locked gazes with me, then leaned forward, that soft hair brushing across my face. I'd wound it in my hands the night before while I'd kissed her, touched her and made her moan. It had been so hot when she'd touched and rubbed my dick, as if she'd done it a hundred times before. Her concern that I get mine after I'd given her hers was actually rather sweet.

And very much appreciated.

She pointed to one of my sheets of paper. "Why not make it a medieval shooter and sniper game? There is no Player vs. Player feature in Dragon Epoch so why not give the people a chance to fight each other in this game instead? The forts they build can be the old medieval type. There could be a phase for gathering resources, like in Minecraft. And building. And designing terrain. The game could start on common ground and then branch out to player-designed areas."

"And what exactly are they shooting if they don't have modern assault rifles?"

"Oh that's easy. The usual fantasy fare—bow and arrow, crossbows, magical wands and staves. You can shoot out magic missiles, meteor showers, fireballs or even some steampunk version of an early hand grenade. Or just anything—spears, throwing stars, boomerangs. Whatever."

I sat up and stared at her for a moment. Then grabbed the nearest empty sheet of paper and started writing that down. It was damn brilliant. She started talking again. "You could even tie it into Dragon Epoch. Let people take things they've built or won into the main game as incentive after they've earned a certain amount of points or kills or whatever. And they could somehow integrate their creation back into the Dragon Epoch game, if they want."

She kept talking, and I kept taking notes.

"And you know, for the next phase, you could try to go with a mobile app. Like our own version of Pokemon Go. People could walk around their neighborhoods and find treasure or weapons or building materials to integrate into the game. Keep the flavor a medieval fantasy so it's all seamless and builds on the other games. You can reuse the lore from Dragon Epoch that way, too. Have intertwining stories and crossover quests. That way it encourages our existing player base to branch out to other Draco products instead of being something completely new like a contemporary shoot 'em up or something futuristic. Besides, there're already tons of those. You don't want to compete with them."

I nodded, scribbled, nodded some more. She quietly watched me. "Or you can just completely toss this idea. I won't be offended."

"Why would I do that? It's a good idea."

She flipped her hair back over her shoulder, a waft of stunning coconut smell followed the action. "Well your idea was good to begin with, I was just building on it."

I said nothing, just continued taking notes.

I felt her gaze on my face. "You're really stressed out about this, aren't you?"

I flicked my gaze up at her while continuing to write. "I really want the job, Kat."

She nodded. "I know you do. Believe in yourself a little. You have a very good shot at it."

I blew out a breath.

She grinned. "Well at least you have a trust fund to fall back on if you don't get it." She made a face as if she meant to duck or hide from my reaction to her tease.

I narrowed my eyes and shook my head. "You're lucky I know you're joking."

She bit her lip. "I am a bit curious. How much is that bad boy worth, anyway?"

I stared at her sidelong. "You honestly don't want to know. I spend very little of my time thinking about it anymore."

She sat down on the table, facing me, swinging her free leg while the other braced on the ground. "Why is that?"

"My father has relied entirely on his inherited fortune to make his way in life. I'm a better man than he is. And I sure as hell don't need that inheritance to succeed."

She folded her arms across her chest and studied me with a tilted head. "So you're proving yourself."

I laughed. "I've got nothing to prove to him. He's pretty disgusted with the choice I made to leave that life behind and get my hands dirty working for someone else."

She shook her head, smiling good naturedly. "No, not proving yourself to him. But you've got a lot to prove to yourself."

I blinked, returning her speculative stare. "Maybe."

"I've got a good feeling about this. I think you're in. And no, not because I'm Mia's friend either. It's just a feeling."

"Well I need more than a feeling to feel better about all this waiting."

"Just do your best to convey your vision, because you have a great one. Adam may have started out as a programmer. But in reality, he's a *visionary*. This company, this game were products of his vision. And you *can* be the visionary he wants to see. Doesn't matter that you're QA and Jeremy a dev."

I quirked a smile, somewhat heartened by her pep talk. "Thanks."

She stood. "When you finish the game design document, I'll be happy to look it over if you want me to."

She put a reassuring hand on my shoulder, then let it slip off, and partially down my arm, which she squeezed before letting go. Her touch burned me through my shirt and I swallowed hastily.

Then she turned and was gone. I stared at the doorway for long moments, wondering why I was finding it hard to breathe. Like the fresh air had been sucked out of this room and had followed her sunshiny presence as she left.

With our unwanted guests out of the house, we met a few more times with them. Once to take them up to Hollywood for some Walk of Fame tourism. And once to Disneyland, which we spared half a day for and left them to enjoy the rest.

Shortly after that, they disappeared. But I'd noticed that Kat had chosen never again to be alone with her brother. He did mention several times how much he wished she'd come back to Canada soon. Every time he said it, she got tense.

So, I was relieved when they finally hit the road a few days later.

Our time together as husband and wife—post the unwanted guest era—regressed to its new normal. Kat retreated to her room at night, thank God, and I slept alone. Though not that well. I lay in bed for hours each night craving her next to me, craving the feel of her body beside me, beneath my hands. Hungering to touch that silky hair. She'd only been in my bed two nights but I'd quickly gotten used to it.

We were cordial, but each kept our distance. Kat left the discussion about getting physical at that and I didn't touch it with a ten-foot pole. She was already too much of a delectable temptation and she now slept dozens of feet away from me with a wall in between.

But some days I'd walk into the living room. She'd be in the middle of doing yoga, leggings and a tank top on, her tight little ass in the air. Or on weekends, she'd walk around with her robe half open revealing something lacy underneath.

To say nothing of the incident where she'd tried to fix a leaky faucet in the guest bathroom and had splashed water all over her thin t-shirt. Her hardened nipples were as easily visible as if she'd been topless when she innocently came to me to ask for my tools. Jesus. I had a nice hard tool I desperately wanted her to handle. *Again.*

Even the sounds of her moving around on the other side of that wall were enough to keep me up at night. I'd obsess over what she was doing, what she was wearing, if anything. What position she slept in.

Goddamn. Sexual frustration seemed to be my normal mode these days. Rubbing one or two or three out in the shower just wasn't doing it for me. I wanted her day and night and it was starting to drive me slowly insane. And cold showers did not help one bit. That was a huge ridiculous myth. Talk about society's great lie. All cold showers did was leave you shivering and pissed off and yet still sexually frustrated.

To combat these temptations, I kept long hours at the office and we started going to and from work separately. We established a relaxed but distant pattern to our living and marital arrangement. I tried not to think too hard about why it wasn't as satisfying as it was comfortable.

The summer was in its final weeks when we were summoned into the immigration office for our inevitable interview. If things went well, it would be our only one. And as we were easily able to prove a long-time relationship of over a year before the wedding happened, things went smoothly. No need to memorize what kind of face cream she used or toothpaste or—god forbid— how often we had sex or whatever else.

The immigration officer assured us he saw no problems on his end and would recommend for Kat's green card. We celebrated over smoothies after the interview, then headed back to work where we both burned the midnight oil to make up for our afternoon off.

Things were going along smoothly and our expiration date, whenever that was, drew near. I'd counted on a feeling of relief. But it never came. Instead, it felt like a weight in my gut. Like waiting for the other shoe to drop.

Because the past had ingrained that into me. Just when things might get comfortable, something was bound to happen to screw that all up—even if that something was brought about based on my own stupid decisions.

Here's hoping that shoe wouldn't drop down on top of either one of us.

Chapter 16
Katya

WE RECEIVED OUR FIRST PIECE OF NON-immigration office mail as a married couple. The oversized envelope in thick parchment paper was addressed to *Mr. and Mrs. Lucas van den Hoehnsboek van Lynden* in in perfect calligraphy. The envelope itself was lined with golden foil and the invitation inside was engraved in gold embossed printing. Was someone getting married?

My eyebrow twitched in irritation at the old-fashioned style of address on the envelope—Lucas's name only, not both names. Then both eyebrows climbed my forehead and practically stayed there when I noted inside that we were referred to as Baron and Baroness.

Like, whoa... it wasn't just some weird ass joke. I really had temporarily married into a European aristocratic family. And they had titles and shit. And *I* had a title. Like... whoa. And like, I'm sure none of them ever said things like, *like whoa.*

It turned out, as I read further, that this wasn't a wedding invitation at all, but a summons to the Napa Valley family reunion that I had committed us to. The Van Den RicherThanGods family apparently sent out engraved invitations to their own children. Complete with titles and all.

Crap. In my anger, I'd committed us to attending this crazy thing. That had been over a month ago when I'd felt cornered and purposely left in the dark about Lucas's family situation.

I'd since calmed down but we were, alas, still committed. And I had to admit I was starting to feel a little panic about it, especially when I showed it to Lucas when he got home. He glanced over it, shrugged, and went to dump his stuff in his bedroom with nary a word about it.

"So... we could always back out," he said when he got back and sank down on the couch beside me. "I've blown them off before. It's no skin off my back."

My mouth twisted in a crooked smile. "I'd totally take you up on that, but this came, stuck to the inside envelope." I handed him the sticky note I'd found.

It read: *Please, please say you'll come and not leave me alone to face the wolves. Please! –J*

He laughed. "Huh, looks like Mother made poor Julia do the mailings."

I blinked at him. "Is it that bad? I mean, she seems to fit in well with that lifestyle."

Lucas turned to me and bit his lip. "Appearances can be deceiving. No one can really know how someone else struggles just by looking on the surface of things. She and my mother have never gotten along."

I thought about that for a moment, wondering about his sister. The one time I'd met her, she'd appeared to have stepped straight out of the old TV show *Gossip Girl*. She had it all, complete with costly designer clothes, a trust fund, It-Girl looks, and even an aristocratic European name to complete the picture.

I guess it was easy to think someone who had all that was happy with their life.

"Well, I'm sorry I got us into it but I guess this means we're committed now?" I asked, raising my brows and silently hoping he'd contradict me.

But no, apparently he really didn't want to leave Julia to the wolves. *Sigh.*

He shook his head. "We'll go. If we're lucky, we might be able to break away early."

My eyes skimmed the itinerary of planned activities and I could feel my anxiety level rising. Apparently, it would be a week-long affair complete with field trips, sightseeing, sports competitions, game tournaments, wine tasting and... some kind of themed ball? Well, crap. I guess this was Karma biting me in the ass for wanting to take some potshots at my new husband. *Mea culpa.*

At that point, Max jumped up on the couch between us and shoved his nose under my hand, begging for scratches. Before Lucas could demand he get off, I wrapped my arms around the shaggy pup and pulled him to me. "I have an idea. How about you go and wave the family flag and I'll stay home and doggy-sit Max."

He sent me serious side-eye. "Whoever smelt it, dealt it. You got us into this. I sure as hell am not showing up without you. Besides, Max gets to go to doggy camp, and he loves it."

I snickered. "If you let me out of this, I'll promise not to tell our co-workers that you call it doggy camp."

He got up from the couch, pulled out his phone and began scrolling through it. "Not a chance, Cranberry. I tried to warn you. You got us into this mess so you're coming."

Max shoved his head against me, lifting it for chin scratches and I complied as I stared at my husband's receding back until he vanished through the kitchen doorway. Then I turned to the dog. "Well, doesn't he just suck," I muttered.

"Heard that!" came the distant call from the kitchen.

My mouth twisted in frustration.

Fine. But if I was going to do this shit, I was going to have to do it right. Perhaps I should have been more Zen about it. After all, they were only going to be my in-laws for a short time longer. For some reason, I found myself caring more than I probably should have.

It was at a much less formal affair the following weekend that I was able to gather my posse and bring them in for help in the matter.

Adam and Mia held a Friday night pool party for their closest friends, which meant me and my new hubby, too. Lucas seemed a little nervous about joining the "inner circle." But hey, it gave him a taste of what I'd soon be experiencing during the festivities with *his* inner circle.

It was a hot evening in late summer and, quite honestly I was thrilled to see my peeps again. We hardly had time these days. Mia was going hard at medical school. All the Draco people were burning the midnight oil to get the new expansion ready. And my girlfriends, Jenna and April, were busy finishing up their schooling.

Jenna was regaling us with stories from her student-teaching experience as she was about to earn her certification. She was months away from being able to teach science in public school. She laughed, pale blue eyes flashing. "Yeah, it was weird to be asked for a hall pass at a school where I'm teaching. The guy refused to believe that I wasn't a student until one of my students saved me from getting sent to the principal's office."

Jenna, April and Mia were all chilling in the hot tub, each holding a glass of white wine. I sat on up on the concrete around the pool with only my legs inside the bubbling hot water. Mia caught my eye, her dark brows creasing in a frown. "Come sit in here with us."

I shook my head. "I'll melt. Canadian blood can't take the heat." It was already a hot August evening, and I'd been sweating it up since we'd arrived. The guys had the right idea. They were in the cooler, more refreshing water of the pool either floating on lounges or sitting in the shallow end drinking beers.

Someone plopped down right beside me with her own glass of chilled sangria. Alex looked tanned and gorgeous in her aqua bikini. "Hey you. I haven't even had a chance to ogle your rock yet, you know that?"

Obligingly, I held out my hand for her to check out the gorgeous antique ring that Lucas had given me. I got to sport it for a short while longer while I still had my role of pretend-wife.

"Ooh this is gorgeous! So unique. Is it an antique?"

I wiggled my fingers to make the diamond glitter. "Yes. It belonged to Lucas's great-grandma in the Netherlands. They got married during the Roaring Twenties."

Alex bent to take another look. "Soo pretty. So detailed. I can imagine parties and beautiful beaded dresses with fringe and low waists and gentlemen dancing the Charleston."

I brought the ring up to my own eyes. "Me? I'm most curious about the woman who wore this before me. What were her hopes and dreams? Was she happy? I wonder about the man who gave it to her. Did he truly love her and want her for ever and ever, even when she had aged out of her beauty?"

Alex smiled. "Who would have pegged you for a romantic, Kat?"

I ducked my head, abashed. "You caught me. Please don't spread that around. I have a reputation to preserve."

"I'm so glad you're happy. I'd heard that you and Lucas didn't get along at work. But damn I don't blame you for coming 'round. Your hubby is a *snack*."

I almost forgot to thank her for the compliment because I was distracted by a movement off to my left. I turned my head, feeling watched. Sure enough, I caught Lucas's gaze. He was sitting nearby on the deep-end step beside Jordan, sipping beers. But he wasn't that far away from us. The way he looked at me, then glanced down at my ring with a smile made it clear he'd heard what I said.

And for some reason, that made me suddenly shy. Especially if he thought I was getting all romantic and gushy about things the way Alex claimed I was being. Ugh. Not a good time for tough Kat to show her gooey marshmallow center. I worked so hard to keep that all hidden. But nowadays, the gooey seemed to want to ooze out and take over.

Not long later, on my way back from the outdoor patio washroom, Heath accosted me. "Come grab something to munch on so we can talk."

I followed him to a table arrayed with every kind of yummy appetizer imaginable. Chips and dip, salsa and guacamole, crunchy veggies and different types of salads. Cold cuts and deviled eggs and fancy sandwiches.

"Is everything okay?" I asked Heath.

Heath was looking better than I'd seen him in a long time. He'd put on most of the weight he'd lost with his horrible breakup last year and had clearly been working out again. His body was finely tuned without an ounce of extra fat on it anywhere. With him looking so good, I had no doubt he wasn't lacking for bed partners these days. "It's fine. It's just that you and I haven't talked lately."

It had been weeks, as a matter of fact. Which was weird because we used to see each other every day as roommates. I felt a pang of regret that I hadn't reached out regularly. Soon it would probably be like that with Lucas, too. What would it be like when we weren't seeing each other every day—outside of work? I felt a pang to think about it. Regret? Apprehension? Who knew?

"I'm so sorry. Work has me crushed. And all the other stuff—the immigration interview and all of that."

I nodded toward the hot number Heath had brought with him. An *extremely* fit and very good-looking Hispanic man in his mid-twenties with dark curly hair and gorgeous straight white teeth. He'd attracted the female gaze in his Speedo. "Who's the hottie you brought with you? You never introduced him to me."

"Because you and your hubby got here late. That's Adan."

"*Another* Adam?"

"No, *Adan*. With an N. We've been seeing each other for a few weeks. He'll probably hang out in the pool all night. He's a big swimmer."

I waggled my brows at Heath. "Hopefully he's big elsewhere too."

Heath gave me a "duh" look. "Of course. He wouldn't be here otherwise."

We snickered, and I plopped some green olives on his plate. Heath hated green olives, so he swore at me and threw them back onto my plate. "Speaking of which. I need you to spill the tea on that cute hubby of yours. What's he packing in his boxers? Have you found out yet?"

"Very clever, Hank." I grinned at him giving him the irritating nickname we sometimes teased him with. It had originated as a misspelling on his coffee cup at Starbucks one time. People sometimes had trouble with his name and thus, Hank had stuck. I soon had Mia and all the rest calling him Hank and the more it irritated him, the more we used it.

He ignored the nickname and stuck to his favorite subject— penises. "Don't tell me you haven't taken a ride on his disco-stick yet. I thought it would only take a week of living under the same roof together."

I heaved a long sigh. "A lady never tells."

"Good thing you're not a lady then."

I rolled my eyes. "I got nothing to tell."

"Come on... not even some heavy petting? The sexual tension between you two is as *thicc* as Henry Cavill's thighs."

I eyed him skeptically. "You picked that up from across the pool?"

"A fucking deaf-blind service dog could pick it up, babe."

I shushed him when William joined us at the table, grabbing some chips and dip on a paper plate. He nodded at both of us. "How are you?"

"Hey William, I have that money I owe you. You take a check, right?" Heath asked.

William frowned. "I distinctly recall telling you I would do the work pro bono."

My brows rose. What was this? Heath flicked me a glance. "He did some artwork for a website I just redesigned." He turned back to William. "And no, I don't accept that. Artists shouldn't work for free."

Adam's cousin shrugged at him. "It wasn't work. It was a favor for a friend."

"I'll mail you the check then," Heath said to his back.

William halted and called over his shoulder. "I'll shred the check."

Heath muttered under his breath about the man's stubbornness. I kept my eyes on William where he sat beside his beloved Jenna, sharing the chips and dip with her. She rewarded him with a peck on his neck and he smiled.

He'd come a long way. Back in the day, he'd be the one insisting on always following the rules. Do the work, get the pay. But he'd loosened up a lot in the past year. Jenna's influence at work, no doubt. My eyes flicked back to my blond friend wondering what his influence had done to her. And was it always like that?

Had Mia changed Adam or vice versa? Or what about April and Jordan?

And would Lucas end up leaving some kind of lasting effect on me, too? Or were we destined to part ways and become strangers to each other once again? It seemed so weird to think about that, even now. We weren't intimate, but I felt I knew him at least as well as my other friends, or in some cases, better. Would we stay friends? Or would we go back to being the office rivals? Or maybe, if we never saw each other much, we'd become strangers.

I was still grazing at the table when Heath left my side to go dive-bomb Adan with a cannonball in the deep end of the pool. Mia joined me soon after. She looked gorgeous in a black bikini with thin silver stripes, her long dark hair pulled back in a high ponytail. Her husband didn't seem to find it necessary to hide his obvious ogling of her no matter where she was in the backyard.

She noticed, too, and wiggled her fist at him, thumb and pinky extended in a "hang loose" gesture. He laughed and turned back to his conversation with April.

Suddenly the music on Adam's 80s playlist clicked over to the familiar beginning beats of *Never Gonna Give You Up*. Ah, only Adam Drake would rick-roll his own party. I caught Lucas's eye and pointed toward one of the speakers. He appeared to understand, laughing. *They're playing our song,* I wanted to say. But that would be letting everyone else in on our little in-joke.

Although when you thought about it, our entire marriage was our little in-joke, wasn't it? Too bad it didn't feel like too much of a joke when I was lying in bed at night alone. In my hot and bothered memory, I relived the memory of his kisses, his hands on my body.

Mia beamed at her husband then turned to me, shaking her head. "I can't take that boy anywhere."

I nodded, duly impressed. "Eight months of marriage and you two are still full-on horn-dawgs. I love it."

She elbowed me. "Don't you judge. Every time I catch your hubby looking at you, he reminds me of a starving wolf staring at a bloody steak hanging just out of his reach."

I could feel the heat roast my face immediately and knew that I was blushing like a cherry. Sometimes being a ginger was such a detriment, especially when trying to hide certain emotions.

"Is that so?" I shrugged and smirked as if I knew full well what she was talking about despite the fact that I didn't. I flicked a glance in Lucas's direction but he was now deep in conversation with Jordan.

"How is everything going? How are you adjusting to married life? I mean... it was all so sudden for you. I'm still amazed by that."

"Well, I guess I have some impulsive tendencies—like when I came down to see you the minute I found out you were sick, remember?"

She smiled and threw an arm around my shoulders. "You have no idea how much that meant to me. It was an amazing gesture and so selfless. You dropped everything in your life just for me. When we'd only ever met in person once."

I shrugged and looked away. I had been happy to do it when I'd found out that Mia had cancer. But what I'd never told her was that it suited my purposes too. I'd needed to get out of town—hell, out of the country—and avoid my own problems back home. To avoid the impossible situation that my family was pushing me into.

What Mia saw as a show of selflessness was actually cowardice in action.

I returned Mia's hug. "Well, you know, I was happy to do it. And now I'm here."

"And here's where you met your true love!" she smiled at me. And again, I avoided her gaze. My true love. *Yeah.* A fresh chord of some sharp emotion stabbed at me. It didn't hurt so much as stated it was there and was too strong to be ignored.

"What's going on over here?" April asked, suddenly appearing at Mia's shoulder. "A mutual appreciation society and I'm not invited?"

April was gorgeous in a deep violet one-piece swimsuit complete with sparkly sequins, a garment made for showing off her curvy figure at the beach rather than actually swimming in. And given that her shiny dark hair looked perfect, it was clear that she'd done more floating than swimming.

Thank God for the perfect excuse to change the subject. "Dude, you have to try the guacamole," I said. "Alex's mum made it and it's to die for."

She pressed her hands to her flat belly. "Ugh. I'm so full I can't eat anything else for a while. Hey is Jordan looking over here? I want to freak him out by oohing and ahhing over your wedding ring. It's beautiful by the way, but I'm not going to put on the big show unless he's my lowkey-terrified audience."

Mia snickered. "You're so deviously brilliant."

April winked at her. "Any chance I can get to tweak my Beast, I'll take it."

"I'll let you know when he looks over and we can start the big show." I laughed along. "Meanwhile, can we talk about how weird it is that Heath is dating a dark-haired, dark-eyed hottie named Adan? Is he dating your husband by proxy?"

Mia's mouth creased as if the thought had already occurred to her. "I would never in a million years say anything to him about it, but it is a little awkward."

"Just make sure Adam and Adan aren't locked in a room alone together. The close contact might cause the universe to implode, like the clash of matter and anti-matter," I cackled.

"Maybe he's just Bizarro Adam—like Bizarro Superman," Mia tossed back and we both laughed while April frowned at us.

"Put a jaunty goatee on him and he could be Mirror-Universe Adam!" I shot back.

April gave us both a look. "You two are way too geeky for this book nerd."

Alex and Jenna soon joined the rest of us girls around the snack table while the guys stayed in the pool. Once we discreetly caught Jordan's attention, I made sure to extend my hand while April blatantly ogled my ring. When we looked again, Jordan had his head turned away from us. We laughed anyway.

"So what's going on over here?" Jenna asked as she refilled her glass of lemonade. "Are you two comparing notes about married life?"

Mia and I exchanged glances, and I sipped my own iced tea. "Sure."

"Any insights into the 'species male' that we can take wisdom from?" Jenna asked.

Mia's mouth twisted. "Being married is kind of like seeing how the sausage is made."

All of us snorted at that while Mia who apparently heard what she'd said on delay, blushed as red as Jenna's bikini. "I didn't mean *that* sausage."

"And you, Kat? What insights have you discovered about your new hubby?" Jenna asked.

"Well the biggest shocker was finding out that he's actually European nobility," I deadpanned. All the girls thought that one was yet another hilarious joke. I disabused them of that notion.

April's dark blue eyes widened like two big shiny toonies. "What, for real? What kind of nobility?"

"His dad is a Dutch Baron, I think?"

Two seconds later, April had a phone in her hand. Who knew where she'd been packing that thing. Did her swimsuit have secret bra pockets in it or something?

"His last name is Walker, right?" Her manicured fingers started flying over the glass surface of her phone. "Doesn't sound very Dutch."

"Uh, no actually that's his middle name."

Mia's head jerked in my direction. "What, he's got like a secret identity?"

I shrugged, glancing toward where he sat talking with some other guys in the deep end. Would he mind having this fact divulged? He never said anything about keeping it a secret.

"I guess he feels it's easier to use his middle name. And he doesn't want anyone making a big stink about it, so please promise me none of you will."

The girls nodded or stated their agreement all around and then April handed her phone to me. "Just to satisfy our curiosity, though…"

I typed Lucas's family name into Google after scouring my brain to remember how it was spelled. It was ridiculous that I hadn't thought to Google the family myself. Once the phone was back in her hand, April hit the search button and her eyes widened. "Holy cow! You weren't joking. Ancestral family mansion in Utrecht. That's a castle, not a mansion. Wow, it's gorgeous!"

She passed the phone to others who scrolled down the search—society pages, headlines, Julia's personal lifestyle brand and social media accounts.

Jenna clicked on one of the links. "This is about your wedding!"

I frowned. That was incredibly odd. "Really?" Had his family announced our marriage somehow? I held out my hand for the phone after Jenna had scrolled through the page clearly looking confused.

It was Lucas's wedding, all right. His first one. To Claire. And it appeared that the family had spared no expense on that affair. As in at least a seven or eight figure expense. Wow. Her dress looked like something straight out of the Duchess of Cambridge's inner circle. Almost certainly a designer gown, probably custom-made.

How glamorous. And he was stunning. What a beautiful couple they made, standing under an arch of gorgeous flowers near a gazebo in the family vineyard. Something tightened in my gut.

I clicked on the X to close out the window on the phone's browser. I did *not* want to explain all that tonight. "Ah, must have been a cousin." I handed the phone back to April.

She pocketed the phone. In that brief glimpse I got, however, I'd seen, alongside pictures of the happy couple, their formal announcement of marriage. Clearly, from the details, it had been the ultimate society wedding with a massive budget to match.

And he'd looked so young in those photos. Fresh-faced and so far from the cynical present. He was *so* handsome in that tux and *smiling*. It made me ache to think he'd sat stoically across from me and signed papers in a hamburger joint for our wedding. Not even a glimmer of a spark of a reflection of any glamor whatsoever. I wonder what that younger, less cynical and stoic Lucas had been like?

The girls were talking about European vacations now. They were wondering what it would be like for us if we went "back" to the Netherlands where other branches of his aristocratic family lived. Mia had to chime in how much she'd loved her short stay in Amsterdam several years ago.

"His family reunion," I muttered almost as if to myself. Heads turned.

"What?" Mia asked. "Are you going to the Netherlands? Meet the royal family?"

"No," I shook my head. "Napa Valley. His family owns a vineyard and winery there."

April and Mia met gazes, their mouths making perfect O shapes. Then both turned back to me. "When is that?"

I grimaced. "Week after next. I'm kind of jittery about it and I'm positive I don't have the right wardrobe." And that meant more now, after having seen his damn wedding on the internet and realizing how dazzling they'd looked together. I suddenly vowed that I'd show up there looking at least twice as dazzling, if possible.

April perked up, suddenly interested. "The doctor is in and I prescribe retail therapy."

I rubbed my forehead. "I don't know. I need some kind of Roaring Twenties attire."

"For a theme party?" April's eyes illuminated like the Disneyland fireworks. "A deco dress… low-waisted with lots of beads and sequins and a matching feathered headdress. With shoes dyed to match… and silk gloves that go up past your elbow! Oh my gosh you would look so cute with your hair pinned up, so it looks like a bob. Jewel tones—any color but red. With your hair color, emerald green or brilliant blue would look amazing. Black would wash you out too much with your pale skin."

I blinked at her. "Can I borrow you to go shopping sometime soon?"

Her smile widened. "I thought you'd never ask. But I'll only go if you back up my fib to Jordan that we're going to look at wedding dresses."

We all busted up in laughter and all heads turned toward Jordan who gave us a deer in the headlights look from across the pool. It made us laugh even harder. A short while later, we set a date to meet the following weekend for an excruciating little shopping trip. April was going to be my fashion advisor and Mia was coming along for moral support.

Thank goodness for my girlfriends.

As the pool party wound down, people started saying their goodbyes. Heath and Adan were the first to leave, obviously moving on to greener pastures—probably some hot club—for the evening. Heath enfolded me in one of his signature bear hugs.

"Remember not to think too much," he muttered into my ear when no one was listening. "Just bust that disco-stick."

I hit him. Hard. Then I laughed as he walked away, his hand on his date's ass.

***

The following weekend, true to their word, Mia and April met me at Fashion Island in Newport Beach—which was often not-so-lovingly referred to as Fascist Island. The place was the very antithesis of me, who bought most of my clothes in second-hand and thrift shops.

I knew that Mia sympathized. She'd once been a starving student and was more in tune with my world at her core than she was to that of being a Newport Beach billionaire's wife. She was there to be my moral support and hold my hand. April was acting as my own personal shopper and fashion advisor.

And man, did that girl have an eye. She asked the shop attendants to bring out a selection of what we were looking for based on her description. Then, with authority, she vetoed anything she didn't approve of before I even saw it. I was happy to let her take over, and she was definitely very accustomed to this world.

And after a few hours of trying on things, I handed over my credit card. It might have squealed a little when they swiped it through the machine. My limit would allow it. And I had more than enough in my home purchase savings to cover it. But it was my condo fund... my dream of having my own home in a place where condos cost the equivalent of a small island nation's GDP to purchase.

"All right," April declared as she dusted her hands on a job well done. "Next we'll hit up downtown Orange antique shops for costume jewelry and then we can finish up at the lingerie store."

I blinked in alarm. "Lingerie?"

"Agent Provocateur, I think." She winked. "You said your mother-in-law wants to give you the honeymoon you didn't have, right? Just what else are you going to wear under that gorgeous flapper dress, anyway? Might as well kill two birds with one stone and knock off your hubby's socks—to say nothing of his other undergarments."

I gulped. I could do with owning some pretty underthings. It had been a while since I'd thought outside the box of serviceable, long lasting and comfy cotton to catnap in while pulling all-nighters in the Den. But I wouldn't be buying them for Lucas to see and appreciate.

My marriage was the long and dry sexual desert. Not by my choice. But I had to accept that Lucas had put his foot down and said no. And no meant *no*.

I bought the lingerie anyway. So what if only I knew these gorgeous things were under my lavish dress? They'd make me feel prettier, sexier, more confident. Thus, they had value to me even if no one else ever saw them.

My poor credit card had taken quite the beating today. But if it meant I'd have a taste of my own glamor and wouldn't be an embarrassment to my secret European aristocrat hubby, then it was worth it.

As we walked out of that last store, April bit her lip, eyeing my shopping bags. "Ahhh it's every bit as good as a fairytale. Almost brings a tear to my eye."

CHAPTER 17
LUCAS

THE WEEKEND AFTER THE POOL PARTY, JORDAN TEXTED me, asking to go on a run with him and I obliged. We met at his fashionable beach house in the Wedge area of Newport Beach. If it hadn't been such a distance, I might have walked, since finding parking near his house was usually almost impossible.

It was a perfect warm beach day, and the surfers were out en masse, taking advantage. I half wondered why Jordan had opted for a run instead of surfing, his preferred method of exercise. That question answered itself once we started talking. I guess you couldn't do much chatting while hitting the waves.

He pumped me thoroughly about my progress on the Great Project that would Wow the Board's Socks Off ™. And then, satisfied with what he heard, as we stood on his porch after the run, he guzzled water and handed me a towel to wipe off my sweaty face.

"So I heard through the grapevine that you are royalty or something."

I frowned, shaking my head, then tipped my water bottle to my mouth, gulping enthusiastically.

Jordan kept talking. "I knew your Dad was loaded but didn't know he had a noble title."

Just before I swallowed, I took a breath too soon and began sputtering and coughing, which spawned more gasping, which prompted Jordan to begin unhelpfully slapping me on the back.

"Stop it!" I finally rasped when I could catch my breath enough to talk.

I wiped the tears from the corners of my eyes brought on from the coughing fit as Jordan watched me carefully. "You have a drinking problem."

I rolled my eyes. "Very funny. Who told you about my father's title?"

Jordan tilted his head. "Bro, your wife spilled it to her girlfriends at the pool party last week. Women talk. Nothing you can do about it. They've all since told their significant others."

My eyes narrowed. *Damn it, Kat!* "She told Mia?"

Jordan followed my train of thought. "Don't sweat it, Lucas. I doubt Adam gives a shit about your aristocratic blood. The girls were duly impressed though, to hear April talk about it. You missed the boat on using that nice little factoid about yourself to get laid as much as you want." He shrugged. "Ah, but your wife is hot, so I guess it wasn't a total loss."

I sighed. "Not everyone thinks like you do, Jordan."

I mulled over this new bit of info as I drove home, annoyed with Kat for having spilled the beans—yet again. Though as I searched my memory, I really hadn't explicitly told her not to tell anyone, either.

Kat made us dinner, and I decided not to bring it up then. What was the point? I'd let her know how I felt about it, eventually. But the pesto Alfredo and Caesar salad were beyond delicious so I'd let my irritation simmer down before I said anything. I truly hadn't eaten as well in years as I had since Kat had come to stay. "Thanks for making dinner. I'll get the dishes," I told her after a quiet dinner where we didn't talk much.

From the kitchen, I heard Kat pad her way into the room where she'd set up her gaming and streaming equipment. As I cleaned up, my mind tried to go over the things I needed to work on that evening for the proposal and game design document.

Once back at my desk in the den, I sifted through the pile of mail I hadn't looked at since Friday. In it, I found yet another legal letter addressed to Kat, marked urgent in big red letters on the front of the envelope.

Hmm. She'd mentioned having shredded the others unread, willfully keeping herself in ignorance. Was she truly in trouble somehow? It definitely involved her brother but why were they after her? And did this have anything to do with Derek's motivation to get Kat back to Canada? My fingers hesitated on the seam of the letter, tempted to open it myself and have a look.

My conscience got the better of me, though. Even if we were truly married in every sense, I had no right to confiscate her mail and read it if my name wasn't also on the envelope. And it wasn't.

The best I could do was to hand it to her in person and ask her directly about it. She owed me an honest answer, after all, since she'd blabbed my not-so-secret to her circle of friends. I wasn't as upset now that a few hours had passed but at least I could use it as leverage to get some answers out of her about this.

I knocked on the door and she called for me to come in immediately. She turned from her computer monitor and smiled. "Hey."

She was in full gamer girl mode, despite the fact that she wasn't streaming on her channel. Her brand new and very impressive Sennheiser headset was perched on her head, mouthpiece poised just over her plump lips. Her gleaming hair was pulled back into a serviceable braid. And she had on a pair of tiny Daisy Dukes that exposed miles of pale, curvy leg for my eyes to feast on.

She was not making this sexual frustration situation any easier, god damn it. And now I suddenly regretted coming in here.

"Are you in the middle of something?" I glanced at the screen, eyebrows shooting up. She was logged into Dragon Epoch. From the background, I could tell that she was using the live version and not the unpublished test material for the expansion. Besides using the testing server from home was difficult and required permission—because of possible security leaks. She actually played this game for fun?

"What's up?" she said, nudging back one of her earphones from her delicate ear. "No, no I'm asking the hubby what's up, not you, dork," she spoke again into the mouthpiece. "Hold on a sec. I'm afk. Besides, the other two aren't even logged in yet so hold your horses." She turned back to her PC and clicked the mute button.

I shook my head, eyes glued to the monitor. "How are you not sick as shit of this game since you work on it all day?"

She shrugged, her smile widening. "My regular group—the one I started playing with ages ago back during the open beta— is logging on tonight for a rare game night. I wouldn't miss it. You wanna join us? Do you have a character on the Omni server in the upper level range?"

"I have no idea. I, uh, need to talk to you about your mail, if you have a minute."

She gave me a questioning glance, then pulled off her headset and swiveled on her chair to face me. I grabbed a nearby stool to sit at her level. "Yeah, I've got about ten minutes before the other two long in."

I handed her the envelope. "You got another letter from the lawyer and I really think you should open it."

She frowned, then darted a look up at me. The question unspoken. What business was it of mine?

"Please, if you would? Put my mind at ease. You said you had no idea if you were in trouble. I'd like to know. I'd like to help."

Her big blue eyes fixed on me for a long moment, unreadable, before she blinked and took the letter from me with a slight shrug. Sliding a finger under the lip of the seal on the envelope, she tore it open. The thick linen paper spilled out onto her lap.

She swallowed, picking it up as if it were a snake that might bite her, then she unfolded the sheet and quickly read the page. Once finished, she crumpled the paper in one hand, clenching her jaw.

"Is everything okay?"

She raised a cinnamon brow at me and then round-filed the crumpled letter and envelope. "I'll only tell you if you say you'll play with my group tonight."

I frowned. "Dragon Epoch?"

She snorted. "No, Donkey Kong. Yes, of course, DE."

I stared past her at the screen. The thought of playing DE for fun honestly did not excite me but I shrugged. "What the hell." My eyes flicked back to her. "So now tell me what's going on."

"I'm not in any trouble. And you aren't going to understand because it's a big long story but they want me to go back to Canada for a case that my brother is involved in. They are threatening to issue a subpoena but I don't care because I'm not in that country anymore. And I have no plans to go back after I get my green card. Satisfied?"

I leaned forward. "You're exiling yourself from Canada? That seems drastic."

"I answered your question." She swiveled back to the monitor where her gaming group was now forming up. "Get back here with your laptop and use your admin privileges to port a character over to Omni."

Fully aware that she'd evaded giving me any important details whatsoever, but at least cognizant that she'd somewhat put my mind at ease, I did as she asked. In no time, I returned with my laptop and headset to sit beside her. It only took a few minutes to have a character of the appropriate level ready to group up with them.

I was about to meet Kat's regular gaming group and for some reason, I was nervous about it. After clicking to accept her group invitation, I adjusted my headset. Kat said, "Hey guys, it's my new hubby online as the darkling assassin, Teakwood."

Huh, I hadn't even paid much attention to the character's name. I had literally dozens of them, mostly used for testing the game post release on my own time. But this character's name seemed very apt considering the constant state of things below the belt during most of my waking—and sometimes my not-so-waking hours. And mostly because of the sexy woman sitting beside me.

I cleared my throat and spoke into the mic. "Hey everyone."

"Hey Woody," said a man's voice. "Good to meet Mr. Persephone at last. I'm Fragged, the tank. We've got crowd control, Eloisa, our spiritual enchantress. DPS is that funny looking monk over there, FallenOne. And of course, not to forget our group healer, your beloved bride."

I frowned. This dude's voice sounded familiar. Kat gave me some side-eye with a weird grin on her face, probably waiting for me to embarrass myself. "Well, I'm a team player and I'll go with the flow. What quests are you working on?"

From there, we got to know each other over the next quarter of an hour. The other two were also friendly. But crazily enough, the obvious didn't dawn on me until we made our way through a particularly grueling fight.

"We keep getting adds. Mia, lock them down!" Fragged, the tank, said.

My head jerked in Kat's direction and she started laughing uncontrollably even as she was pounding the keys to dole out heal spells. Mia, huh? No wonder all these people sounded so familiar. I already knew them.

"So I'm guessing that FallenOne is Adam? And Fragged is Heath then," I muttered at Kat who just barely had the time to get off a heal on Fragged before he fell down dead.

"Damn it, Kat. Not so close next time, please?" he groused.

"I was distracted," she said between laughter and tears streaming down her face. "The jig is up, guys. He knows who you are."

"Took you long enough," said Mia, aka Eloisa. "Heath is the one who blew it, though. Too much nagging at me using my real name."

"If you'd been able to control the adds, there wouldn't have been a problem," Heath shot back. "They were starting to aggro on Kat."

I rubbed my forehead, puzzled. "Do you guys play together a lot?"

"We used to," said FallenOne-slash-Adam. "It's rare nowadays since our schedules are all over the place."

I blinked, surprised. Adam and Kat especially shocked me. They still got this level of enjoyment out of a game that we all toiled on during the day as part of our regular jobs. Especially Adam. Wouldn't he be aware of the game's every secret? Wouldn't his group members weasel it out of him?

"I need the story on this," I said to Kat after we'd logged off. I began to gather my things. It was starting to get late, and we had another long and exhausting day ahead of us tomorrow.

She frowned at me, clearly consternated. "Don't you ever just get on to play for fun?"

I sighed and shook my head. "Occupational hazard, I guess. I've kind of lost that initial love I had for DE."

She shrugged. "Well you know, it doesn't take that much to fall back in love with it. Especially when it's more about the people you're playing with than the game itself."

"Is that how the four of you met? In the game?" I asked.

She nodded, then her face clouded, and she shrugged. "Actually Heath and Mia have known each other forever. Since preteen days. They started playing DE together in the beta. I got the beta and played while I had a really annoying job working overnight in a data center. We all played odd hours."

"So... Adam was just playing his own game, and he ran into you all? Did you know who he was?"

She shook her head, smiling. "Nope. Fun, huh? That Adam and Mia would hook up over the game like that. So many romances have been made and broken playing this game."

I laughed. "You know people who've broken up over the game?"

She nodded. "Oh yeah. People in our guild even. Big time drama. This married couple played the game together. They were power players, on all the time. The guy was our raid leader. His wife started grouping with other people, then started falling for one of the other guys in the guild. Eventually she decided to leave her husband over it. Like, they were halfway across the country from each other so it wasn't really an affair but—"

I stiffened. "It was an affair." My gut twisted at the familiarity of the story. I identified all too much with the raid-leader husband. Busy, caught up with all he had going, probably with work, real life demands and that of the game, which can also become like another job. And she, feeling neglected, sought comfort somewhere else.

Yeah, I recognized that story all too well. "Cheating is cheating. Emotional affairs can be just as damaging as a physical one." With a little more heat than I'd intended, I snatched up my things and stood. Kat rose with me, setting down her headset so hurriedly it crashed to the floor. She ignored it.

"Whoa, hey! Are you okay?" she asked.

I jerked my head back to her. "What? Why wouldn't I be okay?"

Her eyes widened, and she blinked. "Because you're talking *very* loud and it's obvious that your blood pressure just shot up about a hundred points. You're also as flushed as a lobster."

Instead of answering, I bent to scoop up her pricey headset with my free hand and set it gently back on the desk.

"Did—um, did your ex cheat on you?"

I clenched my jaw and then released it. "Depends on if you think an emotional affair is cheating or not."

She frowned and looked down. I didn't want to talk about this anymore. I could feel a headache threatening at my temple and I was exhausted from the long day.

"Goodnight," I muttered quietly and left without another word, depositing the armful of things onto my bed.

I hadn't even had time to grab my things out of the dresser to get ready for bed when I noticed a movement in the doorway. Kat stood there, still looking gorgeous in that tight pink t-shirt, those short-shorts. Her chin was tilted down, her blue eyes huge and full of apologies.

"Lucas, I'm so sorry."

I halted where I stood and watched her approach me. "You have nothing to apologize for."

She shook her head. "My words hurt you. I've never been cheated on—that I know of—and I have no idea how it feels. I-I'm sorry."

I looked away, avoiding her gaze. "It's not just about being cheated on. It—well that was a crappy time of my life all the way around. I still had no idea who I was as a person and I took on way too much. In the end, it was too much to handle and..." I shook my head. "I guess you could say I overestimated how strong I could be. At least that's what everyone else around me told me at the time."

She frowned so deeply her forehead puckered. "What— people blamed you for her cheating? And called you weak? That's messed up. I hope you didn't believe them."

I took a deep breath and let it go, distantly recalling those days and the wretched aftermath. And the feeling in my body that everything was so heavy that I didn't want to move, couldn't get myself out of bed to even do the simplest things. And how that had made me feel even worse.

My voice was hoarse when I spoke again. "It was not a good time."

Kat took another step toward me, big eyes still rounded with empathy. She reached a hand toward my face, then seemed to think the better of it and slowly let it drop. "It's the past and you are awesome and should never feel down on yourself for that shit again. You deserve so much better, Lucas."

Something inside me was moving, changing, melting. The walls I'd built around those deep feelings to keep me safe trembled just slightly. I swallowed. I wanted nothing more than to reach out and pull Kat to me, feel her hug me in return, smell her hair and rub it against my cheek. Bask in the comfort her presence was offering me.

I should tell her to leave. I should push her away. She was standing less than ten feet from my bed and looking *that* amazing. One whiff of that sweet, warm smell of her hair. All I could think of was how much I wanted her in my bed again with no clothes between us at all. I just wanted to forget...

I wavered, and she took another step toward me. It was like we were connected—like some invisible rope was drawing us together, slowly yet surely tightening the knots.

I blinked, trying to break the spell. "It's late. We should hit it."

She bit her lip and nodded slowly. "Okay." Then blew out a sigh. "But first..." She went up on tip toes and wrapped her arms around my neck, pressing that luscious body to mine in a tight hug, her hair kissing my cheek. The warm smell of salty coconuts. *God.* "Good night, Lucas. Thanks for everything."

Our chests rubbed together. Her nipples beaded through the light fabric of her t-shirt. Those hard points pressed against my chest made me instantly aroused. *Damn it.* I pulled away from her.

With a small, self-conscious smile she ducked her head and turned to leave the room. Something inside me half felt like it followed her out. Things were so much easier when we were grousing at each other or finding buttons to push to make the other one annoyed or pissed off. Things were easier when she was at a safe distance.

When I could openly admire, if just to myself, how awesome she was in just about every way, with the barrier of our snarky insults safely erected between us.

But man, those walls, they were coming down. And fast. It didn't matter how much I reminded myself about everything I'd gone through last time. It wasn't just Claire's betrayal, but her dramatic appeal to my family members to take her back. Then the universal pressure and the finger pointing. All that was nothing to the sudden realization that I'd been living some other man's life for twenty years. That I'd spent every second of those years trying to please everyone around me, failing and trying even harder.

Only to find that I'd erased myself in the process.

The months of soul-devouring depression, the long hard road to pull myself out of it. The ties I'd had to cut in order to make it happen.

I would never—*could* never—allow it again. And yes, Kat was not Claire. But... she could hurt me so much worse.

Every day it got harder to resist her. No pun intended. And tonight, that fantasy of the hot gamer girl with a heart of gold made real, the stakes had shot through the roof.

Tactical retreat. That's what this was. Anything less than distant from Kat was the danger zone.

I prayed she got her green card soon. Because if not, I was either going to end up giving in and going for it with her with all its potential to really screw up our lives.

Or maybe I was just going to fucking lose my mind.

CHAPTER 18
KATYA

THE FLIGHT TO SACRAMENTO—A NEARBY COMMERCIAL airport to Napa Valley—was only ninety minutes. Shortly thereafter, we were on the road, driving a rental car for the two-hour trip to the family vineyard. On the way to meet the parents... once again.

Hopefully, things would go better this time. I was now armed with knowledge. Though I didn't know everything, I at least had a better handle on the dynamic than I'd had that disastrous night of the family dinner party.

"Have you heard back about the promotion yet? I mean, I know you'd tell me if you knew you got it but... I was just wondering what the progress was on that."

He had his eyes on the road but his mouth thinned briefly, shoulders stiffening. He was obviously tense about it. Had he heard something?

"I submitted my proposal to Adam and Jordan this morning. The entire presentation with slides, mission statement and sample game design documents. They have everything they've asked for. Jeremy has done the same, so we wait. I'm guessing it won't take long for them to make the decision."

I nodded. "Well for what it's worth, I'll cross my fingers for you."

He shot me a look out of the corner of his eyes and quietly thanked me

Since I was prone to car sickness, I didn't read on my phone and instead watched the countryside speed by. Unlike much of the Southern California urban sprawl, this was much more pleasant scenery to look at.

But this lack of anything to do led me to think. And fidget. Okay, maybe I was a little nervous. I shifted in my seat, laced my fingers together, unlaced them. I had a lot of fun twisting my wedding ring around my finger over and over again.

"That's going to go flying off your finger if you don't stop it. I knew I should have had it resized to fit your finger better."

My brows shot up, and I glanced over at Lucas. I was unaware that he'd taken his eyes off the road for even a microsecond. He was a bit of an anal-retentive driver, hands at ten o'clock and two o'clock, textbook foot position, regular glances at the rearview mirror, the whole shebang.

"I promise I won't lose it. It would kill me. It's so beautiful and has so much history. Plus it isn't even mine."

I held out my hand again and wiggled my fingers to catch the light on the diamond. Then a stray thought occurred to me and I tossed him a glance. "Did... did Claire wear this when you two were married?"

Instead of getting upset at me for bringing her up, he snorted and rolled his eyes. "I proposed to her with that ring. That's, I think, the last time she ever saw it. She rejected it and insisted I get her a new one."

I pulled my hand back to look closer at it, completely baffled. The ring was exquisite and unique and just... I shook my head.

"She wanted a bigger diamond and apparently doesn't like old things. That one has the original stone in it and I'm glad I saved it because you seem to appreciate it a lot more than she ever would."

I blinked, stared at it again. I appreciated it, yeah, but I was probably going to be giving it back in a little while. No way would I think of keeping it no matter how much I liked it. I felt a strange twinge of something, an ache of loss. Weird that I'd feel that way about a ring.

"I heard you talking about the ring to your friends at the party. Those were some nice thoughts, about my great grandmother and all. That's the whole reason I wanted to save it for my future marriage. But to be honest, I'm glad Claire didn't accept it, so it's not tainted by that whole mess."

I kept my eyes on the ring. "Did she... did she end up with the guy she cheated with?"

"Nuh uh," he snorted again and shook his head. "All that mess and it resulted in nothing. Not sure if he didn't return the same feelings or if they both lost interest once I noped out. She did come crawling back to me, though, begging for another chance."

I frowned but didn't say anything.

"I'd already come back to the US at that point. With all the shit going on, I'd been removed from the active team on my rowing crew. I also ended up failing my classes. So, I hopped on the next plane and left. She called my family and claimed I'd abandoned her all by herself in England."

I blinked. "Wow."

"Yeah. And instead of going back to her parents in New York, she flew to California to get my family to pressure me to take her back."

I stared at his handsome profile, fascinated by the story. "What did you do?"

He took a deep breath and let it go, darting me a sidelong glance. "I was having some... health issues at that point and all that was making it worse. So I left, didn't tell anyone where I was going, just vanished, as far as they were concerned."

Okay so *that* sounded incredibly familiar. Because I'd done nearly an identical thing. For a completely different reason, but still. It was almost eerie how much our lives had paralleled each other. We, nearly the exact same age, born in different countries and vastly different social classes. Yet, our lives had spiraled and turned as parallel lines, never intersecting in that same plane. Until the one fateful point in which they did. Like serendipity and geometry combining to form this weird thing that was Lucas and me. This ephemeral, temporary connection we'd created.

Only soon to spiral back away from each other once again. Perhaps we'd return to the parallel, never to intersect anymore.

My chest suddenly felt heavy.

"What's wrong? You look pale. You hated my story that much?"

I smiled faintly to reassure him but chose to deflect instead of share what was really on my mind. "So, when you left your family and disappeared, is that when you changed your name to Walker?"

He glanced away, almost as if he knew that I was evading. "Walker was always my name. My middle name. I just dropped the last name."

"You mean *all* the last names. Those are a lot of names." I cleared my throat, deepening my voice to imitate the monologue at the beginning of every episode of *Arrow*. "My name is Lucas

Walker. And I went to Lian-Yu because I had to become someone else. Become *something* else."

He cracked a smile to match mine but otherwise did not respond.

"So basically you're a secret identity for a superhero."

"Hmm. I guess that's a step up from Jedi Boy. I'll take it."

We rode in silence for a stretch of five or ten minutes. Our bodies swayed in unison with the twists and turns of the road and the land, the slopes and the dips. We were going through some hills now and the road was getting twistier. Since it was late summer, what should have been green and grassy hills were dried and yellowed landscape against a pale blue sky. Like all the colors had been washed out.

I needed a little air, so I cracked my window a smidge. The ends of my hair started dancing around my shoulders like copper-colored snakes and I couldn't help but laugh.

He laughed with me.

I darted a furtive glance at him. "So... I lied to you just now when I said I was wondering about your name change."

He raised his brows but showed no other surprise. "Oh?"

"Yeah... I was being shy. Because I was thinking deep thoughts about how similar we are. I did the same thing you did, left my family's place and just disappeared as far as they were concerned. I did come to California because Mia was sick, but I was going to leave, anyway. Circumstance only gave me the answer to where I should go. But I knew I had to go. Even if just because of my cowardice."

He didn't even blink, still staring at the road. "I don't think you have a cowardly bone in your body, Katya Ellis."

"I do when it comes to my family. Leaving was easier than saying no."

"What did you say 'no' to?"

My stomach dipped. Oh, God. Would he judge me? Would he think I was as terrible a person as my family—and some of my friends—did? Sometimes I thought myself a terrible person, too. It wouldn't take much effort on my part to prevent Derek from unpleasant consequences. Even if he did deserve them.

"My brother got into trouble and my family is upset with me because I refused to help him when they insist that I could. Instead of sticking up for myself, I left home." My heart hammered. Wow. I'd never talked about this to anyone in my "new" life. Why was I volunteering this information now?

Maybe because he'd poured out his soul to me? For some reason I kept feeling it was incredibly important to square with him on everything. And not just the sexual stuff. Although staying equal on the sexual stuff was a lot more fun.

Which reminded me, I still owed him one orgasm.

"Wait, what? How were you supposed to help him? And what kind of trouble?"

I took a breath and blew it out. "Long ass story and one I'm not super proud of," I hedged.

He darted me a sharp look though I couldn't tell if he was annoyed with me or with my family, per my tale. "Sounds like whatever's up is hardly your fault."

My stomach twisted, I grabbed up my Big Gulp cup and, though I knew it was empty, loudly slurped up the very last of the ice juice in the bottom. Why had I said all that? I'd only managed to make myself look like a complete ass and a weakling on top of being a coward.

"You should know by now that I've got a perfection complex. I mean we've been working together too long for you to deny that you've noticed it."

He gave a slight nod, eyes still glued to the road. "Oh, I've noticed it. I've also greatly benefited from it."

"I always put this immense pressure on myself to be perfect at whatever I do—my job, even my gaming. That came from growing up in the household I was in. Everything revolved around Derek and his fuck-ups, *everything*. In college I even had to cancel an important lab for one of my classes because my parents scheduled family therapy at the same time and they wouldn't change it. And of course the family therapy was for Derek. To help him get better. So how could I say no?"

"Was it fair of them to do that to you?"

I snorted. "You should know better than anyone that 'fair' doesn't even come into it. And some of that pressure to be perfect came from inside, you know? Like we were one grade apart. We went to the same high school, and I had many of the teachers he'd had the year before. He'd acted out in class, skipped, fell asleep or was a general pain in their ass. Walking into class on the first day of school the following year, wasn't easy. Let's just say those teachers did a lot of pre-judging, expecting me to be a screw-up just like him. I had to work that much harder to prove I was nothing like him and get them past their initial prejudice. Some of them never did."

Lucas tilted his head to the side, considering, but didn't say anything. That was enough encouragement for me to continue.

"I guess what I'm saying is that I get it when you say that you were trying to please everyone around you but yourself. I was doing the same thing, though I never really thought about it like that. Somehow I got the idea that I had to be perfect because my brother was such a disappointment. He got all the attention, regardless."

Lucas pulled his eyes off the road to spare me a long, speculative glance. There was something weighted in that stare of his. It wasn't haughty or judgmental. It wasn't expectant or even defensive. There was something there, when I glanced up and met that composed gaze of his. A *click* so powerful that you could almost hear it happening.

An exchange of... quiet understanding not without a speck of emotion. A *breakthrough.*

He nodded thoughtfully and returned his gaze to the road. On a weird whim, I rested my palm atop his right hand, which sat on the gear shift. Almost immediately his thumb lightly stroked my pinky. A quiet and simple gesture of solidarity. Of thanks.

When he broke the silence and spoke, it was almost jarring to interrupt that wordless understanding we'd come to. His voice sounded different, as if there were some emotion behind the words. "You're too hard on yourself. I recognize it because I do the same thing."

"You do. I mean, you told me the night of your parents' dinner party that you were a shitty husband. You can't blame yourself for her cheating."

He blinked. "I'd like to think I'm mature enough to say that we were both at fault for the failure of that marriage. Sure, her cheating ended it but it was never all that great to begin with. I'm the one who initiated it and then was too busy to really take care of the relationship. That part was my fault. She was a crappy wife, sure, but that doesn't mean I was any less a shitty husband.

That whole thing taught me one thing. I was never meant to be a married man—well in the real sense, anyway."

I bit my lip, mulling those words over and for some reason, annoyed at this turn of conversation. Time to change it. "With us being so fixated on perfection, it's no wonder we both ended up as game testers. Obsessed with finding and cleaning up every imperfection."

He smiled in agreement. "I doubt the devs see it that way."

"Ah, fuck 'em. They're all a bunch of whingers." I snorted.

For the first time during our entire trip, Lucas threw his head back and laughed. "You get half my next paycheck if you tell them all that to their face when we get back."

As we left the greater Sacramento area, the radio had clicked over into an oldies station. I'd paid little attention to the songs until the familiar synthetic beat of one started up. Yup, it was the crooning of Rick Astley to his lover, vowing he was never going to let her go, disappoint or leave her.

I couldn't resist. I turned up the volume and sang along before elbowing him. "Dude, they are playing our song. Doesn't it get you all misty-eyed and nostalgic about our burger shop wedding and all the fancy dancing we didn't get to do?"

He sneered. "I fucking hate this song."

"Lean into it, Lucas! It's our wedding song. You just don't like it when the QA geeks plot and make it their life mission to rick-roll you whenever you annoy them with the schedule and deadlines. They need some sort of harmless retaliation for when you kick their incomplete bug reports back to them."

He shrugged. "The curse of perfection."

"Speaking of weddings, I have to admit that I saw some of the pics of your first one on the internet. I mean... how many small villages could you have supported for a year on that wedding budget?"

"Not my idea. And the fact that you Googled me is creepy, by the way." He straightened his shoulders and tossed his head like a haughty woman throwing her hair around. "Why are you so obsessed with me?" he asked, imitating Regina the Mean Girl's voice.

I doubled over immediately, gasping for air. He smiled, seeming satisfied I'd found him so amusing. These times had been rare up until lately.

"That impression was uncanny, by the way." After I wiped my tears, I turned down the radio volume, sparing his ears any more suffering.

"I do have a bone to pick with you, though. You told your friends about the noble title." His voice was flat and his face dead serious.

Oh shit. Well that got back to him fast. I bit my lip turning to him. "I'm so sorry. Are you mad?"

He threw me side eye, then quirked a lopsided smile. "Well, I'm not entirely happy about it. But no, not exactly mad. Just don't do it again."

I frowned. "Who ratted me out?"

"Jordan."

I let out a breath. "Completely unsurprising. I will find it necessary to get revenge on him."

He shook his head. "Not 'til after I get my new job, please."

"If I absolve myself of all culpability?"

"Cranberry, you have a shitty track record with keeping secrets so far."

My mouth twisted. Hmm. "Good point." He hit a bump and suddenly with a rush, my bladder did its level best to remind me it was there and it was full. That damn Big Gulp was already coming back to haunt me. "So, uh, don't be mad but... I need a pit stop."

With an exaggerated roll of his eyes, he acknowledged my request. "You're getting to be more and more of a pain, you know that?"

I held out a placating hand to him. "I'll make it up to you, I promise."

A dark brow shot up fetchingly. God, he was hot. "Hmm. I'm interested. How?"

"I'll figure it out. But it will be good."

At the next turn off, he exited the highway and found a tidy and nearly deserted rest area in almost no time. My bladder was ever-so-grateful for it.

We were now just about a half hour out from the vineyard, so Lucas informed me when he checked the GPS. We both took the opportunity to stretch our legs a bit. Lucas didn't seem in much of a hurry to get to our destination any earlier. Kind of like a condemned man facing his doom.

On the way back from the washroom, I bought him a small box of Lemon Oreos from a nearby vending machine and presented it to him. "Behold, my making it up to you."

To be honest, I had zero idea if he liked Lemon Oreos but I'd become addicted to them since coming to the States. Canada only had the more boring flavors of Oreos. As it turned out, my new adopted country was a great haven of all things Oreo and I had indulged in tasting 17 out of the possible 25 flavors.

Lucas, apparently, was not a fan. I wasn't too hurt, though. Because that meant I got the entire pack to myself. "You'll just have to find some other way to make it up to me." He narrowed his eyes at me.

"Oh, I have a few ideas. But they are all on the no-list, according to you." I gave him a wink, then licked my top lip suggestively. He deserved a little tease.

He scowled in response, even while reddening. Then he jammed his sunglasses back on his face.

Before getting back into the car, I did a three sixty to catch the surrounding view. From the vegetation and the landscape views, it hardly seemed like we were still in California. I took in a deep breath, appreciating the fresh, sweet-smelling air. And there were actually trees here other than the ever-present palms and Italian cypress down south. I raised my hands into the air, stretching and relishing the feel of a fresh breeze on my face. Was the summer cooler up here, too?

I caught Lucas's gaze and jerked to a stop, mid-twirl, unaware that he'd been watching me. Our eyes met, and I felt... something.

My heart sped up a little. My blood might have rushed to my face, warming the skin there pleasantly. I may have smiled at him. And the little devil on my shoulder might have danced a little jig and whispered some naughty ideas into my ear. She was a bad seed, that one.

Breathlessly, I explained myself. "I just love that there are so many trees here. It's so different from where we live."

"We're five hundred miles away from home."

Behind the protection of his shades, that weird stoicism had returned. That same distant coldness that wasn't unkind... more like guarded.

I frowned. "What's wrong? Are you really upset about me talking about your title?"

He blinked and turned from me, clicking the car unlocked and gallantly letting me in my side before taking his place behind the wheel.

I didn't expect him to answer my question given the delay. But as he pulled out of the parking spot and headed toward the on-ramp back to the freeway, he did.

"No," he finally said. "But if it comes up at work, you are doing the clean-up on that, got it? I don't care what story you give them. It was a joke, you lied, whatever."

I nodded, watching him carefully. "Okay. Fair enough"

We didn't talk while I munched my cookies. Lucas exited the highway to make our way down the twisty and two-lane Pope Valley road, passing even more trees. Here, I could see the vineyards right up next to the road. Lush green bushes that seemed as if they were planted on every square inch of soil that would hold them. They were stacked neatly in rows and climbing the natural swells of the landscape and the hills. Like undulating waves of a huge and fertile green ocean reaching up to the sky.

And sadly, I'd get a glimpse every so often of a distant hill or chunk of land that still bore the scars of a devastating wildfire. They'd torn through the valley in recent years, leaving barren, burnt paths in their wake. Being from British Columbia, I was no stranger to the devastating effects of wildfires myself.

I turned my head from side to side, bending forward to peer up and out of the windshield at the blue, blue sky dotted with fluffy clouds. The horizon to both the left and the right was trimmed with distant ruffled blue mountains. "It's lovely here."

"Don't get too attached to that nice weather you just enjoyed down at the south part of the valley. Groenveld Vineyard is at the furthest north end of the valley and in the summer, it can get hotter than hell."

"Wait, I thought your dad said it's called Turning Windmill?"

"That's the winery, the place where they make the wine. The vineyard is where the grapes grow."

We'd passed many of the larger vineyards and wineries on the main highway. Some were vast and opulent, one looking like a massive Tuscan medieval castle, others resembling romantic European estates.

My eyes drifted to his hands on the steering wheel. Those sexy, strong, veined hands were currently white-knuckling the wheel. Dude was *not* happy about having to hang out with his parents for a week, clearly. My mind raced to get his mind off of it. A good gamer girl always knew how to draw upon her maximized skill set to get things done.

"So how does a Dutch aristocratic family come to own a winery in California? Why not the south of France or something?"

"My grandfather fell in love with northern California when he attended Stanford. He's the one who acquired the winery. His father helped him buy in, since he was still young and he was a silent partner. He went back to the Netherlands but wasn't happy there so brought his wife and children out to California to live here. Father was born in Utrecht but grew up here. He had zero interest in just sitting in the countryside growing grapes. He got out when he could and now he treats it like a side gig. Just one small part of his own vast business empire."

"Hmm, a real life old school mogul, eh?"

"It's so predictable, isn't it?"

My mouth twisted. "That's not what I was thinking, but you know them and I don't." I shrugged.

"I mean... what about them is not a cliché? Father was successful taking his old money and multiplying it as a driven businessman. Mother was a magazine fashion model. They met at some high society event and got married six months later. They had the requisite two children—one of each—and proceeded to live a high society life together. Father treats the people in his life like props and trophies. No one can stand him but everyone pretends to."

Eek. That was harsh. Lucas's sexy lips had a curl to them, as if he'd just tasted something horrible and couldn't get rid of the bitter flavor in his mouth.

I put my hand over his once again, this time curling my fingers around his. "You know, there's more to family than the people whose house you were born into. There's the family you are born to and then there's the family you choose."

He raised his brows but didn't look at me, eyes still on the road. My fingers tightened around his. "I know this between us isn't real. But for the time being, we are for real married. And while we're married, we're family. *Chosen* family, which is more special. And as long as I'm your family, I'll have your back."

He said nothing, but I knew he heard me loud and clear when his fingers tightened around mine. He took in a deep breath, let out a long sigh and then swallowed visibly, as if coming to a decision. Then he turned his palm and our fingers laced around each other. He didn't have to thank me, didn't have to tell me he appreciated the gesture. His fingers around mine said all of that just as well. *Better*, in fact.

And hopefully this diluted some nervousness he'd been feeling for the days leading up to today. I assumed that this trip would be the longest amount of time he'd spend in his family's company throughout the previous six years. Since he'd left his old life behind.

"Same goes for me..." he began in a quiet voice.

"I already know that. You had my back, with my brother. I was very grateful."

Shortly thereafter, Lucas released my hand to return it to the steering wheel. Then he slowed the car, turning down a single-lane paved road that led toward a set of buildings in the distance. We snaked down the long lane, lined with gorgeous old growth California live oaks. They curved and stooped to shelter the drive with their leafy shadows. But this was no ordinary driveway. It took us a while to even be able to see past the thick dark trunks and the comforting shade to emerge into dazzling sunlight.

Holy shit. The central building was massive and... resembled a palace straight out of the Loire Valley during the French renaissance. I was suddenly glad that I was no longer holding his hand. That would have been some serious sweaty embarrassment on my hands—literally. When I thought he wasn't looking, I clandestinely wiped my palms across my jeans.

Well here it was, large and complete with a massive circular drive; a towering façade peppered with parapets, friezes and cornices. *And* a huge white fountain depicting naked Greek gods in full frolic. Massive proof that I'd married way *way* above my own social and economic class. Not intimidating in the least bit. Nope. *Not at all.*

"You okay?" Lucas was apparently taking in my paleness and the way I was gripping the edge of my seat.

I turned to him, wide-eyed. "Gotta paper bag handy for some healthy hyperventilation?"

He laughed. "You made the bed, Cranberry. Time for us both to sleep in it."

Gulp. And that was another thing. We were probably going to have to share a bed again while we were here. And, well... last time had almost led to spontaneous consummation of our nuptials.

He'd made it perfectly clear, though, that there would be none of that.

And it didn't matter how great his butt looked in those jeans or the way that t-shirt hugged his well-developed biceps. Or the way those dark lash-fringed sleepy brown eyes watched me like he *wanted to eat me up.*

It wasn't happening.

But a girl could fantasize, right?

A butler and driver greeted us at the walkway. The driver took our car to park it God only knew where on this massive estate. And yeah, that's right—a *butler.* Not just the main butler, but *our own personal* butler, apparently.

I elbowed Lucas on our way into the house as we followed our butler, Mr. Deleon, inside. "Why do we have a butler?"

"Because we're in the guesthouse and that comes with a butler." As if that's just how it was, as if that was enough to get me to understand. And I *did* understand, more than I had at any other moment before this, that Lucas and I were from two completely different worlds.

I blinked. "Oh."

Inside, we were formally received—for that is the only way I could put it in such a place as this—by Lucas's mother and his sister, Julia. His father was out golfing, apparently.

A camera clicked incessantly as we approached the reception line. My mother-in-law leaned in and air-kissed me on both cheeks, her ring-bedecked hands resting lightly on my shoulders as if the material from my t-shirt might soil them. Her perfume wasn't overwhelming but much stronger than I normally encountered. And she wore some type of designer pantsuit, full makeup and heels as if having stepped out of a board meeting instead of being on vacation.

"Ah, here they are at last!" The camera clicked some more and then one of the group near the photographer approached. She asked if Lucas's mother would kiss me again so they could catch the angle from the other side.

I glanced at Lucas and he was staring at the group like they were Martians just landed in their flying saucer. So clearly this wasn't a typical occurrence.

I mean, were they that over the moon that Lucas was here that they had to professionally document the occasion for all posterity?

"The prodigal son has arrived." Julia enfolded her brother into a hug, grinning. "Time to kill the fatted calf."

Elaine van den Hoehnsboek van Lynden turned a baleful glare and an arched eyebrow on her daughter. "Julia, *please.*" Her mother darted a pointed glance at the photographer and the other two who stood nearby, one of them scribbling notes onto her tablet with a stylus. Elaine turned to the woman taking notes and plastered on a wide smile. "She's our little joker." Then to Lucas and me she muttered under her breath. "Pay no attention to her."

Elaine tilted her cheek up for an expectant kiss from her son, which he dutifully delivered.

Huh. My gaze bounced from Julia's quiet amusement to Lucas's stiffness to their mother's cool formality. The Awkward was strong in this family.

Elaine raised her voice so she could be easily overheard. "I am so excited to put you both up in the Lover's Villa. I hope you love it, Katharina." Oh, yeah, Lucas had warned me about the full names thing. His mother didn't believe in nicknames. She waved the group of three over. "This is Georgina Weldon and..." Elaine hesitated.

The new woman, Georgina, stepped in. She was short and stocky, mid-forties with a mop of short, curly brown and gray hair drooping onto her forehead, but shaved at the sides. "My photographer, Gary Spencer. And assistant, Sarah." She pointed to the other two, a hipster-looking guy complete with beard and man-bun in his early twenties. Beside him stood a thin, college age girl with straight dark hair wearing a denim jacket over her mini-dress. "We're so excited to work on the feature from *New American Monthly* periodical on your family reunion. It will be a long form article on nobility in America. And you're the newlyweds! I'd love to get some time to do a short interview with you both."

Okay, what was this now?

Lucas looked no less confused than he had before. And for that matter, I was right there with him. We both turned to

Elaine. What was the point in not warning us about this? She must have known, for months probably.

Unless... unless the reason she didn't tell us was because she didn't think Lucas would come. And the reason she needed Lucas and I here so badly was for this. I remembered the things Lucas had told me in the car, about how appearances meant everything to them.

Well, shit.

We must have obviously had that escaped prisoner-in-the-floodlights look about us.

My mother-in-law had a huge but very fake smile pasted on. "Come, let me show you around. We can talk about all this later. We have all week."

I took Lucas's hand and followed her as she walked into the entry hallway of the main building. He was rigid beside me, clearly upset with his mother. I glanced up at him. Regardless, he hid it well.

"I'm sure I will. I love everything I've seen here so far. It's amazing." I cast a glance around me at the frosted glass windows above the doorway. It was all so bright with gleaming white marble everywhere, the onyx statue on an alabaster plinth in the center. Gorgeous paintings hung on the wall of a quality that belonged in a museum. No doubt authentic and incredibly expensive.

And the chandelier! The opening at the top, an oculus, allowed sunlight in to catch light on all the crystals. It wasn't electric, as far as I could tell. Just brilliant and gleaming in the sunlight, leaving mini rainbows on the shimmering entryway floor and walls.

Lucas's mum caught me staring at it gap-jawed. "That's from Austria. Swarovski crystal. It's powered by the sunlight."

"Holy crap. Oh, I mean—um, how cool." Elaine stared back at me, blank-faced. The camera clicked away from the doorway and I squirmed. I looked up at Lucas, silently pleading with him to get me out of this weird awkward situation. "I mean—I've never seen anything like it. It's amazing, um, and—"

Lucas squeezed my hand. "We're a bit tired and we'd like to freshen up..."

Elaine's expression brightened. "Of course, of course. Deleon has taken your things to the villa already. You remember where it is? Do you want the golf cart?"

"We can stretch our legs."

Lucas ushered me through some kind of fancy parlor that looked like a set out of *The Crown* and out some glass doors onto a balcony. It overlooked an extravagant French garden complete with shrubs cut into geometrical shapes, tiled walkways and bursts of color from carefully designed flowerbeds.

I couldn't help it. I had to let loose a few more expletives. Instead of shushing me, Lucas laughed. "I kinda wish I could see all this through your eyes right now," he said in a low voice.

"My eyes are a bit bedazzled, to be honest."

He said nothing, but watched me, his grin widening.

Off to the left side of the parkway, I caught glimpses of a huge gleaming swimming pool ringed with pale rocks and what looked like a complex waterfall system. Directly in front of us at the far end of the long garden were more buildings and, off toward the righthand side was what looked like an old-fashioned carriage house. Lucas pointed in that direction. "The villa is over behind the carriage house."

"That's a hike."

He blew out a breath. "In a few days, you'll be so grateful for the privacy, you won't care about having to walk out there to get it."

I shot him a glance. "Speaking of privacy, what do you think about that reporter and photographer thing going on?"

He shook his head, smile vanishing. "I'm thinking that's the real reason she was practically begging us to come to the reunion. I thought it was weird at the time, how insistent she was being. I figured she was all up in the night about how it would look to the cousins and uncles that we weren't there. Something like this never even occurred to me."

"So weird..."

"Yeah." He nodded. "Hopefully they'll be so busy with all the other people here, they'll leave us alone or just pay minimal attention to the young people. Not many people our age even read that magazine, anyway. If any magazine at all."

"Good point. Besides, if they don't, we can always demand our privacy, since this is our 'honeymoon' and all."

The stroll went quicker than I thought and our *butler*, Mr. Deleon, greeted us at the door. How weird, the thought of us, who regularly spent the night fully clothed slumped over the ratty couch at our office, had a butler for the next week.

Mr. Deleon promptly gave us the tour. The villa was actually bigger than the house I grew up in. Full kitchen, formal dining room and a sitting room, office and exercise room on the bottom floor. Bedroom and a recreation/game room on the second floor. And on the top floor, the best part of the amazing place, a rooftop garden patterned after an Italian garden villa. I'd only gotten a glimpse of it, but was determined to explore it later, once I had the time.

As it were, we had just enough time to freshen up for a casual dinner with the early arrivals. Most of the guests would be arriving later tonight or tomorrow morning. The dinner seemed uneventful though Lucas did not appear all too pleased by the presence of not only his ex-wife, but her parents, too.

And I thought *my* family was weird.

Fortunately there were enough people to provide a barrier, but I couldn't help but marvel at the insensitivity of Lucas's family to have them here. To treat them as if they were still family and give more deference to their feelings than to their own newly re-married son and new daughter-in-law.

After dinner, we went on another walk, then back to the villa. I collapsed into bed that night while Lucas was still in the shower. And by the time he came to bed, I barely registered him lying down. I was in that lucid land where my reality was mostly a product of my own silken dreams. Like... that feather-light touch on my face was most certainly a figment of my imagination. And maybe even that sensation like a thumb lining the edge of my jaw as if that thumb had edged that jaw every night for the past year. When clearly it had not. Which made it almost certainly a dream.

Almost. Certainly.

As a result of my early night, my eyes snapped open just before dawn. And try as I might to close them again, I couldn't. The thoughts had started racing almost the second I'd reached consciousness. Lucas's breathing was still that calm regular inhale-exhale of deep sleep. I slipped out of bed as quietly as I could and dug out a pair of shorts and a t-shirt.

Normally, I'd prefer to do some yoga to help myself wake up. But this morning, I had an even stronger desire to be outside. I was excited to explore the grounds and the bigger parts of the gardens I'd only caught hints of the day before. The air was fresh and cool for now and I started by winding my way through the artfully designed "forest trail" just off the main garden. It was nothing like the forests of the Pacific Northwest, but this forest grove included a few giant Sequoias, which thrived in California. None grew further north due to the cold. They were impressive trees, even to this girl who had grown up amongst trees all her life.

The grove was bordered on all sides, but one, by the carefully arranged grapevines in their fields. On the fourth side, I found myself walking the loamy gravel path of a French garden. There was even a shrub maze.

The sun had risen and was gleaming in the sky hours later as I made my way by the side entrance of the main house. I almost turned away before stepping onto the pavement until I heard a muffled huff of disgust and a swallowed sob.

Too curious to stop myself, I did an about face and peeked around the corner near a service driveway. There stood Julia, Lucas's sister, dressed in designer jeans, Prada boots, a carefully arranged Hermes scarf and a Louis Vuitton bag over her shoulder. Her phone, complete with bedazzled case, was in her hand and she was stabbing at it desperately with her pointer finger.

I cleared my throat. "Hey! Fancy seeing you here."

Julia's head jerked in my direction. Her eyes widened, and she lost some of her color, as if horrified that I was here, witnessing whatever I was witnessing. Perhaps she was about to make her own great escape? Perhaps it was her just acting like a normal person and getting caught in the act. Who knew...

She seemed to recover herself and gestured stiffly at her phone. "Can you believe that Uber won't send a car out here? It's too far out in the tules."

"The *where?*"

She sighed. "I don't know how Canadians say it. East Egypt? The boondocks?"

"Oh," I nodded, suddenly understanding. "We say the boonies."

I frowned. Why did she need an Uber? Did she not have her own car—or cars, most likely—or even one of several drivers on the estate who could take her where she needed to go? Most likely on some shopping emergency or another.

"Do you need a ride? Your mum said a driver could—"

She held up a hand. "I don't need my parents to know everywhere I go, thankyouverymuch." She looked down at her phone as if deep in thought, biting her lip. "It's, uh, it's something I really need to do without them getting nosy about it. Especially with that reporter sniffing around."

My eyes caught on a flash of color clipped to one of the rings of her shoulder bag. A red disc of some kind. Something about it seemed familiar.

"Well, I should be—" I took a step back

At that same moment, Julia stiffened as she punched at her phone. "Shit, at this rate, the meeting will be over by the time the stupid car even gets here."

Meeting? I tilted my head, glancing at the red disc again, picking up the shape of a triangle on the surface.

A sobriety chip. Julia was in recovery. The red one meant sober for one month. And she had a meeting. I suddenly felt bad that I'd discounted her need to get away as a shopping emergency. I was as guilty of being quick to judge as anyone else, I supposed.

"Cancel the Uber," I said, holding out my hand to her. "Lucas and I rented a car. I could get it from the valet and drive you."

She looked up, eyes widening. "Oh could you? Thank you. I'd just need to..."

I drew a figurative X over my heart. "I won't say a word to anyone."

Our gazes locked, and she smiled. Then she informed me how to go about getting my car and flagged down a nearby staff person to help. In short order, we were on the road and I was relieved that Lucas had rented the car in both our names.

"Do you have the address? You can put it into the GPS."

"I've got it here on my phone." She pressed a button on her phone and suddenly we were hearing the robotic directions being dictated to us in an androgynous voice.

The drive back to the city of Napa from our part of the valley would take a little over a half hour and we drove in silence. Julia spent most of it scrolling and typing on her phone.

I dropped her off outside a small community church in town. She gave me a few suggestions of what I could do while she was gone for the next hour.

"Don't worry, I'm good at finding something to do." I smiled. "Have a good meeting."

She furrowed her brows, then thanked me and walked off with quick urgent steps, bouncing on her heels across the pavement. I walked down the main thoroughfare in town, the shops having just opened and the streets starting to gather tourists.

My stomach growled, yet I passed no less than three coffee shops. I wasn't much of a coffee drinker but could use a good cup of tea. Unfortunately, Americans were tea-impaired. I hadn't had a good cup of the stuff since I'd left Canada.

To kill time, I went into the tourist info center and grabbed a printed booklet for anything that looked mildly entertaining. I needed to have a plan in place for when Lucas lost his patience— or his mind—because of his family. We could go hiking or tour a vineyard or even go up in a hot-air balloon or to a natural spring in Calistoga.

I left with a thick handful of glossy pamphlets and an apology on my lips to all the trees that had given up their lives in the creation of them. Then I dipped into a cheesy souvenir shop, determined to grab something for Lucas. Near the back, there were living succulent plants with names of local places colorfully painted on the tiny pots. I grabbed two mini ball cacti with a snicker and paid for them quickly.

Heading back to the church shortly thereafter, I idly wondered how crowded the meeting was. It was an AA meeting being held in the heart of California's wine country, after all... Maybe it was a particularly concerning problem here?

A little over an hour later, Julia and I were in the car and headed back to the family estate. She seemed much more at ease now, thankfully, and I hoped her meeting did her some good. But I didn't pry.

"If you, ah, if you need to come back here again over the next few days while I'm here, I'm happy to give you a ride again. It's a lovely drive, and I enjoyed walking around town."

She fiddled idly with the strap on her bag while staring out the window. Her phone must have been out of battery. She turned slowly to me. "I take it you know what the meeting was?"

"I saw the red chip on your bag. I, ah, I used to attend Al-Anon. I recognized it." I kept my eyes firmly on the road and avoided her gaze so I wouldn't make her uncomfortable.

I caught movement in my peripheral vision as she must have moved her hand to the coin in question. "Hah, so funny. I put it there to flaunt it to my parents. Not that they'd know what it meant, anyway. They didn't want me doing the program because of my 'high profile.' Someone might get word of it, the horror! And write about it where prying eyes could see. Lots of pearl clutching. They wanted me in a private and isolated rehab instead."

I blinked. "They aren't, uh, supportive?"

She flicked a lock of her dark hair over her shoulder. "Understatement. Especially the 'bad timing' of it, what with the reporter here and all the other extended family members. I'm in this all on my own. Not even my friends approve. Because I'm not *fun* and I don't *party* with them anymore. As if that's all there is to life. Claire and Liz haven't stopped whining about it since they got here."

Huh. Another reason to dislike Lucas's ex. Those reasons seemed to be piling up rather easily. "I'm sorry. That must be so hard. And with the big party coming up."

"Yeah, exactly. I need all the support I can get and I'm not getting any. Claire has already told me I should take a 'night off' and just enjoy myself."

I knew this was overstepping my bounds, but I just had to. "Is it wise to have her here at a family reunion when you are so early in your recovery?"

Julia shot me a speculative look. She probably thought it was just a typical case of the second wife being self-conscious about the first. I also realized that she probably didn't know the same story I did about how bad that marriage had really been.

"It's complicated. She's my friend. But her family is also close with mine. I mean... I think my parents feel somewhat responsible for the dumpster-fire that her and Lucas's marriage turned out to be."

My absolute puzzlement and disbelief must have been written all over my face because she spoke again to attempt to answer my unasked questions.

"I mean, no one blames Lucas. He wasn't in the best place emotionally and whatever. But it was hard on Claire, too. When things got ugly with his depression, he just walked out and disappeared. None of us knew whether he was alive or dead for almost a year. Especially with his struggles. He might have done something to himself, you know?"

I blinked. What the...? I knew about the disappearing part. And Lucas had mentioned something about concern for his health but I'd understood that to be his physical health—not his mental health. This sounded way more serious than he had presented it.

Julia obviously read my confusion on my face. She put her hand over her mouth. "Jeez I have such a big mouth, spilling the tea like that. Maybe he didn't want you to know."

I forced a smile and a shrug. "Oh no, we are totally open and tell each other everything." When the hell had I become such a great liar, anyway? "I just feel sad whenever I hear about that time in his life. How sad he must have been."

"Situational depression is no joke."

I swallowed. "No, definitely not." Taking a deep breath and letting it go, I vowed to have a talk with Lucas. I needed to make sure he was fine and not slipping back into any of that while he was here and exposed to his rather insensitive family members.

I turned back to her again. "So, do you have a strategy about the party? Is your sponsor available for you to contact?"

She nodded. "Yeah, yeah. She told me I can call her whenever I need to this weekend. Even if it's two in the morning. I did rehab because I got a DUI. My license is suspended. That's why I can't drive myself to these meetings." Her shoulders slumped as if remembering all that suddenly was making her sad.

"But you're doing great work," I encouraged. "Over a month sober is amazing."

She nodded, fingering the chip again. "Thirty-five days, to be exact. It's a work in progress. But as far as Mother and Father are concerned, that's the end of it. That's all I needed to do to 'fix' myself. They just don't get it. No one here does."

"I'm here. I know we don't know each other very well but I can be your support. And your brother—"

She held up her palm to me. "Do not tell Lucas. Please."

"Oh," I turned my head to gaze at her and she looked a little panicked. "Don't worry. I'm good for my word. I won't tell him. But I think he'd definitely be supportive. He'd also be proud of you."

She let out a long sigh and turned to look back out the window. "Yeah, well, that might have once been the case but we haven't been close in a long time."

I had zero idea what to say to that so I just turned my attention back to the road. If she wanted to continue the conversation, she would.

And it didn't take long for her to do just that. "So, do you mind if I ask who you attended Al-Anon for?"

I hesitated for only a split second. She'd spilled so much to me. I might as well return the favor.

"I went because of my brother. And our parents aren't too different from yours." Minus all the bank accounts stuffed with money, I didn't add aloud. "They want it all to go away without really doing the work for it. But he only paid lip service to the program when he attended." I didn't want to go into detail about the numerous times he had stopped and started. Along with other attempts at recovery—all of them empty promises on his part.

Recovery was hard. It was something that had to be fought for and Derek had never had to fight for anything ever in his life.

"Did your parents attend with you?"

I shook my head. "I did it for myself, actually. I was starting to feel resentful toward him."

She nodded as she dug around in her bag for her phone, then pulled it out, checked the screen and put it down. "Did it help?"

I shrugged. "Yeah, a bit. Family relationships are tough to begin with. Adding addiction into the mix..."

She sighed. "Yeah, exactly the reason I can't really face talking to my brother about it."

I nodded. "You might find he won't judge you the way you think."

"Yeah, well." She shrugged. "I'm actually envious of him. He was the smart one. Everyone keeps blaming his mental state at the time but he did what he had to do, jumping out of all this crap before it could trap him. He remade his life so he wouldn't have to change himself to conform into this one."

"Surely it's not too late for you to do the same thing."

After a pause. "Maybe not."

I seethed on her behalf for the rest of the ride home. For the lack of support from both her parents and her friends. How come people's dysfunction and dependency were so much more welcome than their fight to live their best lives?

It reminded me that such was the case for my parents as well. But instead of doing the work, they wanted me to pay the price to protect Derek. It was always about coddling and protecting Derek. About arranging all of our lives around the monster that had him clutched in its talons. Derek was an addict and until he made the decision himself to do what needed to be done, there was nothing they or I could ever do to change that. And in the meantime, we'd just progressively ruin our own lives to stumble around after him and be there to catch him when he fell.

I'd made an irreversible decision to change that destiny my parents had written out for me. But that had meant cutting out everything that was toxic. Sickness, regret and exhaustion over the entire thing swirled in my gut like the ingredients to a perfect storm, pulling everything inside itself, tighter and tighter. I'd never felt more alone in my life than I had on the plane ride to California, leaving my friends, my family even many of my most prized possessions behind.

We pulled up near the garage instead of the front as Julia had indicated, in order to stay away from prying eyes. She smiled and thanked me, then she did something strangely surprising and also endearing.

She reached out and touched my shoulder. "I love your hair. It's such a gorgeous color. You have a costume for the Gatsby theme party?"

I nodded.

"I've been hyper focused on the theme and all the details—to get my mind off the partying part. My makeup artist and hairdresser are coming over in the afternoon. Can I send them over to you? I want to do something nice as a way to say thank you for today."

I smiled. "Julia, you really don't have to buy my silence. I promise—"

Her eyes widened. "Oh, I know you won't say anything. I just... I'd rather you benefit from their expertise than my unsupportive friends. Let them do their own hair and makeup."

And with that, she opened the door and was gone. I watched her go, confused and even a bit overwhelmed by her.

And by her brother and what she'd casually revealed to me about his mental health after the divorce. It was so hard to tell what went on beneath the surface of my husband's very calm exterior. He kept everything inside—except maybe the gruff and grumpiness.

Jeez. No wonder he'd been so upset with me about going over his head to agree to attend this reunion. I swallowed a big ball of guilt. I owed him an apology. And I owed him some openness, because it wasn't fair for me to expect it from him and not give it in return.

When I got back to the guest house, I had a throbbing headache, a frighteningly grumpy attitude. In addition, I was in bad need of a nap despite the long hours of sleep the night before.

And very little time to attend to any of the above.

CHAPTER 19
LUCAS

I SLEPT IN TOO LATE AT THE VILLA AND WHEN I WOKE UP, SHE was gone. I got up, brushed my teeth and went through the usual morning routine. Workout on the rowing machine in the gym room downstairs. Breakfast from a selection of fruit, pastries and coffee left for us by the butler.

Still no Katya.

I checked my phone but there was no text from her. So I sent her one.

She walked in the front door about five minutes after I hit send without having answered my message. With an exasperated sigh, she flopped onto the couch in the front sitting room. I found her there, sprawled out on the couch, her long copper hair splayed out around her beautiful face.

"Hey," I said as she kicked off her tennis shoes and put her feet up on the glass coffee table. "Where were you?"

She rubbed small circles into her forehead. "It's already starting to get hot out there. I went for a walk earlier and ran into your sister. She needed a ride to Napa, so I took her in our rental car."

I rolled my eyes. "Shopping emergency or Instagram photo op?"

She straightened and looked at me, already appearing tired and it wasn't even noon. "You should cut her more slack than that."

I frowned. "Uh oh, were you two bonding?"

She sighed and pressed the heels of her hands to her eyes as if she had a headache. "Do we have any aspirin?"

"I'll check." I looked in both of the bathrooms—the downstairs one and the one off our bedroom—and both medicine cabinets were empty. So I texted Deleon asking to bring us some. She had aspirin and a cold bottle of water in her hand less than ten minutes later.

"Do you need to lie down for a bit? I can get us out of whatever is on the itinerary this afternoon. A tour or wine tasting or something, I'm sure." She hesitated for a moment. I sank down on the couch beside her. "I'll text my mother to let her know you aren't feeling well."

She straightened and turned to me, her face inches from mine, as if she were looking for something in my eyes. Or my nose, chin or the rest of my features up close and personal. She smelled like sunshine and warm coconuts.

"Tell me honestly, Lucas. Is being here with your family for a week going to trigger you?"

I blinked. "Trigger me into doing what? Wearing black and listening to Barry Manilow?"

"Your depression," she answered quietly.

Huh. Well, I guess Julia'd had time to do some damage. I let go a long breath and settled back against the couch. "I'm not sure what Julia told you but I'm fine."

"*Now.*" She blew out a long breath. "But I feel responsible, for getting us into this and bringing you back into this environment.

I didn't know, but even so, I was being petty because you annoyed me, but I'm sorry. Can we—"

"Stop it, Kat. I'm fine."

She blinked. "I just wish you'd told me. I could have—"

I stiffened and faced her. "There's a lot we haven't told each other, now isn't there?"

She blinked, her eyes darting to one of my eyes, then the other. I took a minute to appreciate how pretty and blue they were. It was difficult to discern her mood. She seemed wound up but also sad.

"You're right, there is. Like I haven't told you everything about what's going on with me. So I shouldn't have expected..." Her voice died out.

I tilted my head, studying her. She was acting *really* weird. "Are you all right? Were you out in the heat too long or something?"

She drew back and continued that expressionless stare that was actually starting to worry me. Maybe there *was* something wrong...

"I'm pretty sure if I go back to Canada that I might be in serious trouble." She drew in a long deep breath and let it out, as if this fact had been some great burden to her for some time. Maybe it had?

I blinked. "Okay, what did you do?"

She bit her lip. "It's not what I did. It's what I didn't do."

I shook my head. "I'm confused."

She stared up at the ceiling in contemplation, rubbing at a spot between her eyes, like her headache was still bothering her. "A few months before I left Canada, my brother got mixed up in something that was way over his head. He had this group of friends that we barely knew. I suspect they were the ones supplying him with whatever shit he was on. Anyway, I don't know the exact circumstances, but he was involved in a robbery and caught on surveillance with a few of the others."

Wow. I frowned. Derek hadn't struck me as the sharpest tool in the shed but he hadn't really screamed *criminal* either. I nodded encouraging her to continue.

She clenched her teeth together for a moment as if remembering something that particularly angered her. Then she began twisting a long strand of coppery hair around her index finger. I watched her wind and unwind and rewind it again, strangely fascinated.

"The thing is, all the images of him were blurred or the lighting was bad or something. He wasn't immediately recognizable though some of the others involved were. But the guys who were caught were happy to name him as part of the group for whatever reason—maybe they got a plea deal or something."

I shifted in my seat, eyes still on that coil of hair. "How does this involve you?"

Her mouth thinned grimly. "I'm getting to it... so the people naming him, of course, didn't have any concrete evidence that Derek was with them. He'd been smart enough not to text them about it and there was no other documentation of him being in on it. Or any of the usual forms of evidence. But Derek didn't have an alibi, either. He swore to us up down and sideways that he was innocent but I could tell by the way he was suddenly flush with cash that he was likely involved. I found it hard to believe that his friends would just hand over the loot from their crime without him being in on it. Of course, my parents believe him one hundred percent."

I blew out a breath. "Well they'd better get a rowboat 'cause they are clearly deep in denial."

She snorted at that and looked up. To my dismay, she dropped the coil of hair and began twisting her wedding ring instead. "That's a new one."

I didn't say anything else, and she returned my stare. I half wondered if she was going to continue with the story and if she veered away from it, then should I try to pin her down? She was silent so long I almost thought she wouldn't finish the story.

But she finally took a long and noisy breath, almost as if she was fighting back some emotion. "They're so convinced he's innocent, that they hired a really expensive lawyer to take his case. They've had to take extra loans and a second mortgage on the house and work more hours to pay for the legal stuff."

Her voice tightened, somewhere between anger, frustration and grief. "But Derek didn't have an alibi that night. And he needed something airtight. Something documented. So the lawyers did some digging and realized that I was livestreaming on Twitch the evening in question. Exactly when the whole thing went down..." She took in another ragged breath, and I sat up, concerned. "So they said that I could be an important witness if I spoke up and swore that Derek was in the house with me all night. Our rooms at home are right across the hall from each other. In theory, I would have been able to see him—or evidence he was there—while I was livestreaming."

"But he wasn't there..." I said between clenched teeth, the sinking in my gut telling me clearly where this was going.

"He wasn't there. In fact I didn't see him the entire day from the time I got off work in the morning—I was working a graveyard shift job then. I'd come home, eat and then crash until midafternoon usually. Then I'd get up, do stuff around the house or work out and get on my Twitch. Since I had that night off, my livestream went longer. I never saw Derek until the next day."

"So of course the lawyers are pushing you to vouch for him."

She shook her head. "They merely suggested it in a roundabout way. 'If she were to tell the authorities he was with her all night...' sort of thing. But my parents clamped onto that and ran with it. They insisted that that's what I needed to do."

I blinked. "Oh yeah, no big deal, just perjure yourself."

She reached up and scratched her jaw with a shaky hand, swallowing fiercely. If I didn't know her better, I'd say she was close to tears, and it did something to me deep inside to see it. If her father were in the room right now, I'd probably punch the asshole. Her parents, the people whose job it was to look out for her instead expected her to put herself in legal danger to save her worthless brother's skin.

"When I said I wouldn't do it, they flipped out. My mum screamed at me and my dad threatened to take my car and my electronics away, my computer, everything. Mind you, I'd paid for almost all of it with my job. The only reason I was living at home was because I'd had to move out of my cheap student housing when I graduated. It costs a king's fortune to live in Vancouver. I was planning to save up for my own place. It was the biggest mistake of my life, moving back home, because all the problems with Derek were still there and even worse."

I sat up and took her hand, which was visibly shaking, and covered it with my own. "I'm sorry. That was incredibly shitty of them to put that pressure on you."

"It's the pattern of things that went on all throughout our lives once he started using. They always gave him a safe spot to land, no matter how bad the mistake. And it only enabled him to keep doing it. I put my foot down. And because he had some minor things on his record, if he got convicted, he'd likely get some real time in jail. The parents guilted me with that. 'Do you want your brother to rot in prison? What kind of person are you? It's just one quick thing to tell them and you can save him.'

"And the more I refused, the more they freaked and threatened. So finally I just grabbed a suitcase and packed it up one night and took off early in the morning when everyone was still sleeping. Then I got on a plane for LA."

"So the letters from the lawyers... that's them trying to get you to come back and testify?"

She nodded. "Yes, they want my deposition to provide his alibi. They hadn't been able to find me for a while. Then somehow all of a sudden, the letters started showing up. I think they must have used an investigator to track me down."

I blinked. "I'd lay down money they're also the ones who tipped off US immigration about your work situation. The government had a flag on you when they ran your passport that day you came back into the country from Adam and Mia's wedding."

A small crease appeared between her brows and she blinked. "Yeah, I've suspected that, too. And lately the letters have been getting worse. They're saying if I don't respond to the subpoena, then it will become a warrant and I'll be arrested or held in contempt of court." She bit her lip for a moment then let out a light squeak. "I just can't believe they'd take it this far. That my parents would rather see me arrested than Derek. I never did anything wrong. I don't even speed, for Chrissake."

"Come here," I said, moving closer to her and pulling her shaking body into my arms. She wasn't crying, but clearly upset. I held her shivering form close to mine, closed my eyes. That silky hair rubbed against my cheek. There was a feeling pooling in my chest, sympathy, understanding and solidarity for her. And something more, I wanted to protect her from these assholes who didn't deserve to be related to her.

Didn't deserve to have her in their lives at all.

Fuck 'em. Fuck. Them. *All.* My arms tightened around her reflexively and her body immediately relaxed against me. "I know what it's like to feel betrayed by your own parents, Kat. It fucking sucks. You have the right to be upset."

"You don't judge me?"

"Judge you? Why would I judge you? You did the right thing."

"Because it wouldn't take much for me to save my brother from something that could be very bad for him."

"From facing consequences... It's like my parents screaming at me to take Claire back when she had consequences of her own to face. And in no way caring about my own well-being. They saw that time as some kind of weakness or lapse. I was 'mentally ill' according to them and they couldn't handle it. When it's something that happens to thousands—probably even millions—of people in this country."

I drew back so I could look at her. Aside from some paleness, she seemed fine and dry-eyed.

I took her shoulders in my hands. She looked up at me with those beautiful big blue eyes of hers. I met her gaze with my own, holding it steadfast. "When they stop caring for our welfare and happiness, they are no longer worthy of being acknowledged."

Something shifted inside of me then, or opened. Like a stubborn, rusting lock clicking its tumblers, the hinges whining as if forced to move after being practically rusted shut in a closed and locked position. And the key that had managed it so quickly? Her raw and open honesty. Her sharing that deepest darkest fear inside of herself with *me*. Her trusting me that much...

I took a shaky breath and dropped my hands, then pulled away completely. That warning I'd repeated to myself when she'd first moved in was screaming through my mind. She was dangerous. I'd grow too close to her and the danger warnings were no longer just paranoia talk in my head.

It was reality, damn it. I hadn't heeded my own warning.

She blinked and put a palm on my cheek. "We're family, Lucas. At least for a little while longer. And I've got your back."

My throat tightened and some strange and unknown emotion welled up. All previous exasperation toward her dissipated. I leaned forward and, without realizing until I was doing it, I kissed her on the forehead. "You're sweet."

Then I did the next logical thing and ran like hell. Okay, I didn't really *run*. Instead I got up slowly and calmly left the room, as if I'd make a bathroom pit stop my excuse to extricate myself from her hold on me.

There was a myriad of emotions swirling in my chest and I needed a minute or a thousand to sort them out. I didn't do emotions well and so it might take a good moment to deal with them before I could stuff them back into cold storage again.

Unfortunately, she rose and followed me up the stairs and into the bedroom. *Damn*. I'd have to come up with an excuse to get some distance between us, and quickly.

In the next second, she was beside me, her arms wrapped around me. She lay her head on my shoulder and I stood there, wooden, my arms dangling at my sides. "Thank you, Lucas. For being there for me. And I want you to know that I'm here for you."

"For the short little while we have left, right?" I had to say it. I had to remind us both that this wasn't something meant to last. That it never had been. Something deep down inside wanted to contradict that. But *this*... this was my head reminding the rest of me that we'd set this in stone at the outset. "You know... since our divorce is practically on the calendar as soon as you get your green card."

She pulled back and looked into my face, her eyes searching mine. There was no offense. She clearly understood what I was saying, but she didn't draw back. Instead, she rose up on her tiptoes and kissed me on the cheek. "I can't reach your forehead so that will have to do. There, now we're even."

I fought a grin, dipped my head and kissed her again on the cheek. That soft, fragrant cheek. Her luscious hair brushed my face and heat surged. "Nope, we're not."

Her face clouded, and I caught that gleam in her eyes, that same one that ignited whenever we were in competition. Hell, who was I kidding? The two of us, we were always in competition. Before I could even think, she was on her tiptoes again, this time kissing me on the lips. It was a long, lingering kiss. Warm, inviting, but close-mouthed.

When she sank back to the flat of her feet, I followed her down, my mouth never further than an inch from hers. I'd been wanting to kiss those lips again—craving it like a man underwater too long craved oxygen. Like a child, lost and searching, craved home.

Her lips parted quickly, easily, and I pushed my tongue into her mouth, aggressive, needing to taste her. My hands clamped tightly around her upper arms, unwilling to cede this newly found treasure. I plundered her, a ruthless pirate unwilling to stop until I got everything I wanted.

She bumped against me as she angled her head to meet my demands, responding to them just as eagerly. That rushed intake of air, that breathy sigh. I was rock hard and aching for her in seconds.

She was just too goddamn sexy for her own good—*and* mine.

She was also caring. And honest.

And sweet.

And Kat...

She was *her* and, as I'd known for the entire duration of our acquaintance, she was irresistible in practically every way. And I'd fought a good fight.

But I wasn't going to fight anymore. We both knew the boundaries of this, the end date. I wasn't going to resist what we both wanted so much. Until then, there was too much to explore, too much to savor.

My hands were under her shirt, palming the soft skin of her waist and back under it. She pressed against me, sighing, sifting her fingers through my hair. Slowly, without taking my mouth from hers, I guided us to the bed.

She caught on quickly and moved with me. Our kisses deepened, became more heated and desperate. I wanted—no I *needed*—to be inside her. I needed it like I needed water, food and air. And I felt that need all over my skin, where it tingled—inflamed, achy, and feverish.

I'd never wanted a woman the way I hungered for her.

This way lay danger, like those old antique maps that were lined on the edges with pictures of mythical beasts and the warning *Here be dragons.*

She was danger, right before me in the form of a diminutive, curvy redhead with the biggest heart I had ever known. Brains, beauty and compassion. A fucking dangerous combination. And I had full sails open to the wind, ready to cruise right over the edge of the map, dragons or no.

And I didn't fucking care.

With a quick tug at the collar, I pulled off my shirt and dumped it on the floor. I closed my eyes and savored the feel of her hands as she explored my body. Her palms smoothed over my chest, my nipples, down across my stomach, around to my back, my shoulders. She left nothing untouched.

"I want you," she whispered to me. Three simple words that entered my system like a drug straight to my blood. *Feverish.* I might boil over if I didn't plunge myself into her soon.

My hands reached up, tangling my fingers into her silky fire hair. Gently, I pulled her head back to look into her face. "I'm going to fuck you, Kat."

Her eyes darkened, dilated wide. They were such a pale blue that I could see the reaction immediately. *And* the way she swayed against me. *And* the way her breath hitched. In seconds, her shirt was off. Then she reached around and her bra followed onto the growing heap of clothes on the floor.

Then her hands were on my fly, trying to ease the zipper down. Things were tight down there and her hands brushed my erection. I couldn't suppress the groan. I helped her undo the pants and kicked them off as quickly as if they were on fire. It certainly felt like my skin was.

Kat reached out and palmed me through my boxers and I grabbed her again, pulling her flush against me. Then I tilted us toward the bed, coming down on top of her as gently as I could. I was naked, and she was almost there, still wearing her shorts.

They'd come off soon enough, but I had some catching up to do. My mouth sank to her breasts, taking a nipple in my mouth while I fingered the other one. I sucked fiercely, feeling my entire body come alive as she gasped and arched her back, her nipple beading instantly.

Holy fuck. How had I managed to stay away from her for so long? Weeks ago, she'd made it clear that she was willing to have sex with me. She'd slept in my bed in nothing more than a thin nightie. And yet, idiot that I'd been, I'd mostly kept my hands off. I'd had no idea that I'd had that kind of strength of will. It had never been tried like this before.

But I'd have to have a will stronger than Iron Man's suit and more powerful than Thor's hammer, Mjolnir, to resist this. Her sighs, her smooth skin, her arched back, her fingers digging into my shoulders.

How long had it been since I'd left to come up the stairs—to remove myself physically from the temptation of her? Hours? Minutes?

It felt like time had stopped and she and I were in our own little pocket universe, oblivious to the motion of the clouds, the sun and the stars; the entire natural world all around us. Just enjoying each other's bodies. No words necessary.

Her other nipple responded as eagerly as the first and now she was grinding her hips against me, moaning. My hand slipped between her legs and I rubbed her firmly through her shorts.

Suddenly, with a rushed intake of breath, she sat up, a hand on my shoulder.

This was it, I thought. This was her being the sane one and putting on the brakes to the out-of-control bus rushing down the mountainside at ninety miles per hour. In spite of the rational thought, an onslaught of disappointment nearly smothered me.

Until I realized that she was rolling me onto my back so she could straddle me.

Holy shit. Just when I thought things couldn't get any hotter, they did.

She bent and kissed me ferociously, luscious lips enveloping mine, her tongue delving into my mouth, hands on my shoulders, slipping over my upper arms. Slowly she moved to my jaw, kissing over my neck. Her hair fell over my skin like liquid satin. It felt goddamn amazing. My hands dipped into it, threading it between my fingers.

Then her head moved lower, across my chest, mimicking my actions with her. My hands reached up to cup her generous breasts. They were perky, so soft, the nipples a pale pink against her glowing skin. A visual and sensual feast.

Let me drown in this ocean, swept over that dangerous edge. I couldn't imagine a better way to meet my end than deep inside this woman.

Then her mouth hit my stomach, tracing over my navel, dipping her tongue inside. And lower. Her fingers wrapped around my cock and suddenly she was licking me like an ice cream cone she couldn't get enough of.

I sucked in my gut, the tension inside me suddenly skyrocketing. *Fuck.*

Her gaze fixed on mine, taking in my reaction with relish as slowly she pressed her puffy lips to the head of my cock and opened them. Heat and pleasure washed over my body like a warm wave of that same ocean that threatened to drown me. I wanted to close my eyes and relish the sensation of her mouth and hands on me, but I couldn't take my eyes away from hers. They looked hungry and predatory, like they belonged to a she-wolf.

Not only was she giving me the most amazing head I'd ever experienced in my life, but she was also clearly enjoying the hell out of it. Add that to her already impressive list of achievements.

"Your cock is amazing," she murmured when she'd pulled her mouth away. "I can't get enough of it."

I tilted my head back and looked up at the ceiling, catching my breath enough so I could respond. Her mouth was far more amazing than my cock, that was certain. But before I could, her mouth was on me again, pushing me in deep, her tongue sliding along the underside.

I looked again, watching that copper head bob up and down over me, her occasional moans accompanied my rushed breath. She knew when to slow her pace and when to speed it up again. As if reading my cues.

It had been a long time since I last had sex and that meant this might not last. But she seemed to know how to handle that too.

My hips jerked, and I wanted to take control, wanted to push her head up and down. I wanted to come in her mouth and that was about to happen any second now. My eyes rolled back and...

That's when the knocking and doorbell ringing started.

Fuuuuuuuck.

Kat's head jerked up. It was like dousing my entire body in ice cold water. "Who's that? Should we—"

"Fuck no!" I bellowed in frustration, putting my face in my hands.

"But—"

"Nooooo," I cut her off again. Christ. It had felt so good.

Then my phone started ringing. Because *that* was just what I needed. I ignored it.

Kat scooped up the phone to read the caller ID. "It's Julia."

"Lucas?" A voice called from down below. My mother's voice.

Katya was off the bed and scrambling to get her clothes back on as fast as she could.

I just lay there, pressing the heels of my hands to my eyes. Great. Yet another reason to resent my mother. Add cockblocking to the long list. Why not?

Apparently I hadn't read the schedule right, as I discovered when I'd dressed and rejoined Kat downstairs. My mother, sister and a few others waited with her near the kitchen. Kat had already offered them cold drinks, and they were chatting about something.

Julia smiled, then laughed when she saw me. "Wow, someone has bed head still." Her eyes flickered to Kat then back to me, clearly speculating.

Well we were newlyweds as far as they were all concerned. Let them speculate that we were about to fuck each other's brains out.

And how goddamn disappointed I was now because it hadn't happened.

But that didn't matter, because we had to run off and join the rest of the large group for a "fun" tour around the vineyard and winery. In addition to attending a tasting before dinner.

I'd rather have private time inside my wife's pants. Because now I was obsessed with getting inside them.

When she sat next to me in one of the big hayride-style trucks that had been rented to drive us around, I could only stare at her gorgeous profile. She tilted her head toward the sun, closing her eyes and letting that river of ginger silk run down her back.

"The colors in the landscape are so beautiful here," she said. "See how they are layered? The bright green of the grass and the vineyard, the yellow and brown hills, those deep bluish mountains and the pale blue sky. It's like a painting."

"Yeah," I stared straight at her and ignored where she was indicating. "Incredibly beautiful."

When she returned my gaze, she smiled, clearly understanding I had no interest in the beauty of the landscape.

"Be a good boy," she whispered to me.

"I've done that for far too long..." I replied before the truck started bumping on one of the back roads and her attention was turned elsewhere.

The wine tasting went as well as a wine tasting could go. I usually found them boring and overly pretentious, though I could appreciate the wine itself.

From across the patio where we stood, grouped at different bar-height tables, I caught a glimpse of Man-Bun hipster photographer. Which meant the reporter was nearby somewhere, probably commandeered by my mother. I skimmed the selection list, vaguely aware that the camera had been pointed in our direction for some minutes. When I glanced up again, I realized the camera wasn't focused on *us*. Man-Bun was clearly taking pictures of Kat. Every time she turned in profile or in his direction, there was a distinct and fast-paced click-click-click which made it obvious.

She, however, was completely oblivious that she'd become the photographer's latest obsession from afar. With a laugh under her breath, Katya admitted, "I have no idea what I'm doing with this." She stared down at an empty wine scorecard.

I moved to the other side of her, blocking the photographer's shot with no small feeling of satisfaction. *Don't even think about it, Man-Bun. She's mine.* Foiled, he turned his attention to something else. I turned over the scorecard and began a quick game of tic-tac-toe with her.

"Not to worry." I set down my first X. "Almost everyone else here is in the same boat. They're just faking it."

Her brow raised, clearly doubtful. She scribbled an O. "Really? Show me...."

I dropped the game and picked up a fresh tasting glass of our 2016 Cabernet Sauvignon by the stem. Then I swirled it, holding it up to the light with a snobby flick of my wrist. "Deep violet color. No hints of browning."

Then I raised a brow and with my nose in the air, I sniffed at the rim, making my best douchebag impression. She laughed, and it was like music to my ears. "Well developed bouquet. Full bodied with hints of berry, cedar and coffee notes."

"Coffee...?" she repeated, leaning forward to sniff, then wrinkled her cute little nose at me. "I don't smell nothing like that."

"We're playing along, pay attention."

She grinned and nodded again. "Okay and...?"

I took the tiniest of sips, swished the sample in my mouth for a long time, puckering my lip. Making the most purposely inane face possible, I wrinkled my nose while she giggled at me. "And the taste? Pure... cranberry. I can't get enough of the cranberry."

Her brows shot up in surprise and our eyes met. Mine burned into hers. If I'd had an excuse to take her by the hand and go find a private shed somewhere, I'd do it in a heartbeat. Because damn, the door between us that I'd firmly kept locked had been smashed opened. And the only thing I wanted to do right now—and for the next couple of days at least—was fuck my wife. *And* make her come, all while moaning my name. As many times as possible.

"Yeah," I continued. "I love the taste of cranberry. It's all I want to taste for the next few days... or even weeks."

Her gaze on me grew heated and suddenly there was tension in the air. She visibly swallowed and then bit her lip.

"You look a little afraid right now," I observed.

One corner of her mouth quirked up. "I am, kind of... because I think I've created a monster."

I hooked an arm around her waist and pulled her against me, uncaring if anyone was watching us. We were newly married, after all. Maybe Man-Bun would back the hell off if he got an eyeful of us all over each other. I whispered in her ear. "It's possible that you have. A monster who wants nothing more than to hear you moan... and beg for more."

Her eyes widened and for a short moment, she melted against me until we were interrupted. Julia had bottles of chilled water in each hand. "I'm the water girl today. Do either of you need to wet your whistle or cleanse your palate?"

Unfortunately, Claire was standing right beside her and her full focus was on Kat. Uh oh.

"Why aren't you partaking of the grape?" I asked my sister.

She and Kat exchanged a long look and then she shrugged, wiping the condensation from her hands as we took the water bottles. "I'm taking a break from winetasting."

"Forever," Claire muttered with a slight roll of her eyes.

Kat lowered her wine glass to the table and clinked her water bottle with mine. "I think I'm going to join Julia on the wine break."

Julia beamed a smile at her, then leaned in to give her a big bear hug. What the hell was this? They spent a few hours together this morning and suddenly they were BFFs? Something dark collected in the pit of my stomach. Was this an innocent bit of bonding or was this history repeating itself?

Claire watched them, too. And she didn't even attempt to disguise the fear in her eyes. Then she shot a look of pure venom at Kat before grabbing Julia by the arm and jabbering about some gossip she saw posted online.

Kat sipped at her water bottle as she stared after them with a puzzled look on her face.

"I'd stay as far away from that mess as possible if I were you," I said.

She turned back to me. "Your sister isn't a mess. She's trying hard to be better. She'd probably love your support."

My brow twitched up. "I was talking about Claire. I know that look she gave you. The claws are going to come out any time now."

Kat quirked her head to the side with a cocky smile on her gorgeous lips. "Oh I'm not afraid of her at all. Bring it on."

That's my Cranberry, I thought almost automatically before I realized that I was thinking of her as mine. That, in a way, I had been all along

Nothing phased her. She was pure tough girl… except when she wasn't. That night she'd cried in my arms had been proof positive that not too far beneath that hard exterior was a vulnerable, compassionate woman.

And beneath those hip-hugging jean shorts she wore was one sexy body that I wanted to get to know intimately over the next few days. Starting the minute we got back to the guest house tonight.

We didn't have lots of time left. Why not take advantage of what we did have?

Except we didn't get back to our place until late. There was swimming at sunset, a late dinner and a ridiculous game of charades. All of these dumbass activities placed barriers between me, her, a few orgasms and a whole lot of naked fun.

At around ten p.m. Kat headed back but my mother commandeered me to help with an odd job for the dinner party tomorrow evening.

It didn't take long for me to figure out the real reason I was there. In the middle of reading off names for her to write down on the place cards, she lay a hand on my wrist.

"Has the reporter set up an interview slot for you and Katharina yet? Also, be aware that after Sunday's small brunch for the five of us, we'll be doing a photo shoot. Be sure to arrive dressed ready for that."

"I don't have much to say to reporters. Fair warning that I'm not going to be talkative."

She jerked her head away, clearly annoyed, but did not argue the point. Through my own clenched teeth, I read her a few more names. She then interrupted me again. At this rate, we wouldn't be done until three in the morning and I was dragging ass already.

"Also, please make an effort with Claire and her family. It would look so much better, especially with our guests around."

I fought rolling my eyes—and sarcastically asking why Claire and her parents were even present at our family reunion. Especially given that she hadn't been a member of this family for six years now.

"You made the choice to have her here. There are consequences. She brings drama to everything. And somehow, I'm supposed to do something to mitigate that?. Well, I did do that six years ago. I divorced her. Now she's your problem." I set down her dumbass list on the table. I was *done.*

Nodding goodnight to a cousin from the Netherlands who was helping out my mother, I turned and left. Then I was out in the cool night air, hoping that taking a moment and inhaling some of it would help calm me down.

My mother never ceased to get my blood pressure up but the lengthy walk did some good.

When I got back to the guesthouse, Kat was fast asleep in our bed.

Admittedly, I made no effort to be quiet when I went about my bedtime routine—shower included—in hopes she might wake up. But she never stirred. She must have been exhausted from the day's full schedule. But, damn it, this persistent and aching hard-on wasn't going to let me sleep.

When I joined her in bed, I turned my back and forced myself to think of everything *but* her. I couldn't help that awareness, though—of the weight of her next to me. I listened to the sound of each inhalation and exhalation, savored the feel of her breath on the back of my neck.

My last thought was that if I didn't get inside her very soon, I might *actually* lose my mind.

When I woke up, again late, she wasn't in bed. *Damn it.* Was I going to have to tie the woman down in order to get some?

That thought didn't help my morning wood at all. I imagined strapping those wrists down above her head while I had my way with her body...

God damn. I ran a hand through my hair, then rose to dress. Another day doing the bullshit family reunion, smiling through a dull and ridiculous party and with no damn time penciled in, literally, to seduce my own wife.

Today was spa day. Great, *just great.* The semi-naked couples massage and the alone time in the private sauna together did nothing to help the tension. Though I did manage to start a hot— literally—naked make-out session with her in there until she cried uncle.

"My poor Canadian blood can't take this heat," she gasped as she left, wrapping that white towel around her generous chest and hips and... *damn.* She was just so sexy.

"To be continued, then?" I asked.

She sent me a sly grin. "Oh, yeah."

Aaaaand I was sporting uncomfortable wood again for the rest of the afternoon.

While she disappeared to get ready, I logged into the VPN and did some work. My outfit and I were relegated to another guest room for the preparations.

I'd asked the butler to prepare us before-dinner cocktails at the bar—Sea Breeze, vodka with cranberry juice—that I'd deemed period-appropriate for the occasion. Then I'd given him a few semi-secret instructions for the afterparty. It was about time we enjoyed that private rooftop garden. If—no, *when*—I could pull her away from the party to enjoy it.

Deleon also acted as my valet, old school style, when he helped me with my tuxedo. In keeping with the Gatsby theme, it was a vintage 1920s style tailcoat with a white tie, authentic as possible, right down to the rented diamond-studded art deco cuff links.

He was just brushing off my coat when Kat came down the stairs followed by the hair and makeup artist that Julia had sent over to help her.

And, holy shit, she was downright fuckin' beautiful. I hadn't thought that perfection could be improved upon but here she was.

The dress hugged her curves and was cropped above the knees. Each step she took or movement she made was accompanied by black fringe dancing to her command. The dress itself was peacock-blue with gold, green and violet sequins sewn in the patterns of peacock feathers. Her shoulders were covered with short cap sleeves, adorned by more of the fringe. And the bodice dipped low, showing off the curve of her generous bustline. She wore satin gloves in a matching color that went up past her elbows.

The hair stylist had pinned Kat's shimmering hair up to make it resemble a 1920s style bob cut. And the bandeau across her forehead was a rhinestone-studded glittery number festooned with peacock feathers.

Delicious.

And, to my dismay, I realized that tailcoats were useless at hiding erections. Since I was going to be with her all night, plotting ways to get her into bed, I'd have to get creative covering for it.

CHAPTER 20
KATYA

MY HUSBAND WAS FLAT-OUT GORGEOUS TONIGHT. Not a sentence I'd anticipated saying to myself at the very beginning of this year but... this definitely hadn't been a typical year in my as-yet short life. The tuxedo tailcoat and white vest underneath displayed his fit form perfectly, hugging broad crew-trained shoulders and tapering down to his slender waist and hips.

He looked like the perfect gallant gentleman—tall, dark, wavy hair. Even fitted white gloves on his hands. *Dayum.*

"Well, Mr. Baron van den Hoehnsboek van Lynden." I said, taking the drink he offered me, then bringing it to my lips as I did another once-over. He was hot... so very hot.

His brows twitched.

I blinked up at him. "I thought I finally pronounced it right?"

"Yeah you did. But no 'mister' needed if you're doing the title, which I rather you didn't, anyway."

"I won't use the title if you don't like it." I moved in front of him, pressing my chest against his. "But tonight, you look every bit the part of a European aristocrat."

His hand came up to my chin, angling my head to peer into my face. "And you just look fucking gorgeous."

He said it with such intensity that I almost felt those words pass through me like fiery arrows, igniting a heat deep inside. Honestly, it threatened to melt my panties right there on the spot. My eyelids drooped and my throat burned. For a second, I fantasized about going back upstairs, peeling these fancy clothes off each other and have our own fun for a while.

But no, playing Roaring Twenties pretend would be fun, too. And how often did two game testers for Draco Multimedia Entertainment get to be glamorous and step into another world?

"Don't even ask how much this dress cost me."

His eyes scorched a path down the front of my dress from neck to knee. "Whatever the price, it was worth every damn penny."

I grinned, and he stepped away, holding his arm out for me to take. As it was still very warm in this part of the valley tonight, I didn't need the wrap I'd bought to go with the dress. Oh well. I'd go in, bare shoulders, exposed cleavage and all. Given his current reaction, it wouldn't be too shabby of a grand entrance.

I took his arm, and he guided me through the door. To both of our amusement, Mr. Deleon was waiting for us at the wheel of a golf cart to usher us to the main house ballroom. We laughed and made jokes as he drove us through the vineyard.

"I've been hearing a lot of Dutch spoken around us since we got here."

"Well, I have a bunch of family here from the Netherlands."

I frowned. "You never told me… do you speak it?"

He shook his head. "I understand a lot of it and only speak enough to be mildly conversational."

"Hmm, I don't think I know any Dutch at all. Wait, no. I learned a word from watching *Friends*. Gunther called Ross an *ezel*."

He laughed. "Donkey? Don't think you'll need to use that one tonight."

I raised a brow. "You never know. Okay, how do I say hello?"

"Tonight you can say *goedenavond*. Good evening."

I practiced that a few times until he said I had it down.

"Okay, now quickly tell me how to say goodbye for when we have to go."

"You're going to be in a hurry to go?" He raised his brows feigning surprise.

"Don't pretend you aren't going to be, Jedi Boy. Now tell me."

"Okay, goodbye is *tot ziens*." And I practiced that one too.

My hand rested lightly on my husband's thigh... until he gently removed it. Judging from the obvious bulge in his pants, it wasn't hard to understand why. I vowed to be a good girl tonight, mostly. I'd given the little devil on my shoulder the night off until later. No need to torment him until we got back to our place.

And even with as much fun as I anticipated having at this fancy party, I hoped that would be soon. No time like the near-future to get on with the more rewarding parts of a marriage, right?

The grand ballroom was breathtaking. Every lamp was lit, every chandelier gleaming, the massive expanse of parquet floor shining golden under their light. Huge stands of flowers stood at studied intervals. Elegant banners in colors of a summer sunset— deep rust, gold and plum—hung from the mezzanine. There, onlookers clustered at the wrought railing to watch the floor below.

We were even announced by the main house butler, given titles and all. The reporter stood nearby, and the photographer caught it all. Even though it was a one-off, being announced as a baroness in front of a crowd of people was the deep thrill I never knew I wanted. Heads turned as we made our way down the stairs into the main room. It was all so Downton Abbey that I expected to see Carson's nod of approval or Mrs. Hughes's proud smile. I shook my head to wake myself up from the dream.

This was the world that Lucas had been raised into—and had summarily rejected. Because it didn't allow for someone to break away and be their own person. It was enjoyable as a one-off, but I couldn't imagine this being my life.

The party was just getting started when we arrived. Cocktails and appetizers were served on the back patio as the sun sank in the sky, our long shadows stretching out opposite the spectacular colors on the horizon. A classical quartet playing the airs of Vivaldi accompanied us in our Roaring Twenties glamor as everyone socialized.

I made sure to stick by my husband's side and ordered another Sea Breeze in honor of his thoughtfulness. A few sips of the one back at the villa had given me the beginnings of a pleasant buzz. To say nothing of a boost in courage to get through this event surrounded by dozens of people I didn't know.

Julia showed up right as Lucas went to fetch our drinks. He hesitated as if to ask her for her drink order, but I interrupted him, telling him I had to speak to Julia alone.

She took my hand and squeezed it. "Thanks." She was wearing a red dress with silver sequins and lots and lots of floaty red feathers everywhere.

"*Goedenavond,*" I said to her with a grin, ready to impress.

She smiled wide. "*Goedenavond! Hoe gaat het me je?*"

My smile vanished. "Uhh. You exceeded my Dutch limit."

She laughed. "Did Lucas teach you that? Did he tell you we had to go to Dutch school for years when we were younger?"

I frowned. "He says he can barely speak it."

She laughed. "He's lying. Anyway, I came over here to tell you how amazing you look! That dress. Those colors on you are... chef's kiss." And she held her bunched fingers to her lips and made a kissing sound, spreading her fingers.

I reached out and smoothed one of the feathers at her shoulder. "Well so do you! Man, sometimes I wish I lived in a time when women got to dress like this all the time. Until I remember the details like no women's suffrage, no birth control and the horrors of segregation."

She grinned. "We should start a movement to bring twenties fashion back without all the awful things that came along with the era." She studied my face. "Violet did an amazing job with your hair and makeup. I'm going to needs some shots for—"

I held up my hand. "No social media for me, if you don't mind. My Discord server has been full of people complaining that I haven't been streaming enough lately. I'd rather not advertise that I have a life outside of my job and my online streaming. They might riot."

She shook her finger at me. "You're allowed to have a life outside of what your followers think you should be doing. You can't work twenty-four-seven. Look at me..." She punctuated with a shy smile.

I put my hand gently on her upper arm. "We kick-ass women have to stick together. You're doing great, Julia. Keep it up."

Her free hand went to rest on top of mine. "I've only barely gotten to know you and already you're an amazing sister-in-law. Thank you."

Yeah, that was the first moment I felt a pang of guilt. Because I knew that this was temporary, sure, and had never fooled myself into thinking otherwise. And Lucas was also conscious of it, as he'd stated it yesterday.

But Julia didn't know. Was it fair for me to be forming these relationships I'd had no intention of continuing once I had a green card in my hands?

Almost predictably, Claire then appeared right at Julia's shoulder, glancing from Julia to me and back again. "Aw, what's this? Sister-in-law bonding time?" She turned to Julia. "Remember all that party crashing we did back when I first got engaged to Lucas? I can hardly recall the details but what I do remember is that it was a ton of fun."

I pasted on the fakest most ridiculous grin that I possibly could. "Yeah, blacking out and waking up in puddles of vomit all over your designer clothes has got to be *the best.*"

Julia stifled a full-on bust of laughter and Claire stared wide-eyed at me like I was a visitor from the Planet Blergh.

Thankfully, my extremely handsome and debonair husband appeared with our cocktails. I winked at Julia and said, "Excuse us."

"What was that all about?" Lucas asked when we were alone.

I took a sip of my cocktail and looked up at him. "Oh, just shooing away the pest."

Lucas's gaze traveled in the direction from which we'd come. "You may have figured it out by now, but she's a very persistent pest."

I raised my brows up at him as I sipped again. "Not to worry. You got rid of my pest for me, maybe I can do the same for you."

He laughed. "Good luck with that. She's got her claws firmly sunk into this family."

That comment troubled me and I was still mulling it over when we were summoned to the table. Clearly Claire wasn't on board with Julia's self-transformation and was acting as if she was under some kind of personal threat from it. Of course if Julia stopped partying, then what role would Claire fill in her life? Maybe that's all their friendship was based on.

Dinner was lovely, and I was thankful that we'd been seated next to each other this time. I flirted shamelessly with Lucas, resting my hand on his thigh in between courses. He left olives on his plate and when I asked to have them, he picked up his fork.

"No... feed me with your fingers," I murmured so that only he could hear.

If he was shocked or surprised, he didn't give any indication of it, plucking up an olive between thumb and forefinger. He held it up for me and I leaned forward, taking it and half his fingers into my mouth. His lids drooped, eyes smoldering into mine as I slowly pulled back. Then, without breaking his gaze, I chewed and swallowed.

Without being prompted, he picked up another one and did the same. People saw, I was sure, but neither of us cared. We were both too obsessed with the thought of what was going to happen the minute we were alone together tonight to care.

Because after nearly seven months of marriage, it was finally *on*.

There was dancing after dinner and though Lucas firmly declared that he was not a dancer, I coaxed him to try a few of the slow ones. He was a good dancer which surprised me not at all. He seemed to be the type of guy who was just good at whatever was required of him. Or at the very least, competent.

At one point several of his cousins came to chat. I took that as an excuse to go powder my nose—as they said in the Twenties. I heard one of them tell him, "Dude, your wife is a smokeshow. Lucky dog."

Flattering as it was, I pretended not to hear, hit the ladies' room and then lingered at the bar to give him a little time to catch up. Because we were leaving, soon. If I had to fake a goddamn twisted ankle or brain-pounding headache, we were *so* leaving here and taking our much-needed alone time.

I was in the middle of fantasizing about stripping every piece of that tux off his body when I sensed someone beside me. A dark-haired woman.

She was wearing seashell pink and silver. I turned and looked at Lucas's ex as she openly gave me the once-, twice-, and thrice-over.

I sipped my drink and smiled. So here it was at last, my chance to do a little pest control. But I wasn't going to be a bitch unless she was a bitch first.

The first rule of bitchiness. Don't bitch first. But if bitched to, then don't be afraid to go all-out bitch. Because she who bitches loudest and bitches best, bitches last.

I nursed my drink and pasted an innocent smile on my face while Claire continued her overt inspection. "All danced out?" she finally asked with what I supposed was an ironic laugh.

"Not yet but getting there."

She raised her eyebrows. "Oh. You actually got him to dance?" She scooped up her drink the moment it was placed on the bar before her, then made a faux-toast in my direction, drinking deeply of her martini. "Well, kudos to you if you've managed to thaw the great iceberg that is Lucas. Mr. Emotionally Unavailable himself."

If, said with a heaping helping of skepticism. I sipped again, considering that. "I've never found him to be an iceberg. More like still waters running deep. He's deep but if a person never bothers with what's below the surface, they'd never know."

She narrowed her eyes at me and finished off her martini, setting down the empty glass. Then she moved in closer, as if to start a prolonged conversation. *Hell to the no*, this drink was almost finished, and I was leaving the minute the last drop hit my tongue.

She raised her chin, as if speaking as some kind of relationship authority. "Well, I wish you all the luck with the iceberg or the still waters or whatever. More luck than I ever had, believe me. I sincerely hope he'll take better care of you than he did of me." She placed a hand on her heart as if to emphasize that "sincerity."

"*Take care* of you?" I stared at her in disbelief. "What, did you want a husband or a daddy? Thanks for the well wishes, but there's no luck needed. I'm mad about him. *Tot ziens*." I sucked down the rest of my drink, setting the glass down. And, because I'm a petty bitch, I added, "*Ezel*."

She looked completely confused as she stared after me. *Good.*

Wow, no wonder Lucas thought he'd been a bad husband to her. Who in the world would put that kind of expectation on a nineteen-year-old kid? To "take care" of another fully grown—at least *physically*—adult? I couldn't conceive of the idea of seeking a mate to parent me. I already had two parents, and they were mediocre at best. What a weird notion of marriage. I shook my head. She wasn't even worth losing another thought over.

I found Lucas minutes later and whispered in his ear that I was about to twist my ankle terribly. I strongly urged him to get me out of here before that happened. I also managed to get my hand inside his tailcoat and run my nails down his back.

He wasted no more than thirty seconds in which he set aside his own glass, leaned in to tell his cousins something, then wrapped his arm around my waist.

His hand was on the small of my back, guiding me carefully as I stepped down the stairs in my heels. It felt comforting and made my insides quiver a little with anticipation. It wasn't a short walk back, and he was carrying my shoes once we hit the small sidewalk because no way was I doing that walk in my heels. Despite all of this, we said practically nothing to each other, basking in anticipation.

I was aware of his breath, of each brush of our limbs, the backs of our hands as we walked. Each touch sparking a new point of heat between us. The only sound other than the night around us were his footsteps. And when we hit the edge of the lawn in front of our villa, he scooped me up and carried me that last little way.

I wrapped one arm around his neck as he steadied me against his chest and held me like I weighed no more than a bag of fast food. "Why Mr. Walker," I drawled in my best southern belle accent. "I might be in danger of falling for you if you keep this up."

He laughed as we reached the doorstep and he fumbled to try to open it while his arms were full of me. I ended up summoning help by knocking loudly. Deleon's replacement butler showed up in a minute to let us in. By then, Lucas had set me down, but I still stood pressed very close to him.

"Everything's ready for you upstairs, Mr. Lucas," he said with a nod.

I turned to Lucas who was studiously removing his cufflinks. He smiled and nodded at the butler. "Thank you. And you can have the night off now. Thank Deleon for me."

He smiled. "Certainly. You have my number if you need anything."

I waited until he was gone before turning back to Lucas, who had a very smug smile on his face. He finished undoing his cufflinks, plunking them loudly into a glass dish, then took off his jacket and began rolling up his sleeves.

I raised a brow at him. "What was that all about?"

He grinned even wider. "You'll see."

I frowned at him. "I'm not used to you smiling this much. I think I need to be afraid, very afraid."

He slipped off his own shoes, setting them beside mine and then removed his bow tie. He still had on the white vest and shirt and his black pants, complete with satin stripe down the sides of his legs. Now he'd rolled up his sleeves, showing off the strong muscles in his forearms.

The panty melting process had officially begun. I licked my lips and thought about how we'd never been able to complete our unfinished business yesterday. He was undoubtedly even less happy about that than I was.

Now he was pulling off his tie and unbuttoning the top two buttons of his collar. Then he reached out toward me, his hand open. "Come."

I arched a brow at him and took his hand. "Yes, as a matter of fact, I *really* want to."

He laughed and tugged me toward the stairs. We went up to the bedroom level, and I pulled off my long satin gloves and threw them on the bed. Then Lucas tugged me up another flight of stairs and we were in the private rooftop garden. One side was dominated by a small but beautifully tiled infinity pool that abutted the edge of the roof. It allowed for a swimmer to look over the edge from inside the pool. And around three sides were large wooden pergolas draped with gauzy fabrics and festooned with gorgeous hanging flower baskets and vines. They were backed with low walls to afford privacy, though no other buildings this height were nearby.

Several fountains contributed to the otherworldly effect, complete with Greek goddess upending a bottomless jug of water into the pool. And one involving concentric steel bowls that sang in low tones as they filled up. The constant sound of trickling water relaxed me almost immediately.

Damn I could live up here. It would be no hardship at all.

Lounge chairs bordered the pool but Lucas led us to an area that couldn't be seen from anywhere below or around us. A thick soft futon mat had been laid down under the stars and covered with blankets and pillows. A nearby food and drink tray, stood complete with shiny ice bucket and a champagne bottle. There were bits of cubed cheese and frilly pastries, fancy chocolates and macarons every color of the rainbow. Everything was laid out in the undulating golden light of short pillar candles.

Wow.

Like... I mean... he had pulled out every stop. "This is gorgeous," I breathed as I stared around me with wide eyes. And *damn romantic.* Not even previous boyfriends had ever done something like this for me. The best it'd ever got was sunset and a bag of White Spot fish and chips on a blanket at English Bay Beach.

I'd dated some pretty damn unimaginative guys in my past. Or Lucas just eclipsed them all. Seemingly effortlessly, too.

I shivered a little in anticipation as he moved to the blanket. He looked back, missing nothing. "Cold? I can wrap a blanket around you."

I smiled at him coyly, my chin down and my eyes tilted upward toward him. "I think I'd rather have your arms than a blanket."

He returned the smile and opened his arms so I walked into them. I wasn't really cold but the warmth of his body immediately melted mine. He smelled amazing, woodsy—like cedar chips. I buried my face into his shoulder, covered by his dress shirt.

"Sorry if I dragged you away from something," I said.

"I'm not," he replied, then shifted his head, and I was almost certain he kissed my hair. I pulled my head back to look up at him, heart beating in my throat. I smiled shyly, and he returned the smile before dipping his head to kiss me.

He quickly pulled away before it could get any more involved than that. "I want to take your hair down. But I have no idea how."

I laughed and reached up, pulling out several of the bobby pins the stylist had used for the up-do. I wasn't even finished before he was weaving his fingers through my hair with a long sigh. "So beautiful. Your hair is gorgeous."

I quirked my mouth into a twisted smile. "My best feature."

He met my gaze again, dead serious, his hands stopping their motion. "Not even close to your best feature, Cranberry."

I tilted my head back and closed my eyes, relishing the feel of his hands there and bathing in the warm glow of his sincere compliments. We'd been fencing and jousting for over a year instead of waging a true battle. All this time, neither of us would have admitted that it had been foreplay.

Before I knew it, his mouth was on mine again, pressing it open, first gently. He tasted of whisky and cinnamon. And when his tongue entered my mouth, that kiss grew in intensity like a sports car hitting the open road, the driver flooring the accelerator. And just as if I might be a passenger in said car, my stomach dropped. I couldn't catch my breath and the world turned as he kissed and kissed and kissed it from me.

We were both breathing hard when he pulled away just enough to talk. "I really *really* just want to give in to what I've been craving for months now."

"Then do it," I said in an equally breathy voice. "Because it's exactly what I've wanted, too."

"Our time is short, Kat."

"Mmm, so then we know ahead of time when it ends. That isn't so terrible..."

He inhaled again through his nose, as if he was smelling my hair again. "We should have rules."

I laughed. "No more rules, Jedi Boy. It's time to get naked."

His hands fell to my shoulders, cupping them tightly, urgently before he brusquely spun me around so that my back was to him. He slowly unzipped my gown and the cool air hit the bare skin on my back, evoking goosebumps. One of his warm hands smoothed down the curve of my spine and his mouth sank to the valley where my neck met my shoulder. Violent tingles raced down every nerve ending with electricity so powerful, I trembled. I arched my chin away, giving him exposure to more of my neck. His hands slipped inside my dress.

"You were the most beautiful woman at the ball tonight. Every guy there was looking at you and I was the smug bastard who knew it was my wife they were ogling."

I laughed. "You're such a liar. There were plenty of gorgeous women there."

"None that I was aware of," he shot back while his mouth glided up my neck multiplying the goosebumps by at least a factor of four. Sensations were overwhelming me faster than I could process them, sending molten lust straight down to my center.

"The only thing I was thinking about was how hot you look in your tux. Oh, and the other thing was how much hotter it would be to peel it off you and get you naked, finally."

He laughed.

I turned around and faced him, reaching up to smooth his jaw. "I also couldn't stop thinking about how amazing it's gonna be."

Those brown eyes darkened with lust. "Fuck yeah," he breathed before brushing off my dress with two determined sweeps of his hands at my shoulders. It fell to a puddle at my feet.

Now I was only wearing my 1920s-inspired sexy lingerie—a see-through black lace bra and matching barely-there panties. A black lacy garter belt around my waist hooked to the top of my black stockings. And to think when I'd bought them, I never thought he'd lay eyes on them.

He was doing a lot more then just laying eyes on them. He was practically eye-fucking me. His gaze burned with fevered hunger and I could have sworn he stopped breathing then. "Jesus," he rasped.

I stepped out of my dress but before I could bend to rescue it from the ground, he stooped and reverently draped it over his arm. Then he took it to the nearest lounge chair and laid it down gently. He quickly unbuttoned his white vest and did the same. He then pulled aside the black suspenders that had been holding up his pants and returned to me.

"I was impatient to get you naked but now I think I want to enjoy you like this for a while. " He grinned.

My hand flew to the front of his shirt and I commenced unbuttoning, fingers flying to each successive enameled button. He pulled off his shirt and tossed it back to the lounge the moment I'd finished the last button. Then his undershirt, which he tugged over his head and similarly discarded. He was shirtless at last, thank all the gods.

It had been so long since I'd gone to bed with a man I almost wondered if I remembered how to be good at it. He'd certainly enjoyed the BJ yesterday until it had morphed into fellatio-interruptus by his family's invasion of the guesthouse.

My hands smoothed over his fit chest, reading him with my fingertips and learning more with each passing minute about how and where he liked to be touched. He directed us over to the spread out-blanket and pillows.

We lay down on the futon, facing each other but neither one of us reached for a blanket despite the chill. Our mouths connected again and his hands traveled over my shoulders, my back, cupped my ass and pulled me against him. His erection was rock hard and, as I already knew, larger than normal.

"I can't wait to feel you inside me," I groaned against his neck.

His cock surged, like I hadn't already been aware of him. *Wow.*

His fingers slipped inside my lacy bra, pushing it aside to get at my nipple, where he mercilessly toyed with me until I cried out and squirmed. Molten sparks crackled down every nerve.

His mouth soon replaced the fingers, teeth scraping gently against my sensitive nerve endings. "I was doomed the minute I told you we shouldn't have sex," he breathed against me. "I didn't have a hope in hell of resisting you."

"Mm, you sure do know how to say all the right things." I grinned, then slipped my hand underneath his waistband to cup his taut ass. Jeez even his butt muscles were more toned than anything on my body. I might have felt self-conscious and admonished myself to start working out more. But he was quite overly vocal about how much he liked my body exactly the way it was.

Lucas reached around and with a practiced flick that told me he was more experienced than he let on, he undid my bra. I pulled it off, and he took several minutes telling me without words how much he liked my body, most specifically, my boobs. Like he wouldn't leave them alone and I enjoyed every minute of it. With one nipple in his mouth, I enjoyed the harsh swirl of his tongue and nip of his teeth. He rolled the other firmly between his fingers.

I could only lie there and gasp between moans because it was overwhelming. My lacy panties were now soaked, and I was dry humping him through his tux pants.

"I swear if you aren't naked in the next ten seconds I'm going to shred those trousers right off your legs," I ground out between clenched teeth.

He pulled back and smiled into my face. "As you wish."

He unbuttoned his fly and squirmed out of them. Then, as he leaned back to toss them onto our discard pile, I reached down and palmed his erection through his boxers. Now it was his turn to gasp.

"Time to get down to business, Jedi boy. Unsheathe your lightsaber."

He threw his head back and laughed heartily. "That was bad, Cranberry. Completely dorky."

"Whatever gets you naked and inside me as quickly as possible, I'm willing to do."

He then eased out of his boxers and reached down to undo my garter belt. Amusingly, he had much more trouble with that than with the bra. Understandably. I doubted many of his previous partners donned a garter belt and stockings very often. I helped him along so it would go faster.

Once the garter was unhooked from my stockings and off, I lifted my butt and eased my panties off as well.

And at last, we were both naked. At the same time. In the same place. And pressed against each other. He was hard, and I was wet. And, barring any freakish natural disaster such as an alien attack or giant meteor falling from the sky. Barring—god forbid—a major earthquake or tsunami, this was going to happen.

At fucking last.

I kissed my way down his chest, as I'd done yesterday, but he stopped me before I arrived at my intended destination.

"No." He rolled us over, bringing my mouth to his. He was now on top of me, easing a leg between my knees. When his head came up, he impaled my gaze with his own. His eyes were dark with lust and glowing with reflected candlelight.

"No more waiting. I'm going to finally do what I've been fantasizing about doing for over a year."

I gulped almost comically. It was so loud that it was probably heard in the next postal code.

"I hope you brought your highest DPS weapon to this raid." I laughed. Yeah, I was *that* person—the corny nerd who cracked gamer jokes during sex.

"Oh?" he said, his face a mixture of amusement and confusion.

"Yeah because you're gonna need it to wreck me."

He laughed and then lined my jaw with more kisses, his tongue slipping out to add more heat. "I think you were perfectly aware of what my *weapon* can do when you put it in your mouth yesterday."

"Mmm. Yeah. It's gonna feel amazing."

"You're about to find out."

And now he was between my legs and easing himself inside of me. So slowly. Like I was a virgin, and he was afraid of hurting me. I pushed my hips up to disavow him of that notion, should it actually exist.

Once he was inside, I did have to suppress a gasp of surprise. He was big, as I already knew, and there was no denying that the feel of him was satisfying But not enough yet. He was still, watching me. I moved against him first.

We both moaned in unison and my eyes closed. I shut out everything but the feel of him. His weight on top of me, his cock inside of me, stretching me and making me burn with a sweet tension, craving that euphoric release.

"God, you feel so good," he ground out breathlessly as he quickened his movements.

By this point, I was beyond the capacity for verbal reply.

Soon, however, we were speaking a conversation full of meaning, sensation and even emotion but completely without words. The statements, questions and responses where the desperate sweep of hands, the movements of mouths and tongues and the building pressure of our hips gyrating in unison.

The rise in tension started immediately and, as if he could sense that I was close, he quickened the pace. He lifted up on his arms, giving him the momentum to thrust more forcefully. His lips locked on mine, muffling moans of pleasure.

The tension tightened to a degree that had me calling out his name, against his mouth. An intricately twisted knot wound tighter and tighter, pleasure washing over my entire body as it crested and washed out in intense, pulsating waves. My back arched, though his body pressed me down, and I undulated against him as the spasms rippled out, like the concentric rings around a pebble dropped in water.

My eyes rolled up into my head and I hardly noticed when he stopped moving, pulled out of me. I wasn't even sure he'd finished, but I lay, listless and glowing with the aftermath, unaware of anything. Suddenly I realized his head was between my legs, his tongue finding my clit. My entire body tensed and he pushed my leg aside without a word, continuing the contact until I was coming again within minutes.

This orgasm had me forgetting how to speak, hell even forgetting how to breathe. He moved to lay beside me once more, but reached out to gently roll me onto my side, my back to him. I immediately noticed that he was still hard. I hadn't been so oblivious as to think I'd missed his orgasm. It hadn't come yet.

He slipped into me again from behind, spooning me closely. He whispered dirty things in my ear about how he couldn't get enough of me, what a turn on it was for him to listen to me come, how good I felt. I clenched every muscle below my waist and he lost it then, letting out a stuttering breath and stilling, coming to his own climax.

Yeah, he only came once to my multiples, but I could tell it was a good one. It took a long time for him to come down, tense and hovering over me for long moments until he was spent, falling against me, consumed.

Neither of us said a thing for a good ten minutes as we stared up at the black sky, the faint, twinkling stars, as we processed. He nudged me awake when I began to doze off. And we took turns in the nearby washroom cleaning up before we ran back to the blankets. Once there, we snuggled against each other naked under a warm blanket and slept.

My last thought before slipping into the black... how much I could not *wait* to do it again.

CHAPTER 21
LUCAS

THE NIGHT HAD GOTTEN COLDER. THAT WAS THE FIRST thing I noticed when I woke up. Reaching for my watch, I saw that it was actually early morning. She was fused to my side, huddled as if she were cold though it was warm under our blankets.

But it was no fun getting up to use the bathroom while still buck naked. With no desire to squeeze into the discarded tuxedo again, my options for clothing up here were limited. But when I came back to our little love nest on the roof, she was shivering in her sleep.

I put a light hand on her shoulder and whispered into her hair. "Kat, c'mon, let's go inside."

She held the blanket even tighter to herself, shaking her head sleepily. "Don't wanna."

"Come on. Let me help you. The bed'll be more comfortable."

"Mmm," she moaned, but hooked her arms obediently around my neck, her eyes still fused closed. I gathered her in my arms, stood and moved to the stairs to take us down to the bedroom level. By the time we got there, she was awake and quietly watching me.

I lay her down on her side of the bed but she didn't unlatch her hands from around my neck as I tried to stand up.

"What's wrong?"

She blinked, staring me straight in the eyes.

"Need some water?"

She cleared her throat and tugged on her arms where they held my neck, drawing me down to her. "Need... more."

My mouth met hers and we kissed, her chest rose as if searching for mine to press against it. When I did she cried out in protest, saying my skin was cold against hers.

"That's why I was trying to get us down here."

A lazy smile crept across her beautiful face. "Let me warm you up, then."

When I lay down beside her, she pushed me onto my back and spread her warm skin across mine. It felt fucking amazing and without a second thought, my arms went around her waist and cinched her to me. That long, silky hair that smelled like a tropical garden draped over my face, my neck, my shoulders. Jesus. I went from being cold to igniting on fire in less than a minute.

She straddled me again, much as she had yesterday, but instead of going down on me, she inched her hips down to lock with mine. Then she slid against me until I entered her, as hard as if I hadn't just had extremely satisfying sex a few hours ago.

Aching with need every bit as much as I had before, I was like a bottomless pit of lust for the feel of her hips underneath my cupped palms. They slid and gyrated over me. Slicing through her wet heat like a forgotten jungle, I was giddy and euphoric with the exploration.

Her hands locked on the headboard behind me as she quickened her movements and I cupped those bouncing breasts with my hands, teasing, rubbing, holding. They were so soft, giving, like the rest of her. But at the base, she was all strong, ferocious woman, unabashedly thrusting for her pleasure.

Her back arched, her breasts sliding from my hands. As she cried out with her climax, I guided her hips over me again and again until I was cresting and falling with her.

Free fall. Unable to breathe, unable to think, I held her fast to me, pushing all the way in until I was spent. Then, exhausted with a buzzing afterglow, every sense alive, every muscle went completely slack with ultimate release.

I watched as she moved off of me, falling on the bed beside me breathless, sweaty. Who the hell was she and what was she doing to me?

What had she already done to me, against my own better judgement?

Sucking in a long breath that felt like the first I'd drawn in years, I felt my lids grow heavy and weary. She was saying something in a quiet voice but I was already fading from the world and too far gone to reply.

"Maybe everyone back at work was right after all. Maybe we *did* just need to fuck and get it over with."

The morning came all too quickly. We woke with less than half an hour to get ready for the eye roll-worthy family breakfast on the main house's back terrace. Since I'd completely forgotten to set an alarm, it was a miracle we hadn't slept through it. This woman had worn me out completely and every muscle felt blissfully used and sore.

But there was no denying that euphoric feeling of having had amazing sex the night before. Especially following a long period of having gone without.

After a quick prep—in which she'd taken hardly any time to look beautiful—we were on our way to breakfast. Kat stopped us in the vineyard, her hair loose and curling about her bare shoulders. She was wearing a sleeveless dark blue skater dress with white tennis shoes.

Our path edged the lush, green vines heavily laden with purple grapes. And she, herself, looked rejuvenated and fresh as a sunny spring morning. When she stopped and looked all around her, mouth opening a bit in awe, she darted a look at me. "It's so damn pretty here." With her signature wicked grin, she held up her phone. "Selfie time!"

She pressed close to me, holding the phone out at arm's length to capture us both. The scent of her hair was so intoxicating that I nearly wavered where I stood.

"Ugh I hate this angle, but I want to get the sky in the background." She cheesed for the camera. "Come on, smile, for heaven's sake. It's a picture, not your funeral."

She pressed the button multiple times, admonishing me to smile more. "We're having yet another meal with my parents, why on earth is there reason to smile?" I sneered between my teeth.

"C'mon, grumpy. One might say you need to get laid but I know *that's* not true anymore."

"Maybe I'm angling for another BJ later today." I snuck a peck on her neck and she snapped that one too.

"Just a few more. We need to do duck lips."

"Duck lips?"

"Yeah, it wouldn't be a social media-worthy photo if it doesn't have duck lips."

She stuck her lips out like she was about to kiss a porcupine. "C'mon duck lips."

"That looks more like BJ face to me."

She rolled her eyes. "Duck lips or your chances of BJ go down 100%."

I shoved my lips out as far as I could in the most ridiculous imitation of the goofiest billed waterfowl I could imagine. "You can call me Daffy Duck for the rest of the day if that's the price for a BJ."

"Motivation. It gets things done," she chirped happily. "And here I just want to see you in your dark blue PJ's again."

"You liked those, did you?"

She laughed, swiping through the photos we'd just taken and looking at each one. "Yes! I miss them." She flicked her pale blue eyes up at me. "Just tell me one thing, were those a gift?"

I smiled. "As a matter of fact, they were."

"From your grandma?"

I shook my head, puzzled. "My aunt."

"For Christmas?"

"What's this all about?"

She grinned as she tucked her phone away. "I was just curious. But I wasn't kidding about wanting you to wear those tonight. So I can peel them off you."

"Done. Don't have to ask me twice when you ask me like that."

Kat led the rest of the way back to the main house. I watched her, her hair gleaming fire in the sunshine, her hands tucked into the pockets of that airy dress. I'd never seen her wear dresses before we got married. I'd had no idea what I'd been missing before, despite the fact that she had the finest ass ever in the faded jeans she favored for work attire.

My eyes slid down her slim waist and settled on that full, round butt. I couldn't stop thinking about the hot sex between us the night before. All that talk of BJs had me imagining that gorgeous redhead bobbing over me. That was all it took to get me as hard as someone who hadn't had sex in weeks.

Fuck breakfast, I wanted to grab her hand and turn back to the guest house and spend the entire day screwing my wife in every position I could imagine. Hot and sweaty. Electric and tireless Naked and writhing underneath me.

I'd opened that pandora's box last night.

But in spite of those hot memories, other, darker thoughts rose up unbidden. It was the way my brain worked now, as this older, more cynical version of myself. I couldn't ignore the sick feeling at the pit of my stomach. The alarm somewhere deep inside told me this could—and if the past had been any indication—probably *would* go south. And when that happened it would be bad, *very bad*.

Which was why I felt the need for the constant reminders— to myself and to her—that we had an expiration date. And the fact that once we left Napa, we had to leave that behind, even if it took still more months to get her green card.

Because if things blew up between us, then it could quickly evaporate into nothing.

I wasn't going to repeat the past. I wasn't going to put myself in that position again and have to do the therapy and all the other, difficult work. I'd had to rebuild my life. *Another* life after the wreck left by another wife.

Though I *felt* different, I was still the same man who had been a shitty husband to Claire. And I'd vowed I'd never do it again.

Yet here I was. I'd set all the rules in place to prevent it but...

Last night and this morning, no one would've ever been able to tell that this had been intended to be a marriage only on paper. Because we sure were doing a wonderful job of acting like it was the real thing.

We arrived at the upper garden, as instructed. A glass and wrought-iron round table had been set up under an even larger umbrella. The spot was perfect—at the top of the stairs near a trickling fountain and surrounded by blooming flower pots. Staff had set the table to perfection as if it were the centerpiece of the perfect garden party, complete with nameplates for each of us at assigned seats. Nearby, another table was loaded with food for a buffet-style service.

For just the five of us. Well this was totally Mother's style. She never did things halfway, and she had an even more important reason than usual to go all-out. The reporter, her assistant and Mr. Man-Bun, the photographer, were waiting nearby, of course.

My parents, however, were nowhere to be seen.

Julia arrived soon after we did, her dark hair tucked into a ponytail under a black satin baseball cap. Her eyes were hidden behind giant mirrored sunglasses and she had cherry red lipstick on to match the cherries printed on her romper. In the past, those shades would have hidden a hangover or bloodshot eyes, but it occurred to me that I hadn't seen Julia drink a thing since we got here.

Julia had a thick copy of French *Vogue* tucked under her arm. She laid the magazine down beside her place setting and pulled off her sunglasses to set them there too.

"Hey! Good morning, lovebirds," she crooned in as chipper a voice as I'd ever heard from her. Wow. She seemed like a different person than the sullen and cynical teen I'd known so well. My little sister was apparently growing up.

Julia then snatched one of the colorful cloth napkins that had been neatly folded, she placed that near her arrangement. She angled her head this way and that, looking at her little still life before holding out her phone to snap photos. All she needed was the requisite flute of champagne to complete the image of *Lifestyles of the rich and internet-famous.*

Then Julia aimed her camera at me and Kat. "The happy newlyweds breakfasting," she muttered the caption as she snapped.

"That's *not* getting posted. Having those guys hovering around constantly is annoying enough." I pointed with my eyes at the cluster of three hovering by the massive shrubs, apparently waiting for my parents to show up. Man-Bun already had his camera pointed at my wife, however.

I was going to have *words* with him shortly.

Julia twitched a brow. "I don't post every picture I take. Sometimes I just want to snap one, in the moment. Besides, your wife is beautiful."

I flicked a glance at Kat. It was true, of course. I'd always thought she was beautiful. But this morning, in this sharply angled morning light in that dress with the slightest of breezes making the long ends of her hair dance, she'd never been more beautiful.

Nevertheless, my favorite was still her naked and spread out on a blanket underneath me.

Julia sat down and began immediately scrolling through the photos she'd just shot. Out of the corner of my eye, I saw one of the magazine people approach our table. I jerked my head around, about to give Man-Bun an earful when I saw it was the reporter instead. What the hell was her name again?

"Katharina and Lucas? I was wondering if we could schedule some time with you after brunch? You're staying at the Lover's Villa, correct? Would two p.m. work for you? I promise we won't take much of your time, just some candid photos of you in conversation and a few prepared questions. Your mother has read through them and pre-approved of them."

I met Kat's gaze and hesitated. She looked almost as thrilled about this as I was. "Well—"

"They're free. There's nothing on the reunion itinerary until this evening. Our bridge tournament and fireworks aren't until after dinner." My mother intoned in her snobby upper class accent. It had been her life's work to eliminate the midwestern prairies of her childhood from her persona. Looked like she showed up just in time to commit us to this stupid thing against our will.

I narrowed my eyes at her. "How do you know we don't have our own plans?"

Mother completely ignored me as she scrutinized the table-top from behind her jeweled Bulgari sunglasses.

"Julia, refold that napkin and take your things off the table! They'll be photographing all this and I had it set this way for a reason," she ordered in *that* voice. The one that instinctively made both my sister and I snap our spines perfectly straight before we could even think about what we were doing.

Kat's wide blue eyes went from me to Julia and then back again. The reporter spoke up then. "Oh just go about your breakfast and we'll make this candid until you get to the toast. Then we'll do some posed shots."

A toast? Suddenly there was a uniformed staff person beside Katya pouring champagne into a glass while another stood behind him with a pitcher of orange juice. mimosas. Great. I loathed champagne.

Julia sprang from her seat, motioning Kat to come with her to the nearby buffet table to fill their plates. I followed behind while Mother gave some instructions to the reporter and Man-Bun.

"No one touch the champagne, it's for the toast," Mother commanded.

What the hell was this toast, anyway? Was she trying to pass this off as some kind of upper-crust custom we held regularly?

We sat in silence while the parents took their time to carefully select their food. Man-Bun danced around the table, snapping photos. Oh this was over-the-top annoying. When he moved in close to focus on Kat drinking from her water goblet, I quickly scooted my chair, deliberately setting the leg right on his foot.

"Ouch!" he yelped, hopping backwards and shooting me a dirty look.

"Apologies," I muttered, hiding a smirk behind my napkin. Hopefully he understood the warning to back away from her. Otherwise I'd have to get more obnoxious. Kat seemed to have noticed his fixation, too. Did I sense some gratitude in her eyes when she looked at me and smiled? After that, she pointedly angled herself away from his line-of-sight. Only then did he move on, turning to take wide shots of the garden. I glared at his back. *What a tool.*

Beside me, Julia appeared nervous, fidgeting at her seat and sending occasional glances at our parents' backs. We all watched as the two eldest family members return to the table with their laden plates.

Mother carefully positioned her plate on its setting, then rearranged the flatware. "Arent, the toast?" She said to my father, then waved her hand toward the reporter woman and her lackeys. "We're about to start."

Father's features hardened as if he weren't on board with this show of—whatever it was. Upper crust grandiosity? With thinned lips, he set down the fork he'd just barely picked up. Expelling a long sigh, he stood and cleared his throat.

Reporter-lady stepped in. "Okay, we're just going to ask you to cooperate for just this first part, the baron's toast to his family. We'd like to get shots of everyone holding their flutes up in unison and try several angles because of the light. So if you don't mind moving slowly and holding when we ask you to? And then when it comes time to drink, take small sips and hold your glass in place. Once we're done with this part, we'll let you get to your brunch as normal but we really think the toast would make a great set piece for the feature."

Ugh. Whatever. It would be a miracle if I wasn't rolling my eyes in every single goddamn shot. But I'd been forced to do more inane things than this and it would be over soon.

And I had Kat here to endure it with me, thank god. But she wasn't looking at me. She was instead frowning and watching Julia carefully.

Father swept up his champagne flute and tilted it toward us, prompting us to do the same. I was sure that the next speech to come out of his mouth would be cheesy and inauthentic. Unless he deigned to surprise me.

"Does anyone mind if I toast with my water goblet instead?" Kat blurted just as Arent was about to let go his self-important expulsion of hot air. My father stared at Kat. From his expression, you'd think she'd just asked him if she could eat a clod of dirt from the flower bed instead of the breakfast on her plate.

He blinked and Mother scoffed. "It would be better if you had the flute..." She turned to Man-Bun to reaffirm, and the reporter agreed that it would look better with everyone holding a flute. Kat made a face and set down the goblet, picking up the flute. She appeared troubled, deep in thought.

What the heck was going on? Maybe she just really hated mimosas.

Father droned on about the family reunion and the place of his childhood and our family's connection to the land, honoring our heritage and blah blah blah. Blather blather blather. Finally with a curt nod toward Kat he said. "And welcome to our newest family member, Katharina. We hope you are here for a good long time." I blinked. What he left unspoken was obvious—*unlike the last one.*

"Okay and can you just start taking some slow sips?" The reporter intervened. "We'll move around the table and get the shots, want to do some effects so give us about five minutes or so?"

We all held the flutes to our mouths except for Julia. But Kat, seeing Julia's hesitation, then put her flute down.

"Is there a problem?" Mother asked.

Kat calmly folded her arms over her chest. "I'm not going to drink and actually I think there must be enough nice photos in what they just took that they have plenty to use. So you don't need to make anyone else here drink, especially, if they don't want to. Or at least just let them fill their flute with orange juice."

Mother seemed to lose all her color as she jerked her gaze at Julia. My sister hadn't said a word but was looking down, her shoulders hunched, appearing very uncomfortable.

Father blew out a breath. "You know I really would like to eat my breakfast sometime in this next century."

At the same time, Mother shook her head, fixated on her daughter. "Now is not the time to be making this all about you, Julia. We have a *journalist* here. Now stop making a big deal over a few swallows of champagne and just be a team player."

I set my glass down, too, but not so much in solidarity as that my arm was getting tired. What was Julia's problem? She seemed emotional, close to tears.

The reporter and the photographer were staring at each other. Katya flushed deep red and had a look in her eye I recognized instantly. Often times in the past, I'd had that look directed at me. This did not mean good things for my mother. And I was suddenly very curious as to what my parents would do when confronted with Kat's full wrath.

"Why is everything so difficult? You're getting to be as bad as your brother," Father growled. And with a forceful thrust, he plopped his own flute down on the table. It tipped over and the orange spread across the pristine white tablecloth and soaked part of his toast. *Good.* Karma was a bitch, old man.

"For once I'd just like to see my progeny succeed at something instead of being whiney spoiled brats wallowing in their sorrows. Especially when they've been handed everything they could ever want."

Wow. The asshole was pulling no punches today. I bit my tongue. No point in losing my cool now. I had nothing to prove and I sure as hell wasn't going to sit at this table and keep eating after that outburst. As far as I was concerned, breakfast was over. I pulled my napkin out of my lap and dumped it on the table then reached out for Kat's hand. But she wasn't looking and I doubt she was even aware of my presence.

If looks could kill, I'd be an orphan right this moment. Kat's eyes were practically shooting blue-hot flame. "I think you'd have to be completely ignorant not to see that your children are succeeding right before your eyes. *In spite of* you." Her gaze flicked to my dumbstruck mother whose mouth was hanging wide open. "And you."

Father stiffened, unaccustomed to being challenged. My first instinct was to warn Kat that he wasn't worth the effort or the breath she'd waste.

"Lucas is on the shortlist for a very prestigious job heading up a brand new division of our company. He's one of the best employees we've got. And one of the smartest, too."

"Now is not the time for this!" Mother hissed. The journalist group had backed off, but the reporter was taking notes in her tablet and Man-Bun was subtly snapping photos of the confrontation.

I was inclined to agree with my mother but more for Kat's sake than for theirs.

Apparently Father didn't give a crap about the audience and only cared about verbally slapping down my wife. "I'm glad to know you think so highly of him for the short time that you've known him. But before you did, he failed at just about everything, including a marriage to a very nice young lady. I just hope for *your* sake, Katharina, that he doesn't sabotage what he has now. He's already thrown out all the advantages he's had in life to go incognito in some useless cubicle job. We won't talk about the times when just getting out of bed was too difficult for him to accomplish."

Kat blinked at him, astonished, her blue eyes blazed azure death. I wrapped my fingers around her wrist and tugged. I was not engaging in this bullshit and if I could help it, neither would she. "It's not worth it," I muttered. Julia nodded her agreement with my statement but Kat yanked her hand free.

"*You* are worth it." Kat looked at Julia. "And so is your sister."

Then she squared off with my father. Mother was frozen in horror, glancing over at the journalists. I could tell she was trying to figure out a way to herd them out of here.

Kat looked like a bull who'd just been taunted with a gigantic scarlet banner.

"Why are you saying such terrible things? You're being abusive."

"Of course I'm not," the old man shot back.

"Then pull your head out of your ass and stop acting like this to your own kids."

Mother dropped her flute on the ground and it shattered everywhere. That didn't stop the confrontation, though. All it did was bring more people running, staff to clean it up. The journalists weren't budging.

"And I've only known Julia a few weeks, but I know what you said about her, too, is wrong. Maybe if you bothered to even *know* your children as people, you'd know how fucking clueless you are. But you'd probably never admit that because you don't even care about them."

Father was losing his cool now, face flushing. He made a jerky gesture in my sister's and my direction. "I care enough to be disappointed that one is a drunk and the other a mopey sad-sack. He couldn't find the motivation to get himself out of bed for weeks and had to go change everything about himself in order to function in life. Give a child everything he or she needs and they waste it, apparently."

Julia's head shot up, her mouth agape and tears glistened in her eyes. "I can't—" she cut herself off when her voice trembled. Then she scooped up her sunglasses and put them on.

Kat was on her feet and, if it were possible, she might have even gotten in his face if it weren't for the six-foot round table in between them. "How fucking dare you?" she all but screeched.

Father's eyes almost bugged out of his head as he drew back, nostrils flaring. At least that outburst appeared to render him temporarily speechless. Too bad it wasn't permanent.

"Julia and Lucas are doing their best to get better and they are doing great—"

"—If you believe in consolation prizes, yes—"

"I *do* believe in toxic parents and you sure as hell are one. You care more about how 'bad' it looks having your children in recovery than worrying about how you can help them get better.

Or what *you* did to contribute to their problems in the first place."

Then she turned to my mother whose mortification wore all over her face, her body language. She didn't move, visibly terrified.

"You should both be on your knees sobbing with gratitude that Lucas and Julia have the strength to face their demons and overcome them. Some families aren't so lucky. *Tough love* is bullshit. And it's not *love*. So if that's what you're trying to do, *you're* the ones who are failing. *Hard*."

I was now on my feet beside her, noting how she was shaking. Father had this bizarre look on his face, a mixture of horror and satisfaction. I took her by the arm. "We're done here. If you ever want me present at a family function again, you'll apologize to her and stop baiting my wife as a way to get to me."

"Your wife has an interesting vocabulary."

"My wife is interesting in every way, which is more than I can say for you and your bland predictability. But be content that you are middle-aged, mediocre and have nothing going for you but the money you inherited from your hardworking ancestors." With that, I wrapped my arm around Kat's shoulders and guided her, still shaking, away from the table. Julia threw down her napkin without a word and followed us.

I couldn't resist a parting shot. "Oh and my trust fund that you've been so worried about? It's going to the charities of Kat's choice. Every last bit of it. And I'll enjoy the thought of you stewing on the fact that you can't do shit about it."

Julia accompanied us back to the guest villa, and it was a silent, heavy walk where no words were spoken. We each seemed to be lost in our own thoughts and, perhaps caught up in the aftershock of that heated and unpleasant confrontation.

When we got to the villa, I turned to Julia. Beneath her sunglasses, her cheeks were stained with tears. I pulled her into a hug. "I'm sorry. I didn't know you were going through all that. Don't listen to that asshole. I'm so proud of you." Then I held her while she sobbed.

I sat her down on the couch in the sitting room, holding her until the sobbing calmed. Kat must have discreetly stepped out, leaving us alone to talk. Once Julia's crying calmed, I fetched my sister a bottle of water, then we sat and talked. *Really* talked. Talked like we hadn't talked in years.

About… everything.

Hours later, when Julia had washed her face and left to go pack, I found Katya. She was on the bed Skyping with Mia on her tablet. When she saw me come in, she turned the tablet toward me. "Say hi to Lucas!" she said.

On the screen, Mia laughed and waved. "Hey there, Lucas. You having fun drinking all the wine?"

I grimaced and returned her wave. "Hey Mia. Not enough wine in the world can help with family issues."

She laughed and looked away. I was suddenly stricken thinking Adam might be in the room and had maybe just heard that. I didn't want to give him the wrong impression—whatever that might be. Good God. He'd had that presentation on his desk for five days now and I hadn't heard anything. Not that I'd expected to hear back that quickly.

Fortunately I'd been too busy, mostly happily, to worry about it while here in Napa. But seeing Mia on the screen suddenly reminded me as my stomach bottomed out. I'd know whether I got the job. And likely very soon.

"So hey, I should get going," Mia said. "We'll get together for lunch one of these days, Kat?"

Kat turned the screen back towards herself. "Absolutely mandatory. Next week."

"It's a date. Have a safe trip home in a few days."

Kat sighed. "I wish we were coming home sooner."

"Eh, why, so you can get back to work?" she laughed.

Kat commiserated and ended the call, setting aside her tablet. The skirt of her dress had ridden up her shapely pale thigh as she lay on the bed, barefoot. She also looked a little rumpled, as if she'd napped earlier. Her hair was an untidy cinnamon cloud around her shoulders and there was a warm glow to her skin, pink in her cheeks. She looked absolutely...

Fuckable.

And I wanted to do just that. *Again.* As soon as possible. Just remembering how those strong legs felt wrapped around my hips while I was buried inside her made me hard again. Instantly.

To cover for my bodily reaction, I sat down on my side of the bed.

"How's Julia?" She rolled onto her side to face me.

I smiled. "She's fine. Had a good cry. Thanks for giving us the time to talk. I—it's been a long time. I guess I'm as guilty as my parents are for not appreciating that she's a lot deeper than I thought she was. I can visibly see the change in her.

She bit her lip and watched me with wide eyes. "So neither of you are mad at me?"

I frowned, drawing back. "Mad at you? Why would we be?"

"Because I could tell you two just wanted to blow your dad off. But I engaged anyway. I couldn't stop myself. I'm sorry but when I see someone mistreating another, I just have to stand up for them. I got so pissed, I couldn't back down."

"You stand up for others being mistreated, but not when you're the one being mistreated..."

That adorable crease between her brows reappeared, and she looked off into the distance, considering. "You're right. I hadn't thought about it that way. I guess maybe because my parents always sided with Derek, I got tired of fighting against it? It's... it's easier to stick up for others than for myself."

"Somewhere along the line you got the idea that you weren't worth the trouble."

She looked up at me. "I'm glad I had you there last time. I guess today makes us square."

I laughed. "That's very important to you, isn't it? That we stay even at least, or that you're ahead. You can't stand it when I'm the one ahead."

She nodded. "Accurate."

"Well, anyway, neither one of us is mad at you and Julia is super grateful you stuck up for her. She's going to take some time to figure out her next step regarding the parents and she'll be asking me for advice with that. I think she's going to be fine."

Kat kept her eyes focused on mine, her stare intensifying. "I like Julia a lot. But I didn't do it for her."

I returned that gaze, seeing... *something* deep in the sky-blue depths of her eyes. Suddenly there was this rush of feeling—like freefall, an exhilarating, heart-pumping breathless sort of feeling that almost overwhelmed me.

She did it for me.

I cleared my throat after far too long of a pause "Well... thank you."

She smiled and reached out her hand to cover mine. "I told you, we're family. Even if it's temporary. And family sticks up for each other. And supports each other. The good kind of family, anyway."

I twitched a brow, staring at that hand covering my own without making a move to respond to her touch. I was also, curiously, finding it difficult to even talk.

She tilted her head toward me. "We both got a bit of a bad draw in the family department. But you and me, we're smart and kind and good people. We can be there for each other."

I swallowed in a thick throat, surprisingly moved by her sentiment. I chanced a glance up to meet her gaze and when we connected, she smiled sweetly.

Without even realizing what I was doing, I reached up and smoothed her soft cheek. God, she was amazing—and not just to look at, and not just in the sack. And I realized that as much as she'd rubbed me the wrong way in the past, it had been because I'd known this all along. She was amazing. Too amazing for me to brush off or ignore so I'd decided I'd needed to push her away. Over and over again.

So she wouldn't upset that carefully won balance I'd achieved in my life.

"I can do the same for you, you know. Be there for you if, for example, you go back to Canada, face your family. I owe it to you for all the shit you just had to endure this weekend."

This time, her smile showed off her even, white teeth. "Maybe I'll take you up on that when it's legal for me to leave the country."

"I'll go with you. You can buy me one of those famous donuts you used to go on and on about. Tom something-or-other."

"Tim Hortons." Her grin widened, and she leaned forward, throwing her arms around my neck with the exuberance of a little girl. The silken fresh scent of her hair washed over me, and it hit me, almost like a physical blow. When she pulled back, I fought to keep any reaction off my features.

I had secrets, yeah. Secrets from her and even some from myself. Like what the hell even was this that I was feeling right now? It was like some part of my brain was screaming in panic and the rest of me was just frozen, at a complete loss for what to do or think.

My phone chimed. Welcoming an interruption to this disturbing internal development, I stood from the bed to fetch it from the dresser. It was a text message from my sister, which I read and then laughed. I knew there was a reason I loved my sister.

Kat frowned. "What's up?"

"I have no idea how she did it, but Julia commandeered the private jet my father chartered. She's getting the plane to fly out tonight and wants to know if we want a ride."

Kat brightened. "So we won't have to stay three more days? Sweet. Let's go."

I made a cutting gesture with my hand to stop her while I texted the butler. "Well, Deleon will want to pack us up but I'm going to have him return the rental car for me instead. We can throw our stuff in the suitcases easily enough. But the plane doesn't leave 'til midnight, which means we don't have to leave here until ten. Which leaves us with the problem..." My gaze flicked up. "That we have nearly six hours with nothing to do."

A slow smile spread across her face. "Oh, I'm sure we can think of something to do to pass the time."

Oh yeah. How I was hoping she'd say that. Inside, every muscle seemed to tense with anticipation. I folded my arms across my chest. "I seem to recall how you like staying even with me or even ahead, but—"

"But?"

"We aren't exactly even in the oral sex department, are we? And I still haven't had a chance to find out about that hidden talent you once bragged about."

Without hesitation she rose, walked over to where I stood beside the dresser and put her hand on my chest. Where she touched me, it felt like fire. When she tilted her head up to look in my face, her open admiration was visible. "Well we definitely can't have that. Brace yourself, because I'm about to blow your mind, Jedi Boy."

I grinned. "Would you call that a... Jedi Mind Trick?"

"More like Jedi Mind Fuck." Next thing I knew, her hands were on my belt buckle. As she continued to stare into my eyes, she undid the buckle, licking those luscious lips of hers. With practiced ease, she dropped my trousers, then pushed my boxers down right after. My body thrummed with arousal and my throat was so tight I could hardly swallow. I was almost overwhelmed in anticipation of her mouth on me. Of watching her on her knees in front of me. Of her taking in my length as she tightened those lips around the base of my cock.

She palmed my erection and blew out a breath as we held that stare. Then she sank to her knees slowly, as if floating. I leaned my head back when I felt her hot breath on my sensitive skin, my cock so hard it was almost painful.

When the heat and moisture of her mouth closed in around me, I almost lost it right there.

"Fuck," I gasped, so unprepared for the sensations despite having anticipated exactly this. As with everything, the reality far outweighed anything I'd ever fantasized about her. I placed my hand on the dresser beside me to brace my weight against it. I didn't think I'd get so carried away that I might fall over but *damn*, you never knew. Once her tongue got involved, I wouldn't be responsible for my actions.

She slid her mouth down on me, taking more in and I swear to God, I couldn't watch her do it. If I did, this would be a lot shorter than I wanted it to be. We'd fucked twice within the past twenty-four hours and that hadn't even taken the edge off. In fact, I wanted her more now than I had before I knew how incredibly hot it was between us.

I reached down and threaded my hand into her soft hair, relishing the way it slithered and snaked around my fingers. Her tongue slid down the underside of my cock and in less than a minute, I was seconds away from coming.

My fingers curled into her hair. I gently pulled her away, sucking in a deep breath and trying not to hate myself too much for pulling away her hot, luscious mouth. But I had to do something or this would be over embarrassingly fast.

I pulled her up, and she had the most puzzled look on her face. Obviously no one had ever done something like this before— turned down one hell of an amazing blow job.

But I wanted more. More of her creamy skin, more of her sighs and moans of pleasure, more of those silky thighs wrapped around me. I wanted her clit in my mouth, throbbing with anticipation. Her orgasm at *my* command.

"I want to taste you," I said in answer to the unspoken question on her face.

Her expression melted from puzzled surprise into dreamy arousal. My hands went to the back of her dress, pulling the zipper down as far as it would go. She slid it off her shoulders and then turned back to the bed, pulling me along with her. When we got there, I pulled off her underwear and quickly shed my own shirt.

Then, with a hand on her shoulder, I pushed her to sit down on the bed, kneeling in front of her between her legs. With another forceful push, I laid her flat in front of me, her long legs dangling over the side. She sucked in a quick breath of surprise but widened her legs, apparently ready to roll with it. I wasted no time positioning myself between those soft, pale thighs. I bent and covered her clit with my mouth, sucking in. The muffled squeak of surprise, the gasp for more air, the long moan as I slid my tongue mercilessly over her. These were all the reward I sought.

My body ached with need as she took each fevered breath, rasped each declaration of my name.

My arousal ratcheted up, tense and painful, my entire body on high alert. Her thigh muscles tightened and relaxed. She grabbed aimlessly at the bedsheets, twisting them in her fists. Her breathing was heavy, labored, punctuated by almost animalistic moans of pleasure. All of this, every bit of it was my doing. *And my undoing.*

And in this moment, I classified her exquisite response as one of my greatest accomplishments.

"Lucas, I'm going to come!" she said about half a second before arching her back, tensing everywhere, her breath stuttering. I sucked some more, and she screamed. *Loud.* "Oh God. Oh, holy shit." She repeated over and over again like a mantra.

Yes. She should have known I would never let her get ahead of me in this little game of ours.

As I pulled back and looked at her, sweaty and spent and tangled in the sheets, I felt a hunger, a truly intense ache I'd never recalled experiencing before. I needed her again to a degree that might have scared me if I let myself dwell on it.

But all I wanted to do now was sink into her heat and feel her, hot and writhing underneath me. She'd barely recovered, finally opening her eyes to look up at me with a sweet, blissful smile.

I took hold of her shoulder and without a word, roughly flipped her over, urgently pursuing my own need. Bending, I hooked an arm around her waist, tugging her hips toward me. Then I angled myself in for a sharp, quick thrust.

I'd fantasized more than once about taking her like this. I pushed into her with every bit of pent up frustrated energy built-up of a year's worth of heated and unfulfilled desire for her.

Kat exhaled sharply. I'd literally taken her breath away. *Good,* because that made two of us. With hard, violent thrusts, I drew back from her and pumped into her again. Again. Again. Fast, fierce, sharp. And when she fell forward, I yanked her up against me once more, only to pound her back down again. Grind, Push. Thrust.

My mind went somewhere, lost in the sensation of her, tight heat wrapped around me, the feel of her sweaty skin under my hands. I closed my eyes, happily lost in her.

CHAPTER 22
KATYA

FUCK. OH HOLY SHIT. THIS WAS... I COULDN'T COLLECT MY thoughts. I was drowning in pleasure so soon after the mind-blowing orgasm he'd given me. Now he had me rolled on my stomach, maintaining a merciless pace. The sensations were so intense I couldn't catch my breath.

Who knew that calm, cool and distant Lucas could be a frenzied animal in bed?

I sure as hell hadn't suspected it, though I may have fantasized about it more than once. He was definitely fit enough to sustain this breakneck pace and right now, I was just holding my own, along for the ride, so to speak.

My arms ached from holding myself up, pushing back against him to meet each fierce thrust. In spite of that, I could feel that tension building again. With shock I realized I was close to coming again.

And almost as if he sensed it, he stopped so abruptly that I gasped. Gently, he hooked a hand around my throat and pulled me up. I was kneeling, now, my back pressed to his heaving chest. He was winded. Sweat coated our skin, fusing us together. And though he wasn't moving, he was still inside me. I twitched against him and he wrapped his other arm around my waist to hold me still.

His mouth was at my ear. "You are so smoking hot, Kat. You blow my mind."

Instead of responding with words, I tried to move against him again. I'd been close again, damn it, and greedily, I wanted my next orgasm. The way he was holding me, his thumb tracing the column of my throat but not holding too tight... Somehow I found it incredibly arousing.

"Tell me what you want," he rasped.

"Make me come, damn it."

"You want to come? Again? So greedy."

I reached up and over my shoulder to grab his head. Tilting my own head back, I pull him into a hot, fevered kiss, my tongue plunging into his mouth. All the while, our chests moved in unison, gasping for every spare bit of air. On the way from pulling back from the kiss, I let my teeth sink in. He liked it... I could tell by the way he surged inside of me.

"Fuck me," he murmured.

"Yep, it's what I'm doing right now. Now fuck me hard."

He pushed into me again, then stopped, holding himself in deep. "You like this? You want more of it?"

I bucked against him. "Don't get cocky." Then I laughed at my own joke and he laughed with me.

Without further hesitation, the hand holding me at my waist released me and went to my clit instead, rubbing me there as his hips turned shallow circles. Oh God, more pleasure ripped through me. It took less than a minute as that build toward orgasm felt like a tornado, screaming vortex forming out of nowhere to suck me in. My back arched, I shouted his name. He surged again and threw his head back savoring the feel of my orgasm as he muttered his own hoarse, "Yes."

I collapsed forward on the bed and he supported me while he drove himself to his own finish. With a stiffening and a quick intake of breath, he was coming. And I could feel it... everywhere. At the juncture where we were joined, on every square inch of my skin, in my core.

When he settled beside me, he didn't say a word... just spooned me, pressing the length of his body to my own. We lay there, enjoying the fresh afternoon breeze that blew in through an open window. I dozed off with no other thought than this must be what true contentment felt like. I'd never had this before and had to admit. I could use a lot more of it.

I dozed fitfully for maybe a half hour before stirring to awareness. I was starving, never having had any of that cursed brunch and we hadn't eaten when we got back.

Lucas wasn't in bed with me. The door to the washroom was shut, and the shower was on. I got up and raided the fridge, happily finding the leftover treats from last night's rooftop escapade neatly packaged away there. Thank goodness for the unseen angels otherwise known as personal guest butlers.

Wow, was this for real? Was this my life, even if for a short while? High fallutin' theme parties, romantic rooftop poolside sex and private airplane trips?

Livin' the high life! Who'd a thunk it? Little ole Kat Ellis from PoCo, the burbs of Vancouver, a baroness and flying in private jets.

Soon after snacking, dressing and packing our things, we were ready to catch a private car to the airport. But I'd almost forgotten about the very special souvenir I'd purchased from Napa. "Hey, there, *husband*," I crooned. "I got you a special gift."

He arched a brow. "Why do I feel like I should be very afraid right now?"

I sent him a cheesy grin and pulled my hands out from behind my back, each one holding a miniature ball cactus. "Look, friends for Cocky! We can arrange them in a very... suggestive fashion, if you will."

His eyes narrowed, landing on my gift, but I could tell he was fighting laughter. He didn't want to give me the satisfaction, but I could tell he was highly amused. "Someone might think you have a penis fixation."

I made a face at him. "That's the stupidest thing I've ever heard. *Of course*, I have a penis fixation. Jeez. You of all people should know."

There was a look on his face then. I couldn't exactly read it—more amusement, for sure, but also something like admiration. I made sure to wrap the newfound treasures up safely so they'd survive the flight and be able to join their friend Cocky the Cocktus as our centerpiece.

Getting home was as simple as I-commandeered-my-private-Gulfstream-with-personal-pilot-and-flight-attendant. It was just a ninety-minute flight from the exclusive Napa airport followed by a quick zip up the freeway to get home.

Once home, we collapsed, exhausted, at nearly three a.m.

We didn't sleep in, unfortunately. So the next morning, both of us moved around the house like zombies. Lucas had got up earlier than me, making a run to get a few groceries so we'd have some toast and milk for breakfast. I was tidying up the house when the doorbell rang.

Michaela called out on the other side and I ran to open it. Max almost bowled me over in his excitement, tail wagging, mouth open and full of slobber. I knelt down and gave the dog a big hug and kiss. "Hey, puppy! Did you have fun at doggy camp?"

Michaela laughed. "He had a blast. Even has some new lady friends."

I unclipped Max's leash from his collar and took it from Michaela. "Max, you're such a dog!"

"I think he was bummed to leave early but Lucas texted me yesterday telling me you guys would be home ahead of schedule. I knew he'd really miss the dog, so I decided to do him a favor and get the pup now."

I stroked the dog's head. "Come in. Lucas will be back any minute with breakfast."

Michaela shook her head. "I'm starting a new job at the university and I have to get over there, so I can't stay. But I figured you'd want your mail." She handed me a grocery bag that had been slung over her shoulder.

I took it from her and wished her well. Lucas was coming up the walkway as she turned to leave. They spoke for a few minutes as I went and dumped the bag of mail on the table. Lucas came into the kitchen shortly afterward with the groceries. *And* a box of donuts.

They weren't half bad donuts. I realized after spying the address on the box, that he'd driven out of his way to get them. After the discussion about Timmy's donuts yesterday, this struck me as a sweet gesture.

Yet when I acknowledged it, he gave a gruff shrug, blank-faced. He refused to admit that he'd done something nice. I studied him with serious side-eye. He seemed to be falling back into default grump-man mode. Like the weekend had never happened.

But I knew better. Because it *had.*

Lucas proceeded to sift through the mail Michaela had collected while we were away. He arranged them in piles. Sales circulars and junk mail. Bills. And then without a word, he took one thick white envelope and plopped it on the table in front of me as I finished my last donut.

I read it, blinked, and read it again.

"Immigration office? Oh shit, what if it says that your country doesn't want me?"

He arched a brow at me. "Have you done anything in particular that would make them not want you?"

I bit my lip nervously and darted him a fearful glance. My heart was hammering like I'd just knocked over a liquor store and had made my great escape on foot. I could feel it in my throat. "What if they want another interview? What if they think we're lying about the marriage?"

He grimaced. "I suppose we could send them a sex tape."

I shook my head. "This isn't funny. Besides, none of them deserve to see me naked."

"True enough." He gestured at the envelope. "Stop speculating about it and open the damn thing."

I just couldn't do it. I was so scared that I suddenly needed to pee. But if I stood up, my knees might be too shaky. And... without another word, I shoved the envelope at him. "You do it and be quick, before I barf everywhere."

He stared at me for a long moment, then frowned. "Will the news—whatever it is—be any better coming from me than from a piece of paper?"

"Lucaaaaaasssss, please!"

He let out a long sigh and picked up the envelope. "Fine, fine."

He tore the envelope open, unfolded the letter and began to read silently. Like, I'd never seen someone read that slow, honestly. Or so without reaction. He was like a statue reading that thing. And you would have thought it was printed on a ticker tape or something. Like he was waiting for it to scroll across his line of sight one word at a time. He read. And read. His eyes slid all the way to the bottom without saying a goddamn thing.

I couldn't hold it in any longer. "Lucas!"

He put the paper down, laced his fingers together and looked at me with dead seriousness in his eyes. My stomach dropped. "Well, they've decided... to allow you to stay in the country."

I didn't trust my ears. "What?"

"Your green card is coming via certified mail in the next forty-eight hours."

My mouth opened, but no sounds came out. I was frozen. So... this was it?

Now he seemed really concerned. He leaned toward me and spoke really loudly. "You can stay, Kat. You're legal."

I snatched up the letter and read it over and over again. Nope, he definitely wasn't bullshitting me. Every muscle in my body sagged with relief. But something deep inside me though thankful and happy also felt more than a little guilty. I set the paper down, reflecting on that.

"Even though this took months to go through, it seems like it should have been so much harder. When you watch the news..." My voice cut out, suddenly choked up, remembering the images I'd seen on the news. People held at the border seeking asylum after having traveled for thousands of kilometres to get there. Separated from their families, their little kids.

Tears poked at my eyes. I should be happy for myself, right? But why? Was I any more deserving than any of them, to have this conferred on me relatively easily? That same thing they fought tooth and nail for their basic survival? I clenched my jaw and released it.

Lucas appeared puzzled. "You seem sad."

I shook my head. "There are so many people trying to get into this country. So many facing hardship and needing asylum. Why was it so easy for me?"

He reached out and grabbed my hand. "I'd hardly call it *easy*, though."

I pushed the letter away from me, suddenly feeling a little sick to my stomach. "I'm speaking relatively. I had advantages... because I'm white and speak English as my first language. I have an education and was able to afford a great lawyer."

He nodded. "Yes, you had a lot of advantages going into it. But I understand why you're feeling upset."

I shrugged. "I just wish I could do something. I feel helpless."

"Hmm. Yes, well a green card means you get to stay here but you don't get the right to vote. But there might be other good things you can do."

I began to twirl my finger through my hair, ideas racing through my mind. I knew I should be happy. And that made me feel ungrateful. Just arghh.

"I feel bad. I want to help others."

He blew out a breath with a lopsided smile. "Well you can't marry anyone else until after we get our divorce."

I knew he was cracking jokes to try and cheer me up. Or maybe he thought I was ungrateful for what he'd done for me— which was a lot. I reached out and took his hand. "Thank you, I so appreciate what you did for me. But now I need to find a way to pay it forward. I'm thinking volunteer work. And when I get my bonus for the year, I'll donate it to a legal relief fund or civil liberties union."

He tilted his head at me. "Or you can help me decide which charities we can send my trust fund money to. That wasn't just a parting shot at my father. I was serious. I don't want that money."

He almost took my breath away. I needed a moment to recover. "You would do that?"

"Yes. I agree with you. We should help where we can. Why don't we ask Jenna her opinion on what to do? Doesn't she work at a refugee center? I bet she'd know where monetary help was needed."

I stood up, bent and hugged him. "Those are great ideas. Thank you."

He reached up and stiffly patted my arm as I hugged him, clearly uncomfortable. I hesitated. It was obvious that being back at the house after our weekend away was weirding him out.

We'd been in each other's company constantly over the past four days. Perhaps he needed his space. I pulled away, ready to back off and maybe go lock myself in my gaming room for a while to get over this weird funk I was feeling.

As I did so, however, he caught my wrist and held me in place. "You didn't look at all your mail."

I glanced down at the table to see no less than three identical envelopes in the same bone-colored fancy linen stationary. I recognized them instantly. They were from my brother's lawyer. Wow, they were getting more prolific in their mailings.

"I'll run them through the shredder." I sighed.

"I think you should have a look at them first. I'm worried, now that I know what exactly you're facing up there... I don't think it's a good idea for you to just ignore it. What if they decide to contact the U.S. government and threaten your green card?"

I blinked, feeling another weight drop. Lucas's conclusion that these same people might be responsible for my troubles with U.S. immigration had me thinking. If that was the case, they wouldn't be above trying to get my newly won green card revoked, either.

I immediately slumped back into my seat, feeling like a tire that had just lost all its air. He was right.

I leaned forward, rubbing my forehead. The mere thought of doing anything about this exhausted me.

"When you get your green card, you'll be able to leave the country and get back in with no problem." He stated what I already knew. "What is your plan, Kat? Are you just never going to go back to Canada again?"

Without another word, I scooted the letters into a pile in front of me and began to systematically tear them open and read through them. As I read a letter, I handed it to Lucas, then tore into the next one while he read the previous one. After the third one, I sat back, feeling more exhausted than before. Each one got more insistent. The last one stating that the Crown counsel had been given my address and other information. I would shortly be subpoenaed for an examination of discovery, if I hadn't already.

Lucas shook his head, squinting at the last letter, then picking up the one before it to skim again. "I'm not understanding these Canadian legal terms. Crown counsel? Examination of discovery?"

I licked my lips. "Well, I'm no expert on the American system but I did binge watch *The Good Wife* last year. A Crown counsel is what you call the prosecutor in the States. An examination of discovery is called a deposition here."

"So..."

"The Crown counsel wants to know if I'm a viable witness for the defense. And if I am, they want to know what I know for when they cross-examine me in a trial."

He stared at me. "But you know and I know that you're not a witness for the defense. You have no idea where he was."

I bit my top lip and locked my arms across my chest tightly. "Correct."

"So if you go there, and you tell them this, then they'll be off your back about it."

I locked gazes with his and as we held that stare, my chest tightened and my heart thrummed. Yes, he was trying to show me how easy this could be. How I could be free of this monkey on my back forever.

But there was another monkey and, much as I was frustrated, angry and hurt, I wasn't sure how to deal with that one. Crazy, really, to think of your own family as a monkey on your back. Once I did this, I'd be effectively cutting them off, possibly forever.

"Kat," he said in a low voice.

My jaw clenched and tears prickled the backs of my eyes. I blinked fiercely. "Don't," I said in a low and shaky voice. "I know what you're going to say."

He reached across the table, holding his palm up for my hand but when I didn't give it to him, he slowly retracted. "I care about you. I want you to be free of this. I know you want it—"

"It's not that simple," I murmured back.

To my surprise he was silent for a long moment before continuing. "I know that too. Your situation is different from what mine was but there are definite similarities. One important difference, though, is that you're not alone. I'll be there with you every step of the way."

It was difficult to swallow, and I was about to become very emotional. And damn it, I'd already lost it once in front of him. He would not be witness to that again. That ugly-hideous cry had been enough for any man to have to put up with for a lifetime.

"I need to go think about this for a bit. I think I'm going to log on and go kill some stuff on the game. That always helps me think."

He grinned, straightening. Only a true gamer would understand that sentiment and Lucas was absolutely a true gamer.

Hours passed, and I watched the clock, soloed my way through two challenging dungeon quests and used that time to think through every scenario with my family situation. It all sounded so easy and logical the way Lucas had put it. There was no denying it.

And Lucas himself. How amazing was he? Yeah, he was acting a bit weird today, but I put that down to our return to the real world. To say nothing of the harrowing confrontation with his parents the day before. Anyone would be distracted after that.

But his kindness, his admission that he cared, his offer to be there with me when I finally faced my past demons.... Those things I couldn't stop thinking about.

Somewhere inside my heart, emotion churned, and I wondered, questioned and theorized. Not only were my thoughts racing and spinning like a stock car down a tight track, but my feelings were overflowing and mixed up. The old and the new. The having to cut ties with my former life and face the strange and thrilling prospects that this new one held.

Was I ready?

I was tough. I'd done so much alone. But I didn't want to do this alone.

Hours later, it was early afternoon. We'd walked the dog in silence and then grabbed some lunch. My eyes drifted toward the clock, aware that I could settle this with a phone call. The phone number was in each one of those lawyer letters sitting on the kitchen table.

I chewed my lip and glanced at Lucas who had pushed me no further since I'd told him I needed time to think. "So... if I made that call. I'd have to go to Canada. Pretty soon. Like in the next week or two."

He nodded. "Yes."

"But we have work," I hedged.

"Well we asked for a week off and we're back three days early. We could opt to go in tomorrow and explain that we need a few days next week. It's a fairly short flight, isn't it?"

"About three hours."

He nodded, thinking. "We could fly up early in the morning and you could go straight to the pros—er—Crown counsel's office. Just walk in, answer their questions—"

"For the examination of discovery, my brother's lawyers would also be involved. They'd be there to cross-examine. And Derek would have the right to be there if he wanted."

"But not your parents, if it's done the same way as it is here. Or anyone else, right?"

I nodded.

"And you would in no way be obligated to speak to his lawyers before you make your statement."

I let go a long sigh. "All right, I'm going to call them and see when they can take me in before I chicken out."

To my dismay, my phone was completely out of power so Lucas unlocked and handed me his phone. "You've got this, Kat. Remember how badass you are."

I dialed the number, put the phone to my ear and without realizing what I was doing, I reached out and grabbed his hand. He squeezed it tightly, reassuring me silently that he was here. He had my back. We were family, and that's how we rolled.

My hand squeezed his tighter when someone answered and I asked for the person listed in the letter. The phone call ended up being shockingly short, but they were more than willing to be accommodating. I had an appointment to do the examination of discovery the following Thursday at one p.m.

Derek's lawyers would be notified, as would Derek and they would have someone there to cross examine me after my statement and questions with the counsel.

Lucas watched me carefully the entire time I spoke, then asked me clarifying questions the moment I put the phone down.

After a moment, we sat in silence, then.... Then he blew out a breath and stared at me with that look of open admiration again. The one that had done things to me the last time he'd looked at me like that.

"You are amazing, you know that?" he said quietly.

And suddenly that emotion was flush to overflowing again. The stinging in my eyes, the heaviness in my throat. Everything twisting and tangling inside of me. I leapt out of my chair and threw my arms around his neck. He grabbed me, held me as I landed right in his lap.

I hung on so tight I didn't ever want to let go, burying my stinging nose into that freshly laundered shirt—that soapy smell of *him*. The feel of those strong arms around me, that confidence in my strength. For those same things I'd been criticized for over and over as I grew up, Lucas was openly showing me those qualities were admirable, desirable. Appreciated.

My head turned and suddenly I was kissing his neck, his rough cheek. The masculine scratch of his whiskers scraping against my skin ignited a new passion in me. I needed him. I needed to be in his arms, to feel his hands and mouth and body on mine. I needed to worship and be worshiped by him.

We kissed long and heatedly. It wasn't lust-driven. No, there was something more there that hadn't been there before. I knew in that moment what it was.

Oh God. I'd fallen for this man. *Hard.* And yet it had happened so slowly and gradually that it almost seemed to have started the moment we'd met, well over a year ago.

But it was no mystery to me anymore, what this was between him and me, and what it had been for a long time without my idiotic heart recognizing it.

Love. Simple, unadulterated admiration for this man and all that he was and all that he'd done for me, whether selfless or not.

I opened my mouth to him, deepening the kiss until his hands pushed gently at my shoulders, forcing us apart. We were both out of breath and he looked... stunned, torn, and not a little confused.

He frowned, slowly shaking his head. "We can't. It's..." His dark eyes locked on mine. "We're not going to be together for much longer."

I swallowed, taking in that expression on his face. "Yeah, that's what we agreed on at the start, wasn't it? Stay married until I get the green card. But..." My gaze dropped to his rising chest, thinking through my next words.

His breath caught at my *but*, but he didn't say anything.

My eyes returned to his, locked onto them with fierce determination. *Remember how badass you are, Kat.* His words came back to me in that moment. And he was right. I *did* have the courage to say this, damn it. I did.

I took a deep breath, determined to just get it out. "Lucas... I'm in love with you."

CHAPTER 23
LUCAS

I F EVER THERE WAS A MOMENT WHERE I HAD NO IDEA WHAT I was going to say, this was it. Holy shit. That was the last thing I expected to come out of Katya's mouth and there it was. *I'm in love with you.* Those five words hung in the air between us like barriers, like smoke bombs, obscuring everything.

I expelled my breath slowly, sounding a bit like a balloon that had been let go before tying it off. My chest rattled. I blinked. "I, uh. I have no idea what to say to that."

She blinked and drew back, watching me carefully with rounded eyes

Whoa, good going there...Ezel

"You don't have to say anything. I just—in the moment it felt like I had to get that out."

My chest tightened, heart racing, palms sweaty. Classic fight-or-flight reactions.

Her eyes widened. "Lucas?"

I swallowed. Was it harder to breathe in here or was it just me?

"Lucas? Are you in there? Are you okay?"

My eyes darted up at her. "I, uh, I think I'm going to take Max for a walk. I need to think."

She rolled her lips into her mouth, biting at them, then nodded. "Okay, heaven knows he'll be thrilled." In fact the dog, having heard that W-word came trotting up to me, tail wagging expectantly. We'd just been out, but he was a greedy bastard and apparently wanted more.

I grabbed his leash and clipped it to his collar. Katya followed me out into the front room on my way out the door. "Before you go..."

I stopped and turned to her, waiting.

"I want to say that there's no pressure for you. I mean... take all the time you need. We can wait to talk about it until you're ready."

Fuck. Would I ever be ready to have that conversation with her?

I grunted something at her and left with the dog, pounding down the sidewalk faster than normal. Max was a little annoyed he couldn't stop and sniff every tree, but he trotted along obediently to keep up.

If I'd only stuck to the rules with her—those carefully laid-out rules—we would be fine right now. Nothing like this would have happened.

Yeah, right. Because *that* was how hearts worked. Goddamn it.

I had no idea how hearts worked but I *did* know that I couldn't do this again. I couldn't disappoint her and I inevitably would because the past had proven that I sucked at being a husband.

In addition, there was no way I could face being disappointed by her, if it so happened.

Not that I thought she'd do to me what Claire did. *But*—and this was a big *but*—once this thing between her and I failed, and it inevitably would, I could *not* imagine what that would do to me.

The pieces I'd had to pick up after Claire and the whole fallout from the family drama.... Those were nothing compared to what it would do to me to lose Kat that way. I was jogging now, and I glanced down at Max who happily kept up.

Max had been part of my therapy, part of my getting better. I'd gone to see a counselor during those first few months after leaving my family home and setting myself up at a new university. It had taken time to heal and in some ways I still hadn't. Taking care of the puppy had helped. And I was grateful that Max had been there for me and was still here for me.

Why hadn't I just stuck to the original plan? The plan that had meant to keep us at a distance, that had seen us parting on friendly terms.

Yeah, I'd screwed up the rules, but it was time we went back to them. We'd always had an expiration date, Kat and I. So things wouldn't go down in flames.

So that we'd still be able to maintain some modicum of a friendship after this. So that we'd be able to be productive work colleagues. So that I wouldn't hurt her as I inevitably would. This had to end like it had been planned.

Even as I said that to myself, my trainers hitting the sidewalk with regular thumps, I knew it was a lie. When I told myself there were no feelings to return, I knew *that* was a lie. When I said that Katya meant no more to me than a trusted and respected colleague.... It was a lie.

Was it love? Who knew? I didn't believe I was even capable. Love wasn't for me. Marriage sure as *hell* wasn't for me.

She was back in her game room for most of the night. I ate dinner on my own and I wasn't sure she ate at all or what was going through her head. But like a coward, I avoided approaching her and just left her to do her thing. And I did mine.

The way it was always meant to be.

In the morning, when we got ready and went to work, as agreed, she was kind and cordial. It was almost like we hadn't had the previous unfinished conversation. *Almost.* Something was a little off.

She was quieter than she would be. Or she didn't look at me as much—or in the same way. Or, fuck, maybe it was all just my imagination.

We talked about other stuff as I drove us and the dog to work. At least we had the work day to occupy us so I wouldn't obsess over what I'd say to her when we addressed this subject again.

My mind was soon tied up in other things.

Word got out quickly that we were back from vacation early. I received a text from Jordan that he wanted to see me in his office as soon as possible. I showed up at the inner atrium area where the executive officers and directors had their fancy offices. His assistant wasn't at her desk, so I knocked on his door.

Jordan whipped it open but didn't wave me inside. "We're going next door."

My eyes immediately darted toward Adam's office. "You didn't say anything about meeting with Adam."

I was dressed ordinarily for work. Jeans and a concert t-shirt for an obscure band that had broken up a decade ago. I smoothed my hands over it, suddenly feeling self-conscious. Not how I wanted to appear to the big boss who had yet to decide if I'd get the coveted job.

Jordan grabbed my shoulder to usher me toward the CEO's office. "It will be fine. Just go."

"If he says something about how I'm dressed, I'm kicking your ass at an arm-wrestling match in front of your girlfriend. *Then* I'm pouring ice cold beer down your shorts," I ground out.

"Fine by me. April doesn't keep me around for the biceps, if you know what I mean." He winked obnoxiously. Without knocking, he whipped Adam's office door open.

I gritted my teeth and darted him a sharp look as I moved past him to enter the office. "Everybody always knows what you mean, Jordan."

Adam was finishing up a phone call as we entered but did not appear surprised or shocked that Jordan had barged in like that. In fact, he was acting like Jordan did it every day.

Adam turned toward the window, finished the call and then stuffed his phone into his pocket. To my relief, he was also dressed casually today, jeans and a collared golf shirt.

"So, Lucas, how are you? You look like you need some coffee."

I ran a hand through my hair self-consciously and tried hard to ignore Jordan's snicker at my side. I'd get him back later—even if it meant plastic-wrap over the urinal in his personal office. I'd resort to frat house tricks if I had to.

"I'm okay." When my voice cracked, I cleared it and said. "I'm doing fine. Just had a late night."

Adam smiled. "That new wife of yours keeping you up too late?"

That was the case, yes, but not in the way Adam was implying, unfortunately. No, I'd been obsessing all night about how I was going to get us out of this situation unscathed and without breaking her heart.

All solutions had pointed toward *impossible.*

Nevertheless, I began to fumble over an appropriate reply. Both Adam and Jordan met gazes and started laughing. "It's all good, Lucas. I was just giving you a little shit." Adam grinned.

Hopefully this wasn't the shit appetizer to a shit serving of some bad news. I cleared my throat and fidgeted in place while Adam appeared to scrutinize me.

"So next Thursday is the quarterly Board of Directors meeting..."

I nodded.

"I'd like for you and Jeremy to present your vision statements and slides to them."

"Which means wear a suit that day," Jordan cut in unhelpfully.

"Okay, I can do that. Is there a timeline, um,..." I hesitated to ask the question outright.

Adam grinned. "Well, just between the three of us, and I'm asking you in strictest confidence not to say anything, but the officers have agreed on your vision and designs. The board wants to see the top two contenders to make their recommendation, too. Jeremy has some good news coming his way, though not the news he'd anticipated about this job. But keep quiet on that, too. I'm going to speak to him about it shortly."

I shook my head, not understanding. "You mean..."

"You got the job, padawan—" Jordan said.

"—Pending the board's approval, *if* the meeting goes well. Yes, you've got it. You'll be the new director of Draco VR," Adam concurred.

A rush of... something raced through me even before I consciously registered his words. Victory? Disbelief? Relief or heady thrill?

Some or all of the above mixed into one intoxicating concoction. I shook my head and almost asked him to repeat his words. For their part, Jordan and Adam appeared to watch my reaction closely. Jordan put a hand on my shoulder. "You, ah, need a minute?"

I shook off his hand and bumped fists with him instead, then took Adam's extended hand. "Welcome aboard, Lucas. It's going to be one helluva ride but I hope it's a good one."

Suddenly I couldn't restrain my grin. My cheeks were aching with it. Whoa. *Whoa*. This was... whoa.

My mind was racing with all the things I had to get done before I took on the new job—and all the people I needed to tell.

I halted, mid-thought. "About not telling anyone—"

"You have to swear her to secrecy," Adam replied, immediately understanding who I meant. "Under normal circumstances I wouldn't have any problems with a spouse being told right away, but she works here. And she has some good news coming her way as well but I'm going to wait and tell her that directly, if you don't mind."

I nodded. "Sure, sure." Hopefully that meant she was getting that brand new white box testing job that they'd been talking about creating just for her. She'd be so good at it.

Jordan walked me back to the Den, rattling off "invaluable tips" for the board presentation. I couldn't fault him. So far his advice had been good enough to help me get the job—or maybe it had been my own hard work.

He slapped me on the back just before I opened the door. "Congrats again, Lucas. Adam was lit with all your ideas. Especially that take on a Draco version of Pokemon GO."

One thing was certain, there was no way I would have gotten this job without Katya. Both with her help pushing to the deadline—the original reason I married her to keep her here. And afterward, with her input into my design. Her suggestions had been spot on and I'd used them all, sometime embellishing here or there. I wondered if there was a way I could thank her. If I could buy her something special or...

Maybe when we were in Canada, I could take her out to dinner somewhere nice.

That was assuming she still wanted to even be around me after how I'd reacted to her admission of love yesterday. She had to be mistaken. She had to be confused. Those were the only things I could think of. Love was never meant to spring from this.

I decided to wait and spill the beans on the drive home. Best to keep in private. Especially since the secret hallway was now compromised, as she inadvertently proved all those months ago when news of our marriage had gotten out.

As it was dark, it was a little hard to read her face. But she seemed to be acting normal if not quite her usual exuberant self.

"So, this afternoon Jordan pulled me aside," I began.

She looked up from her phone and turned toward me. "Yeah? Did he have any news?"

"Well, when I got to his office, he ushered me into Adam's office and—"

"Oh my God! I knew it. I knew you'd get it."

I frowned at her. "What? I mean how—"

"If you were telling me this story because you hadn't gotten the job you would have been acting like Scrooge and the Grinch's love child. That used to be your norm, actually."

I blew out a breath. "Accurate... I guess."

"Oh, I'm sorry, did I rob you of your moment telling me the good news?"

I shook my head. "No, it's fine."

"Well, you're driving, so I'll save your congratulations hug for when we're out of the car."

I smiled. "Thank you."

"Also, on my break, I got us our plane tickets for next week and a reasonable hotel room that isn't in a divey part of town. Man when did hotel rates in Vancouver go up so much? I suppose I could have looked in PoCo but I don't feel like possibly running into people I know."

"PoCo?"

"Port Coquitlam. It's the nickname for my hometown."

I nodded.

When we got out of the car and I freed Max from the back seat, she came around the front end of the car, arms open wide. "I am sooo excited for you. You deserve this. This week has been good to us so far!"

She wrapped her arms around me. Her happiness was genuine and infectious and only made my current joy surge. I pulled her tight against me, closing my eyes briefly, relishing the smell of her hair against my nose, the feel of her lush curves pressed up against me.

Something stirred in me and the words hovered on my lips. My expression of gratitude, my strong sense that we had done this together. The teamwork I'd felt with her, and more.

But yesterday's admission of her feelings stood like a giant road barrier between us. With crossed boards painted in garish colors and yellow lights flashing warnings. But I could still see, on the other side of that road barrier, us. *Together.* Happy. Making it last.

A sharp pinch of almost physical pain squeezed my chest when I thought of coming back to this house after a long day of work alone. And her living somewhere else. I'd have to rattle around between those four walls alone. My throat felt thick, and I cursed my stupidity for not keeping her at a distance. For allowing myself to feel.

Because right now I wanted to ask her to try with me. To stay. To see what we could make of this. It felt like the tiny spark of the beginning of something great. Could it be?

Or should we stick to plan A and quit while we were ahead?

I followed her into the house while she chattered a mile a minute, demanding details about the job—of which I had a surprising few.

"Well, it's not official yet and—speaking of that, Adam specifically asked me to swear you to secrecy."

She made the sign of an X over her chest. "Mum's the word." She plopped down on the couch and began scratching the dog who was whoring for love, as usual. "When does it become official, anyway? We should have a party."

I sighed. "Well they're making me do some dumbass presentation to the Board of Directors Thursday morning. I'm not super thrilled about it but—"

I stopped. Her face had instantly darkened. Had I said something wrong?

"Thursday morning as in... next Thursday morning?"

Oh shit. My stomach dropped, remembering what I should have realized much sooner. I rubbed my forehead with my palm. "Kat, I'm so sorry. I didn't even realize."

She blinked and her body language was such that she was immediately closing off. She pulled her hand away from the dog who kept poking at her with his nose.

"Max, go lie down," I snapped.

The dog did as he was told, shooting me a look in transit. Kat bolted up from the couch and followed him, then zoomed right into the kitchen. When I got in there, she was pulling a bottle of water out of the fridge. She uncapped it and drank half of it while I watched.

"I'm sorry. We can call tomorrow and reschedule the deposition—"

She shook her head. "No, I can't do that. Derek's lawyers have confirmed and will be there, too. They've ordered an independent court reporter and videography crew to document it. I also have the plane tickets and the hotel reservation. Can't you ask Adam to change the Board Meeting?"

I blinked. Not only could I not ask him. I *would* not ask him. "Those meetings are set up months in advance. The people on the board are CEOs and execs of other companies. It would look horrible for me to—"

She blinked. "To what? Leave the country on urgent family business? They wouldn't get that and cut you some slack?"

I took a pained breath in and ran my fingers through my hair. Well shit. I'd promised her I'd be there for her and now... now I couldn't.

"I don't know what to do, I'm sorry."

At that moment, I felt like one hell of a crappy friend. And the shittiest husband ever. Why break that track record, right?

Just one look into her pale face, her wide eyes as she contemplated doing all that she had to do alone made my gut twist.

This was it. This was the reason I should never be a married man. I let the women in my life down. And I'd left Kat down after setting her up to do something she so feared that she'd planned on never going back to Canada again rather than do it.

Now here I was, backing out on her.

But I honestly could see no other way, barring cloning myself.

I shook my head. "Kat, I'm sorry."

When she blinked, there were tears in her eyes. "Well you warned me, didn't you? That you weren't good at being a husband. Too bad you didn't take this opportunity to be better."

An invisible punch to my chest. It knocked the wind out of me. It was nothing more than I'd told myself—and her—several times before. But for some reason hearing her say it to me—in that shaky, hurt voice, pierced me like an arrow.

If she had just hauled off and kicked me in the nuts straight out, I don't think she could have delivered a lower blow.

CHAPTER 24
KATYA

LUCAS LOOKED LIKE I'D JUST PUNCHED HIM IN THE FACE. I had to admit, I kind of wanted to, even though part of me kept scolding myself for being mad. It was an honest mistake. It still sucked that he wouldn't even consider finding a way to make it work.

Not that I could think of a solution right at this moment but damn. I didn't think I was being *that* unreasonable by expecting him to at least try. He clearly didn't want to try.

And sure it probably had something to do with my telling him I loved him yesterday. What had I been thinking, blurting it out like that? He'd probably been inwardly screaming since yesterday and counting the days until I moved out. *Shit.*

I'm not gonna cry. I won't cry. I'm not gonna cry.

Lucas blinked and looked away, catching his breath, then seemed to come to some sort of decision. "I told you at the start. I reminded you in Napa. This always had—"

"An expiration date, yeah, I know. Looks like this marriage has aged like milk."

His Adam's apple bobbed as he swallowed. "About yesterday—"

I shook my head. "I don't want to talk about yesterday and neither do you. You're too busy living out a self-fulfilling prophesy and I want no part of that." He looked completely puzzled, so I elaborated. "You've convinced yourself deep down that you were a crappy husband to Claire and thus you'll be a crappy husband to anyone. That means you don't even want to try."

"I'm not going to deny that. I also told you that all along, too."

I threw my hands out in frustration. "Lucas! You were nineteen years old--a *kid*. She expected you to take care of her, like a child. You weren't her daddy, and you didn't deserve that expectation put on you. You were still trying to figure out how to be an adult, start your college life and everything else."

I took a deep breath to collect myself. My voice was getting louder, and I didn't want to make this a shouting match. But *damn* this man and his stubbornness were frustrating me. "But you're a grown man now. A self-made man who knows what he wants. You threw off all the trimmings and advantages that came with your family and childhood. You chose to make your own way, built a career and you're succeeding. You're not the same person who walked out on your first marriage. And *I'm* not your first wife. I'm a grown ass woman who doesn't need or want some man to take care of me. I take care of myself."

He opened his mouth to protest, but I held out a hand to stop him. I hadn't yet said my piece.

"You're a game tester, you know what a logic error in programming is. Well human brains get those, too. And you got a big logic error somewhere in your brain when you divorced Claire. You invented this belief that because of that one instance with that one woman, you couldn't do it. Or you wouldn't."

He shook his head. "I've told you where that left me, where that failure, among all the other failures, had me on the floor. It took everything in me to pick myself up again. I just can't risk doing that again."

I shook my head sadly. "There are no guarantees in life, ever. You know that old saying, the only sure way never to win a game is to never play? This is you taking your ball and going home because you're afraid."

He gritted his teeth, speaking through them. "There's nothing wrong with being afraid. There's nothing wrong with not wanting to disappoint the people you care about. I don't want to disappoint you, and yet it's inevitable. This whole situation is me disappointing you. See? Prophesy fulfilled."

"Well, I'm afraid to go to Canada and face my family. But you know what? I'm going to do it. And now it looks like I'm going to have to do it alone. Screw it. I'll do it. I'm terrified, but I'm doing it."

He shook his head, watching me, true emotion crossing his features for the first time. I even thought I saw something in his eyes, perhaps I imagined it. Or maybe just wished I saw them for real—unshed tears.

His hand tightened into a fist and landed on the counter beside him. "I can't be responsible for another person's happiness, Kat. That's what sunk me the first time. Letting down all those people. I can't and I won't be responsible for your happiness."

I blinked back my own tears, but they slipped down my cheeks anyway. I refused to wipe them away. "Of course you aren't responsible for my happiness. But you are absolutely responsible for *your* happiness. And in your heart only you know how to bring that about."

I drew in a deep breath and much to my horror, it sounded like a sob. Pressing the back of my hand to my mouth, I turned and left the kitchen, heading to my room. He didn't stop me.

The minute I hit my bedroom, I knew that there was no way I could spend another night in this house. I just couldn't. It would hurt way too much. It was bad enough that we were going to have to cross paths at work every day. Maybe once he got his feet wet with the new division, he wouldn't be around as much. But until then...

No, I had to get out of here. I whipped out my phone and texted Heath and without waiting for a reply, I pulled out my large beat-up camp duffle bag and began stuffing essentials into it. My clothes for the next few days, everyday items I'd need. If Heath couldn't take me in, then I'd reach out to one of my other friends. Or, hell, I'd dig into my house savings and get a hotel for the next week until I left for Canada.

I went into the washroom and gathered things in there, too. A lot of my items were still packed up from the trip to Napa so that made it a bit easier. I'd try to get back here and grab a few more things before my trip. I'd definitely need my warmer coat, since autumn had undoubtedly hit the northwest while it was still very warm here.

I was almost done when a shadow drifted across my peripheral vision and I turned to look. Lucas stood filling up the doorway, hands braced on each door jamb.

I zipped up my duffle and straightened, pushing a strand of hair out of my eyes.

His eyes zeroed in on the bag, narrowing. "You're leaving?"

"I thought it would be best," I said quietly. "You know, since we're about to expire, anyway."

He blinked, his mouth set. He looked like he might protest. "You don't have to go."

"I do. We don't have to pretend anymore. The good thing is that we both got what we wanted, right? I have my green card. You have the job. We should just get back to our real lives now."

His brow furrowed. "Real lives?"

"Our previous lives, yeah."

My phone chimed, and I picked it up. Heath's reply expressed some confusion at my asking if I could crash with him for a few days but he was more than happy to house me. That was all I needed. I typed out a reply and hit send.

Lucas hadn't moved.

"Where are you going?"

"Back to Heath's until I have to go to Canada. And after that..." I shrugged. I waited, and he still didn't move, watching me with those intense dark eyes of his. I glanced down to check that I had everything and caught sight of the flash of diamond on my left hand.

Oh, yeah. Well, damn. I had to give that back now, didn't I? Shit.

I reached up and slid it off my ring finger, then held it up so he'd see that I was laying it carefully down on the empty nightstand. "Remember to put this away so you don't lose it."

No response. He was like a statue. It was an awkward and heavy moment. I looped the handles of my duffle over my shoulder, grabbed my purse and my backpack and headed toward the door.

And him.

And he didn't move. I stopped short, looking up at him. "Can you step aside please?"

His eyes were full of emotions and unspoken words. They boiled in there like a stew—like a pressure cooker with no outlet.

"Stay," he said quietly.

I frowned. "But why?"

"Because I don't want to be that guy who threw my wife out into the street. You can stay here until the divorce is final."

Wrong answer, buster. "There's no reason for me to stay. I want to go. And you aren't throwing me out. And I won't be in the street." I hesitated, then swallowed. He still hadn't moved.

"Let me go, Lucas," I finally said.

His jaw tightened, and he stepped aside, watching me pass through. I hefted the unwieldy load and dropped them at the front door while I fished out my keys.

I turned back to him. "I'll, uh. Is it okay if I keep the rest of my stuff here for a little while? Until I figure out where it's going?"

His face was expressionless, those eyes still burning, his body language was stiff, defensive, with tense shoulders and stiff arms and clenched fists. "That's fine."

"This is for the best. And now you can go back to your single life as quick as you want."

He blinked. "I'll have the divorce papers drawn up and ready to sign when you get back from Canada."

I probably should thank him for that. After all, it would likely be a bit of a hassle to wade through the legal paperwork. I should have thanked him, yeah. But I couldn't.

"Goodbye." And I left.

A half hour later I was stepping out of the car into the parking lot at Heath's condo.

I heaved a sigh, then pulled the bags out of my trunk. This was for the best, as I'd told Lucas. The clean break would give me time. For what, I didn't know but... Time healed wounds, didn't it?

Heath greeted me by pulling me into a big bear hug and fixed me some of my favorite tea. We caught up on the latest goings on and I explained to him why I was there.

"So what does this all mean?" Heath said. "I mean... You've got the green card, he's got the job. Everything worked out just like you wanted, right? Why are you looking so damn sad?"

I studied him over the top of my mug while I took a long sip of the fragrant, hot liquid. Damn, I missed tea. *Real* tea, not the usual American facsimile.

"Wow, this is imported, isn't it? It's so good." As good a way as any to sidestep a question.

He frowned. "You totally fell for him, didn't you?"

I blinked. Wow, there was no preamble, no warning. That accusation just thrown out there like that, ringing off the walls and flat surfaces of his condo.

I shook my head. "I don't—"

He grinned. "Yeah, you do. What happened when you told him?"

I took a deep breath and let it go. "He went and walked the dog and was gone for an hour. Then we just didn't talk about it."

"Hmm." Heath scratched his goatee. "Classic case of denial."

"Denial of what? He doesn't have anything to deny."

He looked at me like I was an idiot. "Oh no? Girl, every time we've all been together, I've watched him. That guy is bonkers for you. Has been since long before this marriage thing. Why would he have gone for it otherwise?"

I shook my head. "He needed me in the country so I could help him get his job. I mean, it's really nice of you to say this, Heath. But right now I can't be like some lovesick sorority girl with daisy petals in my hand saying 'He loves me, he loves me not.' I can't play that game. Not with everything I've got going on."

Heath looked at me, completely lost. "I think you need to fill me in."

So I took an hour—and another full cup of tea—to catch him up on everything. My brother's visit. The reason why I had to go to Canada. Everything.

"Holy shit," he muttered when I was done. "That's..." he shook his head. "Girl if it wasn't such short notice, I'd take the time off and go up with you. You could show me around. I've never been."

I leaned in to give him a big hug. "I'd love it. But you know what? I think I'm getting used to the idea. It isn't my favorite, but I'm just going to go up there and get it done and stop being afraid. And stop having to run away. Like a badass."

He gave me a hug. "I'm sorry about the unwanted love advice. I don't know why I always end up in this position of romantic advisor, lately, but there ya go. Blame it on Mia."

I laughed. "Poor Mia."

He made a face. "No, poor *me*. Mia's just fine. But seriously, someday soon, one of you girls needs to become *my* romantic advisor when I meet the hot hunky man of my dreams."

"You don't want me as an advisor, I assure you!"

Soon after, I crashed in my old room on an air mattress in Heath's house.

At work I laid low. We couldn't exactly avoid each other, but we really made no effort to chat, either. Two days after I'd left, he handed me an envelope, telling me he'd signed for my green card when it came.

So here it was, my way back in the country once I'd left. That was a burden lifted from me and I felt a little heady with the relief from it. That was one less worry to deal with regarding my Canada trip.

Once the weekend rolled around, I decided to cash in a few extra sick days and not go back to work again before I left. It was just getting too hard to see him there, knowing he was in the process of going back to the way things were before. That he was getting divorce papers drawn up. That he was moving forward with his life.

Hopefully once I got back, he'd be working at his new job in the other building and those chance happenings would be rare.

I took the time to find an Al-Anon meeting in the area and attended, and for once, told an abbreviated form of my story to the group. They were supportive, and I found some strength in that. I was doing the right thing.

The days ticked down and with each passing one, I was getting more and more anxious to get on my way and get this done and over with.

And behind me. Hopefully other things would soon follow and become part of the distant—but safe—past.

CHAPTER 25
LUCAS

KAT WASN'T SHOWING UP TO WORK. WHEN I discreetly talked to HR, they informed me that it was sick leave. Since it was the Monday before she was to leave for Canada, I assumed she was giving herself the week off.

But still... not knowing where she was slowly drove me insane. Kat didn't do personal social media, part of the whole paranoia and lying low thing. Since all her equipment was at my house, her gamer persona and Twitch channel were dark.

And so was I... completely in the dark, losing my mind.

I was working on my presentation for the board, yeah. But I wasn't sleeping and definitely wasn't eating like I should have been.

And that empty house, but for clicking of dog toenails on hardwood floors and other normal household noises, was driving me insane. Everything was bland, gray and empty.

And she was gone. She'd left a Katya-sized hole in just about every aspect of my life.

Well this was what I wanted, right?

Because I was a gigantic fool. Because even now, after all of this, I had no answer to her open, guileless admission. *I'm in love with you.*

For the thousandth time, those words, in that clear, brave voice sounded in my memory. Indelible as the feelings it evoked. Fear, panic, a rush of... relief? Satisfaction? Denial.

I was on the couch, paging through my slides again on the night before the big meeting. I'd brought home some fast food for dinner and then walked the dog. Now I was listless and exhausted and flat. I scrolled through the tablet, mind blanking, forcing myself to focus when someone knocked on the door.

For one split second of misplaced adrenaline laced with hope, I thought it might be Kat. I knew she'd be catching her plane early in the morning, but maybe she'd swung by to pick up some of her things?

When I looked through the peephole however, it wasn't her. It was Julia. Taking a moment to curb the profound disappointment, I opened the door.

My sister entered the house for the first time in months— since before Kat had moved in, anyway. Had that only been less than two months ago? So much had changed since then.

And I was now measuring my life into Before Kat and After Kat. What did that mean?

Julia's glance darted around nervously before I invited her to sit down. She wiped her palms across her pant legs, as if drying them and sunk to the edge of the couch. "Hey there, how are you doing?" she finally asked when I took the chair diagonal from her. "I'm sorry about just showing up. It was.... Well I've been trying to get up the nerve to do it and figured just getting in the car and driving over would be the easiest way to get it done. So I'm sorry to pop in with no warning. Is... is this a bad time?"

I shrugged. Having Julia here might help break me out of my dark mood and wash away the sense of emptiness in the house. "No, it's fine. What can I do for you?"

Julia's gaze shot toward the kitchen then back at me. "Is Katya home? I'd love to chat with both of you, actually. In fact, she's a big reason I'm even here."

I frowned but fidgeted, the lie springing to my lips quickly. "She's not here, no. She's getting ready to visit her family in Vancouver tomorrow."

Her eyebrows scrunched together. "You aren't going with her? You haven't even met your in-laws yet, have you?"

I waved a hand. "I have an important presentation tomorrow. A big meeting I can't miss. The new job I want so badly hinges on it. She understands." And though I completely sucked at lying, Julia bought it. Usually she could see through my crap but Julia seemed preoccupied tonight. And more nervous than I'd ever seen her.

I'd offer her a glass of wine but now, thanks to Kat, I knew better than to do that.

"Well, I can talk to just you, too. I wanted to... make amends."

I twitched my eyebrow. "What? I thought we covered that when we talked at the guest villa at the vineyard. You're good. You don't have to ask my forgiveness for your alcohol issues."

She shook her head vehemently, dark hair whipping her shoulders. "No, this is more specific. I wanted to apologize about Claire."

I sank against the back of my chair and quirked a brow. "What has she done now?"

Julia almost laughed. "No. I mean... I just feel badly. All these years I've kept her in my close friendship. Mother and Father encouraged all that at first but then she became someone I could count on for a good time. Someone I could party with."

I shrugged. "An enabler?"

She nodded. "Yeah. And through it all, even though I knew how much it hurt you, your marriage falling apart along with your depression. I was selfish and kept her around for my own reasons. Sure, I was helping the family save face by making your split seem amicable even though it wasn't. I'm sure the parents were hoping you and her would patch it up again eventually. They blamed you for it all. And Claire's let enough slip to me over the years that I know that wasn't the case. But the parents, they just care about how everything looks. And the two of you splitting up five months after a twelve million-dollar highly publicized wedding was the ultimate egg on their face."

I rolled my eyes. "Tell me something I don't know."

She bit her lip and looked up at me with wide eyes. "I played a big part in hurting you. I'm sorry."

I took in a deep breath and then let it go, unwilling to sort through the stew of emotions churning inside. "Apology accepted."

She rubbed her hands over her knees. "You're letting me off the hook too easily."

"You're my sister. I love you. And I want you to get better."

Suddenly her face clouded. "Thank you but… it's hard not to feel guilty about how I didn't support you when you needed it."

I clenched my jaw. "I've never had a problem with you and how you handled things. We've handled things as best we could. We were too busy trying to live up to their vision for what we were supposed to be to figure out what we really wanted for ourselves."

A tentative smile tugged at the corners of her mouth. "But you figured that out a while ago. You're doing so much better and I'm proud of you for that. And I can't tell you how happy I am that you've found someone who makes you as happy as Katya does. Even though I really like her a lot, I'm also a bit jealous of what you two have."

Gut punch. There it was. *Her* name. *Her* essence. Even this conversation with my sister was made possible because of Katya's presence in my life. In the few short months we'd been living together as a couple, she'd left her indelible mark on my life.

I must not have hid my thoughts as easily as I'd assumed because Julia tilted her head at me and frowned. "Is everything okay? With her?"

My gaze darted toward Julia and... I considered maintaining the lie. I wanted to. But in the face of her complete raw honesty with me, I just couldn't do that and feel like a worthy human being at the same time.

I hesitated, biting my lip and Julia held out her hand. "You don't have to air your private business with me I just... whatever it is, I hope you work it out because you two are so good together and—"

"It was fake," I uttered in a monotone.

Her mouth shut and opened again, then she frowned. "Wait, what?"

I took in a deep breath to fortify myself, then let it all out. Once I'd broken the seal on the dam, it all rushed out in a deluge.

"We got married for... convenience. It helped us both out in our jobs." She didn't need to know the details. "It was just for appearance."

She blinked, so I continued to babble.

"It was her idea, initially. I was happy to go along with it as we both gained from it. It was just meant to be a secret, but— well you don't need to know all that. And please if you would keep this just between us—"

Julia's face had clouded during my monologue but suddenly she burst out in the middle of it with, "Bullshit."

I frowned. "Excuse me?"

"No, I won't. There's no way that was fake."

I rubbed my forehead with my palm, threading my fingers through my hair in frustration but said nothing. The last thing I wanted right now was an argument with my sister. Especially when part of me—a reluctant part—agreed with her.

"Look, I'm not going to dig into your personal private life. It's not my business why you two got married. But if you split up believing it's fake now, then that's just dumb."

"Gee, thanks," I breathed.

She made a cutting gesture through the air. "I'm not trying to be mean, Lucas. I'm just saying that if you let her go, then you're throwing away something good. It was rotten with Claire and even worse when everybody tried to pressure you to stay with her. So I really don't want to overstep my bounds now. But... you love her. And she very clearly loves you too."

I looked away, unable to deny the tightening in my chest. And the pinch I'd felt when Kat had admitted those very feelings to me. I ran my hand over my face to buy me some time with my sister.

I wish I could just throw Julia out. Or maybe give her strong hints that she should show herself out.

As if reading my mind, she stood up. "I can't and shouldn't tell you how to run your life. I'm sorry. You were always kind to me in that regard."

I stood to show her to the door and suddenly found myself wrapped in my sister's arms. "You've been a good brother to me," she murmured into my shoulder.

"I've been average at best," I replied.

She stepped back and looked at me. "Don't sell yourself short, Lucas. You deserve to be happy. You deserve to get on with your life and ignore the BS our parents have put us through. You deserve Kat. She's the best thing that's ever happened to you."

I swallowed but said nothing and she averted her eyes, flicking her dark hair back from her shoulder.

After an awkward pause I sighed heavily. "Move out, Julia. Get away from them and find a group of supportive friends. Do what makes you happy, not them."

She smiled. "I'm already on it, big bro. Plans are in the works."

I grinned and tapped her shoulder. "So don't you worry about me, sis. I'll be fine. Just concentrate on getting better."

She stared at me for a few moments longer and I could tell that there was a ton more that she wanted to say. Mercifully, she kept her mouth shut, and we hugged out a goodbye while making a plan to get together for lunch next week.

Hopefully by then she would have dropped the idea of me chasing after Kat to save a fake marriage that she never should have known about in the first place.

This aching feeling, this missing Kat was friendship. Nothing more. Definitely not that mythical unicorn called *love*.

I wasn't prepared to examine this any closer. Even now. The hurts of the past, the potential for another deep dive into depression was all too real. I couldn't let myself go there. I couldn't let myself feel that. Not now. Never again.

I resisted the urge to text Kat before her flight early on Thursday morning. Instead, I got ready, wearing my best suit, while running over and over in my mind the talking points I wanted to emphasize for the board meeting.

Every single time I thought I was in the zone, something reminded me of her. Something she left around the house, the *Lord of the Rings* mug that she liked to use for her tea sitting beside the sink. Or stray strands of long red hair on a throw pillow.

But I forced my thoughts away from dwelling on her, or wondering where she was or what was happening. I found it too damn hard to concentrate.

And sleep wasn't much better.

Everything sucked without her, but I refused that truth, insisting that this feeling was temporary. She'd be back soon enough, and we'd establish a different sort of relationship—a consciously uncoupled one, to use the vapid vernacular. Yeah *conscious*. Yeah, *uncoupled*.

Ugh that thought didn't bring me much comfort at all.

I was at work very early, waiting for the board to convene. I'd been paging through my slides at my desk when Warren approached. Damn it, I wasn't in the mood for any more of his Canadian sex position jokes.

I held up a hand without looking at him. "It better be important or I'm doubling your work load starting five minutes from now."

He paused, holding his phone. "Well, um, it's weird. It's a text from your wife but I have no idea why she sent it to me. And I have no idea what it means."

I snatched the phone out of his hand without another word. Then, of course, had to unlock it. I held the screen up to his face and the message immediately flashed up.

Kat: Hey Warren, Can you pls inform whoever's now in charge of QA that I'm going to need an extra week off? I've already alerted HR but I'll need to hand off a couple projects or delay them.

"What does she mean 'whoever's in charge of QA'—that's you, isn't it? Did you lose your job?"

I checked the time stamp on the text—a little over half an hour ago. Then gave him back his phone, mumbling something at him to make him go away. My stomach churned and I could feel the blood drain from my face.

What the hell was this? And why would she text Warren instead of me? Well that was a stupid question, she obviously didn't want to communicate with me. Or she thought I was already in the big meeting or...

If I remembered right, she'd already be in the air by now, or soon would be. I whipped out my phone and keyed in her contact info to call her.

It went straight to voicemail. Taking a deep breath and as calmly as I could, I asked her to call me back at her earliest convenience. She probably wouldn't be doing that for quite some time. She'd have other things on her mind today.

I suddenly had a mental image of her flying in that plane alone, probably sandwiched between gruff businessmen or a noisy family while her nerves ate away at her. I remembered how she'd trembled when she'd told me the entire story of Derek's constant bad choices. And how her entire family—the people whom she'd presumably most trusted in the world—had stood by, expecting her to commit a crime in order to cover for him.

None of her friends here in California had any idea what she was facing. Only me. And I'd vowed to be by her side. I'd put her up to it in the first place.

What the fuck are you doing sitting here while she's on a plane, Lucas?

And why did she need the extra time off? What was she going to do? Was she thinking about staying in Canada now that she had some money saved up and could get her own place?

Maybe find herself an exciting new programming job or.... My mind raced, slides forgotten. She was *not* staying there. I'd go and get her and bring her back, first.

Before I even realized what I was doing, I'd gathered up my things and headed straight to Jordan's office. He was usually in early, anyway, and though the meeting wasn't for another hour, I needed to reach out to him.

His assistant, however, was not in, so I found myself knocking on his door yet again. He called out for me to come in. He was standing at the doorway into his bathroom in front of a mirror tying his tie.

"Padawan! Good to see you all nicely dressed up for your big day." He turned back to his tie. "I didn't feel like wearing all this shit into the office so I came in casual." He pulled the last loop on his teal-colored tie. Then he examined it in the mirror, straightening it and adjusting his collar.

I swallowed. "I have to go," I rasped.

He frowned and stepped away from the mirror, motioning toward the bathroom. "I have no idea why you walked all the way up here to use the restroom but fine, there it is. You'll soon know what it's like to have a private bathroom of your own."

I blinked and adjusted my stance. "No, I mean I have to leave. I have to get to the airport. Please, can you... can you just tell Adam I'm sorry? And... I gotta go."

Jordan was now staring at me like I'd spontaneously burst into flames.

"I have no idea what just came out of your mouth right now but you aren't going anywhere."

I drew a deep breath, trying to figure out how I was going to explain this to him without violating Kat's confidence. "Yes I am. I'm going now. Kat had to leave the country this morning on urgent family business. I need to be there for her. I'm just going. Do what you need to do." So I turned and left.

Jordan jumped into action, reaching into his desk drawer. He grabbed his keys and phone and tailed me. "Tell me on the way to the airport. And you're gonna help me figure out how I'm going to keep Adam from going nova and giving Jeremy the job."

As we walked out, Jordan's assistant was just getting into the office, setting down her case. "Jordan, wanted to let you know I'm here a little early to get everything together for the board—"

He held up his hand. "Susan, grab a pad of paper and a pen. First off, delay the meeting by at least thirty minutes, more if you can manage it." Her mouth opened, but he rode over her. "Next, I need you to find me the next flight to...?" He turned to me.

I spoke to Susan. "Vancouver, British Columbia."

Jordan clenched his jaw. "Shit, an international flight. I forgot she's a Canuck. I have to run him up to LAX. There's probably only one flight a day there out of John Wayne." He checked his watch. "We have to leave *now*. We can use the carpool lane, and it's early on a Thursday so it might not be that much of a clusterfuck. Find him the earliest flight two hours from now." He turned back to me. "You need your passport, bud."

I swore. It was at home. "We'll have to take a detour."

Jordan turned toward the entrance, following me while calling back to Susan. "Stay close to your phone! I have more things you need to do."

Then we booked it out of the building, into the parking lot. Jordan refused to drive my "old piece of shit." Screw him, it was a perfectly maintained Mercedes 500 SL.

We got into his ginormous SUV instead. It would have been ideal if we'd had to take some mountain roads or ford some raging rivers on the way. As it was, the thing acted like a tank on the freeway and the minute he hit his blinker, cars got out of the way. Good enough.

"Tell me what the hell is going on now," Jordan asked me. He'd just finished barking more orders at Susan on his speaker phone and told his car to text Adam to delay the meeting. With a knot in my stomach, I watched the screen on his dash, expecting the reply any moment now.

"I let her down. She... she's facing some tough stuff she has to take care of at home and I'd promised her I'd go. We made the arrangements last week, the day before I got back to the office..."

"Which was the day before you found out about this meeting and the presentation. Okay, but can't you fly up tonight and meet up with her then? Why right now?"

I ran my hands through my hair. "Because I'm an idiot and should have just been on the plane with her in the first place. It's legal stuff, she's doing it this afternoon, and I promised I'd be there for her."

He shook his head, clearly not pleased. "I just wish you'd told me all this in the first place. I'm not sure what we could have done but it would have been better than *this*. Honestly, bro, I'm not even sure I can save your job when Adam finds out about this. He's not going to take it well. I hope you liked your old job in QA."

I tore my eyes from the dashboard to look at Jordan. His face was dead serious now, not his usual joke-cracking, devil-may-care self. I believed every bit of what he was saying. But seeing my future back in QA versus the future I had been envisioning for the past few days only made me more sure. My throat closed with emotion and I had to clear it before I could speak.

"You know what? I'd choose to be a bug-hunter until I retire rather than live the rest of my life without her."

Jordan's brows raised, and he nodded. "Seems legit. You're reminding me of a last minute red-eye flight I once took from New York to LA for similar reasons. Right, full speed ahead, then." His foot went down and by now he was clearly breaking some speeding laws.

"I'll try to see what I can do with Adam, but don't hold out too much hope, all right?"

I nodded. "I understand. I'm willing to accept that." Then, when I went to thank him, the chiming on the dash interrupted me. There were multiple messages coming in all at once—from Adam, from Susan, even one from April.

Not long after that, he dumped me off at the terminal curb for the airlines where Susan had reserved my ticket. I had my passport, wallet and my work case with a laptop and tablet in it. And pretty much nothing else.

As luck would have it, I was on a plane forty-five minutes after checking in. But Katya was now three hours ahead of me, probably touching down right as I took off. She'd be heading straight to the Crown counsel office in Port Coquitlam.

Fortunately, I'd been able to get that address with some simple Googling. So I'd know straight where to head once I touched down.

I'd definitely arrive too late to be there for her during her deposition.

I hoped to God, though, I wouldn't arrive too late for *us*.

CHAPTER 26
KATYA

WITH COLD, STEELY DETERMINATION, I STEPPED OFF that plane, made my way through customs with my carry-on rolling luggage and hit the curb to summon a taxi. Here I was, back in the hometown again after a couple years away. My gaze drifted north, as it often had on clear mornings like this. Along the horizon, my eyes traced the familiar outline of The Lions in their vigil over the city spread out below them. These two peaks in the North Shore mountains were all the sign I needed to know that I was home.

Any feelings I might have had, looking at them in any other circumstances, were currently muted by that strange numbness inside. With single-mindedness, I reminded myself I couldn't waver until this last task was over. Until I'd cleared up that outstanding business I'd outrun almost two years before.

Perhaps I'd left this city a scared little girl, but I was stepping back into it a grown woman. A badass.

Remember how badass you are, Kat. And though it hurt to think of Lucas, his words helped get me through, running on repeat through my mind like a mantra.

As I'd planned, I got to the Crown counsel office in PoCo over an hour early. They stored my bag for me. The showed me to the questioning room, where I'd asked to be seated early. My family would no doubt come. Though Derek had the right to be in the room when I was questioned, my parents did not. I didn't want to hear their guilt trips. I didn't want to be subjected to the pressure they'd no doubt put on me. I didn't want to be so deeply disappointed in them once again.

I just needed to get this out. The truth. *My* truth. And be done.

People trickled in and out, a court reporter set up her machine, videographer doing the same, making sure lighting and sound were optimal. The prosecuting attorney and the defense lawyer team soon arrived. I kept my eyes down and sat and did what I was told until it came time to answer the questions.

Derek tried to approach me before the questioning, but I'd kept my eyes down, hadn't spoken to him, hadn't even looked at him. I couldn't. Because I knew I'd waver and my heart would hurt. And I'd want to do anything to help him. Like I had, over and over, all throughout my life.

But putting myself in legal jeopardy wasn't the answer. And it sure as hell wouldn't help him. So after they swore me in, I spoke my truth. Only then did I dare look at Derek. Our eyes met for just one brief second before he buried his face in his hands. It was over, finally. And he knew it.

I blinked tears from my eyes, aware of the shakiness, though whether it was from nerves or lack of having eaten a thing since the night before, I didn't know. Soon the questioning was officially through and people packed up their things and began their side conversations, I was in the middle of it all, alone.

"Are you all right, dear? Is there anyone we can call for you?" I looked up at a kind-faced middle-aged woman, part of the prosecuting team.

I shook my head. "I'm alone but I'm fine."

Nevertheless, she fetched me a cup of cold water which I sipped. Derek had left the room by then and now all I needed to do was call a taxi to take me to my hotel. Then who knew what? I was off for a week.

Maybe I'd look up some of my old friends, go visit my aunt.

It was altogether possible that I'd never step foot in this beautiful city ever again.

Outside the conference room, I glanced around under my eyelashes while keeping my face pointed toward my phone. I was Googling numbers for a taxi service but also trying to avoid accidentally bumping into my parents.

Much to my shock, they weren't there and my brother was gone already, too. It was entirely possible that Derek had had a friend drive him here. Perhaps the parents didn't even know. Though that would seem odd. Suddenly I felt light, giddy with relief.

I was only a few kilometres from home. It would have been nice to be able to go pack up a few boxes of my things. But did I want to chance the inevitable confrontation with them?

With firm strides out the door and into the sunny afternoon, I decided it wasn't worth it. I'd lived without those things this long, I could go longer, perhaps forever. This strange mixture of relief and loneliness was doing things to me, however. As I made my way down the overabundance of concrete steps toward the curb, tears prickled the backs of my eyes.

This too, would pass.

Remember how badass you are.

The minute I thought of that phrase again was the same minute that I saw them. Three figures on a nearby concrete bench. Upon seeing me hit the bottom of the stairs, all three of them stood.

Mum, Dad and standing right in between them, Derek.

I froze and the needles behind my eyes exploded with sharpness and pain. My vision blurred and my throat clogged. Damn it. Not the best time to burst into tears like a little girl.

Not when I was trying to be a badass.

I stood still and slowly they walked toward me, Derek lagging behind the other two. I sniffed loudly and blinked my eyes, then admitted to myself that I needed to give my cheeks a quick swipe with the back of my hand.

Dad stood right in front of me. Mum off to the side, a little behind him.

"Katya," he said. "How are you doing?"

With another self-conscious sniff, I tore my eyes away from the scrutiny on my mum's face and looked at Dad. "I've been better."

"I missed you, girlie. Why didn't you ever call?"

I swallowed and stuffed my hands into my pockets. "I was under the impression that *You stick with this family or you're gone for good,* meant, yeah, that I was gone for good."

He flinched, clearly not appreciating his own words repeated back to him across almost two years. Mum spoke up at his side. "Derek was just telling us you came all this way back home just to tell everyone you won't help him."

I cleared my throat and turned to her. "I came back to tell the truth. I don't know where he was that night. And I had to get this over with because your very expensive lawyer tracked me down and was trying his hardest to get me kicked out of the States. I didn't appreciate that trick, either. Maybe now you've learned that I'm not a little girl you can intimidate anymore. Maybe you haven't missed me at all. Especially if the first things you have to say to me are how upset you are that I didn't commit a crime just to cover Derek's ass."

Mum started shushing me and that just pissed me off more.

"No, I'm not going to quiet down. Even now you have no notion whatsoever that what you asked me to do was heinous and wrong. I'm your daughter, goddamn it!"

"Kat, don't speak to your mother that way," Dad snapped.

"Then she shouldn't be speaking to me the way she is. She seems to forget she has two children, not just one."

Behind both of them, I could see Derek begin to pace, wringing his hands. I tore my eyes away.

"Was there anything important you needed to say? I'm going to leave," I finally said.

"Don't leave. Come to the house, girlie. I promise we'll be civil."

"There's nothing I want there, anymore. I'm still really hurt by the way you've all treated me so I don't think I can."

Mum shook her head at me with a disgusted curl of her lip. "It's always been all about you and only you, hasn't it, Katya? Why, oh why, did I raise such a selfish girl? Your brother is sick. Didn't you listen for one moment during all that family therapy? He's sick!"

New tears sprang to my eyes and now Derek had stopped and was watching us talk about him like he wasn't even there. "Yes, he's sick. And it breaks my heart—" my voice cut off in a sob. "And it's broken my heart over and over again. And every time he promised to do the work to get better, I hoped against all hope that this one time, that one time would be the time. And over and over again, he'd fall. And instead of learning what you needed to do to be the support network he needs, you enabled him to keep doing it. Derek may be the addict but this entire family is sick. You two are addicted to enabling him."

Now Dad was trying to shush me because my voice was raising and people were on the sidewalk nearby. A mother pushing her baby in a stroller had her eyes glued to us and almost ran into a pole. Some man in a dark suit out of the corner of my eye veered from the curb and headed straight for us. Maybe he was an officer of the court who was going to threaten us with disorderly conduct or something.

This was Canada, after all, didn't the world know us all for our politeness and cheerful friendliness? There was nothing cheerful or friendly happening on this sidewalk right now.

"I told you I'm not going to shush. If you're going to stand there and accuse me of being selfish—"

Suddenly the man in the dark suit was beside me, holding my arm. Dad jerked his head toward the newcomer, his expression angry.

I looked up at the man beside me and almost fell over when I saw who it was. *Lucas.* A rush of so many feelings raced through me—confusion, joy, relief, betrayal. I blinked.

Maybe I was imagining things, and I'd just dreamed him up out of delusion.

"Hello," he said, clearing his throat. "I'm Lucas Walker, your son-in-law." And just like that he was shaking my stunned dad's hand and then my mum's.

Lucas then waved to Derek who was staring at him. "Hi Derek."

My brother dropped his gaze to the pavement. "Hey Lucas."

"I've come to take my wife away from whatever this is. She doesn't deserve this sort of treatment. She is the one who did the right thing. And it was wrong of you all to ask her to do anything else."

Dad looked at Lucas as if he had no idea what to say and Mum was now crying. Great. This family... we'd be a great case for the Jerry Springer show if there was anything like that in this country. And I'd be embarrassed that Lucas was even here witnessing this if I hadn't seen just as bad behavior on his own parents' part.

Lucas tugged my arm lightly, trying to get me to disengage, but all I could do was look at them with these crazy mixed-up feelings. Should I just walk away again without a word—like I had before?

It felt wrong not to say anything.

"You're my family. You'll always be my family. But that doesn't mean you get to tell me how to live my life anymore. I'm going to make the decisions I need to be happy. And if you can't love me anymore, then I'm sorry for you and I'll find the people who will truly love me."

Dad and Mum looked like I'd just set off an explosion in their faces. They were clearly shell-shocked. The only one who wasn't, was my brother, who'd finally stood up straight, watching me.

And the most stunning thing of all was that he had tears running down his cheeks. He slowly approached, and I felt Lucas tense at my side, ready for anything. But I knew Derek better. My brother was messed-up and selfish most of the time but he wasn't violent. He'd never hit me, even when he was high.

He stopped right in front of me, unabashedly crying and making no effort to wipe his face. "Kat," he croaked in a voice that broke. "I'm sorry, sis. I'm sorry I put you through this. I'm sorry I broke this family. I'm just sorry."

Gawd. Now I was losing it again. That feeling like I'd swallowed a handful of nails. I hadn't cried this much in—well since that incident in Lucas's den the previous month. My eyes ached and my cheeks were raw with salty tears.

Ugh. It would be so much easier if I could just hate Derek.

But I loved him.

He was my brother. He was a fuck-up. He was sick. But he was Derek. *And I loved him.*

I reached out my hand and grabbed his, squeezing it and looked him straight in the eye through my tears. I summoned up the lessons I'd learned from all those tenets at Al-Anon meetings and from my own therapy and in my reading. "If you love me... if you love all of us, give us the best gift ever. *Get better.* But don't do it just for us. Do it for yourself."

I'd heard that he might get sentenced to as many as two years in jail if he was convicted. And though the thought of my brother in jail made me ill, I knew that nothing I could have done, even if I *had* lied, would have made him better. He had to decide to fight for it and no one else could do it for him.

Derek's face dropped into his hands and Mum was comforting him. And for once, I didn't begrudge her that. She and I might not ever see eye to eye, but it didn't matter anymore. I was a grown woman, and I had to live my life for me now.

"Good bye, Mum. Bye Dad."

I stepped back and Lucas guided me, his arm around my shoulder. He turned us around so we were walking away from them. They didn't call after me.

And I didn't look back.

Instead I kept walking. And before I even realized it, I was leaning against Lucas, resting my head against his shoulder. His arm tightened, and we kept walking.

I knew that there was a park nearby with a trail. I'd catch the cab for my hotel soon, but for right now, I just needed to be away.

And I needed to know why the hell he was here.

Once we were safely down the thickly wooded path, I stopped. Every fifty metres or so, there were wooden park benches, covered trash cans and those little dispensers for bags to put your dog poop in. But at midday on a weekday, there was hardly anyone here.

I faced him and he stopped, staring at me, allowing me to extricate myself from his hold.

He had his laptop bag slung over his shoulder and began fishing through the front pocket until he pulled out a rumpled but clean In-n-Out napkin.

I thanked him and began mopping up my face and blowing my nose loud enough to summon small animals to my aid. "Wow the napkin is giving me flashbacks to our glorious wedding."

"I've got another one. Here." He tried to take the snotty one from me but I wouldn't let him. Gross. Why'd he want that? "Let me throw it away for you."

I stuffed it into my pocket instead. "Why are you here? What happened with the presentation?"

He hesitated, staring at me and taking a deep breath before letting it go. "It's not important what happened with the presentation. What's important is that I screwed up massively by letting you come up here by yourself after promising you I'd be here for you."

I rubbed at my sore eyes.

"Well, as you see, I managed to do it myself." I took a deep gulp of air. "But I'm glad you showed up when you did. I was feeling mighty alone out there on that sidewalk."

He blew out a breath and shook his head. "I'm so sorry, Kat. I wish I could have been there for you."

I frowned. "In some ways, you were, or at least your words were, reminding me I was a badass. And that I could do it alone."

He hesitated, and I looked up at him. He seemed super nervous. He was staring into my eyes. I'm sure they were a sight to behold—all runny mascara, puffy and swollen. He had no luggage to speak of and I still only had my carry-on which I'd been lugging beside me all this time. "I should probably get going. It's late enough I can check in and I could really use a nap…."

"Can we… can we go sit on that bench over there? For just a minute."

"I think I've had my share of overwrought emotional confrontations for the day."

His face fell. "I don't have anything to confront you with. I just—"

I sighed. "Okay, fine. I'll sit there and hear what you have to say. You've had a long trip, and it doesn't even look like you brought any luggage… Did you have a plan?"

He turned and walked to the bench without answering my question. I tagged along after him, rolling my bag behind me. He sat, and I gave him some space, scooting away to the end.

He noticed, his jaw bulging where he clenched his teeth. You bet, I was still pissed at him. He was here, and that was great and I was grateful but had it really changed anything?

"I need to admit some things to you."

I folded my arms over my chest and cocked my head toward him. "Okay."

"I'm not falling in love with you." I blinked, acknowledging the stab of hurt that sliced through me but before I could say anything, he kept on talking. "Because I already fell for you long ago."

My brows scrunched so closely together they threatened to form a permanent unibrow. "Uh, what?"

"Kat, I think I fell in love with you the first week I met you. I didn't know it then. I didn't acknowledge it because I was so dead set against ever trusting my feelings again. They'd failed me once. And it had been a critical failure that had cost me a lot."

I opened my mouth to interrupt, but he held up his hand. "Please, just let me get this out. Then you can say whatever you want."

I snapped my mouth shut and waved my hand, urging him to continue.

"This entire time we've known each other, I pushed you away. I was an obnoxious prick at times, but it was full on self-preservation mode. I knew you'd destroy me if I let you get close to me." Man, it was hard not to interrupt him or to talk back, but I did as he'd asked.

I thought through those times he was talking about, his gruff, sometimes mean behavior. The insult ping pong game we constantly played. I gave as good as I got—and sometimes better. But all that time, I'd been so sure he hated me—or merely tolerated me out of necessity.

Except those few times I'd caught him looking at me with something other than hate. It wasn't lust, though I'd caught that sometimes, too. Other times he'd look at me with that same expression I'd seen so much on his face lately. Admiration, respect and sometimes even pride.

I shook my head.

"I know it's hard to believe. Believe me, I'm the textbook poster boy for lying to myself. And that's exactly what it was. I... built these huge walls around myself and I was safe there. But I had to keep you away because you'd beat them down like they were never there. Not a wrecking ball, not a steam-roller but a fucking one hundred megaton bomb wrapped in a supernova."

I blinked, those tender feelings from all the emotions I'd felt throughout these past few days were sore. And like anything that was sore, they didn't want to be poked and prodded any further.

I drew back from him, hugging myself. He wanted to talk about walls? Well, I needed some protection right now because I was feeling naked and vulnerable and...

Without another word, he stood up from the bench, took a step away, ran his hand through his hair, then pivoted, right in front of me. He sunk to both knees in front of the bench where I sat.

"You are, without a doubt, the best thing that has ever happened to me. And I was a stupid idiot and pushed you away hard because I was so afraid of what you were doing to me without even trying."

On that bench I stared at him, wide-eyed and stunned. My mouth opened. What could I say? I licked my lips.

He reached out and took each of my hands in his own. "Thank you for letting me get all this out. I don't even deserve you, not after I let you down the way I did. Not after I hurt you. But I'm going to be an undeserving asshole and ask you anyway.... Will you give us another chance?"

I opened my mouth and closed it, stunned. Our gazes locked and held. I couldn't breathe and it sure as heck looked like he was holding his breath, too. Maybe we'd both die from lack of oxygen out here and sometime in the spring, some unsuspecting jogger would happen upon us, frozen and then thawed in this exact position. And they'd launch an investigation to find out why we'd died.

And the cause would be sheer stupidity. On both our parts.

I blinked and bit my lip. "There would have to be rules..." I began.

His brow dipped in earnest and he nodded slowly.

"You know, because I love rules so much..." I continued. "And I can make much better rules than you can."

He blinked, concern clearing. He was on to me.

"Before you tell me what they are, I agree to all of them."

"Is that wise?" He reached into his pocket, pulled something out, then tugged my hand toward him. Without any words, he slipped a ring on my finger. "Your great-grandmother's ring! I gasped in surprise.

"Nope. That's *your* ring. To be resized at our earliest convenience. I can't ask you to marry me because we're already married. And asking you to not divorce me seems backward."

I pulled my hand back and studied the flashing diamond for a moment. "Now tell me about your job, because I have a sneaking suspicion that you were at work to give the presentation and you left to catch a plane."

He nodded. "Accurate."

I raised my brows at him expecting him to elaborate. He didn't. "Well? What happened? Did you lose the job?"

He didn't even hesitate. "I don't know. Probably."

"You don't seem to care all that much."

His eyes fixed on mine, and he looked at me, really looked at me like he was looking at me for the very first time. Like he was laying eyes on an awe-inspiring work of art. His eyes traced the contours of my face, my hairline, my neck, my ears. Like he was soaking it all in.

Something about that, the way he looked at me, stole my words, blocked my throat. And there was this pressure inside my chest, like suddenly my heart hurt with every beat.

"It was a matter of perspective, Kat. I wanted that job, yeah. I *really* wanted it. But fuck if I didn't give a shit about whether or not I had it once you were gone. It was like…." He shook his head. "Like nothing good was worth having if you weren't there to share it with."

Well, talk about melt-inducing. My shoulders slumped and my spine softened and I melted right into him, bending forward and catching my hands around his neck to pull him in to kiss me.

We kissed, and we kissed, my mouth opening to his and our lips fusing together, speaking the language of love that had been so difficult for us to express with our words.

I held his head to mine and his hands clamped on my waist, scooting me close to him. Soon, we were pressed up against each other and breathless. Our lips parted and there were tears on my cheeks. He expelled a breath of surprise and reached up to dry them. "Please don't cry anymore, my beautiful Katya. I'm going to spend the rest of my life making sure you never have a reason to cry again."

"Even though you're going to be stuck with me hunting bugs in the Den for the rest of our lives?"

"Cranberry, if it's with you, it's going to be ten times more fun than anything else."

I smoothed my thumb over his cheek and smiled. "You've absolutely ruined the knees in your suit pants by now."

He smiled. "Worth it." He picked up my left hand, the one that bore the ring he'd given me and kissed it. I noticed, then that he wore his ring, still. He'd never taken it off.

"So if you just walked out of the board meeting and went to the airport, how did you have my ring with you?"

He smiled. "I had to run by the house to get my passport for the trip. I grabbed the ring at the same time."

Suddenly, as I pictured him running around grabbing stuff at the house, another thought occurred to me. "What about the dog? You didn't leave Max alone, did you?"

He shook his head and smiled. "Jordan and April are babysitting him tonight. Tomorrow, Michaela is going to take him back over to his doggy camp to see his lady friends again. I heard one of them is a poodle."

I laughed. "You know, when we first met, I thought you were so hot... then you opened your mouth and said the most complete assholish thing to me."

"You remember what I said?"

I nodded. "Yup. You said, 'There's no reason to be so smiley. We're serious in QA and you'd better be serious, too.'"

"Wow, what an asshole," he concurred.

"Right?" I shook my head. "Jedi Boy."

"Cranberry."

He ran a thumb over my hand again, then pushed to his feet, sliding onto the bench beside me. He held that hand up to his mouth again, kissing it like an old-timey gentlemen would woo his lady-friend.

"It's too late for me to give you the wedding of your dreams, but we can have a big fancy party to celebrate... maybe renew our vows, if you want."

I snorted. "You know me well enough by now to know what I'd think of something like that."

"Sounds like Hell?"

"You got it. Let's just have a nice little get together with our close circle and as for our vows... let's renew them on our own. On a real honeymoon."

He raised his brows, intrigued. "Hmm that sounds like an interesting idea. Any idea when—or where?"

"I have the next week off. Let's go now."

He nodded. "That's very possible. Where should we go?"

My grin widened, heartened with the idea. "Let's test our adventurous spirit. I have hardly any luggage and you have none. Let's just go to the airport and pick a destination when we get there."

He threw his head back and laughed. "You are absolutely insane." Then he shouted to the sky, "My wife is insane! I love her more than anything."

"My husband is too sane. I love him more than donuts. And beer."

He wrapped his arms around me. "But not tea?"

I grinned. "There are limits. But there's always room for growth."

He kissed me again, and we held each other, rocking to the rhythm of the beating of our hearts. He squeezed me to him tight, and I pressed my face to his solid shoulder.

He kissed my hair. "I will never give this up. And I swear to God I will never let you down again. To say nothing of never making you cry. And—"

I pulled back suddenly, staring at him in disbelief. "Whoa, whoa, whoa!" I held up a hand between us. "Don't even!" But there was a wicked, wicked glint in his eyes that gave me my answer. "Dude, did you just… rick-roll me?"

"You know the rules…"

I punched him in the arm. "You fucker. I'm so getting you back!"

He grimaced and rubbed his bicep. "But not right now because right now we're getting a taxi and going to the airport."

He took my hand and pulled me off that bench. Then he grabbed my suitcase. I tried to get him to skip to the parking lot but he refused. He did sing along with me, though it was Lucas's least favorite song in the world.

It was now my favorite.

EPILOGUE
KATYA

Forty-eight hours later...

I WOKE UP EARLY IN THE MORNING FLUSHED HOT WITH arousal. It was still dark, and I'd only slept a few hours, but my entire body was alive and burning for him. When I felt his searing breath skate across my bare skin, I realized that he'd hiked up my shirt while I was sleeping. Now he had his mouth tightly wrapped around one nipple, his thumb and forefinger gently tugging the other one.

It was the most incredible sensation. Without a word, I opened my legs and let him pull off my panties and fuck me slowly, tenderly. His hips swayed against mine and he surged inside of me as our breath swirled and mingled, mixing and melding just like our bodies. I savored the steady, rolling weight of him on top of me, the snug, delicious fit of him inside me. I arched my back and closed my eyes and let him drive this course, happily along for the ride.

This was one of many times to come. And when we both came, it was breathtaking and as natural as the steady rolling of waves against a beach. All in the space of the first few moments of consciousness, our sweat sealed our bodies together. He collapsed against me and I basked in the afterglow thinking I would love many more mornings waking up just like this.

And so we had that before us...

His hand caressed my stomach, my hip as he nibbled on my ear and I turned my head toward him. "Mmm good morning to you, too, husband."

"I think that's my favorite way to wake you up, wife."

"It's also your favorite way to put me to bed at night. And to express your enthusiasm during the afternoon. I'm sure you'll find that's your favorite way to do other things around the house as well."

"Looks like I'm going to have to get even more creative to add to that list."

I threaded my leg between his, my hand traveled down his stomach to rest on his thigh. "How about you show me your second favorite way to get me out of bed in the morning?"

"Mmm." He rolled to face me, his mouth swooping down toward my ear when—

Suddenly his phone rang with a weird sound. I recognized it instantly. A video conference call.

What the *hell?*

I looked at the clock on the bedside. It wasn't even six a.m. Who was calling at this time?

Then I remembered the time difference. It was late afternoon at home.

Lucas was scrambling to pull on a t-shirt. "Fuck, it's Adam."

"Yeah, definitely don't answer it naked. He won't appreciate that."

"I can be naked from the waist down." He turned to me, asking me to straighten his hair, which I did. Then I flipped on the lamp and got the hell out of eye-shot of the camera. Because my best friend's husband seeing my boobs would be more than awkward.

Lucas clicked to answer the phone. "Uh, hello?"

"Hey, Lucas. Did I get you at a bad time?"

"Hi Lucas, I'm here too. It's a 3-way, but not the fun kind." Jordan said. Figured.

"Hi Adam, Jordan." Over the phone, Lucas shot me a slightly terrified look.

"Listen, before I get to the reason I'm calling, I'm on strict orders from the wife to make sure Katya's okay. She was very worried when she heard that Kat had to leave the country for urgent family business."

"She's fine. She's here with me. We've had a crazy past two days." He ran his hand through his hair again. "In fact, uh, I was just catching a cat nap which is why I probably look like crap."

"I wasn't going to say anything but..." Jordan said.

"I'm glad to hear she's okay. I'll pass the message along to Mia," Adam said.

"I'll let Kat know to touch base with Mia, too."

"So, as to why I'm calling. You left us in a bit of a bind on Thursday. The board was looking forward to hearing your presentation. Jeremy gave his, and they liked it and I had to present your slides and designs with only my own explanations. I really was half-assing it but without you or Jordan there..."

"Yeah, Jordan was kind enough to drive me to the airport. I appreciate that, man."

"Glad we got you there on time," Jordan replied.

Adam cleared his throat, presumably to get the conversation back on track. "Anyway, the board was really thrown that you weren't there and let's just say I wasn't in the best mood either. And Jeremy did a really good job on his presentation."

Stone-faced and pale, Lucas met my gaze over the top of his phone. I held my breath and crossed both my fingers. Crap. Crap. Crap. As much as I'd wanted him to be with me when I faced my family, I still didn't want it to be the reason he lost his dream job. Would he resent me for it? Would it turn into a problem further down the line?

"I offered Jeremy the job as head developer and he's excited to accept. And if you're still up for the Director of the VR division, the board has approved that. I guess I didn't fuck up your presentation that badly." *Yes. Yes. Yes!* I jumped up and down, both thumbs up. I could tell that Lucas was paying close attention because he didn't even glance my way to watch my boobs bounce.

"Uh, I, oh, yes, yes of course. I'm sorry you had to be the one to do it but thank you so much. Thank you."

"Glad to hear it. You'll be back from Vancouver on...?"

I had to slap my hand over my mouth not to bust out laughing. That's right. They still thought we were in Vancouver when we were actually on the other side of the world.

"Wednesday night so I'll be back to work on Thursday. Kat, too."

"Great, is she around? I have good news for her too."

My eyes went wide, and I shook my head. Then grabbed the sheet off the bed and covered up. "I'm here," I waved my hand in front of the camera but kept my face far away from it. "I look awful, but yes, I'm here. You can tell me the news without looking at me, right?"

All three guys laughed.

"Yeah, sure. I'll just imagine you being happy when I offer you the new team leader job on the white-box game testing. You get to hire your own team and train them to your specifications."

I dropped the sheet and my jaw and let out a whoop. This time Lucas *did* zero in on my bouncing boobs when I jumped up and down. Good boy... that was more like it.

"Do you want me to narrate? She's throwing her arms in the air and yelling and looking quite happy."

"Thank you, Adam! I'm super excited."

"Good. We'll see you two back next week. I hope all is well with you and your family, Kat."

"It is now, thank you."

"All right, I'll let you get back to your catnap." Adam, ever the professional boss, didn't even put air quotes around that catnap. Jordan totally would have done that.

Lucas signed off with the guys and I ran to him and jumped into his arms before he could even put the phone down. He wrapped those arms around me tight and pulled me off my feet. I went flying up, kicking my legs. "You can run but you can't hide! I'll still be over in the Den and you'll be in the other building, but I'll find you."

"Good, maybe we'll have a quicky in that bathroom off the workshop."

"Gross, that sounds like something Jordan would do."

I gave him a quick smooch. "That's all I get?"

"I'm getting in the shower. More later. Guaranteed." I ran for the bathroom.

"I'm still waiting for the full experience on one of those *next level BJs!*" he called after me.

LUCAS

Five minutes later.

S HE WASN'T IN THE SHOWER THREE MINUTES BEFORE THE phone rang again. This time it was Jordan and just Jordan. "Hey Jordan. I don't know what you did to convince him, but thank God you did it."

Jordan pulled a face. "Don't thank me, thank your wife." I threw and involuntary glance toward the bathroom. "Is she there?"

"She's in the shower. Why what did she do?"

"Well Adam was, as I predicted, damn furious about the whole thing. Your leaving, my leaving. He ripped me a brand new asshole for that one. You owe me huge, junior."

"I'll make it up to you. But… what changed Adam's mind if he was so pissed at me?"

"Mia…what do you think? Probably the only person on the face of this planet who can change his mind about anything."

I shook my head. "And how did… hmm."

"Yes, you've followed the logic trail. Sometime in the last day or so, Kat called Mia and asked her to work her magic on her raging Incredible Hulk."

"'Hey, big guy. The Sun's getting real low?'" I quoted.

523

He laughed. "Something like that. Anyway, I was hoping she was there so I could congratulate her on her ingenious thinking. But since she's wet and naked right now, I better let you go so you can go at 'er."

"Thanks man, I appreciate you letting me know. I'll keep you posted on everything and I will definitely be back to work on Thursday."

"Right on. See ya."

I dropped the phone onto the bed and stared in wonder at the bathroom door. Wow, when had she managed that? How? The only time we were separated in the last two days was during a three-hour flight layover. We'd split up to quickly tackle the problem of my lack of luggage. She'd sent me into a couple clothing and gift shops to buy some replacement clothes and underwear. Meanwhile she'd run to grab basic toiletries like a toothbrush, toothpaste and a razor for me. She must have made the call then.

She was sneaky, my wife. And it was time to give her a taste of her own medicine. Turned out shower sex was now my favorite way to scrub down with my wife.

Hours later, we were fully dressed and in tourist mode, threading in and out of a throng of people. We were in the Asan market scoping out souvenirs. Kat and I were each taking turns nibbling on a piece of *lapsi titaura* candy, savoring the unusual but tasty sweet and sour flavor.

"Mmm wanna know the best part of being on a secret honeymoon?" Kat asked between bites.

"What's that?"

"We don't have to drag home a shitload of souvenirs for everyone." I pointed out a couple of interesting looking shops on the other side of the street and we crossed to that side. She asked, "What made you pick here, anyway? You never did tell me the reason."

I smiled, nipped off another bite of the candy in her hand. "It might have something to do with the first three letters of the city's name."

"K-A-T. Awww, no really? Is that why?"

"Of course it's why."

"Huh, you're just trying to one-up me in the creative department. I'm the one who suggested the secret spontaneous honeymoon in the first place and now you have to one-up me by being all cool with picking out Kathmandu, Nepal. You realize what this means, don't you?"

"You humbly and politely accept defeat?"

"Annnnd you know me not at all! I will find a way to top your top."

Suddenly she stopped walking and pulled her phone out of her pocket. "Hold on, someone's texting me." She read it and then laughed, read it again.

"What is it?" I asked.

She handed me the phone so that I could read.

Mia: Adam just let me know that he talked to you both about your new jobs! CONGRATS!!! Girl, you owe me huge. Which is why you and your hubby are now fully obligated to come to our skiing retreat in December. I'm planning on all our friends being there and it's going to be EPIC. We got an amazing place.... So you're coming, right? Yes. Yes, you are.

Kat and I looked at each other and laughed again. And after sharing another bite of candy and a subsequent sticky kiss, I sincerely wondered how it could ever get more epic than this.

Keep an eye out for the next adventure in the Gaming The System series. A Love, Actually-style romp featuring a ski retreat holiday adventure with the couples you love so well, including Adam, Mia, Jordan, April, William, Jenna, Lucas, Katya and Heath.

BIOGRAPHY

Brenna Aubrey is a USA TODAY Bestselling Author of contemporary romance stories that center on geek culture. Her debut novel, At Any Price, is currently free on all platforms.

She has always sought comfort in good books and the long, involved stories she weaves in her head. Brenna is a city girl with a nature-lover's heart. She therefore finds herself out in green open spaces any chance she can get. She's also a mom, teacher, geek girl, Francophile, unabashed video-game addict & eBook hoarder.

She currently resides on the west coast with her husband, two children, two adorable golden retriever pups, a bird and some fish.

More information available at www.BrennaAubrey.net

To sign up for Brenna's email list for release updates, please copy & paste this link into your browser:
http://BrennaAubrey.net/newsletter-signup/

Want to discuss the Gaming The System series with other avid readers? Brenna's reader discussion and social group is located on Facebook
https://www.facebook.com/groups/BrennaAubreyBookGroup/

Made in the USA
Columbia, SC
18 November 2020

24854679R00321